To Richard and Letitia
With best wishes
Richard Coward

London
January 1997

THE VIENNESE WALTZ

THE VIENNESE WALTZ

by

RICHARD COWARD

LONDON
Richard & Erika Coward
WRITING AND PUBLISHING PARTNERSHIP
1997

First published in 1997 by
Richard and Erika Coward
Writing and Publishing Partnership
16 Sturgess Avenue
London
NW4 3TS

Phototypeset by Intype London Ltd
Printed in Great Britain by The Bath Press, Bath

British Library Cataloguing in Publication Data
A catalogue record for this book is available from the British Library.

ISBN 0–9515019–4–1

To my brother
Ian David Coward

It took no more than a touch of his finger to extinguish the images before him, but Dr Antonin Ziegler did not seem to notice that the television screen had gone blank. He remained expressionless, slumped in his armchair, staring numbly at the vacant grey space where only moments before there had been a vivid procession of light and sound. It was as if he were watching another programme in his mind, a programme which could not be so easily silenced.

His motionless vigil did not last long. It never did, for Antonin Ziegler was a man prone to self-analysis, for whom even the most simple of actions was the result of a detailed process of reasoning and counter-reasoning, and he had long since discovered that he found it easier to think on his feet rather than sitting down. And although the events on the ten o'clock news had not been completely unexpected, it had still come as something of a shock to realise that the constraints which had for so long held his life in some sort of manageable order had so suddenly and completely evaporated.

He rose ponderously to his feet and walked into the small private hallway which acted as a neutral zone between the college rooms which were his home and the wider world beyond. Pulling his winter coat around his shoulders, he slipped quietly out onto the cold stairwell and started down the stairs towards the cloistered court-yard below.

There was a dense November mist outside, so thick he could only just make out the dull yellow glow from the lights on the far side of the quadrangle. Pulling his coat closely around himself, he began to walk around the cloisters towards the small passageway which led to the college gardens. In the carefully controlled fashion which was typically his own, he had resolved that he would not begin thinking until he had reached the tranquillity of those gardens. So as he walked his thoughts remained relatively uncluttered, leaving him free to savour the chill beauty of the fine sixteenth century buildings in which he had so long before found refuge from the tempests of his younger days.

He was just passing the main college gate when he became aware of a voice calling to him through the mist.

"Dr Ziegler!"

He turned and saw one of his third year undergraduate students hurrying towards him, a keen young fellow by the name of Danny who boasted an unusually strong Glaswegian accent for one so clever. Close beside him was a pretty young girl, but as her boyfriend approached his tutor she hung back a few yards.

Danny looked at him excitedly.

"Have you seen the news, Dr Ziegler?" he blurted out.

Antonin nodded dryly.

"So what do you think?" Danny continued.

His face was eager, the eager excitement of a perceptive young man who was astute enough to recognise the significance of history in the making.

"The events remain largely predictable," Antonin replied stoically, as if his interest in the unfolding events in Prague that day was entirely academic.

"Are you going back then?" Danny asked brightly. "You'll be able to now, won't you?"

Antonin momentarily recoiled, shocked by his student's apparent ability to perceive his inner turmoil. But Danny's face showed that he attached no special significance to his words. And it was after all an obvious enough question, for everyone at college knew that Dr Antonin Ziegler had left Czechoslovakia shortly after the Warsaw Pact invasion in 1968 and had not been back since.

"I don't know yet, Danny," he replied. "I'll have to see."

Antonin allowed his eyes to flick towards the young girl with Danny. Danny took the hint.

"Oh well, Dr Ziegler, see you about."

He turned away and rejoined the girl. They kissed briefly and exchanged a few intimate words before vanishing into the mist.

For some reason he found the sight of their mutual affection disturbing. Turning quickly away, he paced purposefully on towards the gardens.

* * * * * *

There was the sound of a woman singing, her clear voice distant and alluring. She sang in Slovak, the lilting melody gently rising and falling like the wind blowing through the nearby trees. Her voice should have been happy, yet her song suggested a great sorrow, a hurt which could never be put right.

A small boy was in a tiny log shelter in the heart of the woods. His parents' house lay on the fringe of a great city, a city of ruins and smoke and anger, and despite his tender years he already knew it was a place to avoid. But here in the scrubby woodland there was a different kind of world, a place of flowers and berries and shrubs where people rarely came to disturb the peace of nature.

His father had built him the log shelter during one of the rare times when he was not at work. It had taken a whole weekend, a long and happy time when the little boy had for once not been alone. He had hoped that this would be the first of many shared times, but instead his father had returned to his endless work in the city and the small boy had been left alone with his log cabin, a wooden memorial to a brief and happy moment. And it was to that log cabin that he would take his toys and create for himself a fantasy world in which he could mask his inner sadness.

The small boy did not have many toys with which to fill his cabin, but there was one which held a special place in his affections. It was a wooden doll which must once have been new but was now very old and worn. To him it was a friend and confidante, a soulmate in the imagination where none seemed to exist in real life. And now he sat talking to it quietly in the corner of his secret home.

The singing was coming closer. The small boy clasped his doll rigidly to his chest and waited silently for his mother to arrive. And then finally the singing stopped.

"Antonin!"

The small boy laid the doll carefully on the floor of his wooden house and clambered outside to stand beside his mother. She smiled down at him, meaning perhaps to reassure him, but there was something about the smile which made him feel uneasy.

"I have exciting news for you," his mother announced in the rather cold and formal way in which she often addressed him.

He looked up at her nervously.

"I'm pregnant," she said proudly.

His eyes were filled with such a confused expression that she must have supposed that he did not understand her words.

"Soon," she explained, "you will have a little brother or sister. And then you need never be lonely again."

* * * * * *

A large beech tree stood alone at the far end of the college gardens, an ancient tree which according to legend had been the source of inspiration for several important discoveries in years gone by. And it was while he paced backwards and forwards under the mist-shrouded branches of this beech tree that Antonin began to think seriously about what he would now do.

3

Danny had been right. The news from Prague was indeed exciting. The discredited General Secretary of the Czechoslovak Communist Party had finally succumbed to popular pressure and resigned. A quarter of a million people had been able to assemble freely in the centre of Prague and listen to a speech by the disgraced figure of Alexander Dubcek, leader of the abortive Prague Spring of 1968, the Prague Spring which had triggered both the arrival of Warsaw Pact tanks in Czechoslovakia and Antonin's own departure. Taken together with the collapse two weeks earlier of the Berlin Wall there could no longer be any mistaking the truth. The long reign of darkness in Czechoslovakia and the rest of Eastern Europe was finally and irrevocably drawing to a close.

Antonin could not help but feel annoyed with himself. He knew he should feel nothing but joy that the squalid regime of tyranny and oppression which he had loathed ever since his schooldays had finally vanished. Yet mixed with his genuine pleasure at the triumphs of his compatriots was a sense of deep anxiety which was threatening to undermine his determined attempts to share in their rejoicing. For the political barriers which had prevented him returning to his homeland for over two decades had also enabled him to evade a difficult personal encounter. They had prevented him from returning to see his parents.

Antonin smiled wryly at the absurdity of his futile attempts to convince himself there was no point in going back, no point in trying to seek their forgiveness for the hurt he had caused them by his departure. He had been no older than Danny when he had gone, scarcely more than a boy, a revisionist cuckoo in the nest of two true revolutionaries. He had known at the time it would hurt them badly when he abandoned both them and the political system which they had strived so hard to build.

His father and mother were both the children of pre-war Czechoslovakia, both from comfortable middle-class homes which were remarkably similar except that in his father's home they had spoken German while in his mother's they had spoken Slovak. But the bourgeois world of their youth had collapsed in the face of Hitler's ferocious onslaught, and somewhere in the resulting chaos they had quite independently turned to communism. It seemed that in the certainties of the Soviet system they had found a strength and solidity which the vaguely good-intentioned liberalism of so many of their parents' generation had so transparently lacked. And so they had ended up in Moscow during the war, both attending a political school for the foreign cadres which Stalin already sensed he would need to govern the conquered nations of Eastern Europe after the war.

It was in Moscow that his parents had met and fallen in love, and despite all the difficulties he had himself subsequently experienced with them Antonin knew that their love for each other was as strong and enduring as their faith in the communist ideal. Even as a child he had understood the strength of his parents' mutual devotion. He had seen it in the looks which they exchanged with each other. He had seen it in the way they touched and talked. But most of all he had seen it in the way they had struggled so very hard to conceal from their first-born child the painful fact that he was an encumbrance they would willingly have done without.

Antonin shuddered. He had not spent much of his adult life in Britain thinking about either his childhood or his parents. He had left them behind at the age of twenty-two and been forced to accept he may never see them again. In the early months of his exile he had written to them, explained to them at great length the reasons for his abrupt departure. He had hoped they would reply. But they had not replied and he had finally been forced to conclude that the hurt had simply been too great. And so he had built his own life, a successful life by most counts, and on the whole he had thought it best not to dwell too much on a painful past which he had believed to be a closed chapter in his life.

But the Czech counter-revolution had changed all that. Just as before there had been no alternative, now again there was no alternative. He could no longer hide behind other people's rules, the rules of a police state which did not invite return visits by those who had abandoned their country to work for the class enemy. And now he knew for certain that before many more months had passed he would have to return and resurrect the buried ghosts of his past life.

* * * * * *

The bright June sun was streaming in through the high windows facing out from his college rooms. Antonin squinted through the glass at the busy street beyond, trying to remember what he had been thinking about the first time he had looked through those windows some fifteen years before. That day too had been a June day, a bright sunny June day when the world had seemed so full of hope and joy. He had been a young man then, not yet thirty years old, newly appointed as Reader in Soviet and East European History at Oxford University.

5

The day he had taken possession of his rooms at college had held for him a special significance. It had represented a symbolic acceptance in his new homeland, for no one could deny that Oxford University lay at the very core of the British establishment. Like so many other central European exiles during the twentieth century, Oxford had offered him a refuge, a place where he could study and teach in an atmosphere free of oppression. It was an appointment which had brought him great satisfaction then, and it had continued to bring him great satisfaction ever since.

With a barely audible grunt, he turned away from the window and walked through to his bedroom. Glancing at his watch to confirm that the awful job could no longer be put off, he pulled a large suitcase down from the top of the wardrobe and placed it carefully on one side of the bed. Then he moved purposely to the chest of drawers and pulled open the top drawer.

He had a carefully laid plan, of course. There was not much in life about which Antonin did not have a carefully laid plan. He would start with the underwear and then work systematically outwards, taking care to allow for each different circumstance in which he might happen to find himself. That way he would be completely safe. If the weather was hot he would have hot weather things, if it was cold he would have cold weather things, and so on. In principle it sounded straightforward enough.

He pulled out a pair of white underpants and laid it neatly on the bed beside the suitcase. He stared at it uncertainly for a few moments and then laid two more pairs beside it. But even this didn't seem to satisfy him, and eventually he pulled out a fourth. The trouble was, it was so hard to know how many to take. There was inadequate information on which to form a reasoned judgement, hopelessly inadequate information. For one thing he didn't know for sure how long he'd be there, and then again he didn't really have much idea about what facilities he would find for washing his clothes. Finally, with a resigned shrug, he pulled out all the remaining underpants in the drawer and added them to the pile.

He carried on in this fashion for several more minutes until he was pretty well certain he had gathered together sufficient undergarments. But the pile of clothes on the bed was already disconcertingly large, and Antonin knew that unless he began to be more selective he would end up with more clothes than would fit into his suitcase. In his mind he decided to revise his original plan, ensuring that he only took those garments where there was a fairly high probability of putting them to good use. Casting his eye critically over the items on the bed, he reluctantly returned his bed-socks to the drawer.

Yet despite the new system, the pile grew inexorably larger. Again Antonin looked anxiously at his watch. In just over an hour the taxi would arrive to take him to the station, but he still hadn't checked through his papers. Throwing a contemptuous glance at the huge pile of clothes lying on the bed, he strode out of the bedroom and over towards his desk in the living room. The clothes could wait. If he didn't check through his papers in good time he would forget something really important.

He had just placed his passport prominently in the centre of his desk when there was a purposeful ring on the doorbell. He looked up with an annoyed expression, well aware that he did not have any time to waste in idle chatter. For a moment he thought of leaving the door unanswered, but then his curiosity got the better of him and he walked through the lobby to release the catch.

No sooner was the catch released than an elderly lady elbowed her way past him into the hallway.

"All packed and ready then?" the newcomer asked in a sprightly voice which belied her advanced years.

"No," Antonin grunted. "I should have started doing it yesterday."

"When are you off?"

"In just under an hour. I've a taxi booked."

"Well in that case it's just as well I came to check up on you, isn't it?"

The elderly lady swept through the lobby and headed straight for the bedroom. With a horrified glance at the mess on the bed she set to work with a will, casting some items to one side of the bed while others were consigned roughly to a heap on the floor.

While she worked she took no notice whatsoever of Antonin, who had silently followed her through to the door of the bedroom. He watched her work with the silent gratitude which was always present when he was in her company. For Vanessa Sinclair was his one true friend, and without her steadfast companionship over the last twenty years he did not really know how he would have coped with life's vicissitudes.

They had met shortly after he had arrived in London following his hurried departure from Prague. It had been at a sort of informal club in London for Czechs and Slovaks seeking political asylum in Britain following the Russian invasion. At that time Vanessa had been a woman in her prime, a lecturer in international law at

London University, and she had offered her services to the group as a kind of unpaid legal advisor. She had worked ceaselessly on behalf of all the refugees, but somehow she had come to form a special friendship with Antonin, a close bond which had now lasted for over twenty years.

Vanessa had never married. She was a spinster of the old school, a kind and caring woman who had never found time in a full and active life for the single-minded devotion required by marriage and motherhood. She was a true citizen of the world, and if she loved anyone, she loved the whole human race. For Vanessa to have given a special place to a husband or to children would have involved her in a kind of betrayal. It was a betrayal she had fought all her life to avoid.

Yet Antonin knew Vanessa almost as well as she knew him. He knew that there was a private price to be paid for the warm-hearted altruism to which she so earnestly aspired. There was an inner loneliness, a secret wish that someone would cherish her with the same single-minded devotion which she denied to anyone else. And in that simple little fact lay the basis of the close friendship that had sustained them over the years.

It took no more than ten minutes and the suitcase was all packed. For the first time since she had entered the bedroom Vanessa seemed to notice he was standing beside her.

"Carry the case to the door, will you," she said in the slightly bossy way which would have made most people cross but just made Antonin smile. He did as he was asked.

When he returned from the hallway she was shuffling through the papers laid out on his desk in the living room.

"Do you still need a visa for Czechoslovakia?" she asked anxiously, flicking through his passport.

"Yes. But it's all up in the air right now. Even the embassy's muddled about the whole situation."

She frowned. Laying the passport down on the desk she turned to face him.

"Are you really sure you're doing the right thing, Antonin? It's been an awfully long time."

He smiled at her.

"Don't you think I'm doing the right thing, then?" he asked.

She shrugged.

"Quite frankly, Antonin, I don't know whether you are or you aren't? But I know you left a lot more behind than either your family or a bunch of stupid Soviet tanks."

8

Antonin winced. That was pure Vanessa. She didn't spare the recipient of her words with any gentle preamble. Straight to the heart of the matter and no messing about.

He walked silently over to the desk and looked down solemnly at the papers.

"Do you reckon it's all here, then?" he asked.

She nodded her head.

He carefully placed all the papers in a small briefcase. And then, without saying a word, he kissed her gently on the cheek.

* * * * * *

The beer was going to his head. But the beer was good, and drinking good Czech beer in the company of a good Czech friend made the inevitable hangover next morning a price worth paying.

Jiri Sebek, whose glass was already empty, pointed an unsteady but accusing finger across the table.

"Still not drunk up, eh, Antonin. So like a Prussian. You drink your beer at such a slow and predictable rate."

Antonin peered into his half-empty glass. Then he lifted it to his lips and with one long gulp it was gone.

"That's rich coming from you, Jiri. If I remember correctly your grandfather was a defrocked Austrian priest."

It was a ritual exchange of pleasantries which masked a close and growing friendship. Antonin and Jiri were both postgraduate students at Prague University, but whereas Jiri had lived in Czechoslovakia all his life, Antonin had only just arrived from the dull and sterile atmosphere of 1960s East Berlin.

Jiri ordered two more beers and then leant forward with a conspiratorial expression.

"I've been told some of the undergraduates have drawn up an open letter. They want to know who'll sign amongst the postgrads."

Antonin frowned.

"What sort of letter?" he asked.

"Most of it's the usual stuff – support for Dubcek and so on. But there's also a bit about the university itself, a list of academic staff who should be unceremoniously sacked because of the way they compromised themselves with the old regime."

"It must be rather a long list," Antonin snorted.

Jiri shook his head violently, as if trying to shake off the effects of the alcohol.

"It's not long. Four names. Just the worst offenders with the clearest case against them. That way there's more chance we'll get results."

" 'We'll'? You sound as if you've already decided to sign this thing?"

Jiri shrugged.

"What the hell. Why not? If the First Secretary of the Czechoslovak Communist Party says it's all right to think for ourselves then I damn well don't see why we shouldn't."

The waiter appeared carrying the beers and they fell silent. Even in the more relaxed atmosphere which had appeared in Prague in recent months it was a difficult habit to break.

Jiri leant forward again.

"Well, Antonin. Will you sign?"

Antonin looked hard at his friend.

"I'd like to. You know that. But I can't."

Jiri scowled.

"Why not? You're not scared of them, are you?"

Antonin stared glumly into his beer.

"No. I'm not scared. But when my parents agreed to allow me to study in Prague I promised them I'd keep my nose out of politics. You might say it was a kind of deal."

"But why should your parents care? You're twenty-two years old. What's it got to do with them?"

"Because they've had a lucky break they've wanted for a long time. My parents didn't like it in Berlin any more than I did. My father was forced to go to Germany after the war because he was from a German-speaking home and all the German-speakers were thrown out of Czechoslovakia in 1945. And then my mother followed him. But they've been wanting to get back ever since. So when that job came up near my mother's village in Slovakia a few years back they jumped at the chance."

"And because of them you won't sign. Because they don't want anyone to rock the boat."

Antonin nodded.

"Partly that," he said. "But if I'm completely honest it's not just that. I want to stay here too, particularly now that Dubcek's changing everything. For you it's all right. You've got a Czech passport, they can't sling you out. But although I speak both Czech and Slovak as well as any local I've got a German passport. If just one idiot official takes the huff then I'm out on my ear."

Jiri frowned.

"We're all taking risks, you know," he said softly.

Antonin looked at him glumly. He knew his friend was right. If it all went dreadfully wrong, if the authorities changed course again and clamped down, then every single one of the students who signed the open letter was risking a secret police report which could blight them for the rest of their lives.

Jiri was sipping his beer thoughtfully, as if something had just occurred to him.

"There's a person I'd like you to meet, Antonin. Someone I think might be able to make you change your mind."

Antonin examined him with curiosity.

"Who?"

"The person who asked me to sign. An undergraduate by the name of Katrina Rostov."

* * * * * *

The door of the plane swung open and Antonin could feel a ripple of excitement running through his entire body. A few more steps and his feet would once again touch Czechoslovak soil. He looked around at the drab uniformity of Bratislava airport and drew in a deep breath. Even in summer it was an unpleasant smell which reached his nostrils, the stench of a major industrial city where pollution controls had never been given high priority, but to Antonin it was a warm and familiar smell, the smell of his past life, the smell of home.

He walked down the steps of the plane and boarded the waiting bus together with the other passengers. Most of them were businessmen in dark suits, arriving like vultures to pick over the bones of communism's crumbling industrial assets. It seemed to Antonin that they looked strangely indifferent to their surroundings, uncaring for the lives they had ostensibly come to transform, yet he knew enough of economics to know that the financial flows they brought in their briefcases would be crucial in undoing the damage which fifty years of brutal oppression had done to this once charmed city.

The bus drew to a halt and Antonin was swept along with the besuited businessmen to the customs building. As he filed slowly past the throng of waiting officials he could see in their faces a kind of confusion, a moral uncertainty at how to deal with this invading horde of capitalist infiltrators. It was as if a part of them were inwardly resisting the invasion, fearing the loss of sovereignty which would inevitably ensue once their country was carved up and sold off to foreigners, while the other part was proud that these busi-

11

nessmen had deigned to come, their presence living proof that their country had been restored to its rightful place on the wide open highways of international commerce.

The formalities did not take long, certainly not the eternity which had used to accompany any movement over international borders under the old regime, and Antonin soon found himself walking out onto a wide concourse filled with people. The foreign businessmen seemed to melt away into the crowd, and Antonin became aware of something he had often supposed he might never hear again, the sound of many tongues all speaking the language which he still thought of as his own. For even during his childhood in East Berlin they had always spoken Slovak in the privacy of their home. For his parents it had been a reminder of their own youth, and now it seemed to him a reminder of his.

"Antonin!"

He turned to see a thin man with greying hair elbowing his way towards him through the crowd.

"Jiri!" he said, a broad smile spreading across his face.

The two men embraced warmly, for although they had often written over the years it was the first time they had been in each other's company since Antonin's abrupt departure for the West in 1968.

"You got my letter, then," Antonin said when they had released each other. "I wasn't sure you would."

"It arrived this morning," Jiri replied. "But you could have phoned, you know. Last week I finally managed to persuade them to give me a private line."

Jiri stood back a pace and looked his old friend up and down.

"You need to go on a diet, Antonin," he chuckled.

"That's Oxford for you. The food's too good. It's about time you came to try it."

Jiri shook his head and smiled.

"One day I most definitely will. But not just yet. First I have work to do here."

Antonin looked thoughtfully at his old friend. He hadn't changed, at least not in so far as the fundamentals were concerned. There was still a hidden intensity just beneath the surface. It was an intensity which had already got him into trouble several times and would no doubt do so again.

"Compared to you I'm a pretty poor Slovak, aren't I, Jiri?" Antonin said with a smile.

Jiri shrugged.

"I used to call you a Prussian, now I suppose I should call you an Englishman. But perhaps you will never be either of those things. Maybe you are a citizen of whole world. Maybe you don't really belong anywhere."

His words were not harshly meant, but despite himself Antonin could not help but feel hurt. For he knew that Jiri had proved his love of his homeland many times over. He had stood up for what he believed to be right and by twenty years of persecution had proved the strength of his convictions. And mirrored in his friend's commitment Antonin could feel his own frailty, a frailty which had made him flee his homeland in the hour of its greatest need. And only now, with over half his life gone, had he finally returned to pick up the pieces he had left behind.

Jiri must have read his thoughts.

"I'm sorry, Antonin," he said kindly, putting his arm around him and steering him towards a nearby bar. "That was not a good way for me to greet a dear old friend who is finally coming home. Let us go and drink a beer together, just like we used to."

Antonin nodded and followed Jiri in silence. A strangely oppressive mood had descended upon him and he began to wonder if it might have been better if had not written to tell Jiri of his arrival plans. In his mind he could see Vanessa standing by the desk in his college rooms. He could hear her words and he could see the concern on her face as she had asked him if he was doing the right thing by returning to Czechoslovakia.

The faint smell of pollution in his nostrils, the Slovak language in his ears, the sight and sound of his old friend Jiri talking to him. There was no way in which a man of his intelligence could any longer conceal the truth. And sooner or later he would have to confront the twisted love he still felt in his heart for Katrina Rostov.

* * * * * *

He climbed the steps towards the uppermost apartment in the crumbling tenement and knocked apprehensively on the door. There was a long silence and he knocked again, this time more firmly. Finally he could hear the faint sound of approaching footsteps on the other side of the door.

"Who is it?"

It was a girl's voice, cautious and apprehensive.

"Antonin Ziegler. Jiri Sebek said we should all meet up here."

There was the sound of a bolt being undone and the door swung wide open. And suddenly there was a slender girl wrapped in nothing but a large white bathtowel standing before him.

Antonin took an involuntary step backwards. Despite the fact that he was now a postgraduate student, he still felt uncomfortable in the presence of girls, never mind pretty young girls dressed in nothing but bathtowels.

"Come in," she said with a smile, as if she had noted his discomfort and was mildly amused by it. "I was expecting you, but not quite yet."

Antonin stepped nervously over the threshold and into her flat. It was a typical student digs, complete with peeling wallpaper and cheap furnishings, but the occupants had done their best under difficult circumstances to make it homely. The girl closed the door and carefully locked it before turning to face him.

"So you're Antonin, are you?" she asked, eyeing him carefully up and down in a way which redoubled his discomfort. For he was making a studious attempt to control his instinctive desire to do the same to her.

"Jiri said there was a meeting here," he mumbled uncertainly. "A meeting about the open letter."

For a moment the girl looked surprised. Then she laughed.

"That's what he said, is it?" she said in a tone which suggested she didn't really believe him.

Antonin was afraid that his face was gradually turning a kind of beetroot colour, but the more he worried about his embarrassment the more it showed.

"I'm sorry," he muttered anxiously, taking a step backwards towards the door. "Jiri must have got in a muddle. I didn't mean to intrude."

The girl put her arm out as if to bar his way.

"It's like I said, Antonin. I was expecting you. It's Jiri I wasn't expecting. My name's Katrina."

She carefully extended a hand from somewhere inside the bathtowel and Antonin had no choice but to shake it. As he did so he tried to meet her eyes, but there was a kind of fire in them which both excited and frightened him. He looked away, yet he didn't want to peer at her body for fear of appearing lewd while looking around the rest of the room seemed somehow impolite. So as a result his gaze started shifting around uncomfortably all over the place.

"Why don't you sit down," Katrina continued. "I'll be back in a minute."

She disappeared into an adjoining room and closed the door. Several minutes later she was back, this time dressed in a rather plain cotton dress.

She smiled again.

"Better?" she asked.

Antonin looked at her with a confused expression. The two minute gap while she had changed together with her more conventional attire had helped him to relax a bit. Yet now her one word question produced exactly the opposite effect.

"Jiri thought you'd be able to persuade me to sign the open letter," he repeated firmly.

"Did he?" she replied thoughtfully, turning her back on him and pouring water into an old kettle.

This time Antonin said nothing. She couldn't see him now because her back was towards him, so he allowed himself for a brief moment to relish the slim outline of her body. She turned and he quickly looked away.

"What else did he say?" she asked.

"Nothing."

She set the water on the gas cooker in the corner of the room and lit the flame. And then she returned and sat down opposite him.

"Jiri's lying, of course," she said quietly. "He told me you were a secret admirer of mine who'd begged him to fix up a meeting. I was curious. So I just told him to tell you to come round and introduce yourself."

Antonin stared at her and gulped hard. For several moments neither of them said anything. But then Katrina started to laugh.

"Looking at all the evidence and taking one thing with another," she said with a smile, "I'd say that you and I have been the victims of a set-up job."

* * * * * *

It had been an odd notion to take the slow train. Antonin gazed out at the tiny village where the train had been standing motionless for nearly a quarter of an hour and found himself wondering why, when he had been just about to climb onto the express, he had suddenly turned around and walked over to catch a train which stopped at every tiny hamlet.

He had already been travelling north from Bratislava for well over four hours, creeping along at a snail's pace in the sweltering mid-summer sun. The train was moving along a wide valley, flanked on either side by distant ranges of low tree-clad hills. The towns through which they had passed had been inconsequential and drab, their potholed streets twisting and turning through what appeared to be a whole series of building sites where work had been started but never finished, while over each human settlement hung a dull lingering haze of industrial pollution. The countryside through which they passed was scarcely any better, living proof of the dead-ening hand of the collective farm, as if every sign of individuality had been carefully and systematically eradicated to make way for vast featureless cornfields.

The combination of the heat and the monotonous terrain should have conspired to make the journey tedious, yet instead of feeling impatient with the train's dull progress Antonin found himself grateful that they were not making better time. And he knew that in that uncharacteristic desire for delay lay the reason for his bizarre choice of trains.

He did not know the area through which they were travelling. When he had visited his grandparents' home in the mountainous uplands of Slovakia as a child they had always come from the north, from Germany via Poland. And later, when he was living in Prague, he had travelled to the village from the west. So he had never had occasion to visit the less mountainous southern districts of Slovakia through which the train was now passing. Yet despite the fact that he had never before seen the village outside the train's window he could already sense that the place he had always thought of as home was drawing ever closer.

In so many ways the village was just like the one from which his mother's family came, a mixture of traditional low wooden houses with broad overhanging eaves and a slightly newer generation of two-storey houses built with large grey breezeblocks. Each house was surrounded by a generous plot of land which looked more like a smallholding than a garden, a valued piece of personal property which played a vital economic role in the lives of the villagers. So functional were these private gardens that even where flowers grew they were arranged in rows, as if they were only being cultivated to be cut.

Just as in the larger towns through which they had passed, the whole village seemed to be one huge building site, for every track and every dwelling seemed cluttered with the debris of a myriad uncompleted construction projects. This was also true in what appeared to be the centre of the village, which lay immediately opposite the railway halt, a scruffy patch of grass beside a weed-infested duck pond and an ancient and abandoned pile of used tyres.

Yet despite the mess, perhaps because of the mess, the overall effect of the village was not entirely unpleasing. It displayed a kind of ragged individuality, where forty years of socialist collectivism seemed to have left little outward mark except for the railway halt itself, a brash concrete shed of angular design painted an incongruously bright shade of yellow.

As he looked at the village Antonin's thoughts turned again to his parents. On one level it was a ridiculous notion that he would still find them exactly where he had last seen them in the summer of 1968, standing together on a railway platform as he had said goodbye and, unbeknown even to himself, left for a new life in a far-away land. And precisely because it was such a ridiculous notion Antonin was puzzled by his own motivation for failing to undertake any proper preparation before setting out to track them down. It would after all have been easy enough to check through telephone directories or approach the authorities to try and establish his parents' current whereabouts.

But Antonin also knew that the dilemma was not a new one. Two decades before, as soon as he had realised that his parents were not going to reply to his letters, he had known that the sensible thing to do was to ask one of his Prague friends, somebody like Jiri, to visit them and find out how they were. He could even have asked someone to act as an intermediary, to approach his parents and try to explain to them on his behalf why he had left for the West. Yet even then he had held back, found a whole heap of excuses for doing nothing. Just as now, even on the duly appointed day, he had chosen the slow train rather than the express.

* * * * * *

The train from Prague pulled into the station.

"Antonin!"

A tall middle-aged man with greying hair began to stride towards him from the far end of the platform as soon as he alighted from the train. Antonin picked up his suitcase and walked towards his father, and as he approached him he noticed a strangely distracted look on his face.

"Hallo, Dad," he said cautiously, puzzled by the look in his father's eyes. He had known it was just possible that news from Prague had preceded him, and all the way he had been half expecting an eruption of anger as soon as they met. Yet something now told him that the odd expression on his father's face was completely unconnected with his son's arrival.

"Hallo, Antonin," his father said in the somewhat false voice he often used when making a determined attempt to be friendly and relaxed. "Did you have a good trip?"

The formality between father and son was usual and Antonin was accustomed to it. Yet his father was normally a very controlled man, and his slightly dishevelled appearance was distinctly odd.

"Are you all right?" Antonin asked. "You look worried."

He could see his father make an inward effort to pull himself together.

"No, no. I'm fine. How is Prague?"

"Prague is OK. There's a lot going on at the moment."

The older man frowned. A communist of the old school, Antonin knew his father held deep reservations about the pace and direction of Dubcek's reforms. But clearly now was not the time for a political discussion.

"I've been overdoing it a bit recently. I thought a few days down here in the country might do me some good."

Again the distracted look had appeared on his father's face, and Antonin was not sure whether he had heard him speak or not.

His father looked at him, as if making an effort to concentrate.

"The car's outside," he said, and picking up Antonin's suitcase he turned and headed silently for the station exit, as if giving up all further attempts to engage his son in idle chatter. Antonin walked along behind him with a worried expression. For the story about wanting to spend a few days in the country had been a complete fiction. He had come to see his parents with the express purpose of breaking two important pieces of news to them, both of which might cause them considerable distress, and he had therefore been hoping he would find them in a relaxed mood.

As soon as he emerged from the station building Antonin caught sight of his mother sitting in the small family saloon. She must have seen them, for she climbed out of the car and walked towards them.

"It's nice to see you, Antonin," she said, kissing him on the cheek. "We've been looking forward to having you stay."

Again the tone was slightly fake, the welcome not entirely sincere, but this time Antonin was relieved to discover that his mother's reactions were completely normal.

His father slung his suitcase into the boot of the car and climbed silently into the driving seat. His wife settled herself down beside him while Antonin squeezed into the cramped back seat.

"How's work, Dad?" he asked, leaning forward between the two front seats and trying to think of something to say which didn't involve talking about Prague.

There was a brief silence.

"You know your father can't talk about his work, Antonin," his mother said presently.

Antonin frowned. He really should have had more sense. His mother was always so insufferably proud of the fact that her husband's administrative work, whether in an East Berlin office or at an obscure Slovakian research institute, was of a classified nature. It reflected her hidden anxiety that despite her husband's unquestioned loyalty to party and state and his undoubted capacity for long hours and hard work, he had not had a particularly successful career.

He gave up the attempt at conversation and leant back silently in his seat. It often happened like this with his parents. He would ask them something about themselves, about their own feelings, seeking some basis for building a human bridge with them, and they would find some way to rebuff him. The rebuff was rarely harsh, and might perhaps amount to no more than a look or a glance, but it was enough to tell him that they did not wish to share themselves with him. It had been like that throughout his childhood. They had always cared for him, provided him with everything he needed, even been concerned for his well-being. But they had never shared their thoughts and feelings with him, never established a meaningful two-way exchange. The wall of silence had always been impenetrable.

Eventually the car clanked into their village and pulled to a halt beside a small house. The house had been in the possession of Antonin's mother's family for many generations and was a picturesque single-storey wooden building, flanked on all sides by overhanging eaves and rows of brightly painted windows. It was surrounded by a large vegetable garden, and bent double in the garden tending a row of cabbages was an old man in blue overalls. Yet if he had heard the car arrive he showed no sign of having done so, because he made no attempt to stand up and come to greet them as they drew up.

Antonin could feel his heart racing, surprised at the intensity of the feelings which now engulfed him as he set eyes on the old man, feelings which contrasted so strongly with the coldness he felt towards his parents.

He climbed out of the car and pushed open the rusty metal gate in the fence.

"Grandpa!" he called out loudly, picking his way gingerly between the neatly arranged arrays of vegetables towards the old man. His grandfather looked up from his work, and the warmth of the smile which spread across his wrinkled face revealed better than any words the love he felt for Antonin.

"Antonin, my boy. Welcome home."

Antonin looked admiringly around at the garden.

"It's looking good this year, Grandpa. You've been working hard."

His grandfather nodded sagely.

"The seeds are doing rather well this year, aren't they, Antonin? We must all do what we can to nurture them."

Antonin smiled. He understood his grandfather's words all too well, for he was one of the few younger people in the village who understood that the old man was not the rather bumbling rustic he had portrayed himself to be for many years. Before the war he had been a local councillor, eventually rising to become mayor of the whole district. Arrested by the puppet Slovakian regime set up by the Nazis in 1939, he had spent most of the war years in prison, but when the war had finished he had resumed his political career, regaining his old post as district mayor and planning to seek election to the federal parliament in Prague. But then, in the early months of 1948, Gottwald's communists had seized power for themselves and his grandfather had quickly realised that his political career was finally over. And instead of struggling on, trying to turn the tide of history and getting himself thrown back into prison again, he had quietly changed into his old gardening clothes and retired to tend his vegetables.

Antonin flicked a wary glance in the direction of his parents to check that they were not within earshot.

"I'm doing what I can in Prague, Grandpa," he whispered. "Many of the students are mobilising in support of Dubcek. Some of us have signed an open letter of protest aimed directly at the university's old guard."

His grandfather smiled, and beneath the rustic exterior Antonin could glimpse the savage smile of a politician praying silently for a long-awaited revenge. But the smile quickly faded and his grandfather poked his face towards Antonin's parents, who were just disappearing into the house with the suitcase.

"Have you told them about your exploits yet?" he asked.

Antonin shook his head.

"Not yet."

His grandfather grunted.

"Rather you than me. I gave up trying to talk about politics with your mother a long time ago. I think the communists must have brainwashed her while she was in Moscow."

Antonin shuffled uncomfortably.

"That's what's worrying me, Grandpa. There's more to it than just the open letter. Many of us are signing that."

His grandfather looked at him with curiosity.

"Oh yes," he said inquisitively.

Antonin nodded.

"I've met a girl. She's a very nice girl, but she's much deeper in than I am, a ringleader you might say. She's goes much further than Dubcek does, wants the leading role of the Party completely scrapped and the liberal democracy of your day restored. And amongst other things she thinks people like my parents should be thrown into prison for crimes against humanity."

A slow smile spread across his grandfather's face.

"Oh dear," he said with a faint grin. "If you're going to say what I think you're going to say, then I think we're all in for a rather difficult weekend."

Antonin nodded glumly.

"Yes, grandpa, we are. Sometime over the next two days I've got to find the guts to tell them we're going to get married."

* * * * * *

"You'll have to get off."

Antonin stopped leaning on the glass and turned to see a uniformed railway official looking at him from the corridor.

"Sorry?" he said.

"Train's broken down. You'll have to get off."

The official turned and started to shuffle away.

Antonin stared after him for a few moments and then stood up and stuck his head out into the corridor.

"Excuse me," he said.

The official turned with a bored expression.

"What's going to happen, then?"

The official shrugged.

"It's already happened. They've sent another train to pull us."

Again he turned to leave. Antonin, trying hard to resist a slight sense of annoyance at the man's inability to communicate properly, stepped firmly out into the corridor.

"If they've sent another train, why do I have to get off?"

The man turned again, clearly puzzled at this passenger's stubborn refusal to comply with a perfectly simple request.

"They're taking this train to the depot. Passengers can't go there. That's why you've got to get off. Now do you understand?"

"But what's going to happen to the passengers."

The official shrugged.

"Wait for the next one I suppose."

Antonin looked at him.

"And when's that?"

The official reached into his pocket and pulled out a small dog-eared railway timetable.

"Well . . ." he said slowly when he had found the correct page, "there's one coming through in ten minutes time . . ." Antonin breathed an inward sigh of relief, for he knew that his decision to catch the slow train had already cost him a lot of time and if he didn't get a move on he wouldn't arrive before night fell, " . . . but it's an express so it doesn't stop here. Where are you going to, anyway?"

Antonin told him. The official looked at him with a bemused expression, as if he were now firmly convinced he was dealing with a complete idiot.

"So what did you get on this train for? You should have taken the express."

"I made a mistake," Antonin grunted, not wishing to engage in a discussion on the point. "And when will the next stopping train arrive?"

Again he consulted his timetable.

"In just over five hours," the official muttered before turning away. This time Antonin let him go. Quietly returning to his carriage, he picked up his suitcase and headed for the exit.

Outside on the station platform the sultry afternoon sun was unpleasantly hot. He looked around to see what the other passengers were doing, but there were no other passengers. Moments later, the train started to reverse out of the station and move slowly away down the line along which it had recently arrived. And then he was all alone.

There was a single wooden bench under the shade of the angular yellow concrete construction he had seen from the train's window. He sat down, grateful for the shade, and looked wryly down the line as his train disappeared into the distance. The village he had seen lay behind him, and on the other side of the track a wide cornfield stretched away into the distance, featureless and forlorn. He found himself staring morosely across its vast expanse, trying to convince himself that someone would think to tell the driver of the express to stop and pick him up.

Ten minutes later he became aware of the sound of a train. He stood up, and far away in the distance saw the express approaching. His experience with the broken down train had sobered him up a bit, made him realise that he had come all the way from Oxford to Slovakia in order to complete some unfinished business. He resolved to stop climbing on slow trains and drifting off into foolish reminiscences. In future, in life as much as on the railways, he would take the express.

There was a shrill screech from the approaching train's whistle. And then, without so much as a faint application of the brakes, it thundered past him and disappeared into the distance.

Antonin watched it go. And then, wearily, he returned to his perch in the lonely waiting room and slumped down on the bench. The yellow walls of the waiting room, which had looked so bright from a distance, now appeared drab and dull, daubed with graffiti which concerned itself more with the sexual antics of the local teenager population than the recent revolution which had transformed the political life of the nation. Eventually, tired of reading the graffiti, he rose ponderously to his feet. Dragging his suitcase behind him, he wandered out of the station onto the village street.

Despite Vanessa's best efforts to dispose of inessentials, the suitcase was too heavy to contemplate a long walk. There were no cafes, no shops, no public buildings of any sort other than the station itself. And if the houses in the village were occupied they showed no sign of it, for there was not a soul to be seen in any direction.

Antonin struggled over to the duck pond and stood for a while watching a large flock of white ducks pulling at the generous quantities of weed with which the pond was infested. Then he sat himself down on the pile of disused tyres beside the pond and tried to work out what he was going to do.

It was already four o'clock. Another five hours and it would be dark. If he switched to an express at the next main station, it would be perhaps another three hours until he arrived at the station nearest to the mountain village where they had once lived. From there he would have to travel either by cab or bus, so he would be unlikely to arrive much before midnight, hardly a sensible time to appear.

He had pulled out a map from his case and was just trying to decide where to spend the night when his thoughts were interrupted by a loud quacking from the general direction of the pond. He looked up and saw the thin frail figure of an old woman in a black shroud. She was standing with her back to him beside the pond and in her hand she held some bread, which she was tearing up and throwing to the birds.

He rose to his feet and silently approached her, meaning to ask her precisely where they were on his map, but before he had a chance to speak she addressed him.

"We are in Gdin," she said softly.

Antonin gulped, for the old woman had not turned to face him and he had supposed she was not yet aware of his presence.

"Gdin," he repeated.

"Yes, Gdin."

Antonin stared at her apprehensively.

"Thank you," he said nervously. For some reason he glanced back at the station halt, its modern concrete brashness now somehow reassuring, for the old woman had succeeded in making him nervous by her manner.

"You need somewhere to stay," the old woman said, turning now to face him. Her eyes were small and dark, yet they studied him intently.

It should have been a question, but the intonation wasn't quite right for a question. It sounded more like a statement of fact.

"Yes," Antonin mumbled. "As a matter of fact I do. But not here. I was waiting for the next train."

The old woman started to laugh, and her laugh was a strange kind of croaking sound.

"I wouldn't wait here if I were you. The night train won't come. The next train will be tomorrow morning."

Antonin recoiled.

"How do you know that?" he asked. "How do you know the next train won't come?"

Again the old woman cackled.

"You can wait and see if you like," she said. "But it won't come."

Antonin stared at her for a moment, trying to persuade himself that she was making fun of him, or perhaps of herself. But her face was perfectly serious, and something about her manner convinced him that it would indeed be foolish to doubt her words. He looked uncertainly around.

"You can stay with me if you like," she continued.

"With you?"

"Yes. I live just there, in that cottage."

She extended a thin forefinger towards an ancient cottage covered in a thick layer of creepers. Antonin gulped, for the cottage looked disconcertingly like a witch's lair in some medieval fairy tale.

"There's nowhere else for you," she said. "Not for miles."

He looked at her hard. Apart from her uncanny knack of appearing to know about things before they happened he had to admit he could see no one before him but a kind old woman.

"Thank you," he mumbled. "That's very kind of you."

Without another word, the old woman turned and started to walk back towards her home. With a last uncertain look back at the empty railway line, he picked up his suitcase and followed her to the door of the cottage.

She pulled open the door and stepped inside. Apprehensively he followed her, for he could see that it was dark and slightly damp within and he could distinctly detect a faint smell of rotting wood. The inside of the cottage was divided into a number of tiny rooms, each of which appeared to be full of the accumulated clutter of many generations, as if people had lived and died in this cottage over the centuries and no one had ever bothered to clean up.

There was an ancient water pump in the narrow hallway, and underneath the pump was an old metal bucket. The woman took the pump in her frail arms and started heaving it up and down. Antonin stepped forward.

"Can I help you?" he asked.

She stopped pumping and stepped aside.

"Yes, you may. If you bring me some water I will make us both some tea."

Antonin pumped the water until the bucket was full. And as he did so, he continued to look around in amazement. Anywhere else in Europe and it would have had a preservation order slapped on it, for it appeared to be completely undeveloped, a medieval dwelling intact at the end of the twentieth century. The floors were of caked mud, the walls uneven and rough, and there was no sign of electricity or gas or, apart from the old pump, running water. And it suddenly became clear to him that this was not the home of a witch, but rather of a hermit.

He carried the bucket into the tiny back room which served as a kitchen. He was about to ask the old woman if she lived alone when she once again spoke.

"I have a cat," she said.

As if to acknowledge its announcement, a sinewy black cat appeared from nowhere and started rubbing against Antonin's legs. He looked down at the creature, and then he looked at the thin old lady stoking up a fire in the corner of the room, and he could not help but notice a certain similarity.

"My cat is my younger self," she said, and again Antonin could hear the faint cackle.

There was a wooden chair in the corner of the room. Antonin sat down on it and looked at her thoughtfully. Once, when he had been a young lecturer in London, he had met a young man who had claimed to have telepathic powers. He had told Antonin that if he thought of a number between one and ten thousand then he would tell him what it was. And Antonin had laughed at him long and hard until he had done precisely that.

"You find it strange that I can read thoughts," the old woman said without turning round.

"Yes," Antonin replied. "It is hard for me to accept."

"It is not always a pleasant thing," she said sadly. "Sometimes you see things about people which you would rather not see."

"Is that how you know about the train?"

"Perhaps. I just know they will not send the train. I don't know how I know."

"It must be strange."

She shrugged.

"For me it is not strange. I have been like this all my life."

The cat jumped stealthily up onto Antonin's lap and promptly curled up. He looked down at the purring ball of fur and a thought suddenly occurred to him.

"Oh yes," the old woman replied. "That is one of the best things about my second sight. That is how I know she is so like me."

Antonin looked up at her.

"You can talk to the cat?" he asked.

"Of course I can. A cat is all feelings. Strong clear feelings. Not nearly as complicated as a human."

Antonin laughed. Suddenly he felt a complete idiot, a fool because he had initially been frightened of the old woman. He had been like a blind man among the sighted, possessed of a foolish irrational fear of the unknown. And if there were any evil spirits about, they were in him, not her.

The old woman cackled.

"You are a clever man," she said. "I see that you do not fight the evidence before your eyes. That is quite unusual in a human."

Antonin looked at the cat. He was already beginning to understand that he didn't really need to speak his mind, but he still found it easier to do so.

"Who do you prefer, then? Cats or humans?"

For the first time since he had met her, Antonin could sense a wave of sadness fill the room, a deep overpowering sadness.

"It is not easy for me to be this way," she said. "When I was a young girl I often prayed that my second sight would leave me. If there had been eyes, I would willingly have cut them out so I could be like other girls."

Clearly upset, she turned away and started pulling some cups out from an old dresser. Antonin looked at her sadly, for he did not find it hard to imagine the suffering she had endured over the years.

It was as if she had felt the compassion in his mind. The sadness seemed to ease and again she turned to face him.

"You have waited such a long time for this day to arrive," she said softly. "And yet you are so very afraid. Why?"

Antonin stroked the cat quietly. It shuddered with pleasure at his touch. Then he looked up at her.

"Don't you know?" he said.

"I know it goes very deep," she said thoughtfully. "It goes back to your childhood. But you don't fully understand what it is that torments you." She smiled, as if she was pleased with herself because she had suddenly solved the riddle. "That's why you're here, isn't it? You want to find out."

Antonin nodded.

"I suppose so," he said.

"Why do you bother to look for them?" she asked. "They didn't help you before. Why should they help you now?"

Antonin looked at her with despair.

"I don't know where else to start."

"You could start with yourself."

"I've tried that. Ever since I went to England I've tried that. Sometimes you think you're making progress, you think you're winning. And then, in the middle of the night, you wake up and realise you don't have a chance."

She looked at him for a long time, and Antonin could tell that she was concentrating hard, trying to see the cause of his suffering. For a moment he tried to resist her gaze, but as he looked into her kindly eyes he could see that she was only trying to help him. He tried to become like the cat, allowing his mind to go blank so that the feelings would shine through.

"There was a double betrayal," she announced at last. "That is why it runs so deep."

He gulped but said nothing.

"First there was the long slow betrayal of your childhood. But you were strong, a resilient child then as you are a resilient man now. You found ways to cope. But what destroyed you was not that first betrayal but rather the second one, the sudden one, the one you couldn't understand. The one you still don't understand."

Antonin could feel the tightly repressed emotion of over two decades surging up within him. He looked at her with pleading eyes.

"Why?" he mouthed, asking a question he had asked himself so many times before. "I just can't understand why?"

With difficulty the old woman knelt down on the floor beside him, laying her hand gently on his cheek and meeting his eyes with hers.

"I don't know," she said. "And that is the strangest thing of all."

* * * * * *

Katrina's fringe was slightly too long. She flicked it away from her eyes and examined the nervous student sitting beside her on her living room sofa.

"Why do you think Jiri's set us up like this?" she asked.

Antonin squirmed uncomfortably under her penetrating gaze.

"I don't know," he replied anxiously. "Maybe it was one of his jokes. But I really think I ought to be going."

"You haven't drunk your tea yet," she observed.

He picked up the mug she had placed in front of him and started to sip the tea. Despite the plain cotton dress with which she had replaced the bathtowel, he was still finding it difficult to sit beside her in such intimate surroundings. It wasn't her fault, for not even the plainest of clothing would have been adequate to mask the overpowering sexual intensity which seemed to exude from every pore in her body. Most men would have jumped at the chance to sit beside such a beautiful young woman, but in this respect as in so many others Antonin was unusual. For he had never had a girlfriend at all, never mind a pretty one, and although he had no difficulty in conversing with girls when they formed part of a wider social group he shrivelled up with embarrassment whenever he found himself alone with one.

So now, instead of grabbing the chance of getting to know her better, he remained perched uncomfortably on the sofa, his eyes downcast, waiting for an opportunity to escape her presence.

After her earlier refusal to dismiss him Katrina had made no further attempt to speak. The silence began to become oppressive.

"So you've got nothing to do with the open letter, then?" Antonin said in a matter of fact sort of voice.

Katrina smiled slyly, and Antonin suddenly became aware that she had deliberately said nothing as if to force him to speak.

"Well . . ." she said, " . . .actually I wrote it."

"But I thought . . ."

"You thought I was going to persuade you to sign. Why should I? Why should I persuade anyone to sign a dangerous document if they don't want to do it for themselves?"

There was a strength in her voice which Antonin found rather frightening. He put down his mug and stood up.

"I really had better go," he said with determination.

Katrina scowled at him for a moment. Then her face suddenly softened.

"You're not very used to girls, are you, Antonin?" she said.

He gulped, completely thrown by her unexpected remark.

"I'd better go," he reiterated, taking hold of the doorhandle.

Katrina took a step towards him.

"Damn it, you stupid boy," she said in exasperation, "if I wanted you to go I could have got rid of you ten minutes ago. Can't you see that?"

He let go of the doorhandle. There was an edge to her voice which he had not noticed before. He turned to face her, and for the first time since he had arrived he allowed his eyes to meet hers. There was a kind of pleading intensity in them which completely disarmed him, and suddenly the fear he had felt since his arrival completely evaporated.

"Please sit down," she said softly.

He lowered himself onto the sofa again and looked up at her.

"Now I think I know why Jiri set us up like this," she said quietly, sitting down beside him.

"Why?"

"I told him once I was lonely. It's not something I often admit."

This time Antonin was shocked. He couldn't help but wonder how such a pretty girl could ever be lonely.

29

"You? Lonely?" he said.

She smiled.

"Yup. You sound surprised."

Antonin nodded.

"You're so . . ." he began.

"Confident?" she finished, not choosing the same word Antonin would have selected.

"If you like."

"It's just a cover. I learnt it a long time ago, when I was a girl. You use a different method, I see."

Antonin looked at her.

"Who said I was lonely?" he asked.

"You're so transparently lonely that you don't even bother to cover it up. I'd have thought you'd have known that much about yourself."

Antonin remained silent.

"Jiri's perceptive, isn't he?" she continued. "He could tell that we'd get on. But he knew we'd never make any headway if we just bumped into each other at some party. So he just shoved you round to my flat on a pretext and hoped for the best."

Antonin could feel a sense of unease returning. He looked at her uncertainly, wondering if he had made some sort of dreadful mistake. But there was no mistake. Katrina was quite definitely making a pass at him.

"Surely you've had lots of boyfriends," he asked uncertainly.

She shrugged.

"A few. But after a while you can tell that they're all after only one thing. That's all most men are after. But you're different, I think. Unusual. You want someone dished up whole."

He smiled weakly at her.

"Maybe I do," he said softly.

She laughed.

"As you see I make quick judgements about people," she said. "It's just the way I am. And now I've made enough of a judgement about you to know that I'd like to get to know you better. If, that is, you have no objection."

Antonin smiled, and perhaps for the first time in his life he could feel a ripple of pure uncontrollable happiness surge through his body.

"I've no objection," he said. "None whatsoever."

* * * * * *

The train gradually picked up speed. Antonin leant out of the window and waved at the frail old woman standing beside a black cat on the platform. She raised her hand and then turned away, heading back towards the village, her black cat following obediently in her footsteps.

She had been an odd interlude in his life, and it had been strange that he should have met her at such a moment as this. For the old woman had been like a lens, focusing his mind on the dilemmas which faced him and enabling him to understand far more clearly the nature of his current quest. For she had seen right through his journey, ruthlessly stripping away the fiction that he was seriously seeking a reconciliation with his parents, and successfully identified the true purpose of his trip. And yet the true reason, his secret desire to understand exactly what had happened to Katrina all those years ago, was an objective beyond his grasp.

He looked out of the window at the dull cornfields passing by. The train was still travelling towards his parents' home, and if he took no action to the contrary he would soon be standing on their doorstep. For all he knew they would still be there, and he would be back exactly where he had been twenty-two years before. They would all be considerably older than they had been then, but other than that precious little would have changed.

Antonin smiled wryly to himself. Living so far away must have made him begin to see his parents through the proverbial rose-tinted spectacles. He had supposed they would be pleased for a reconciliation, that they would actually want him back. But the old woman had exposed that notion as a myth, a self-comforting image of grief-struck parents paralysed with anger at their first-born son's betrayal. During his exile in England the myth had allowed him to view himself as far more important to his parents than he ever had been in reality.

The truth, he now had to accept, was far more humdrum. His childhood memories, when studied patiently and calmly by the mature adult the child subsequently became, were all memories of rejection and denial. He had to accept that his decision to emigrate to England would probably have been a relief to his parents. Their problem – their Antonin problem – had packed up and gone. Provided they didn't reply to his letters, and for that a certain self-generated anger would admittedly have been useful, they could simply pretend he didn't exist any more. The unwanted child could simply be written out of the script.

The cornfields were flying by at an increasing pace, as if the train driver were trying to speed Antonin to his destination as quickly as possible. He scowled, pulled his map out of his pocket, and began to work out where he could conveniently change trains and return to the airport at Bratislava. For the psychic old woman had merely confirmed the message which Vanessa had tried to convey to him in Oxford before he left: it was pointless to seek out his parents, even if they were still alive and he could trace them. And as for Katrina, the girl responsible for the second betrayal, she was far beyond his reach.

Yet despite his decision to return to Oxford, there was still a sense in which he was pleased he had come to Slovakia. Perhaps it had been worth it to dispel the myth that he would one day be able to turn the clock back to his youth and pick up where he had left off in 1968. Perhaps, if he could now accept the finality of his past, he would be able to return to the comfortable surroundings of his college rooms at Oxford and live out the closing decades of his life in peace and dignity.

There was only one snag to his plan, one nagging doubt lingering in his mind. Before it had seemed like a subsidiary issue, something which would resolve itself automatically once he found his parents. For although he had always been estranged from his parents there had been two people in his family at the time of his departure with whom he had once been close and had subsequently lost touch. One of them, his grandfather, would almost certainly be dead. But the other would in all probability still be alive.

His younger brother Stepan was a prize he might yet find.

* * * * * *

There was a distant cry. A cry of pain.

Antonin threw down the book in which he had been engrossed and jumped quickly out of the log cabin in the woods. It was Stepan's voice, the high-pitched voice of a young child, and it had come from some distance away. He had supposed that his little brother was in the house with their mother, but now he was sure the cry had come from the opposite direction, through the dense undergrowth on the far side of the cabin.

"Where are you Stepan?" Antonin screamed.

There was a long silence.

"Stepan!" he yelled out at the top of his voice, but again there was no reply.

He glanced uncertainly towards the house, wondering whether to go and fetch his mother, but then started to run towards the place from which he thought he had heard the cry.

The undergrowth was thick with the new growth of spring, long treacherous brambles protruding into the narrow paths which led deeper into the woods. He pushed them roughly aside with his hands as he ran, fearful that he was already too late, for the cry of pain had carried with it an ominous finality, and now he found the cold silence which met his shouts hard to endure.

As he pushed his way through the bushes he called out again and again, but still to no avail. By now his fingers were bleeding profusely as a result of pulling away the brambles, but he took no notice of the pain. He had to find Stepan.

There was a place where his younger brother might inadvertently have stumbled if he had wandered off alone into the woods. During the war a landmine had detonated nearby, leaving behind a deep overgrown pit with steep sides all round. Possibly, just possibly, Stepan might have fallen in.

Eventually he reached the edge of the pit. He looked down, and as he did so his heart was suddenly filled with a deep and penetrating ache, for there at the bottom, some twenty feet below him, lay the inert figure of his little brother.

Antonin tried to fight off the terror which now engulfed him, for the motionless body at the bottom of the pit was the tiny figure of the five-year-old child on whom Antonin had lavished all his love. And now, as he stared in horror at his brother's twisted form, he wondered how he would survive if he discovered he were gone.

Clinging onto the overhanging brambles, he clambered down into the pit and rushed towards the limp figure. Stepan was unconscious, his legs contorted behind him in an awkward and unnatural position. But Antonin was hardly aware of this as he knelt down beside him and tried to work out if he was still alive.

"Stepan," he whispered. "Don't die, Stepan. I don't think I can bear it if you die."

* * * * * *

Antonin folded away the map and leant wearily against the carriage window, watching numbly as the cornfields flew by. He could still clearly remember the day on which his brother had lost the use of his legs. He could remember the terror he had felt when he had seen him lying at the bottom of the pit. He could remember the moment of dread when he had believed his brother to be dead. And afterwards, when his parents had told him that Stepan would be confined to a wheelchair for the rest of his life, he could remember the almost infinite sense of relief which had engulfed him. For he had supposed his brother might die.

When Stepan came home from hospital Antonin had scarcely left his side. He had played with him and talked to him and sometimes, as Stepan tried to come to terms with his loss, he had cried with him. Feeling a sense of guilt at his own mobility, he had refused to go anywhere without his little brother, pushing him patiently around in his tiny wheelchair wherever he went.

Yet in spite of his disability Stepan soon began to make rapid progress. He was as precocious in his studies as his older brother, yet in many ways he seemed even more successful. For whereas Antonin was a cumbersome and withdrawn teenager, always seeking refuge in his books as an escape from social interaction, Stepan became increasingly gregarious. At school he was regarded by his teachers as a model student, successfully developing a rare knack of displaying enthusiasm for Marxism-Leninism without alienating his less than eager fellow students. As a result he was held up as a paradigm of virtue by the school authorities, periodically paraded across the pages of the local newspaper as a symbol of triumph over disability in a socialist state.

Stepan seemed to thrive on the attention he received. He eagerly joined the communist youth movement and became one of its leading members, so that by his mid-teens it already seemed that a successful career within the Party machine was within his grasp. And with his growing success it became apparent that his parents' preference for their younger child, obvious from the very moment of his birth, was becoming ever more pronounced. Antonin's own achievements, even on the rare occasions when they were recognised, were always set in the context of his brother's greater triumphs.

When his parents had moved to Slovakia, the young Stepan wanted desperately to remain in Berlin. So Antonin, who was already an undergraduate student at the university, had arranged to care for him in the cramped and uncomfortable surroundings of the student hostel which was his home.

Stepan's decision to remain in Germany proved to have been a wise one. His enthusiasm for communism, itself seemingly a replica of his parents' political convictions, had been continuing to impress. The editor of the communist youth paper had the bright idea of seeking a medical opinion on Stepan's condition from the leading orthopaedic surgeon in the land. He had asked him a simple question: if cost were no object, could Stepan ever be made to walk again?

Nobody had ever thought to ask this question before. After his childhood accident, his parents had been bluntly informed that he would have to remain in a wheelchair for the rest of his life. They had not thought fit to challenge this medical opinion and neither had anybody else. So now it came as something of a shock to Stepan and his family when they discovered that something could after all be done.

Shortly afterwards he had been admitted to a leading East Berlin clinic and had begun a lengthy series of operations on his spine and legs. For many long months he had remained hospitalised, only just recovering from one painful operation before being subjected to another. And eventually, triumphantly, he had won through. One fine summer day, in front of the television cameras and the assembled press corps of the East German state, Stepan had been pushed in his wheelchair into the garden of the clinic and proudly handed an ornately carved walking stick by the surgeon. And then, in front of the whole assembly, he had risen cautiously to his feet and begun to walk.

The operations had transformed Stepan's life. His suave self-confidence, already high for a disabled teenager, now reached dizzying heights, and even his pronounced limp he seemed to turn to his advantage. He was sixteen now, a handsome boy capable of turning on immense charm when he wanted to. And now that he could walk, the charm began to work on girls. He gathered around himself an enthusiastic band of devotees who would come back to Antonin's dingy room at the hostel and sit gazing at his little brother with admiring eyes. Stepan had chosen no particular girlfriend but seemed to prefer entertaining in batches, his manner shifting unexpectedly between gravitas and humour. And as if to please him his band of admirers would copy his moods, adopting serious poses when he became serious and laughing merrily when he began to jest.

As Antonin leant on the train's window and watched the cornfield fly by, he could still remember how disorientating he had found the rapid change in Stepan's fortunes at that time. The weak and defenceless invalid brother was suddenly no longer weak and defenceless. And he could still remember feeling a wistful sense of longing for the days when Stepan had been confined to his wheelchair. But he had always tried to rejoice in his younger brother's growing success.

Time had gone by and eventually Antonin's first degree had came to an end. He could have stayed in East Berlin for his postgraduate degree, and in the past had always assumed he would have to stay there to look after Stepan, yet now he decided to go to Prague instead. For despite all his attempts to resist the sensation, he knew deep down that Stepan was beginning to crowd him out.

Antonin had seen his younger brother just one more time before his departure for the West. In the summer of 1968, shortly before the Warsaw Pact tanks invaded, Stepan came to visit him in Prague. He was passing through on his way back to Berlin after a brief visit to his parents in Slovakia. He had been much more subdued than usual, more thoughtful perhaps, and had listened intently to Antonin's description of the unfolding events in Czechoslovakia that summer with interest rather than outright censure. It had been an Indian summer to a relationship that neither could possibly guess would end so very soon.

After his defection Antonin had agonised long and hard over whether to write to Stepan. He had known that Stepan was planning a career as a high-flying East Berlin apparachik. A dissident brother in the West was a dangerous connection. So eventually he had written a long letter to Stepan which he had arranged to be smuggled over the border by a friend and posted inside East Germany. In the letter he had explained the reasons for his departure and asked bluntly if Stepan could risk corresponding with him.

For weeks he had waited for a reply. And then, finally, a letter had arrived. The reply, like Antonin's own letter, appeared to have been smuggled out, for it had been posted in Vienna. In the letter, Stepan had spoken of his great love for him and his earnest wish that they remain in touch. But he had explained that the East German authorities were currently very jumpy about the Czech situation, having called him in for several difficult interviews about his relationship with his older brother. As a result Stepan had asked him not to write for the time being. He had assured him that as soon as it was safe to do so he would contact him again.

And that was the last time he had heard from his little brother.

* * * * * *

He had an uncanny sense of déjà vu. As he walked through the village he could feel the ghosts of his childhood rising up all around him. The old metal swing was still perched incongruously on a patch of waste ground beside the lane, the very same swing to which he had always run with his grandfather as a young child. It was still in exactly the same spot, still the same dowdy shade of green, still as rusty as it had ever been. Beside the waste ground flowed the murky little stream where he had once paddled with his grandmother's colander in the vain hope of catching some tiny fish. And all around him the tumble-down yet strangely quaint dwellings of the high hill village, the squat wooden houses in exactly the same state of dilapidated disrepair as they had been the last time he had seen them. And beyond and above the village, the timeless blue-grey stillness of the vast forest which shrouded the Slovakian uplands still cast its dull presence, just as it had done when he was a child.

It was twenty-two years since he had last set foot in this place. Men had landed on the moon, microcomputers had taken over the face of the world, countless presidents and prime ministers had come and gone, a whole generation of humanity had died and a whole new generation had been born to replace them. But here, in this village of his childhood dreams, his spiritual home, nothing whatsoever had changed.

His family home was still several streets away, for the village had always been a fairly substantial one. Antonin hesitated, and then turned and tramped over the rough ground towards the swing. He lowered his ample form onto the wooden seat, realising with something of an shock that although the village may not have changed he himself certainly had, and began to rock backwards and forwards.

But eventually he rose. The sun, which until a few minutes earlier had been shining brightly, had disappeared behind a bank of cloud. Now a slight breeze was picking up, and Antonin knew it would not be very long before it started to rain. He began to step out briskly towards his family home, fully expecting it to look exactly the same as it had done when he had last seen it.

He turned the last corner and stopped dead. For a little way in front of him, on the site where his family's wooden house had once stood, there was now a large modern two-storey building of concrete construction.

He walked uncertainly down the street. Finding the family home was something of which he had been relatively sure, a fixed reference point. And now its disappearance suddenly disoriented him, made him unsure again about what his exact purpose here might be.

The concrete structure had not just devoured his family's home but also a number of other similar homes to either side. A plain flight of steps rose up from the pavement to a slightly incongruous pair of Doric columns flanking an imposing set of double wooden doors. Other than this rather grand façade, absurdly out of style with the folksy style of the rest of the village, the building appeared to be a plain and unprepossessing modern office block, with neat rows of small rectangular windows set into plain whitewashed walls. Yet of the precise purpose of the building there was no further clue.

Without really knowing why, he climbed up the steps and examined the double doors. There was no brass plaque or other sign to indicate the business of the building's occupants, merely a discreet bell set into the concrete beside the doors. Glancing around uncertainly, he rang the bell and waited.

Several minutes went by. He rang the bell again. This time, since he could not hear any ringing, he knocked sharply on one of the doors as well. As he knocked he could feel the door move beneath his touch. He pushed it more firmly and it swung gently open, revealing a spacious but sombre and ill-lit hallway within.

He stepped cautiously over the threshold.

"Hallo," he called out softly, not wishing to disturb unduly the hushed silence within. For if this was indeed an office building, it was not like any he had ever seen before.

A few moments later a door to one side of the hallway swung open and a short thin man of about sixty hobbled out. He was wearing a faded white coat with a number of pens tucked neatly into his breast pocket.

"Who do you want?" the man asked.

Antonin stared at him uncertainly.

"I used to live here," he mumbled.

The man's eyes narrowed slightly as he examined Antonin carefully.

"I don't recognise you," he said, taking a pace forward and peering up into Antonin's face.

Once again Antonin looked round the hallway.

"What is this place?" he asked.

The old man shrugged.

"You should know. You said you lived here."

"Sorry," Antonin explained, "I didn't mean I lived here recently. I meant as a child, before this building was here."

"Oh," the man said. "I see."

Antonin looked at his blank face. It was not an unkindly face, merely the face of one who rarely had occasion to use his mind.

"So what is this building then?" he repeated.

The man was on the point of replying when there came from

the first floor the sound of a faint cry. He glanced apprehensively upstairs.

"Excuse me for a moment," he said, "I shouldn't think I'll be long."

He turned and started climbing the stairs, leaving his visitor alone in the hall. The cry had been weak, the cry of an old person in trouble, and Antonin wondered whether the building was some kind of old people's home. He wandered over to the small reception desk to one side of the hallway and started idly flicking through a pile of ill-sorted papers, hoping to find out if his theory was correct.

"What are you doing?" came a sharp voice, and Antonin looked up to see a prim middle-aged woman in a white nurse's uniform glowering at him from a few paces away.

Antonin gulped, for he knew he was being rather nosey poking around on the desk and now he felt guilty at having been caught red-handed.

"Sorry," he mumbled. "I was just trying to find out what goes on here."

"Why?" the woman snapped aggressively, and Antonin instantly recognised an East European official of the old school. In his youth he had hated them with a profound loathing, and now he found his hatred had not faded one jot over the intervening years.

"Because I'm interested, that's why!" he replied tersely.

The woman appeared shocked. Antonin knew the sort all too well. They were so used to getting their own way when they growled at people that they didn't quite know how to react when somebody growled back.

"It is an asylum for mentally deranged elderly citizens," she said in a matter of fact tone of voice. "Why do you wish to know?"

"It's as I said, I was curious. A long time ago, when there were just private homes here, I used to live in a house on this site."

The woman said nothing. Now he had told her he felt rather incongruous. His past was of no possible interest to her. He inclined his head slightly towards the woman.

"Thank you for your help," he said faintly, and without waiting for a reply turned and walked towards the door.

He stepped outside under the wide porch and pulled the door closed behind him. It had just started to rain quite heavily and he was still standing under cover of the porch when he heard the door opening once again behind him.

It was the man who had first greeted him.

"Did you say you once lived here?" he asked.

He nodded.

"Is your name by any chance Antonin?"

Antonin stared at him incredulously. For a split second he wondered if he had stumbled across another Slovakian clairvoyant like the old woman with the cat.

"Yes," he mumbled. "I'm Antonin Ziegler."

The man nodded.

"He talks about you a lot. He always said you would come for him one day."

"Who?"

"One of our patients. He said you were his grandchild and that you would come for him. He's been waiting for years."

Antonin could feel his heart pounding. It wasn't possible. Surely he couldn't be talking of his grandfather.

"But he's too old," he blurted out. "It's not possible he's still alive."

"He's not always entirely lucid," the man said, ignoring his remark. "If you've not seen him for a long time you'll probably find him much changed. And you must remember he is not used to visitors. Until you came, there was no one."

Again, Antonin could feel the internal shock, as if someone had hit him.

"No one," he said uncertainly. "But my parents. My brother Stepan. Do they not come to see him sometimes?"

"If he has any family they never come to see him. And he never talks about anyone other than a grandson called Antonin. Frankly, until you arrived I was not sure whether you were a real person or some kind of fantasy he had created to comfort him in his old age."

For a moment Antonin said nothing. He thought he had braced himself for most eventualities, but not for this.

"Is he here now?" he asked.

The man nodded, and then pushed his head inside the building again as if to check who was in the hall.

"If you like I will take you to him now," he said in a slightly conspiratorial tone. "Strictly speaking these are not the visiting hours and you should not be here, but he has waited so long. It would seem cruel."

With a final apprehensive glance inside, he led Antonin in silence through the hall and up the stairs. The woman who had challenged him before was nowhere to be seen, and from his manner Antonin realised that his guide was wary of encountering her. Once upstairs, they walked along a narrow landing until they reached a room marked "Lounge".

"You'll find him over there," his guide said, pushing the door open and pointing with his finger, "sitting beside the window with his back to us. I'll come back and fetch you later on."

The room was warm and spacious, if somewhat lacking in character. It was dotted with high-backed modern armchairs covered in a lurid orange fabric. Several of the chairs were occupied by elderly people in varying stages of decrepitude, most of them female. One or two of the residents looked up at the new arrival, but most of them took precisely no notice. Other than the quiet drone from a television set in the corner, the room was completely silent.

Antonin walked over to the chair his guide had indicated. It was facing a large picture window, through which the view of the nearby village houses and the more distant hills was exactly the same as it had once been from his grandparents' old house. Only the gardens in the foreground were different.

He walked round to the front of the chair.

Sure enough, his grandfather was there. He looked thinner and older than the last time he had seen him, but he was still recognisably the same man. He was asleep, his head leaning against the high back of the chair, and resting on his lap was an open newspaper.

Antonin reached out a hand, meaning to touch his grandfather's arm and wake him, but then he changed his mind and pulled up a vacant armchair. Positioning it so that he could comfortably watch his grandfather, he settled down to gaze at the old man's face as he slept.

For nearly half an hour he waited. Once or twice he noticed his guide appear silently at the door and glance nervously in their direction, but he made no attempt to disturb them.

Finally his grandfather stirred. He opened his eyes and gazed out through the picture window with a lost and distant expression on his face. And although Antonin was sitting only a few feet away from him, he did not yet seem to be aware of his presence.

"Grandpa."

Antonin spoke the word softly, for fear he might alarm the old man. Slowly, his grandfather's head turned.

"Antonin," he said with a gentle smile, but to Antonin's amazement there was no surprise in his manner. His grandfather just sat and gazed placidly towards him.

"You look different today, Antonin," he said in a quiet voice.

"Older. And you have become too fat. You must eat less of grand-mother's puddings and more of my vegetables. Vegetables are so much better for you."

His grandfather's face was still placid and calm, the face of an old man lost in some unfathomable private world. Antonin could feel the tears welling up inside him, fearful that he had arrived too late, too late to break into the hidden world of extreme old age.

But then, just as he was about to despair, a change seemed to come over his grandfather. It was not much at first, just a confused flicker of the eyes, an alertness long since repressed. And then, with considerable effort, his grandfather pulled himself up in his chair.

"Antonin?" he asked, and this time there was an anxiety in his voice, an anxiety which suggested uncertainty.

Antonin could no longer fight back the tears. He rose to his feet and leant down, embracing his grandfather and gently kissing his wrinkled face.

"It's really me, Grandpa. I've come back."

Slowly but surely the doubt seemed to clear. A smile gradually spread across his face.

"You've been a long time coming, Antonin," he said. "I'd almost given up hope of you."

Antonin nodded.

"Too long, Grandpa. Can you forgive me?"

By now the old man seemed wide awake, and Antonin guessed that he was probably more awake than he had been for a very long time.

"Have you come from Prague?" he asked.

Antonin shook his head.

"No. From England. I've been living in England for over twenty years, ever since the Soviets invaded. That's why I didn't come to you, Grandpa. Until now, I couldn't come."

The old man smiled faintly, but although the smile was faint, it held within it all the frustrated savagery of a man who could still remember the shattered dreams of his youth.

"The Soviets," he snarled softly. "They're good and proper buggered up now, aren't they, Antonin?"

Antonin smiled.

"Yes Grandpa. They are. And you had to wait a long time for that too, didn't you?"

The old man looked at Antonin thoughtfully. And as he did so a somewhat impish look appeared, rather like that of a naughty schoolboy. He leant his head towards Antonin with a conspiratorial expression.

"Oh well," he said quietly, as if he didn't want anyone to overhear. "Now you've come you'll be able to get me out of here."

His grandfather remark hadn't been a question. It was more a statement of fact.

"Sorry?" Antonin said, unsure exactly what his grandfather meant.

"I can come to England and live with you and that girl you were going to marry, can't I? What was her name? Katrina?"

Antonin tried to look away, but his grandfather had caught his eyes with a vice-like grip. It was a trick he had always used with him when he was a boy, so that however hard you tried you simply could not look away. The technique still worked just as well as it ever did.

"Didn't you marry her, then?" his grandfather asked at last.

Antonin shook his head.

"No."

"Nobody?"

"No."

The old man looked almost relieved.

"Good," he said. "All the more reason why I can come and keep you company until I die, then. Surely you won't begrudge your old grandfather that."

"What's so wrong with it here, Grandpa?" Antonin asked softly. Yet he already knew the answer to the question. All the other chairs in the room were facing inwards, towards the centre of the room. His grandfather's was facing outwards. That said it all.

"Have you met her yet?" his grandfather grunted, with a venomous emphasis on the word 'her'.

Antonin nodded.

"Yes," he said. "She's a little . . .'brusque', isn't she?"

"She's a veritable witch," the old man snarled. "Sent by the devil to give the new recruits to hell a taster of things to come."

Antonin looked at him sadly. It would perhaps have been better if his grandfather had been like the other senile old folk in the room. At least with them the brain fitted the body.

"I don't know anything about what's happened since I left, Grandpa," he said at last. "They say nobody comes to see you."

For a fraction of a second a sharp flicker of pain seemed to pass across his grandfather's face, as if he had been cut by a knife. But then the pain disappeared as quickly as it had come, replaced by a strangely forlorn expression.

"You will take me away with you, won't you, Antonin?" he pleaded. "I've been waiting for you so long. I always knew you were the only one I could trust."

Antonin flinched.

He hesitated before speaking, reluctant to ask. But he had to know. He simply had to know.

"Are they all dead, grandfather? Was there some accident that I don't know about?"

For several seconds his grandfather stared at him blankly. Then, with an extreme effort, he leant forward in his chair.

"Nobody comes," he whispered. "Nobody ever comes."

Antonin looked at him in despair. It was as if he were floating away again, returning to the safe private world he had inhabited before Antonin had arrived.

His grandfather had closed his eyes again. Antonin rose slowly to his feet. He felt angry with himself for having brought the old man such pain when he should have brought him nothing but joy. But things couldn't be left like this. That just wasn't an option. He bent over his grandfather and gently kissed his weary face.

"I'll be back in a minute," he said softly.

The old man's face was relaxed again, his gentle features calm and placid. Antonin turned smartly away and walked towards the door. Once outside, he marched along the corridor and back down the stairs to the hallway. The officious nurse was sitting at the desk flicking through some papers. At his approach she looked up.

"It's you again," she said. "What were you doing up there?"

"Your colleague realised you had my grandfather here. He's the very elderly man who sits by the window upstairs. He was kind enough to let me see him."

"He should not have done so. Visiting hours are two till four every afternoon."

"I'm sorry. I didn't know. But now I'm here, there are some things I need to know."

She looked at him askance, as if wondering whether to throw him out, but then she thought better of it and remained silent.

"I've been in England for a long time, since 1968." Antonin continued. "I've had no contact with any of my family during that time. Yet when I asked him about them he seemed frightened, as if the memories were very painful to him. It's clear he can't talk about it."

44

The nurse shrugged.

"I wouldn't know."

"But surely you must know something."

From the look on her face he could see that the nurse was rapidly tiring of the conversation. It was brutally plain that she just didn't care. She didn't care about Antonin's plight, and she certainly didn't care about that of his grandfather.

"Do you have a file on him?" Antonin asked. "You must have some kind of file."

The nurse rose to her feet.

"Of course," she said imperiously. "A confidential file. But I could not possibly allow you access to the confidential file. It would be a flagrant breach of the regulations."

"But couldn't you just read the file and tell me more about my grandfather. Surely that's a reasonable enough request in the circumstances."

The nurse shook her head fiercely.

"Perhaps in England you do not understand the meaning of a confidential file. But in Slovakia confidential means just that. It is a medical record. It is private. And now, if you will excuse me, I must return to my work. The normal visiting hours are from two until four every afternoon should you wish to see your grandfather again."

She sat down and deliberately started to leaf through the papers, as if to indicate to him that the conversation had come to a close. Antonin could feel his blood pressure gradually rising.

"Tell me the name of his doctor then," he demanded angrily, taking a step towards her. "If you can't help me then perhaps he can."

The woman looked up at him sarcastically.

"I am the senior psychiatrist" she said. "And as such, I am responsible for all matters relating to the patients in this institution. And now I must ask you to leave the premises. If you wish you may return tomorrow during the stipulated visiting hours."

Antonin stared at her wide-eyed. As a bitter and frustrated nurse he had felt he could just about make sense of her conduct, but as a psychiatrist? No wonder his grandfather had been so fearful.

"I have one further request," Antonin asked slowly, for any doubts he had previously harboured about his grandfather's unexpected request were evaporating with every sentence which emanated from the woman's mouth.

"It is possible I will wish to take charge of my grandfather's welfare from now on. Please can you explain to me the correct procedure should I wish to do so."

For a few moments the doctor looked taken aback, as if genuinely surprised by his request.

"Why on earth would you want to do that?" she asked.

Antonin leant over the desk so that his face was not far from hers.

"I suspect you may find this hard to grasp," he said, "but I actually love him. I always have. He appears to have nobody else who cares for him here and he wishes to be near me during the closing days of his life. I shall therefore arrange to take him back to England with me."

The doctor thought for a minute, as if weighing up several conflicting considerations. Then she seemed to make up her mind.

"It is impossible," she said. "Completely impossible."

This time Antonin was really shocked. He had supposed he would be doing them a favour.

"Why?"

"Because your grandfather was admitted here under a medical protection order. He is not just free to leave on a whim."

Antonin stared at her.

"What are you talking about? What's a medical protection order?"

"Your grandfather was sent here many years ago for his own protection by order of the courts. He was deemed to be a danger not only to himself but also to others."

"Why? What's he done to deserve that?"

"I can't tell you that, I'm afraid."

Antonin swallowed hard, trying to fight his own temper.

"Why not?"

The doctor smiled, enjoying her final revenge.

"Because," she said smugly, "it's in the confidential file."

* * * * * *

It was just as well it was a warm summer evening, because he'd already been waiting there for over four hours, sitting on a tree stump at the far end of the road and carefully watching for any sign of life. The light was beginning to fade and still nobody had left the clinic. Unless there was a rear exit, then both the doctor and her assistant must still be inside. It was getting dark and he was getting tired. Not for the first time it crossed his mind that they might actually live there. His suitcase was still down in the valley, at the railway station, and soon he would simply have to start thinking about returning to town in order to find a room for the night.

It was gradually starting to get chilly. Antonin shivered, glancing at a nearby telephone box and wondering if he should phone to the nearby town for a taxi. But then, just as he was about rise to his feet, he saw the door to the clinic swing open.

It was the elderly assistant he had met earlier. He walked slowly down to the bottom of the stairs before turning away from Antonin and starting down the street in the opposite direction.

Antonin was ready for action, having just had four hours sitting on a rather uncomfortable tree stump in order to plan what to do. He walked quickly down the road after the man, being careful not to catch up with him until he had turned several corners and was well away from any prying eyes in the clinic. Then he stepped up his pace and quickly caught up with him.

"Excuse me," he said in a friendly voice.

The man stopped and turned.

"Oh, hallo again," he said.

"I wanted to thank you. What you did was very kind."

From the grateful look on the chap's face it was clear that he wasn't thanked for anything very often.

"That's all right. You cheered him up by coming." He hesitated for a moment, examining Antonin with curiosity. "But you left ages ago. You haven't been waiting outside all this time just to thank me, have you?"

Antonin decided to take the remark head on.

"No," he said. "Although I am grateful to you, really I am. It's just that I don't know anything about what's happened to my grandfather or the rest of my family. I've been abroad, so I haven't been able to have any contact with them. And now I want to know what's happened, not just to my grandfather but to the rest of my family. I asked the doctor, but she wasn't very helpful. That's why I waited to talk to you."

The man looked at him uncertainly.

"She's my boss," he said with a frown. "I can't go against her."

"I'm not asking you to do anything improper. I just wondered if you could tell me something about my grandfather. He can't seem to talk about his past very easily."

He could see the man was still unsure. The bureaucrat in him was visibly fighting the human being. But finally he seemed to come to a conclusion. The human being won.

"Your grandfather has been with us ever since the clinic was built about twenty years ago. I wasn't here when he arrived but I gather he used to be in a very bad state. He's actually got better over the years – more settled, you might say."

"The doctor said something about a medical protection order."

"That's right, I understand he's in under a court order. It had something to do with what he did before he came here, but I don't know exactly what that was."

"Isn't it in the file?"

"Yes, but the file's confidential. I'm not allowed access to patient files. I just clean up after them when they're sick."

"So who is, besides the doctor?"

The man shook his head.

"Nobody. The files are locked away in her office and only she's got the key. She's a bit odd, you know. Rather secretive."

"She doesn't seem to be a very caring sort of person, does she?"

The man smiled wryly.

"Frankly," he said in a whisper, "I'm inclined to share your grandfather's opinion that she's a witch. But I can't do anything about it, or else I'd lose my job, and with the way things are right now I can't afford to risk that."

Antonin looked at him balefully.

"I'm thinking of taking him back to England with me," he said.

"Not a chance if he's under a medical protection order unless the doctor agrees."

"She doesn't. But what if I applied to the district medical authorities to have the case reviewed?"

The man shrugged.

"They'd refer the whole thing to the courts. Then the courts would ask the doctor. You'd probably be straight back where you started."

"So he's effectively a prisoner."

"That's just about what it boils down to, I suppose. The only real difference between a medical protection order and a prison sentence is that there's no parole."

Antonin could feel the frustration building up within him. Fighting a case through the labyrinthine bureaucracy of the Slovakian courts would take months if not years. His grandfather would probably be dead by the time he finished. And still he didn't even know what his grandfather had done. He looked glumly at the elderly nurse. He had been sure he would know something, yet the fellow seemed to know as little as he did.

"Oh well," Antonin said sadly. "Thanks for your help. Tell my grandfather I'll come and see him tomorrow afternoon."

The man started to walk briskly on. But then, as Antonin watched him leave, his pace gradually began to slow. Finally he stopped, glanced uncertainly over his shoulder, and walked slowly back.

"Your grandfather's a decent old chap," he said. "Over the years he's talked about you a lot. Whatever they say, I know he'll be better off with you."

Antonin looked at him uncertainly. His words could just have been idle sentiment, but his face suggested something more.

The man glanced around, checking that nobody was within view.

"If you really want to take him, bring a car with you tomorrow afternoon at four, right at the end of visiting hours. It's my boss's afternoon off and I'm the only one there. If he vanishes, I promise you I won't notice a thing until the following day. And if you want to take the confidential file as well, you'll find it in the middle drawer of the filing cabinet in the room off the hallway. It's not very strong, so bring a spanner with you and wrench it open. Then take the file you want and tidy up nicely so that I can honestly say I didn't notice that either. Oh yes, and leave a note under his pillow saying that the reason you've taken him with you is because of the uncaring and irresponsible way in which clinic is being run by the doctor in charge."

Antonin looked at the man in astonishment.

"But won't you get into terrible trouble over this?" he said.

The man nodded, a sly grin spreading across his face.

"Probably," he replied, "but not half as much as she will."

* * * * * *

Jiri's flat was half-way up a high but unprepossessing tower block in the heart of Bratislava's vast southern housing estate. Built as the solution to the post-war housing shortage, the estate was one of the largest in the old socialist bloc, a terrible scar on the landscape of what had once been a fine medieval city. For mile after endless mile, stretching away from the Danube towards the Austrian frontier, the huge tower blocks rose upwards towards the sky, looking from the distance rather like some vast Soviet-style Manhattan. Yet any fleeting illusion of grandeur faded quickly as the crumbling prefabricated structures loomed closer, for the buildings were already in a state of advanced disrepair as a result of decades of near total neglect.

Antonin quietly pulled the curtains shut and tiptoed out of the bedroom door, relieved to discover that his grandfather had finally fallen asleep. Jiri had gone out for the evening, attending one of his interminable political meetings in the city centre, and for the first time since smuggling his grandfather away from the old people's home earlier that day he found himself completely alone.

It would be wrong to say that he was cross with himself, yet he was disturbed that he had acted with such an uncharacteristic lack of foreplanning. He had found himself angered and appalled by what he had seen at the old people's home. Perhaps he had found the determination to act so decisively because he had seen in his grandfather's circumstances a glimmer of what might yet be in store for him in the vulnerable years of extreme old age. Yet now, left alone to reflect on his conduct, he could not help but wonder whether he might have been a little rash.

He had not yet formulated any definite plans about exactly how he was going to get the old man to Oxford. He had no passport, no identification papers of any kind. Technically at least, Antonin had now committed at least two criminal offences by absconding with the old man and stealing his confidential file from the doctor's filing cabinet. Yet despite the circumstances he was pretty sure he could arrange it. In the continuing state of political uncertainty nobody would be interested in chasing after a man in his nineties. The Czechoslovakian authorities might well object if he made a formal application for papers, but the body searches which had typified the country's land frontiers under the old communist regime had vanished, making it relatively easy to smuggle him over the nearby border to Austria. Once in Vienna, he could arrange for his grandfather to apply for political asylum in Britain in just the same way he himself had successfully applied some twenty years before. In the circumstances, with the application backed by a well-connected and highly respected Oxford academic, it was unlikely that the Home Office would raise any serious objections.

And there was no doubt that the day's dramatic events had had a beneficial effect on his grandfather. Once away from the home, his health and general mental alertness had seemed to improve proportionately with every mile they travelled. He had become visibly more relaxed, telling jokes and reminiscing about the good times in his life. And yet there was still an ominous gap, and at no time during the day's journey had he referred to the period of time between Antonin's departure from Czechoslovakia in 1968 and his subsequent arrival at the old people's home.

Fearful of upsetting his grandfather once more, Antonin had not probed. Neither had he revealed to him that he had quietly removed his confidential file from the doctor's office. Only now that he was sure he was alone did he carefully lift up his suitcase onto the dining table in Jiri's cramped living room and open the lid. Pulling out a large grey envelope, he extracted the file and started to read.

It was entitled 'Medical Protection Order – Vladimir Kosik' and was marked 'Confidential – For Authorised Medical Personnel Only'.

'This is to certify,' the document began, 'that Vladimir Kosik, formerly of the village of Urbanek in the district of Zilina, is committed under Section 4, Subsection xi of the Restraint of Persons of Unsound Mind Act, to be held in an approved psychiatric institution for a period of indeterminate duration.'

For several paragraphs the document droned on in this standard official language, giving little away other than the fact that two doctors and a court official had signed the restraint order in May 1969, some nine months after Antonin's departure from the country. Antonin read on, fearful that the document contained nothing really useful, until his eye alighted upon a section entitled 'Case Background'.

'Vladimir Kosik was arrested by local militia in the village of Urbanek on 14th May 1969,' it began. 'The fire brigade had been alerted during the night by local residents when they became aware of smoke rising from Mr Kosik's house. Mr Kosik had been living in the house alone since the recent death of his daughter and her husband. By the time the fire brigade arrived, the house was completely ablaze. It was a warm and windy evening, and other neighbouring wooden houses had also caught fire as a result of the blaze. The fire brigade alerted the local militia when they became aware of Mr Kosik staggering around in the garden of his burning house brandishing a large axe. When they attempted to extinguish the fire, Mr Kosik attacked the fire brigade, severing several of their water hoses with the axe. The fire brigade were forced to withdraw from the scene until the militia arrived and disarmed Mr Kosik. Mr Kosik was then taken to a local militia station and administered sedatives.

'Mr Kosik does not appear to have a history of violence. Enquiries in the village, where Mr Kosik has lived all his life, have revealed that he lived there with his wife until her death in 1962. He then lived in the house alone for three years until, in 1965, his only daughter and her husband came to live with him. It is believed that

Mr Kosik became mentally deranged following the murder of his daughter and her husband during a burglary at his home.

'Mr Kosik is convinced that his family committed suicide following harassment by State Security and other government agencies. Yet enquiries with State Security have confirmed that no such investigation ever took place. It seems likely that this paranoid persecution complex might be related to Mr Kosik's own close involvement with bourgeois political movements during the early part of his life.

'It is recommended that in view of his advanced years no further criminal charges be brought against Mr Kosik. However, in order to ensure he does not harm himself or cause harm to others, it is felt that he should be subject to indefinite observation in a protected environment under the terms of a Medical Protection Order.'

For a long time Antonin stared blankly at the sheet of paper in front of him. He had read the words but he could not absorb the meaning.

"They were shot."

With a jolt Antonin swung round and saw his grandfather standing just behind him, looking down at the file. He was still wearing his night-shirt, but his eyes were calm and composed.

"I thought you were asleep."

His grandfather lowered himself into a chair beside Antonin.

"I can see it all clearly now," he said slowly. "Before it was nothing but a blur, but now I can see it all very clearly again."

Antonin pushed the file towards him.

"Is it true?" he asked.

"I haven't got my glasses. Read it to me."

Antonin did. When he had finished his grandfather sighed heavily.

"Most of it is true," he said. "Your parents died in my house. After that I could not bear to live there any more. And one day, when I had drunk too much vodka, I set light to it. I wanted it destroyed. That is why they thought I was mad."

"It says here you thought it was suicide? That they committed suicide?"

His grandfather shook his head firmly.

"Your father was suicide, I think. There was no evidence of a break-in. And when I found them dead he had the gun in his hand. But only the day before it happened I'd spoken to Martina and she'd seemed quite normal. I'm certain she didn't know what was about to happen."

Antonin could feel his throat going dry.

"Are you saying my father murdered my mother and then shot himself?" he murmured.

His grandfather nodded slowly.

"I think so," he said, looking Antonin square in the eye, "although I suppose it's possible someone gained access to the house and then carefully staged it to look that way."

Antonin stared at him uncertainly, trying to convince himself that his grandfather was confused. But he was not confused. That much was plain from his eyes.

"But why? They loved each other. They were with you in Slovakia. It's what they'd always wanted. Why should my father have done such a thing?"

His grandfather poked his finger at the file.

"You just read in there what I think. For some time before it happened your father was very tense and irritable. He was obviously frightened, and I think that he had even stopped talking to your mother about what was on his mind. He thought I couldn't see anything, of course, but I knew that look very well. He had the look of a hunted man."

"Hunted? You mean State Security?"

His grandfather nodded.

"I saw it many times in the fifties. When the communists came to power in forty-eight many of my friends disappeared. Each of them had that same look on his face in the weeks before he was arrested. And I myself was investigated at that time, I too know what it feels like when they are on your tail."

Antonin frowned.

"But neither of my parents were like you. They were always slavishly loyal communists. They had nothing to fear."

His grandfather scowled.

"You should know the communists better than that. They are even crueller to their own than they are to their enemies. I think your father must have made them suspicious about something or other at his work. So they started to turn on the pressure. Eventually he broke."

"Did you understand about his work, Grandpa? He and mother always used to be so secretive. All I knew was that he was the administrator of a research institute."

"It was a venture officially funded by Prague and East Berlin. Some of the staff were German, others Czechoslovak. Your father was a reliable man, he spoke German, Czech and Slovak fluently. I think that was the main reason why he got the job. But he never discussed what he did there."

Antonin rose to his feet and walked over to a cupboard to one side of the room. On it was a half-drunk bottle of cheap Slovakian brandy and some glasses. Pouring out two drinks, he returned to the table. He felt weary, but in a strange sort of way he didn't find himself overly distressed by his parents' death. Perhaps, for him, they had died long before. But it still didn't make sense. His father had had many failings, but a suicidal temperament was certainly not one of them.

He sat down again at the table and turned once more to face his grandfather.

"What happened to Stepan?" he asked at last.

His grandfather scowled. It had always been an open secret that they had never got on.

"He vanished. I haven't seen him or heard from him since it happened."

Antonin looked at him with a puzzled expression.

"He just vanished. Completely."

"Your parents had a will. They left some money to you and Stepan. As far as I know it's still there. After it happened, before I was arrested, I wrote to him many times at his address in Berlin. But he never replied."

At his words Antonin looked up sharply. Then he picked up the file and checked the date.

"When did they die? It says here May 1969."

His grandfather shook his head.

"No," he said. "That was when I burnt the house down. They died long before, the previous autumn. September, I think. Anyway, it wasn't very long after the Russians came."

Antonin swallowed hard. If it had been September 1968 it would have been just weeks after his own defection.

"Did they say anything about me to you, Grandpa? Did they say anything about me going away or about any letters?"

Again his grandfather shook his head.

"No. They said nothing to me. I didn't know there were any letters."

"But there were dozens of letters. I wrote to them and to you dozens of times over several years before I gave up trying? Are you saying that in all that time between September 1968 and May 1969 you never received any of my letters at the house."

His grandfather looked him straight in the eye, a sad echo of a distant sorrow etched on his face. And suddenly Antonin knew that his grandfather's pain, the pain he had seen so vividly on his first visit to the old people's home, had not been caused by his parents' death at all. When his grandfather finally spoke, it was in a scarcely audible whisper.

"As the months went by, I really did begin to wonder if you'd abandoned me too, Antonin. You see, it was you I was waiting for after their deaths. I thought I knew you. I trusted you more than any of the rest of them. I thought you'd be sure to come and help me in my hour of greatest need. And when I finally burnt the house down that night, it was really your memory I was trying to banish."

* * * * * *

Jiri picked up a small stone lying on the pavement and threw it over the side of the bridge. He watched it fall until it splashed into the wide expanse of the Danube far below. Then he turned towards Antonin.

"They could get rid of people just like that," he said bluntly. "They didn't need to drive their enemies to suicide."

For a while Antonin said nothing, watching a huge river barge piled high with coal as it chugged methodically towards the bridge. Only when it had disappeared from view beneath the arches did he look up at his friend.

"But what about the letters? My grandfather lived there for eight months after they died. I wrote to the address frequently, but none of them got through."

Jiri shrugged.

"I suppose they might have stopped the letters because of you," he replied. "After all, you had just defected."

"I was a student. A nonentity. Tens of thousands of young people like me defected at that time. Don't tell me they stopped all their letters home."

Jiri thought for a while.

"No. Come to think of it they didn't. But maybe your grandfather was confused. Maybe he didn't notice the letters when they arrived. It must have been a pretty traumatic time for him."

"He wasn't confused. He was waiting for me to get in touch and help him. He would have noticed one of my letters arriving."

Jiri turned away from the parapet and started walking over the bridge towards the heart of the old town. It would be wrong to say he looked cross, for in point of fact he had been more helpful than could reasonably have been expected since Antonin had turned up at his flat with his elderly fugitive in tow, but he did look slightly frustrated.

Suddenly he stopped and turned on Antonin, who was walking along several paces behind him.

"What's the point of all this? What exactly do you hope to achieve by all this agonising? 1968 was a long time ago, you know. We all know it was a bad time. You had to pull your poor old grandfather out of that psychiatric institution because he's still alive. But everyone agrees your parents are dead. Finding out exactly what happened all those years ago won't bring them back, or help you trace Stepan. You should leave it all behind you and turn a new leaf, just like the rest of us in this country are having to do right now."

Antonin looked away. There was a sense in which he knew Jiri was right. He had lost some parents with whom he'd already had a pretty distant relationship before he'd left. Jiri had lost the best twenty years of his life under communist oppression. It was a moot point whose loss was the greater. Yet despite it all, there was still something eating away at him and he knew he wouldn't be happy until he had sorted it out.

They had reached the end of the bridge now. Nearby was a small park beside the river. Wandering into it, they sat down on a bench facing the river. The sun was shining brightly, but a cool breeze off the water prevented the heat from becoming oppressive. It made it easy to think.

"I met a strange old woman on the way to see my parents," Antonin said at last. "She was some kind of clairvoyant."

Beside him on the bench, he could see Jiri examining him with a look of sceptical detachment.

"It doesn't really matter about her," Antonin continued hurriedly. "The point is that she made me understand my visit here more clearly. She made me see they weren't really the reason why I came."

At this Jiri looked surprised. But still he said nothing.

"They never really cared about me, Jiri. Not properly. When I was a kid, only my grandparents cared, and after my grandmother died there was only my grandfather. So you see I'm not curious about my parents' death because of grief, if that's what you're thinking."

Jiri frowned.

"If it's Stepan you're trying to find, I'd go to Berlin, Antonin. You told me yourself he wasn't too keen on Czechoslovakia. With your parents dead and you gone, he might simply have decided to break the link."

Antonin looked at him sadly.

"It's true I'd like to find Stepan, Jiri. I was pretty close to him when we were little. But with Stepan it was different. He was never a strength to me, only ever me to him. Because he was younger than I was and so terribly crippled as a child he used to be very dependent on me. But later, after he had the operations and could walk again, I could see he was trying to distance himself from me. I'd be pleased to see him again, and he's certainly why I didn't turn straight round and go back to England after meeting the old woman. But I don't think I'd search the four corners of the earth just to find him, because even if I did I'm afraid he might have just carried on growing apart from me. There's an odds on chance it would be a painful encounter."

Antonin could suddenly sense the force of the nearby river as it thrust on relentlessly towards the Black Sea, surging angrily around the obstructive pillars of the bridge. The water couldn't be stopped: however hard you tried, you just had to accept its passage as a simple fact of life. And with Stepan he could accept, had already accepted for many years now, that their relationship was a thing of the past. But as he thought of the last time he had been together with his brother, on that last weekend in Prague, he could not help but think again of the person who had been by his side throughout that time. Her memory was like the river, sweeping forwards and onwards towards the distant sea, but unlike his memories of Stepan, he could not bear to let them drift away.

He turned to Jiri.

"Did you ever find out what happened to Katrina?" he asked, unable to hide the sorrow in his voice.

All trace of scepticism vanished instantly from Jiri's face.

"No," he said softly. "Do you still think of her, then?"

Antonin nodded. He had thought of her on every day of his life since the day she had told him she was leaving. Her departure had been sudden, jarring, completely without warning. With her warm kind-hearted passion she had won him for her own, and then with a silent inexplicable coldness she had thrust him away. And more than the rejection itself it was the profound contrast between the Katrina he had loved and the Katrina who had cast him aside which had haunted him so terribly over the years.

And now it had happened all over again. The same jarring contrast between what had happened and what could plausibly have happened. For Antonin knew in his heart that whatever had happened back in 1968, his father's behaviour in shooting his wife and then himself was as completely inexplicable as Katrina's rejection of him only a few weeks before. It was almost as if the two events were connected.

Jiri was watching him, studying the sadness and confusion in his friend's face. Without saying anything, he quietly pulled out a pen and a piece of paper from his pocket and started scribbling down an address.

"There is someone who just might be able to help you," he said as he wrote, "but I'm afraid you'll have to go to Prague."

* * * * * *

There was a faint smell of garlic hanging in the air as Antonin made his way slowly up the shabby stairwell to the top floor. He was in the heart of the old quarter of Prague, not far from Wenceslas Square, and the building he was in retained a lingering aura of the bourgeois grandeur of a bygone age. The balustrade of ornate iron, the delicate plasterwork on the ceilings, the width and spaciousness of the entrance hall on the ground floor, all suggested that these had once been the apartments of the pre-war Czechoslovakian elite. But it was merely an echo of the past, for the paintwork was peeling and the iron balustrade was rusting, and the flats had long since become no more than drab inconsequential housing units in some ministerial five-year-plan.

Reaching the top floor, Antonin knocked on the door and waited. After a while he heard footsteps approaching.

"Who is it?"

It was a man's voice but high-pitched. He sounded anxious.

"Antonin Ziegler. I'm a friend of Jiri Sebek. He said you could help me."

The door was unlocked and a thin greying man in a jacket several sizes too large appeared.

"Come in," he said, glancing nervously around to see if his visitor was alone.

"Are you Andreas Pitra?" Antonin asked, stepping inside the hall.

The man nodded. Antonin pulled from his pocket a letter of introduction Jiri had written and handed it to him. He scanned it with a quick and intelligent eye. Then, pushing open a door leading to an ill-kempt sitting room, he indicated that Antonin should enter.

"You are a friend of Jiri? An exile returned?" he asked.

Antonin nodded. From the contemptuous look on the man's face he could see that he didn't think too highly of such people.

"I left after the invasion. Now I'm an academic at Oxford University."

He regretted the words as soon as he had uttered them, but it was already too late. The man had turned away and was pouring himself a vodka, making no attempt to offer his guest one.

"And what would a successful Oxford academic want in Prague in 1990 which was not here before?" the man asked, turning again to face Antonin.

Antonin examined him glumly. Jiri had warned him that his friend Andreas was a little prickly, but this was ridiculous.

"Would you like me to leave, Mr Pitra?" Antonin said abruptly. "I only came because Jiri said you might be able to help me."

The directness of Antonin's remark seemed to check the man. He downed the remains of his vodka in one gulp and with a jab of his arm in the direction of a faded sofa indicated that Antonin should sit.

Antonin lowered himself onto the sofa. But his companion made no move to follow suit, and instead poured himself another vodka and stood watching him intently.

"How can I help you?" he asked presently.

In as few words as possible, Antonin explained the circumstances of his parents' death. He felt uncomfortable delivering his monologue with the man hovering over him, and he got to the point as quickly as possible.

"I don't know anything about the research institute where my father worked but I think that my parents' death may have been in some way connected with what was going on there. Jiri thought you might be able to help me find out."

There was a long silence. Then the man suddenly pulled up a small wooden chair and sat down opposite Antonin.

"Did Jiri tell you precisely what I do?"

"He said you were conducting investigations into the activities of State Security under the old regime. He told me no more than that."

The man nodded.

"Do you realise what a job that is? It wasn't the Communist Party which ran this country, it was State Security. They had files on nearly the entire population. Several million cross-referenced and cross-indexed files. Their systems and methods were labyrinthine, and when you start to probe one case you soon discover a thousand others. And sometimes they deliberately introduced lies into the system, covering up for mistakes and laying traps and tests for each other in some kind of sick incestuous game. Finding out the truth about what happened is often a near impossibility even if the events are recent. Twenty years ago and it becomes a thousand times more difficult. You continually have to ask yourself if it's really worth it."

Antonin looked at him wearily. He seemed like a man who had craved all his life to gain access to those files, only to discover when he finally did that they were of absolutely no use to him. Perhaps he had erroneously thought they would assuage his anger.

"Will you try?" Antonin asked.

There was another silence. The man looked at him with a curious expression.

"Is this a strictly personal vendetta?" he asked.

Antonin shrugged.

"My parents killed themselves. I think State Security forced them to do it. I suppose that makes it personal."

The man's eye fell back on the note from Jiri.

"Jiri has done me a few personal favours over the years," he said slowly. "For him I will help you. If you tell me where you are staying I will come to you when I have found something out."

* * * * * *

For two long days Antonin stayed in a drab motel room on the western outskirts of Prague and waited. He could have found a hotel in the picturesque centre of the city, but he had quickly discovered that old Prague held too many painful memories. So after his meeting with the depressive Andreas Pitra he had climbed aboard a rickety tram and headed for a remote suburban district which he had never before visited.

A strange lethargy had engulfed him. Waking early in the morning, haunted continually by dreams of student days in Prague, he stayed for most of the day in his room. He tried to work on a heavy academic treatise he had promised to review on his return to Oxford, but generally his mind drifted away into a neutral void where he was quite happy to leave it. Occasionally he would venture forth to the hotel restaurant to eat a solitary meal, but mostly he preferred to eat alone in a quiet corner of his room.

The motel itself was colourless, functional but lacking in any outward charm. Through the bedroom window, some distance away over rough ground, he could see the reception area of an overcrowded camping site. Sometimes he would sit by the window and watch the arrivals and departures for hours on end. Many of the campers were students, assorted backpackers from all over the world, and once or twice he found himself studying them carefully, hoping that he would catch a glimpse of Katrina. But it was of course a ridiculous notion, because wherever Katrina had gone and whatever she had become she would no longer be the young student of his memories, but rather a woman of mature years, a mother of students herself perhaps, and with a shock he realised that he might not even recognise her if he were to chance upon her in the street.

It was late on the evening of the second day and the light was beginning to fade before there was a furtive knock on the door. Antonin rose from the bed with a start and hastily brushed his hair before opening the door.

Andreas was standing outside, wearing exactly the same oversized jacket as he had on the previous occasion they had met. Under his arm he was clutching a dark leather document file.

"Please come in," Antonin said, standing aside and motioning for him to pass.

Andreas entered the room and without waiting to be asked sat down on the bed. Flinging open the document file he silently pulled out a handful of faded papers.

"So you managed to find something?" Antonin observed.

His visitor nodded.

"As you've probably worked out by now," he began, "I'm no friend of Czechoslovak State Security. For most of the last forty years, if anything underhand or nasty has been happening in this country, you could safely reckon on the fact that they were behind it. So I expected nothing less than to find that your grandfather's version of events was substantially true."

"And isn't it?"

Andreas shook his head.

"No. State Security were as puzzled by your parents' deaths as you were. Even more puzzled, perhaps."

Antonin sank down beside him on the bed. Between them, spread out on the bedcovers, lay an assortment of ageing official documents, each and every one labelled Top Secret. It struck Antonin as odd.

"That's rather a high classification, isn't it?" he said.

A slight smile spread across Andreas' face. He shuffled through the papers and picked out a single sheet which he handed to Antonin.

"Read this," he said. "It is a summary of the situation prepared immediately after the events for the Chief Directorate."

The light was fading fast. Antonin leant over and switched on the bedside lamp before starting to read. The document was headed: 'Report on Events at Oblanov Technical Research Institute'.

'A full investigation of the recent events at the Oblanov Technical Research Institute in Northern Slovakia has failed to clarify many aspects of this situation. Oblanov is a joint Czechoslovak/German Democratic Republic research centre concerned with technological developments in the military communications field. A small group of scientific and technical staff from both countries had been assembled in order to investigate the possibility of using coded sonic impulses to interfere with, disrupt and disorientate enemy ground troops in conflict zones. Reports from the research station's administrator immediately prior to the incident did not indicate that any particular progress was being made in this work at the time when the incident occurred, and this was independently confirmed by our own source.

'On the last weekend of September, reports began to filter through of a series of deaths involving staff working at the institute. In the space of ten hours, between eight o'clock on the Saturday evening and six o'clock on the Sunday morning, twelve people died. The dead included almost the entire scientific and administrative establishment of the institute. All of them appear to have been murdered.

'Subsequent enquiries have failed to explain adequately why these deaths occurred but it seems likely that deliberate sabotage by a foreign power must be held responsible for this attack. We can only suppose that foreign intelligence sources were ill-informed about the progress of work at the institute and took the unusual step of eliminating all those concerned with the research. It should be noted, however, that enquiries with our network of undercover intelligence operatives within overseas security services do not provide any evidence to support this claim. Without adequate corroborating information, it is therefore recommended that no official protest be lodged through diplomatic or other channels at this stage.'

Antonin read and re-read the sheet of paper several times before laying it back down on the bed. Then he looked up at Andreas.

"Is there a list of the dead somewhere?" he asked.

Andreas nodded. Sifting through the papers, he produced several sheets stapled together and handed them to Antonin.

"These are working notes prepared by the State Security investigator. You'll find a report of your parents' death on page three."

The document was a series of individual paragraphs on each of the deceased employees of the institute. Antonin turned to the third page and began to read the entry on his parents.

'Following the sound of gunshots in the early hours of the morning, officials of the local militia found Johann Ziegler and his wife dead of gunshot wounds at their home in Urbanek. Johann Ziegler was the senior administrative officer at the research institute. A career administrator with the government of the German Democratic Republic, Mr Ziegler had been selected for this post because of his political reliability and his fluent understanding of Czech and Slovak languages in addition to his native German. According to colleagues in Berlin his record as an administrator in East Berlin was flawless if somewhat unexciting.'

Antonin moved on swiftly to the other entries. Besides his parents, ten other people had been killed that night. All of them were scientific staff and all of them had been murdered. Beyond that, the entries offered little hard information. Finally he laid down the papers on the bed.

"This is all rubbish, isn't it?" he said, looking up at Andreas. "My grandfather was sure it was my father who had done the shooting. He said he had shot my mother and then turned the gun on himself. And yet it says here quite consistently that all the dead at the institute were murdered."

Andreas frowned.

"If your grandfather's right then it would certainly appear to suggest some kind of cover-up," he said.

"Why should anyone have wanted to do that? If State Security were puzzled by what happened then distorting the truth in these reports wouldn't have helped them to work out what really happened."

Andreas smiled thinly.

"You might think so. But you don't understand how their minds worked. Information about the deaths started to flow into Prague. It didn't make sense so a team was sent to Slovakia to investigate. Their job was to tie up all the loose ends and report back but they couldn't. So somebody somewhere came up with the bright idea of blaming it all on a western intelligence agency. A suicide would have made a shambles of such a neat theory and so it was quietly suppressed before the information was passed on up the line."

Antonin continued to stare helplessly at the papers.

"You mean they never found out what happened? They just buried it?"

Andreas nodded.

"So it would seem. As soon as it was labelled a devilish if misguided scheme by a western intelligence agency it became comprehensible and therefore safe. So it was simply shoved away in some filing cabinet pending further information coming to light."

Antonin picked up some of the sheets of paper from the bed and started flicking through them. Then he put them all down again.

"Well," he said, "is there nothing here which might give us a clue about what really happened?"

"There's not much to go on," he said. "They've been pretty thorough. In fact there was only one thing that struck me as odd. It's on the list of deaths." He picked it up again and handed it to Antonin. "Here. Have another look."

Antonin read and re-read the list several times but could see nothing other than the dull catalogue of killings he had seen before. He looked up uncertainly.

"It's not in the words," Andreas added. "It's in the paper."

Antonin examined the sheets in his hand again. His parents' entries were at the end, on page three, along with that of another younger man. He held the paper under the bedside light and examined it.

"Is page three on slightly different paper?" he asked uncertainly.

Andreas took the document from him.

"Exactly."

Antonin looked at him.

"So what?" he muttered.

"Nothing if you don't suspect anything. But it made me wonder if this sheet had been typed up later, after the other entries had been completed. And look here, in the corner. The first two sheets have been stapled together before and then the staple has been removed, but the sheet describing your parent's death was not attached before. So maybe there was originally another sheet with the true version of what happened to your parents on it, and then somebody switched it."

Antonin rose to his feet and walked morosely to the window. He had hoped Andreas would help him understand his father's seemingly incomprehensible behaviour. Yet now he found himself having to come to terms with the fact that they brought him no nearer to the truth. He turned to Andreas with despairing eyes, intending to ask him if he had any clue how to proceed, but before he could speak he noticed a sudden softening in Andreas' hitherto cold expression.

"You're not alone in all this," he said quietly, taking a pace towards Antonin as he stood by the window. "Really you're not alone."

"Aren't I?" Antonin asked.

"Everybody in Czechoslovakia has to come to terms with their past. The lies, the betrayals, the humiliations. They became so endemic in this country that it will take us a hundred years to wipe the slate clean. My father was a communist idealist like yours. But unlike yours he vanished when I was a child – in the early fifties. Soon afterwards my mother took an overdose, although whether it was because of my father's disappearance or the public disgrace which followed I'll never really know. So with all that in my background I was marked down as a potential troublemaker long before I gave the authorities the satisfaction of actually becoming one."

He spoke softly, speaking words he clearly didn't often speak. And as he spoke Antonin could feel himself engulfed by a wave of fellow-feeling for this mysterious little man in the over-sized jacket. For although the passage of their lives bore as little outward similarity as their looks, it was becoming obvious that they shared the same central core, a rotten diseased core which prevented either of them from fully functioning as human beings.

"Did you ever find out about your father?" Antonin asked quietly.

Andreas smiled, but this time it was a gentle smile, not the biting angry smile which was his usual garb.

"No," he said. "I know he was sent to Russia, probably to the Lubyanka. After that not even my friends in Moscow can find any trace."

The two men were standing beside each other next to the window, both looking out across the rough ground towards the camping site.

"So why do you carry on searching?" Antonin asked softly.

Andreas smiled, and slowly lifting his arm he pointed across the rough ground towards the camping site. There was a small outdoor cafe beside the reception block, and in the cafe several dozen young people were already gathered together at long trestle tables. Somebody must have cracked a joke, for through the warm night air they could hear the faint sound of many voices laughing.

"I'm not searching for me any more," he whispered. "Now I'm searching for them."

The small Bohemian market town of Melnik lay to the north of Prague, a sleepy backwater unknown and untouched by the vast armies of tourists and businessmen flocking into the glittering heart of the capital city. At the centre of the town was a picturesque if crumbling town square surrounded on all sides by ornate arcaded stone buildings, and it was into this square that a small black Lada now drove, bumping and bouncing over the rough cobblestones. Finally it came to a halt beside one of the covered arcades, immediately opposite a large shop window filled with dark grey curtains. Only a lopsided red sign advertising the delights of Budweiser beer beside the door gave any clue that this was in fact a bar.

The door by the driver's seat swung open and a thin angular figure in a scruffy jacket stepped out. From the other side of the vehicle a somewhat overweight middle-aged man in a smart Western jacket appeared. With a silent glance at each other, they disappeared together into the bar.

Once inside, the thin angular man produced a photograph from his pocket and glanced quickly at it before approaching the barman.

"What do you want?" the barman asked moodily, a parody of old style Eastern European service at its finest. He was a podgy man in late middle age, and seemed ill-at-ease in his job.

Andreas smiled.

"You," he announced bluntly.

The barman's eyes flashed menacingly backwards and forwards between the two visitors, the reflex of a lifetime, but then he remembered who and what he had now become.

"What do you mean?" he asked cautiously.

"You are Milos Petrovsk, are you not?"

"What of it?"

Andreas leaned menacingly over the bar.

"Milos Petrovsk, formerly of Czechoslovak State Security," he said quietly.

The man's eyes flicked nervously around the room, checking to see if any of the locals in the bar had overheard. But they were still sitting at their tables, drinking and talking just as before.

"I don't work there any more," he said, turning deliberately away and starting to dry some dishes which were draining beside a sink.

Andreas flicked a glance at Antonin and casually sat down on a high stool beside the bar.

"You've got a nice job here, Colonel," he called to the barman in a slightly raised voice. This time several of the locals looked up. The barman swung round angrily and came over to them.

"Leave me alone," he snorted.

Andreas leant forward across the bar until he was only inches away from the man's face.

"You've got just one choice, Colonel," he said. "We can talk here, or we can talk in private. Which would you prefer?"

The barman put down his tea-towel and led them silently to a small storeroom filled with crates of empty beer bottles and assorted pieces of cleaning equipment. Andreas pulled the door closed behind them.

"Calm down, Milos. We're not here for you."

For the first time Antonin noticed just how frightened the barman had become. He was standing in one corner with his back to the wall, a vacuum cleaner positioned carefully between himself and his unwelcome visitors as if by way of protection. He did not seem to be greatly reassured by Andreas' comforting words.

"You have the eyes of a guilty man, Milos," Andreas snarled.

"What do you want?" the secret policeman-cum-barman asked, attempting a show of bravado but failing miserably.

Studiously ignoring the man's question, Andreas turned to Antonin with a scornful expression.

"You see what they're reduced to now," he said. "A few months ago they were the lords of all they surveyed, and now they are like frightened animals. Believe me it does not make my task of flushing them out from their burrows any more rewarding."

To Antonin's amazement, Andreas suddenly swung round and thrust his index finger into the barman's chest.

"Put your hands on your head!" he jeered.

For a few moments the man stared uncertainly at his tormentor, their eyes locked in silent conflict. But then, ever so slowly, he started to raise his hands.

Andreas relaxed.

"Good," he muttered. "Now I think you're just about ready to talk to my friend here."

Antonin pulled a document from his pocket and handed it to the man.

"Do you remember the work you did in September 1968 at a place called the Oblanov Technical Research Institute in Slovakia?" he asked.

The man frowned.

"Oblanov?" he asked uncertainly.

"It was a communications research facility in Slovakia. There was a series of suspicious deaths amongst the staff and you were sent by Prague to investigate. Do you remember?"

Gradually the man's face started to relax. In his long career in the secret police, it was reasonable to suppose that he had been involved in many far less savoury cases than Oblanov.

"Yes," he muttered, "I remember Oblanov."

"Look at this," Antonin said, handing him the document.

The man took the papers describing the deaths and quickly leafed through them. When he had finished he handed them back.

"I remember," he reiterated.

"What did you find out?" Antonin asked.

The man's eyes were casting backwards and forwards between his inquisitors, as if searching for clues about how much they already knew.

"It's all written down there. You have my report. It was probably the work of a western intelligence agency."

"Hogwash," Andreas interrupted. "My friend and I didn't come all this way to speak to you because we were interested in this waste paper. We want to know what you really found out when you were at Oblanov."

This time the relief was plain to see. Before he had been testing the water, finding out how much they already knew. Now that he knew they had seen through his deceit, the truth was easier to tell.

"Although it was notionally under civilian control, Oblanov was really a military facility, jointly funded and staffed by Czechoslovaks and Germans. The incident really did have all the makings of an unusually crude piece of sabotage by western military intelligence. I really thought I had it all sewn up until I found the two suicides."

Antonin thrust the document back towards him. His grandfather had been certain that his mother had been shot by his father, that he was a suicide and she was a murder.

"Look at the list. Tell me who these two suicides were," he ordered.

The man scanned the papers for a few moments and then stopped on page three.

"This was one of them. This man Johann Ziegler, the chief administrator at the institute. He'd been shipped in specially from Berlin to run the unit. I was almost certain he shot his wife and then turned the gun on himself."

"Are you sure?"

He nodded, and once again Antonin could feel his spirits sagging.

All the man was doing was confirming something he already knew, that his father had for some reason decided to kill his wife and then himself. He glanced uncertainly at Andreas, who responded by leaning over the vacuum cleaner once more and peering aggressively at the frightened man's face.

"You mentioned there were two suicides." he said. "I don't suppose you happen to remember who the other one was, do you?"

"Yes," the man replied slowly. "He was the other one listed on the same page. A young Slovak scientist called Gregor Markov. I said in the report that he was strangled by his assailant, but when I first set eyes on him he was suspended from a light fitting in the bathroom of his flat by his own necktie. Although it could conceivably have been staged, I was pretty sure at the time that he'd put himself there voluntarily."

Andreas grabbed the sheet and quickly glanced at the entry.

"You say you first set eyes on him when you found him hanging in the bathroom. How come the local militia hadn't cut him down long before you got there?"

"It was me who discovered the body. His family were away visiting relatives at the time. They didn't come back till later."

At this Antonin looked up sharply.

"His family? He had a family?"

"Yes. There was a wife, I believe. And a little girl."

"So this other man made no attempt to kill his family. It was only my father who did that?"

As soon as the words passed his lips he knew he had made a mistake. The training of a lifetime had clearly not been wasted on their adversary. A scarcely perceptible smile slowly spread across his face.

"Your father?" he repeated, examining Antonin with renewed interest.

Andreas stepped forward smartly.

"Never mind about that," he said. "Now tell us what you found out about the work at the institute. You must have looked into that."

The man shrugged.

"The report I filed is quite honest on that point," he said. "They were working on a technique to transmit sonic signals over a battlefield in order to disrupt and disorientate enemy ground troops. If it had been developed successfully it might also have had some useful civilian applications, since such a technique could have been used in a variety of social disturbance situations. As far as we could make out from our visits to the site, they hadn't been making very much progress. The administrator was well aware that the funding for the whole project was in jeopardy, so if they had been about to come up with something useful they'd have had every reason to pass it up the line."

Andreas pulled another report from his pocket and checked it.

"It says here you thought some documents were missing. Gaps in filing systems."

The man nodded.

"Someone had been over the place with a toothpick at around the time of the deaths. Whoever it was had been careful, but it was obvious enough. It was probably the same people who did the killings."

"But you never found out what they took?"

"No. All the people with authorised access to those papers were killed. Every last one of them."

"So it's possible they had discovered something important."

"It's theoretically possible but unlikely. As I said, if they had then they'd have had every reason to brag about it."

Antonin could see that Andreas was becoming increasingly curious, like a dog on the scent. His keen eyes were flashing eagerly backwards and forwards between the report in his hand and the former counter-intelligence officer who had written it.

Yet this time it was Antonin who spoke.

"If something big had come up, there must have been rumours floating about. If eleven people had known about a major new development, surely something would have slipped out."

The man shrugged.

"The only people left alive were relatively junior staff, none of whom had full security clearance. The dead scientific and administrative personnel at the institute were all experienced people, quite used to working in sensitive environments and not gossiping about their work. They would all have known the rules and they would also have known that lurking inside every lowly cleaning lady there might have been a State Security informant checking up on their reliability. It wasn't exactly an environment which encouraged people to chat. So I repeat again what I said in my report – it was theoretically conceivable that they'd stumbled on something which hadn't yet been reported up the line. But since they all died we'll never really know, will we?"

Andreas raised his eyebrows.

"But surely you had your own people in there. In a joint project of that importance, Prague would never have relied on a middle-ranking German bureaucrat to keep them in touch."

The man hesitated for a moment as he eyed his visitors with curiosity.

"You two gents are pretty astute," he said. "I can still admire that quality, even if it's in my political opponents. It was smart of you to work out that I'd lied about the suicides, because my bosses never did. So now tell me why you think I faked the information. What on earth do you suppose was in it for me?"

"You wanted to tidy up the loose ends, I suppose," Andreas offered.

The barman smiled.

"But they weren't my loose ends, were they? Why should I have cared about loose ends? But if I'd been caught out lying by the Chief Directorate I'd have certainly been sacked."

Slowly, imperceptibly, Antonin could see that the man was fighting back. With every passing minute he was becoming more confident, as if he were almost starting to enjoy the opportunity of using his brain once more instead of dishing out endless glasses of Budweiser to ignorant Bohemian yokels.

Antonin examined him carefully.

"You must have had a vested interest," he said slowly. "A personal vested interest."

The man nodded, fixing Antonin with his eyes.

"You asked me before about Prague's contact man on the inside, the man responsible for making sure nothing went wrong down there. Well, we had a clandestine State Security contact down there all right, a man who'd been appointed on my personal recommendation in the face of a good deal of high level opposition inside the service from people who weren't too sure of his reliability. I'd staked quite a lot on him."

Antonin stared at the man for a few moments, and then the penny slowly started to drop.

"Oh my," he said. "I think I'm beginning to see what you mean."

The ex-policeman grunted.

"Yes," he said. "My personal recommendation for State Security's inside wire, the very man I'd promised them would be one hundred percent reliable, was none other than Gregor Markov, the very same man I found dangling from the ceiling in his bathroom, the only man besides your father to kill himself.'

There was a long silence. The ex-policeman remained firmly pinned down in the corner behind his vacuum cleaner, but he was breathing distinctly easier now. Eventually it was Andreas who broke the silence.

"You've been most co-operative, Mr Petrovsk. If we think of any more questions we'll call back."

The man bowed slightly.

"And where can I contact you if I remember something?" he asked politely.

Andreas flicked a suspicious glance at him.

"Don't," he said. "Just like you, my friend and I are rather shy."

Again the man inclined his head by way of acknowledgement. Then he stepped out cautiously from behind the vacuum cleaner and held the door open for them to pass.

A few minutes later Antonin and Andreas were back in the black Lada, once more bumping and bouncing across the cobblestoned square. There was no particular reason to turn back, but Antonin did, glancing one last time at the dingy bar with its dark grey curtains. And as he did so he was surprised to notice that the barman had followed them out onto the pavement. He was peering after their car as it drove off, and just before they swung round the corner and out of view he pulled out a little pad of paper from his pocket and started jotting something down.

* * * * * *

As he put the phone down he breathed an inward sigh of relief. It had only been a brief conversation with his grandfather, but it was clear that the old man didn't seem to be overly troubled that Antonin was going to stay away from Bratislava for a little while longer.

It was perhaps not altogether surprising that Jiri and his grandfather had struck up such a close relationship. Despite the difference in their age they were both thoroughly political creatures, people who viewed the world with broad ideological vision. And their vision was the same, for both shared a dream of a Czechoslovakia free from oppression, a Czechoslovakia in which people would be free to live their lives according to the dictates of their own conscience rather than the dictates of a brutal totalitarian state. His grandfather was one of the few surviving architects of pre-war Czechoslovakia, Jiri an architect of the new free Czechoslovakia of the 1990s. Quite a lot of alcohol had probably been consumed while they exchanged notes. And with a smile, Antonin realised that the hard thing to do would be to tear them apart from each other when the time finally came to return to England.

He stepped out of the payphone and glanced anxiously around the large and familiar expanse of the Zelina station concourse. He knew the station building well, for Zelina was the nearest large town to the village where his family had lived and he had often passed through the station when visiting them. And only a few days before he had passed through with his grandfather as he had smuggled him away from the mental hospital.

It was this recent visit which was now the source of his anxiety, for despite himself he was fearful lest he bump into the ferocious doctor from the clinic. It was of course a ridiculous notion, the chances against such an encounter minuscule, but still it made him feel nervous and uncomfortable.

He walked over to a small kiosk on one side of the concourse and bought a street map. Then, clutching his suitcase in one hand and the streetmap in the other, he headed for the station cafe and ordered himself a coffee. The cafe was fairly crowded, a popular meeting point in the town, and it was only with some difficulty that he found a seat at one of the tables. Trying to ignore the bustle around him, he pulled out the piece of paper on which he had written down Mrs Markov's address and tried to locate it on the map.

"Can I help you find your way?"

Antonin looked up to see the friendly face of a man in his mid-thirties looking down at him. He was wearing a smart jacket and tie, and in contrast to most of the scruffily dressed people in the bar he looked like a pretty respectable sort of chap.

Antonin held up the piece of paper on which he had written the address.

"It's this address. I don't know it."

The man examined it for a moment.

"I'll show you," he said, pointing out a street on the map not far away from the railway station.

Antonin thanked the man and turned away, looking down at the map to try and work out the best way to walk. But then he became aware that the man in the jacket was still looking over his shoulder.

"You go out of the station," the man said. "Then turn left, walk on until you get to the second set of traffic lights, and then turn right. The block you want is down there on the left hand side, just after a small row of shops. You can't miss it."

Again Antonin thanked him and made to turn away. But this time the chap didn't hesitate.

"Do you need a room for the night?" he said with a friendly smile.

Antonin paused, slightly taken aback by the man's offer. But the train journey from Prague had taken a long time and it was already late afternoon. He might be quite a while at Mrs Markov's, yet registering at an official hotel after so recently absconding with a psychiatric patient from a nearby clinic might not be so clever.

"You have a room?" he asked.

"I have a very nice room in my flat. It is near the station, and it is clean and cheap. Only one hundred and fifty crowns a night."

Antonin smiled quietly to himself at the man's burgeoning free enterprise zeal. After all, what better place to tout for business than amongst the tourists at a busy main line railway station.

"I'm probably only going to be here one night," he said.

"One night. A hundred nights. It's all the same to me."

Antonin hesitated.

"Very well. If you give me your address I'll come and find you after I've finished my business."

The man eyed his suitcase for a moment.

"Why don't you come back to the room first. Then I can show you the way. And also you can leave your heavy suitcase there when you go out."

Antonin shrugged. Drinking up the remains of the coffee he had ordered, he rose to his feet.

"OK," he said. "Lead the way."

* * * * * *

As Antonin made his way through the city streets towards Mrs Markov's flat, he could not help but feel rather pleased that he had found such a convenient place to stay. The room was light and airy and his host had proved most helpful, insisting on serving him a pleasantly cooked dish of pork and dumplings as well as pressing out the creases in his rather crumpled suit before he went out. For the first time in what had been several rather stressful days, he felt comfortable again.

He had to admit that visiting Mrs Markov was a long shot. She probably knew no more than he did, perhaps even less if nobody had ever taken the trouble to tell her that her young husband had killed himself. Yet there was just a remote chance that she would have heard Gregor Markov mention something about his work which would yield a clue about why he had taken such a drastic step. And if he had, Mrs Markov could just give him the vital clue which would unlock the riddle of his parents' death.

The drab grey tenements of central Zilina rose up on either side of him as he walked. Of all the grey industrial cities of Slovakia, Zilina was one of the greyest, a featureless town which looked like a film set from an early black and white movie, where somebody had decided to save money on paint because the cameras couldn't see it anyway. To add to the dismal effect, the usual collection of clapped out Eastern European cars and lorries coughed and spluttered their way through the streets in the dull evening light, filling the air with the dull stench of half-burnt oil. Yet despite the drabness of the surroundings, Antonin did not feel depressed.

It was a strange mood which now overwhelmed him. He had felt it several days before by the river in Bratislava as he had spoken to Jiri, a kind of excitement which defied logical description. He knew there was absolutely no objective reason to link his parents' death with his half-buried feelings about Katrina, no reason to think that by pursuing the truth about his parents he would uncover the truth about her and ultimately about himself, but nevertheless that was precisely what he did think.

He turned a corner and came into the road where Gregor Markov's wife still lived. Tracking her down had been easy enough, for citizens of Eastern European countries did not move home as often as their Western cousins and she was still living in exactly the same flat as she had done in 1968. A quick check in a telephone directory had been sufficient to establish that she was still there.

The tenement block where she lived looked slightly more appealing than most of the others in the area, its flat grey walls softened by flower-laden window boxes beneath many of the windows. Pushing open the street door, he climbed up the rough concrete stairs, where again someone had tried to soften the effect by arranging pot-plants and little pieces of carpet on each of the landings. Eventually, on the second floor, he arrived at the door of Mrs Markov's flat. Outside the door was a brightly-coloured mat and a particularly fine arrangement of potted plants which suggested that the occupant was the prime mover in the uncharacteristic floral displays which adorned the building.

He knocked respectfully on the door, still not quite certain how he would best introduce himself when she answered. Eventually the door opened, and a pleasant-looking lady of around fifty appeared. She was wearing an apron decorated with a trim floral design and the smell which emanated from the inside of her flat suggested she was doing some baking. She smiled at him in a disarmingly friendly and open way.

"Excuse me," Antonin began, promptly forgetting all the opening lines he had rehearsed before arriving.

"Hallo," Mrs Markov said, looking at him and smiling kindly.

"My name is Antonin Ziegler," he said. "I wonder if I could talk to you for a moment."

The smile half froze and was overlaid with a frown.

"Ziegler?" she said uncertainly.

"Yes. My father was Johann Ziegler. He used to work with your husband a long time ago."

The smile died.

"Come in," she said, standing aside for him to pass.

He stepped inside. The flat was small but immaculate, bright summer flowers cascading from every nook and cranny. But the expression on Mrs Markov's face no longer matched the flowers as it had done when he had first arrived. Instead she looked tense and drawn, as if remembering against her wishes a nightmare she had struggled hard to forget.

She led him into her sitting room and steered him towards a sofa. Then she sat down opposite him and allowed her eyes to meet his.

"How can I help you, Mr Ziegler?" she asked cautiously.

"I've been living in England since 1968," he explained. "I've not had any contact with my parents since then so I've only recently found out about their deaths."

He hesitated, hoping she would offer some comment, but she remained sitting silently where she was, her face rigid and controlled.

"It came as rather a shock to find out how they died," he offered.

Again she said nothing, but she nodded her head slowly. It was as if she were trying to formulate something to say but couldn't quite put the words together.

"I understand your husband was in a similar situation . . ." Antonin continued hesitantly, " . . . so I wondered if you understood anything about why they did it."

The woman looked down.

"It was a long time ago, Mr Ziegler. It was a horrible thing for me and for my little daughter. We try our best to forget it."

Antonin watched her uncertainly. It was clear she didn't like him probing, that she wanted him to go away and leave her in peace. Bracing himself, he took a deep breath.

"I know this is painful for you, Mrs Ziegler, but my father's suicide has come as a terrible shock to me. I need to understand it. And I thought that if you had any idea why your husband killed himself then I might begin to understand why my own father did."

He watched her face intently as he spoke, and as soon as he uttered the words he was sure that she already knew. If she hadn't known she would have flinched, instantly rejected the very notion of suicide. But her face remained set and controlled.

Finally she looked up.

"Gregor didn't kill himself. He was killed by a foreign intelligence agency in connection with his work for the government."

It was a well-rehearsed line, a standard response. She delivered it with great fluency, as if she had used it many times before.

Antonin let a few moments pass before speaking.

"If you know something, Mrs Markov, please tell me. I know it is easier to tell people he was killed, but don't you see I'm in exactly the same situation as you. It was your husband and my parents who died. Surely it would be better if we speak frankly with each other."

He could see her fighting hard to hold back tears. She was a kindly woman who had been sorely abused by fate and had spent over twenty years fighting back. Yet if the flowers in her flat were a symbol of her fighting spirit, he saw now that they were also a symbol of her tragedy.

She rose slowly to her feet, careful not to allow her eyes to meet his.

"I'm sorry about your parents, Mr Ziegler. But I knew nothing about them or my husband's work. And now, if you will excuse me, I have some cakes in the oven which will spoil if I do not attend to them."

Antonin watched her sadly as she edged towards the door. It was clear that even if she did know something she was not going to share it with him. Yet a part of him didn't even blame her for throwing him out.

"I'm sorry I troubled you, Mrs Markov," he mumbled, more to himself than to her, and then he walked quickly past the flowers in her hall and out onto the landing.

The door closed behind him and he could feel his spirits flagging. The carefully-arranged flowers around her front door, which previously had seemed so bright and cheerful, now seemed to mock him. For Mrs Markov had done no more than he had done. She had taken a wrecked life and papered over the cracks, presenting to the outside world a cheerful and outgoing exterior. And whatever lingering torments lurked within her she had resolved to keep as strictly private matters, carefully disguised behind a warm façade of bonhomie and charm.

He looked at his watch, wondering what to do with himself for the rest of the evening. He had supposed he would be with her quite a while, that it would be too late to return to Jiri's flat in Bratislava on the evening train. Yet now that he had drawn a blank there was no reason to remain in Zilina. It crossed his mind that he should pick up his things from the room and leave immediately.

He was just about to start down the stairs when he became aware of the sound of footsteps coming up. Antonin looked up and saw a young girl of about twenty appear around the corner of the stairwell. Suddenly he took an involuntary step backwards.

"Katrina?" he murmured.

The girl looked at him oddly.

"Not me," she said. "You must be thinking of someone else."

Antonin stared at her wide-eyed. She was young, not like Katrina would be now, but she looked identical in nearly every way to how Katrina had once looked. And it was no better when she spoke, for even her voice carried within it Katrina's lilting freshness.

"Are you a friend of my mother?" the girl asked, and suddenly Antonin realised that he was blocking the door to Mrs Markov's flat.

"Yes . . . er . . . no," he mumbled, standing aside. He tried to take his eyes off her face but found he couldn't.

"You don't seem very sure," she said, pulling a small black handbag from her shoulder and rummaging around inside for her doorkey.

"I came to see her," he said. "Her husband and my father were colleagues before they died."

He'd said the words mechanically, more for something to fill up the empty space than because of their particular meaning. But as he spoke the girl's face suddenly changed. The bright and playful expression faded, replaced by a look of violent and savage intensity. Antonin could feel his insides churning around, confused and uncertain. It was precisely the kind of devastating mood swing which had so disarmed him with Katrina when he had been young. One minute she would be laughing and joking about some utter trivia, the next she would say or do something which had the power to eat its way into your soul.

"You knew my father?" the girl said.

Antonin shook his head.

"No," he said. "It was my father who knew him."

The girl frowned.

"Is that what you were talking to my mother about? About my father?"

"I tried to. But it was difficult."

The girl eyed him carefully for a moment.

"You can talk to me if you like, but it's better if it's not here. My mother doesn't like the subject brought up."

Antonin looked at her with surprise, fighting hard to ignore the girl's similarities to Katrina. Then he forced a smile.

"I'd love to talk," he said.

"Meet me downstairs in the street," she continued. "I'll just dump a few things inside and tell her I'm going out for a bit."

Antonin walked slowly down the stairwell and waited in the street outside. He felt excited by his encounter with the girl, but also a little afraid.

"Let me introduce myself," she said as soon as she had joined him. "I'm Nadja."

Antonin inclined his head politely.

"Hallo, Nadja. My name is Antonin. Antonin Ziegler."

She looked at him oddly.

"That's a German name, but you don't sound very German."

"My father was a German-speaker from the Sudetenland. My mother was a Slovak."

"Come on," she said. "It's a nice evening. We can go to the park."

Antonin walked along beside her, unsure precisely what to say. Because of her resemblance to Katrina, a part of him felt immediately close to her. But as a matter of simple fact he knew she was a complete stranger.

"I didn't know my father," Nadja began. "He died when I was still a baby."

Antonin glanced sideways at her.

"That must be hard," he said.

She shrugged.

"I suppose it is, although I don't really know what to compare with. My mother has always taken good care of me."

"I can see that," Antonin observed. "She seems to be the sort of lady who has everything under control."

Nadja laughed.

"It doesn't sound to me like you two hit it off very well," she said. "Do you know, she didn't even mention to me that you'd called."

"I think I upset her. It wasn't very kind of me to walk off the street like that and stir up all those painful memories."

"So why did you, then? Why did you come and see her after all these years?"

Antonin began to explain, but was careful not to mention the true circumstances of either his parents' or her father's deaths.

While he was talking they reached a small city park. Nadja walked over to some swings. Lowering herself gently onto one of them, she started rocking gently backwards and forwards. Antonin sat down on a bench opposite and watched her intently while he talked. As she listened to him, her expression was distant and strangely forlorn. It was only when he stopped that she looked up.

"What do you know about my father's death?" she asked.

Antonin could feel his mouth drying up. The swing started to slow, and all the time she was staring at him, probing for the truth. He had resolved to confront the girl's mother with her husband's suicide, because she might possibly have been able to shed some light on what had happened all those years ago. But this girl had only been a baby in 1968. She couldn't possibly know anything. Upsetting her gratuitously was hardly fair.

"He died . . ." Antonin began hesitantly, seeking a form of words which would mask the truth.

The swing was now motionless.

"You all know, don't you?" she interrupted. "All of you. But you won't tell me, will you?"

"Hasn't your mother told you?"

"My mother has always told me he was strangled by the CIA. But I've always known she was lying."

"Perhaps she's trying to protect you?" Antonin said softly.

The girl rose to her feet and stood in front of him.

"Like you are?" she asked.

"Perhaps."

"Well don't. I give you prior absolution for any hurt you may cause me, but please tell me everything you know about my father's death. It might sound silly to you, but it's just something I need to know."

Antonin looked at her glumly. As a matter of fact it didn't sound silly to him at all. He knew better than most what it was to try and live out a life cluttered up with unexplained history.

"Eleven people working at the institute died that Saturday night," he said at last. "Most of them were scientists like your father, although my father was an administrator. Of those eleven people, nine were murdered."

He hesitated, watching her intently. But her face remained set and expressionless. He rose slowly to his feet and stood just in front of her, unsure how she would react.

"My father shot my mother before turning the gun on himself. At around the same time, in the early hours of Sunday morning, your father went into the bathroom of your flat and hung himself."

For a few moments she remained motionless.

"Thank you," she said at last. And then, without another word, she returned to the swing and resumed her gentle rocking. This time, despite himself, Antonin sat down on a neighbouring swing.

After a while she looked sideways at him and smiled rather limply.

"It makes me feel rather empty inside," she said. "Is that how it makes you feel?"

Antonin looked at her with a perplexed expression. He felt an affinity for Nadja, or was it for Katrina. And if at first there had been no doubt that the girl beside him was nothing but an illusion, the longer she was with him the more difficult it became to disentangle the reality of her presence from his distant memory of Katrina's.

"I have one big advantage over you, Nadja," Antonin replied. "Already when I emigrated to England I knew my parents didn't love me. They always pretended to, but they never really did. Perhaps because of that I never learned to love them either. That knowledge made their death and the horrible circumstances which surrounded it easier for me to grasp."

She looked away.

"My father couldn't have loved me very much either, could he?"

She was rocking backwards and forwards on the swing, as if trying to comfort herself by its motion, but Antonin could see that tears were running down her cheeks.

"You can't say that," he said quietly.

"If he'd loved me, he wouldn't have hung himself. If he'd loved me, he'd have stuck it out for my sake."

Antonin could feel a lump forming in his throat. She looked so vulnerable, so hurt, yet he didn't really know what to do. The best he could think of was pull out a large white handkerchief from his pocket and hold it out to her.

She looked at the handkerchief and allowed the swing to slow down. Taking it from him, she blew her nose loudly.

"Sorry," she said. "First I tell you to upset me, then I reward you by sobbing."

He looked at her thoughtfully, relieved that she had at least stopped crying.

"I find your reaction interesting, as a matter of fact," he said.

"Interesting?"

"Mmm. Because you never knew your father you make various perfectly reasonable assumptions about him which seem to you to square with the facts. Here was a successful young scientist with a delightful wife and a sweet little baby. You'd think he had everything going for him. So when you hear he killed himself you naturally assume that he didn't love you, that he was so obsessed with his own personal misery – his own ego, if you like – that he just decided to finish it. In your shoes I suppose I'd have drawn the same conclusions."

"But?" she said.

"But it's different for me. You see, I knew my father and I know that explanation won't wash. He was a solid and dependable man. And although he didn't love me he was very much in love with my mother. He wasn't an unstable personality who just tipped over the brink into suicide. Something or someone must have pushed him very hard indeed."

"And you think it's the same for my father?"

Antonin nodded.

"I suspect so. Probably the same thing. Something at that institute made them do it. It's what I hoped your mother could throw some light on."

Nadja had stopped crying now. She was thinking intently, as if herself trying to formulate a satisfactory theory.

"What about the others who died?" she said suddenly. "If our fathers were the only suicides, then who on earth killed all the others?"

Antonin looked at her blankly. For some reason he hadn't really stopped to think about the others.

"I . . .I don't know," he said slowly, but the moment he spoke the most likely explanation suddenly dawned on him.

She looked at him aghast, as if she had read his mind.

"Oh no," she said. "You don't think they did it, do you?"

Antonin rose from the swing.

"Come with me," he said. "If we go back to my room, I'll show you the State Security documents I picked up in Prague."

As soon as they arrived at the flat where he had rented a room, he rang the bell and waited patiently for the landlord to answer. Eventually the door opened and his host appeared, still wearing exactly the same smart jacket and tie as before. But at the sight of him, Nadja took a sharp step backwards.

"Mr Siracky!" she exclaimed, obvious surprise in her voice.

The man too seemed to flinch.

"Hallo, Nadja," he said. "How are you?"

"Fine," she replied politely, and Antonin wondered if he had perhaps been one of her schoolteachers.

They walked through the flat and into his room. As soon as Antonin had pushed the door closed, he turned to face her.

"You know him?" he asked.

"Yes," she said. "He used to be a big shot in the Party's youth movement, organising official rallies and that sort of thing."

"Oh," he said.

"And once," she continued, shuffling her feet slightly, "once a couple of years ago he made a pass at me."

Antonin looked at her with embarrassment.

"Oh dear," he said. "I'm sorry. I wasn't to know coming here would be difficult for you."

"It's all right," she continued. "I managed to get rid of him. He's a horrible man. And now he's probably out of a job."

Antonin shrugged. Her description of his landlord did not match up with his own rather favourable first impressions of the chap, but perhaps that was only to be expected.

"Shall we look at the papers," he asked, pulling his suitcase up onto the bed and taking out the documents. He handed most of them to her while he started working his way through the detailed notes on the nine murdered scientists.

They both sat silently reading on the bed for quite a while before Antonin looked up glumly. Where there was an indication of the time of death he had noted it down on a piece of paper. Now he held out his findings to Nadja.

"Look at that," he said.

She scanned the list.

"They all died earlier that night," she said quietly. "So they might have gone round killing off the others and then come home early on the Sunday morning and killed themselves."

Antonin nodded.

"Looks a bit that way, doesn't it?"

She looked at him, and he was pleased to note that curiosity had replaced self-pity as the dominant emotion.

"But why?" she asked. "Why on earth do such a dreadful thing?"

Antonin tried to think about his father. He had been such a silent man, silent and strong. A man of convictions, albeit a form of rigid communist convictions which Antonin himself found repulsive. Nadja's father had been the same. A solid reliable man, a dependable sort of chap who wasn't just a scientist but had also been recruited as a secret police informer. And something pretty awful would have been required to persuade two such sober men to thrash about one night in such a frenzied orgy of killing.

But then, just as he was about to despair of ever finding a sensible explanation, a childhood memory seemed to rise up within him. It was something he didn't think about very often. But now it was suddenly there, as fresh in his mind as if it had happened only yesterday.

* * * * * *

He had only been about ten years old and he had already learned it was wise to avoid the subject. For on the few occasions when he had asked his father about his childhood or his parents, the replies had been so evasive that he had simply given up trying.

But then, one day, something strange had happened. Without warning, Antonin's parents suddenly announced that his father's parents were coming to stay. It seemed they had emigrated to America just after the war and were returning on a brief visit to see their son and his family.

A strange transformation now began in the Ziegler household. As if from nowhere a series of dusty photographs of his father's childhood in Czechoslovakia appeared. They were liberally dotted around on bookshelves and mantelpieces and carefully inserted into photograph albums. And then, shortly before the day of their arrival, his father had actually started talking about them.

They had been, it seemed, ardent Nazis. During the war, while Antonin's father was in Moscow being trained by the communists, they had remained behind in the Third Reich as enthusiastic supporters of Adolf Hitler. After the war, finding themselves equally uncomfortable on both sides of the new European divide, they had swiftly decamped to the United States. For many years they had not dared visit their son at his East German home for fear of trouble with the authorities, but now that they had secured United States citizenship they finally felt it safe to risk a visit.

So one day there had been a knock at the door and suddenly Antonin was face to face with a new set of grandparents. Having rather come to expect a pair of jack-booted Nazis, he had been surprised when they turned out to be perfectly normal people. They brought with them ten dollar bills and real American candy for the children, and were more than delighted to play for hours on end with their grandchildren.

But things did not go so smoothly for the grown-ups. After about a week of gradually rising tension, Antonin had been playing together with Stepan in their bedroom when he became aware of a ferocious row taking place in the living room. Creeping out into the hallway, he had sat anxiously on the floor and listened.

The temporary truce which had accompanied his grandparents' visit had finally broken down under the weight of its own falsehood. As he sat numbly in the hall, he could hear his father angrily denouncing his parents for their wartime collaboration with the Nazis. At the same time, and in equally forthright terms, he could hear his grandfather launching into a bitter tirade against Moscow and all its doings, insisting that even in Eisenhower's America many people now wished that the West had made common ground with the German people to destroy the communist menace.

The row cannot have lasted for more than twenty minutes before his grandparents came storming out of the room. Completely ignoring young Antonin, who was still crouching in the hall, they had swept in silent rage into their bedroom and packed their things. And then, without so much as a goodbye, they had marched out of the house and were gone for ever, leaving in their wake nothing but a numbed silence.

The re-establishment of order in the Ziegler household following this strange episode had been swift indeed. No sooner had these mysterious grandparents left the house than everything had returned to normal. Even as Antonin remained crouched in the hallway the purge had begun. His father, his face filled with silent rage, had walked calmly around the house gathering up all the photographs which had so recently been put on public display. His mother had done the same with the photograph albums. But this time, instead of returning the photographs to whatever cupboard or box they had previously inhabited, Antonin's parents had gone into the kitchen and systematically stuffed the whole lot into the stove. By the end of the evening of his grandparents' departure there was no trace of the fact that they had ever existed.

It was the last time Antonin ever saw his American grandparents. Their disappearance was total and complete, a final break never to be healed. It was as if his father had buried them away in a deep dark dungeon in his mind and then simply thrown away the key.

* * * * * *

"Antonin!"

Nadja's voice interrupted his thoughts.

"Sorry," he said. "I was just remembering something."

Nadja was sitting cross-legged just a few feet away from him on the bed and he found her physical proximity disconcerting. He knew it was not just because she was a pretty young girl, for at Oxford it was common enough for him to find himself alone in the presence of pretty young girls. But Nadja was different. There was a chemistry about her which reminded him so strongly of Katrina, an intense fusion of physical and mental attraction which was hard to resist.

"I think I may have worked out what was going on," he said, adopting a businesslike tone which he hoped would mask his confused feelings towards her. She listened in silence as he recounted his father's final rift with his own parents.

She listened in silence.

"Oh," she said quietly when he had finished, and from her voice and manner he was sure that despite his best efforts she had rumbled him, that she was not listening to his words at all but rather to the powerful emotional undercurrents which he was trying so hard to deny.

"Do you see what I'm driving at?" he asked with resolve, standing up and edging away from the bed.

She smiled at him, the same enigmatic smile that Katrina had so often used.

"Perhaps," she said. "You mean that your father and my father were together trying to destroy all trace of something at the institute, something like an idea or an invention. You think they wiped out everything and everyone involved with it, rather like your father did with the photographs of his parents when he wanted to wipe them out from his mind."

The words were promising, suggesting not only that she accepted the logic of his deduction but also that she had decided to ignore whatever it was she had sensed about his emotional reaction towards her. But the tone with which she delivered the words told a very different story. It was as if she were no longer interested in the death of a father she had never met, but was gradually becoming interested in Antonin himself.

"Why are you looking at me like that?" she asked suddenly.

Antonin gulped.

"Like what?"

"It's like you're trying to see through me."

He took a small step backwards.

"You remind me of someone," he said, unable to think of anything better to say. For a moment he thought he could see her wince, but then her face cleared.

"A girl?"

He nodded.

"Yes. Someone I used to know, but it was a long time ago, when I was about your age."

"A student romance?"

"I suppose you could say that."

She hesitated.

"Here, or was it in England?"

"In Prague."

She nodded thoughtfully.

"She was important to you?"

Antonin nodded.

"And she hurt you?"

Again he nodded. Confronted by this endless stream of questions, he could find no way to respond other than by telling the truth.

"You really must have loved her very much to still be missing her after all these years," she said sadly.

Antonin walked towards the bed and started gathering up the papers lying about. He felt foolish for embarking on such a pointless and rather painful conversation, and a part of him hoped that she would take the hint and leave. But she stayed exactly where she was.

"You're not married then?" she asked abruptly.

He put the pile of papers down on the bedside table and looked at her with a slightly irritated expression.

"You're asking a lot of questions, aren't you?"

"Yes," she said. "But then you're giving me a lot of funny looks."

For a brief second Antonin allowed his eyes to meet hers. And as they did, he suddenly realised that despite the age gap between them the chemistry might possibly be mutual, that she might actually feel attracted towards him. The relaxed way she was sitting on the bed, the endless stream of intrusive personal questions, the tone of her voice. All pointed in exactly that direction.

"In England I'm a university lecturer," Antonin said, standing over her and trying to look stern, "so I'm used to talking to people your age. And if you will permit me to give you a small piece of fatherly advice, I would suggest that you should be rather more circumspect than you are in the way you talk to men. It could easily get you into trouble."

She grinned at him.

"Do you think you're dangerous then? Do you think I'm in some kind of personal danger in your presence because you might jump on me and rape me?"

He shook his head, suddenly feeling rather silly. He knew for sure, had known all along for that matter, that Nadja was perfectly capable of looking after herself.

"Now if you were him," she snarled, jerking her head towards the door and clearly referring to Antonin's dapper landlord, "then I might have something to worry about. But then I wouldn't have agreed to go off alone with a man like that in the first place."

She was still on the bed and his futile attempt at gentle admonishment had clearly failed. There was a small upright chair on one side of the room and Antonin lowered himself onto it. He felt horribly torn, relishing the echo of Katrina's warm presence which he had found in this young girl but also rather frightened. Part of him would have liked to become an observer, watching her with silent curiosity rather than interacting. But that, of course, was not an option. Since she showed no signs of leaving by herself, there were really only two options left. He could either throw her out or let her stay.

"You seem to be a bit frightened of me," Nadja said at last.

Antonin smiled.

"A little perhaps. I told you why."

She thought for a bit.

"Is my resemblance to this other girl physical, or is it more to do with my personality."

"Both. I tell you you're really remarkably like her. It's a bit . . .well, it's a bit disorientating for me, that's all."

She was silent for a while.

"I think I see," she said slowly. "Part of you wants me to be her, but I'm not. Is that right?"

She smiled.

"I can see why she liked you," she said.

"Can you?"

Despite himself he could feel himself thrilled by her words. But whether it was because she had spoken them or Katrina had spoken them was far from clear.

"Yes. You're not just sweet, which you really are. You're also strong inside. But you don't want to use your strength to hurt people, so instead you absorb all the hurt yourself."

Antonin shrugged.

"I mustn't grumble. Most people would say I was a pretty successful man."

Again she smiled.

"Most people. But not you, I suspect."

The upright chair was hard beneath him, but no longer did he feel awkward. He could sense that she was trying to give him space.

"It's rather ironic that I should meet you here," he said. "I'd sensed for some time that there was a link between my parents" death and Katrina, although I couldn't really understand what it might be. And now when I'm poking around asking nosey questions I meet someone who resembles her so closely. It's a bit uncanny."

"A coincidence, you think?"

"Yes. I suppose it must be."

She thought for a bit.

"Both our fathers seemed to think eye-to-eye too. Perhaps it's not as much of a coincidence as you suppose." She hesitated. "What on earth do you think they could have been going to such lengths to conceal, anyway?"

"They must have found something they didn't like, I imagine. It was a scientific research establishment, loosely linked to the military. So it's rather like the old adage about nuclear weapons, isn't it? People are often asking themselves why the scientists responsible didn't just strangle the idea at birth, as if it was somehow their fault that Mankind's grip on common sense is a bit shaky. So maybe this time the scientists came up with something so ghastly that at least two of the people involved – namely your father and mine – decided to stamp it out before it spread."

She said nothing, staring blankly ahead.

"My poor father," she said at last. "If that's true, it's pretty dreadful, isn't it?"

Antonin nodded.

"For him, yes," he said. "But for you, maybe it's better than thinking he didn't love you."

She smiled at him weakly.

"Aren't you curious about what it was?" she asked.

"Curious. Of course I'm curious. But perhaps it's better if we don't know. The whole point of their actions was precisely so that we wouldn't."

She hesitated for a moment. But then, rising to her feet, she got off the bed and knelt down beside the chair where he was sitting. Then she glanced around nervously, as if checking to see that she could not be overheard.

"Antonin," she whispered. "I think there's something you should see. It's something I've never shown anyone before."

Her tone was anxious, and he looked at her sharply.

"My mother told me quite a lot about my father. By all accounts he was a bit of an enigma. He was a brilliant scientist, but he also had many failings as an individual. He was often careless, a bit unreliable. For example, he would mislay things and then not remember what he'd done with them."

Again she hesitated, as if she still had serious doubts about telling him. But then she seemed to make up her mind.

"My mother has a small dacha," she continued. "Well, 'dacha' is rather a grand title for it really. It's just a little wooden house up in the forests north of town. They got it as a perk when my father was alive and nobody ever thought to take it away from us when he died. Anyway, when I was a child my mother and I went up there most weekends in summer. As you can imagine, I used to scramble about all over the place exploring. When I was thirteen, I was killing some time poking about in the attic when tucked away in the corner I found a tatty old briefcase. It was full of my father's stuff. Important stuff, I think, because it had all these security classifications stamped all over it."

Antonin stared at her anxiously. It was obvious what she was thinking.

"What sort of stuff?" he asked.

"I don't know. Mainly incomprehensible scientific papers. A lot of equations, some technical drawings, and a box which looked like some kind of tape recorder."

"What did you do with it?" he asked sharply.

"Nothing. I was going through a bad time with my mother just then. You know, like girls do. So I just pushed all the things back into the bag and put it back where I found it. Later I went back to it a few times. This might sound silly, but when I felt alone I would go up and finger it all, as if it gave me some kind of personal link with him."

"And it's still there?"

"I would think so."

"Will you show me?"

"I wouldn't have told you if I didn't want to show you. Why

don't you meet me tomorrow morning at the railway station at about ten o'clock so we can go up together? It's not far."

She fell silent, still kneeling next to him on the floor. Antonin did not reply immediately. He looked down at her and knew that if he had reached out to her and kissed her she would not have resisted. But instead he rose to his feet.

"Yes, Nadja, I'll meet you there" he said. "And now I think it would probably be for the best if you were to go."

She stood up slowly and went to the door as if to leave, but then she turned and faced him once more.

"There's only one thing I can't understand about that girl you think I'm like," she said. "I can see why she went for you, because I could easily see myself doing just that. But what I really can't understand is why she changed her mind."

And with that she turned again and was gone.

* * * * * *

It was dark except for a narrow chink of light shining through beneath the door from the corridor beyond. Outside, far away in the distance, he could hear the rhythmic chanting of the demonstration. Antonin lay outstretched in the cramped single bed, listening to the distant cry of the students, and tried not to succumb to the guilt he felt for not being with them. Katrina would be there, no doubt, risking her neck for the cause of Dubcek's freedoms, but he himself had not yet broken his promise to his father to avoid becoming ensnared in political activity.

The chanting was coming closer, filling the night air with its rhythmic repetitions, and finally Antonin gave up all attempts at ignoring it. Rising from the bed and going over to the window, he pulled aside the flimsy curtains and peered outside into the warm August air. But except for a few anxious-looking policemen there was still nothing unusual to be seen in the nearby streets.

Yet even though he could not yet see anything he could still feel the tension in the air. The present stalemate couldn't last forever. Sooner or later the crisis would have to come to a head.

Antonin gazed out at the capital city of the country he loved so much. Ever since adolescence he had hated the political system which was Stalin's legacy to his homeland. It was a cruel and tyrannical system, and he knew he really should have had the courage to go out onto the streets and join hands with those who were fighting for something better. But instead he had remained behind in his room when so many of the other students had left, and all just because of a stupid promise.

The noise suddenly became louder and he leant out of the window so that he could see to the far end of the street. And sure enough, the vanguard of the crowd was just coming into view, although still some way away. He strained his eyes to see if he could see her in the crowd. But in the crush of people she was nowhere to be seen.

Most of the demonstrators were young, their eager faces reflected in the yellow glow of the streetlights. The demonstration was orderly, files of students in white armbands marching either side of the main body of people. Held aloft by the crowd were Czechoslovak flags and large banners calling for a strengthening of the reform process, and right at the front of the crowd was a student carrying a loud hailer, a thin angular fellow who seemed to be initiating most of the chanting.

But as the demonstration approached ever closer Antonin suddenly closed the window and held back, hiding his face in the shadows. He wanted so much to see Katrina, but at the same time he didn't want her to see him. Not there. Not hiding away in the darkness when she was fighting so hard to bring light.

Suddenly there was a sharp knocking on the door. He swung round, wondering who could be calling so late, for it was already gone eleven o'clock.

He switched on the light and opened the door to see Katrina standing before him. Her face was still flushed from the excitement of the demonstration outside. Despite her sloppy jeans and tee-shirt she looked radiant, exuding a kind of nervous energy which seemed to contrast so devastatingly with his own sallow reserve.

She stepped into the room and closed the door silently behind her.

"I thought I'd call in and see you," she said, flicking her hair out of her eyes and examining him with that slightly condescending look which made him shrivel up inside.

He breathed an inward sigh of relief that he had not yet changed into his pyjamas.

"That's nice," he mumbled. The noise of the demonstration now filled the air, redoubling his feelings of embarrassment about her finding him cowering alone in his room. "Is everything going well?"

Her face darkened.

"Of course," she said. "Dubcek's not going to stop us, is he? It'll be Brezhnev who does that."

She walked over to the window and flung it wide open.

"You've got a ringside view here, haven't you?"

Her tone didn't sound sarcastic, but nevertheless her words made him wince.

"I promised them," he murmured softly.

She turned to him with a serious expression.

"I know you did. And I didn't come here to have a dig at you, if that's what you mean."

Antonin joined her by the window.

"I know you didn't," he said. "I suppose it was more of a case of me having a dig at myself."

Suddenly, without warning, she turned away from the window and pulled him roughly towards her. And then, before he had really grasped what was happening, he found that she was kissing him full on the lips.

It was a long time before she drew her face away from his. And then, with that sly smile which he had found so irresistible from the day they had met, she began to stroke his hair.

"For such a clever man you're rather slow on the uptake, aren't you, Antonin? Haven't you worked out yet that I love you?"

He looked at her in amazement.

"Me?" he said, his heart pounding in excitement.

She laughed.

"Go on, Antonin. Ask me why."

He risked a sort of smile.

"Why?"

"Because I see through you, and I like what I see."

"And what is it that you see?"

"A kind and thoughtful man with an immense capacity for love. And I know that you are the one I need."

She hesitated, and he suddenly became aware that her lonely eyes were searching his face for some sign that he reciprocated her feelings. And slowly, with an intense thrill of pleasure, he pulled her towards him. He could feel the warm pressure of her young breasts beneath her tee-shirt, the eager throb of her heartbeat. He made to kiss her, but she held him away, her eyes pleading with him to look into hers, and he could tell that she was searching for a mental fusion with him more enduring than any physical act could be.

He met her gaze, and deep inside he could feel something extraordinary happen. It was as if there was a mingling of the soul, a sharing of all times past, present and future, a loss of self and a gaining of another. And he knew at that moment that there would be no turning back, that their lives were merged for all time, that even beyond death they would still be as one. For they were no longer separate people, but had instead become one. And if that was what was meant by falling in love, then that was what had happened.

* * * * * *

Antonin awoke. His palms were sweaty, his bedcovers strewn haphazardly across the floor beside his bed. He could still feel her beside him as she had been in the dream, her warm flesh pressed against his as she writhed beneath his touch, her gaze gentle and tender as their bodies had joined together in ecstasy for the first time. But already the dream was crumbling fast, already the memory of that beautiful August night in 1968 was reverting to the twisted horrible form it had taken for over two decades. Once more he could see another night, another Katrina, the beginning of the long silent nightmare of his adult life.

He rose from the bed and walked to the window, flinging it wide open. In his ears he could still hear a faint echo of that Prague student demonstration so long before, but outside in Zilina it was three in the morning and there was not a soul to be seen. Since that night one revolution had failed, another had succeeded, and Antonin Ziegler had turned from a shy postgraduate student into a successful Oxford academic. But despite all that had subsequently happened, he knew that nothing had really changed.

He turned on the light, hoping that the combination of electricity and fresh air would restore his normally composed manner. For it was not true to say that Antonin was a man in a perpetual state of inner turmoil. In twenty years he had learnt to control his disability, learnt to play to his strengths rather than dwell upon his weaknesses, and he prided himself that on the whole he had succeeded.

He sighed heavily, gratefully drawing the cool night air into his lungs. His dream had been more intense than usual, and he knew that that was largely Nadja's fault. He glanced at the floor where she had knelt beside him only a few hours before and wondered for a fleeting moment whether he had been wrong to push her away.

There were of course many perfectly sound reasons for rejecting Nadja's advances. For one thing she was nearly twenty years his junior, young enough to be his own daughter. And Antonin had always been a man of fairly conservative opinions in this regard. At Oxford he was fully aware that relationships between male academic staff and female students were not at all unusual, almost commonplace perhaps, but in general he regarded these transitory romantic liaisons as vaguely immoral, nearly if not quite a case of exploitation. It was not for no reason that he had recently been appointed Moral Tutor at his college, an ancient if rather quaint office which provoked much fond amusement amongst staff and students alike.

But Antonin also knew that his feelings towards Nadja were different. She carried within her the same taut vibrancy as Katrina, the same burning intensity towards life. And just as Katrina had seemed to form a swift judgement about him so had she, as if she too were jumping desperately at life's meagre chances of happiness before they passed her by.

Antonin tired of standing by the window. He lowered himself slowly onto the bed and stared once more at the place where she had so recently knelt beside him, trying to imagine what might have been if he had reached out and touched her as he had sensed she wanted him to do. Was there even a chance it could have worked, that she could have restored him to what he once was? And if so, had he not been crazy to let that chance pass by?

But as soon as the thought crossed his mind he knew for certain that the answer was no. It was precisely because of her similarity to Katrina that she would fail, or rather that he would fail. For many years as a young man he had tried to fight this terrible thing, this affliction which was Katrina's parting gift. He had struggled bravely and repeatedly, helped by many kind and considerate women, knowing inwardly that it was not his fault and that it was a struggle he should fight and win. And if many years before he had finally given up the fight and resigned himself to a lifetime of quiet solitude, it was only because he had come to learn that it was all utterly pointless, that he would simply hurt himself again as he had hurt himself so often before.

And now he had to accept that it would be no better with Nadja. He dare not even try, for it would only end in fresh despair. Far better to accept his fate freely than confront it once more in such a cruel way. Because ever since Katrina it had always been the same when Antonin had tried to make love. He could fool himself for a long time, right up to the very point when he was almost certain he would find fulfilment. But then, just when he thought he had won, he would suddenly see her face looming up before him, the blank expressionless face with which she had told him she was leaving. And then, invariably, he would fail.

For Katrina's final lingering gift to Antonin had been a cruel yet fitting jest to play on one who had loved her with such profound intensity. She had bequeathed to him a lifelong gift of impotence.

* * * * * *

"It's not much further," she called, flicking a glance over her shoulder.

Nadja clambered up the winding path which led through the forest with the confidence of a lifetime's familiarity. Her pace was swift and Antonin found it difficult to keep up with her. He was breathing hard and as he walked he was slowly becoming aware that his right foot was developing a blister.

"You didn't tell me it was so far up?" he called after her, his chest heaving.

She stopped and turned.

"Sorry," she said. "Am I going too fast? We can wait for a bit before we go on."

She bounced over to a nearby log and sat down while she waited for him to catch up. Since alighting from the bus in the valley below they had already been climbing for over an hour through the dense forest which covered the high Slovakian uplands.

"What on earth possessed anyone to build a dacha up here, for goodness sake?" Antonin puffed, joining her on the log.

"There are lots of them dotted about up here in the hills," she replied.

"But aren't there any roads?"

"There's an unmade forest track. It leads right up there."

Antonin eased off his right shoe and sock and began to examine the place which hurt.

"Might it not have made more sense to drive up?" he muttered.

"We don't have a car."

Antonin scowled.

"We could have hired one," he mumbled, half under his breath.

Nadja laughed.

"Sorry. I do this walk most weekends in summer. It was silly of me not to think of you."

Antonin said nothing but started to pull his sock and shoe back on again. He had found himself becoming slightly annoyed with Nadja ever since they had met at the station that morning. Her gently flirting manner, which the previous evening he had found alluring and exciting, he now began to find irksome.

She looked at him.

"You look really miserable this morning, Antonin." she said. "Didn't you sleep well?"

He flicked a glance at her.

"Not particularly," he said gruffly, tying up his shoelace and setting off again up the path. But he had not gone very far when she overtook him, edging past him on the narrow path so that she completely blocked his way.

"What's the matter with you?" she said, swinging round to face him. "Why are you being like this today?"

"Like what?"

"Acting as though you're trying to shove me aside. Have I done something wrong?"

Antonin looked at her perplexed young face and suddenly felt extremely guilty. Whoever's fault they were, and he wasn't exactly sure, she was certainly not responsible for the difficulties and confusions of his past life.

"Sorry," he said. "I didn't sleep very well last night and I'm always grumpy when I don't get enough sleep. And now to cap it all I've got a blister developing on my foot."

For a few moments she looked as if she was going to say something, but then she stepped aside.

"It's best if you go ahead," she said, "and then we can go at your pace."

Several minutes later they arrived at a small clearing in the trees. It was cradled in a high mountain valley, low shrubs interspersed with open pasture and a profusion of wild mountain flowers. Through the middle of it, hidden from view by the shrubs, they could hear the sound of water crashing and tumbling down the hillside towards the main river valley below. And on the far side of the clearing, at the end of a rough forest track which seemed to appear out of nowhere through the forest, there was a small two-storey wooden house.

"That's it," Nadja called, catching up with him.

She overtook him and started leading the way along the narrow path which snaked across the clearing towards the little house, but when they reached the stream she stopped and waited for him.

"Take your shoe off and put your bad foot in the water for a while," she ordered bossily. "You'll find it helps."

Antonin looked at her and nearly offered some cryptic remark to the effect that he was old enough to look after himself, but then he thought better of it and quietly removed his shoe. As he did so, Nadja bounded off across the springy grass towards the house, pulling out a key from her trouser pocket and unlocking the door before disappearing inside.

He lowered his foot gingerly into the fast-flowing stream. The water was icy cold, but as it flowed around his foot it numbed the pain from the blister. Sitting there on a tuft of grass in the middle of the clearing, he began to understand why generations of Slovaks had chosen to build remote little weekend houses like this. For in sharp contrast to the noise and pollution of the towns, here the air was crisp and clear. A slight breeze was causing the tops of the trees to sway gently back and forth, their leaves making a soft rustling sound as they moved. In the forest the sunshine had been patchy and weak as it struggled to get through the dense undergrowth, but here it was strong and bold, flooding down into the mountain clearing with a tantalising combination of the heat of high summer and the coolness of the high mountain peaks far above.

He looked across at the house itself, a fairytale construction of interlocking logs and tiny square windows. High up on the pointed roof, a rusty weathervane seemed to tell of a long dead rustic past, when life in Slovakia had been simple and uncomplicated, a land of timeless alternation between summer and winter in which people's lives from cradle to grave were as predictable as the crops they had grown and the animals they had reared. To Antonin it had always seemed a lost world, but here in this remote mountain clearing bathed in summer sunshine, it seemed as if an echo of that world was somehow managing to linger on.

Nadja emerged from the house and started walking towards him, carrying in her hands two large plastic water containers. When she reached him, she bent down and started filling them from the stream.

"Your water supply?" Antonin queried.

"Yes," she replied. "We've all mod cons up here, you know."

Antonin eyed the building carefully. After his mistake about the road he had no desire to look even more stupid.

"You've no electricity, presumably," he observed cautiously.

She shook her head.

"No. We use liquid gas for everything."

He shrugged and gingerly lifted his foot out of the water. To his relief he found that not only did his blister feel better, but also that his breathing had returned to normal.

"I must admit it's quite pretty up here," he said.

She didn't reply. Again he could feel the tension rising, that she wanted him to say or do something which would show that he took an interest in her.

"And this is where you found your father's things?" he asked.

"Yes," she replied. "There's a small attic in the roof space. I'll show you."

She stood up and walked off towards the house carrying the water bottles.

The inside of the house was dark and damp, little sunlight penetrating the tiny windows. There were only two small rooms on the ground floor – a living room and a sort of overgrown cupboard space which seemed to serve as both kitchen and storeroom. Between the two was a tiny hallway, and from the hallway a narrow wooden staircase led up to the top floor and two simple bedrooms, each of which was nearly filled with a large wooden double bed.

"Quaint," Antonin observed.

But Nadja took no notice. Standing on an old wooden chair, she reached up and pushed aside a small piece of wood set into the ceiling to reveal the dark space above. And then, without further ado, she lifted herself nimbly up with both arms and disappeared from sight.

Antonin stood uncertainly beneath the dark hole in the ceiling and peered up.

For a few moments he could see nothing, but then he heard the sound of a match striking and Nadja's face appeared at the hole. In her hand she was holding a candle.

"Aren't you coming up?" she asked.

Antonin looked at the chair and then at the hole in the ceiling. They seemed to be an awfully long way apart.

"I don't think I can," he commented unhappily.

She looked at him for a few moments and then scuttled away. But a few moments later she was back, clutching in her hand an old leather briefcase.

"Take it from me," she ordered.

He stood on the chair and took it from her outstretched hand. Climbing down from the chair, he laid the briefcase on the bed and waited for her to join him.

She sat beside him and opened the briefcase, carefully lifting the contents out onto the bed. A few of the things were obviously personal – a photograph of Nadja as a baby, another of her parents together on the day of their marriage, a comb, an assortment of pens and pencils – but most of the contents clearly related to Gregor Markov's work at the institute. There were a lot of papers, all highly classified, and also a small machine which bore some resemblance to an old tape recorder.

Antonin picked up the sheaf of papers and started to examine them. Most were highly technical, written in that strange in-house jargon favoured by academic scientists. As well as written text there were diagrams, tables of data and a great deal of complex mathematics, the whole supplemented from time to time by somebody's hand-written notes in the margin.

He leafed carefully through the sheets of paper, trying to form some sort of impression of what the research might concern. But there were no summary documents, no convenient descriptions of the aim or results of the research. Nothing but endless technical scientific scribblings.

"Frankly," he said at last, "it doesn't make a lot of sense to me. There's a lot of stuff about things called response rates and strike targets and modal transformations, but most of it's just incomprehensible clap-trap, isn't it?"

She nodded.

"I've read it all through several times," she said. "I can hardly understand a word of it."

Antonin picked up the box which looked like a tape-recorder and examined it carefully.

"Any ideas about this?" he asked her.

She shrugged.

"It's got two spools like a tape recorder, although it's not like any that I've ever seen. And it's got what looks like an empty battery box at the back. Once I took it all round Zilina trying to find a battery to fit it but none of the electricians I spoke to could make it work. But even if you could make it work, it's got no tape, has it?"

Antonin lifted the panel off the back and examined the empty space. It did indeed look as if it took batteries, for there were what appeared to be a series of rusty terminals at either end. But other than that it yielded no more information than the papers.

He put it down on the bed again and looked up glumly at Nadja.

"So what do we do now?" he said.

She stared for a while at the things on the bed.

"Destroy them, I suppose." She said it calmly and quietly, as if she took it as self-evident.

Antonin stared at the assortment of objects for a long time before replying. And when he did, he spoke in the slow and ponderous tone which he usually adopted when he was trying to think at the same time.

"If it's true your father made a mistake and left something of importance behind when he killed himself then we've got a simple choice, haven't we? We don't really need to know what they found out. We can either respect their wishes and finish the job or we can take this briefcase back down the hillside with us and hand it over to somebody who might make sense of it."

Nadja stood up and walked over to the tiny window. She gazed out across the sun-lit clearing, watching the trees beyond as they swayed gently back and forth in the wind.

"You're not sure then?"

Antonin sighed and shifted uncomfortably on the bed, eyeing the briefcase and its contents with some considerable distaste.

"If I share my father's judgement on this," he said at last, "then it'll be for the first time in my life."

She turned anxiously to face him.

"So you're saying you think he might have been wrong?" she asked.

"My father's judgement was invariably wrong, Nadja. You're talking about a man whose heroes in life were Joe Stalin and Walter Ulbricht."

She thought for a while.

"I think I see," she said at last. "When you came up here today you were hoping you'd either convince yourself the contents of this briefcase were unconnected with the research or be able to work out exactly what it was they were trying to hide. And then you would have been able to make up your own mind and trust your own judgement."

Antonin nodded.

"I suppose that just about sums it up," he replied.

"Yet now you've looked you've not only convinced yourself that this stuff really might be significant but also that you can't work out what it's all about without expert help. And that means you're having to rely on your father's judgement rather than your own, which is exactly what you didn't want to do."

"Precisely."

They both lapsed into silence. But then, without any warning, she climbed back up onto the wooden chair and jumped up again into the attic. A few moments later she was back with the box of matches.

"Here you are, Antonin," she said, holding them out to him. "Since I never had the benefit of knowing that my father was a rat

I'm voting for a bonfire just on the off-chance he may have been right. But I'm prepared to leave the final decision to you."

He took the box of matches from her and grunted.

"I could toss a coin, I suppose," he observed dryly.

She smiled but said nothing. He looked at her intently for a few moments.

"Something tells me we've got to think about this for a while longer, Nadja. This work, whatever it was, was done by the communists over twenty years ago. It was a different time and a different world. And if this really was a major scientific breakthrough which they'd stumbled across by accident and then deliberately suppressed, we can't just strike a match and let the whole thing go up in smoke without even knowing what it was, can we?"

She sat down again on the bed.

"Why not?" she said at last. "If my father hadn't made what appears to have been a careless mistake and left this briefcase here and I hadn't subsequently discovered it then we wouldn't know anything about it anyway, would we?"

Antonin smiled faintly.

"No. But he did make a mistake and you did discover it, and so now we're both here on this bed with the infernal thing sitting between us. So your noble attempt to extricate us from our moral dilemma doesn't greatly help, does it?"

Nadja examined him thoughtfully for a few moments. Then, abruptly and without any warning, she suddenly stretched herself out full length on the bed and tucked her hands behind her head.

"All right," she said. "I'm in no hurry. If you want more time to think, we'll simply have to stay the night, won't we?"

Antonin looked at her aghast. Once again her meaning was clear, the invitation open and unashamed, if anything more pressing now than it had been the night before in his room in Zilina.

"Well?" she said.

"I don't know," he said brusquely, suddenly angered at the way in which this girl who looked and spoke so like Katrina appeared to be toying with his already confused feelings. He stood up and shoved the papers roughly back into the briefcase. "But if it's all right with you, I think I'll go back downstairs and quietly read it all through again by myself."

He picked up the briefcase and marched off downstairs. In the tiny living room there were several large armchairs, their cushions worn and tatty. Forcing himself to banish all thoughts of both

Katrina and Nadja from his mind, he settled down into one of them and started to read.

At the head of several of the documents were dates which showed that the papers had been prepared only weeks before the killings. That was certainly a sign that they would reveal a meaningful clue to the nature of the work being undertaken at the institute at the time. Cursing himself inwardly that he had never taken a more active interest in science, he forced himself to try and follow the cumbersome text which appeared between the blocks of mathematical equations. For many pages there was nothing he could get a grip on, nothing but meaningless jargon. But then, just as he was about to despair, his eye alighted on one of the hand-written notes in the margin, alongside an incomprehensible table of what appeared to be the results of some kind of experiment. As with all the other hand-written comments, it was written in what was probably Gregor Markov's own handwriting.

"Rubbish" the note stated. "This would imply an absurd level of suggestion."

Antonin stared bleakly at the brief comment, and as he did so he could feel a ripple of fear running down his spine. Despite himself, he clutched the papers tighter in his hand, as if protecting them from an unseen assailant. For although the words were inconclusive, plainly open to all manner of entirely innocent explanations, he could not shake free of the theory which was now beginning to take shape within his mind.

* * * * * *

His grandfather was devoting even more time to his vegetables than he usually did, and sorely though Antonin wanted to join him in his hiding place between the tall rows of runner beans he knew he still had to confront his parents before he returned to Prague. So, shortly after the Sunday midday meal, he allowed his grandfather to slope off alone to the garden while he remained sitting at the dining table with his parents.

His father was still displaying the same distracted manner he had carried with him at the railway station on Antonin's arrival. He seemed lost in some unfathomable world of his own thoughts, and unusually for him he did not appear to be sharing those thoughts with his wife.

"You seem to be worried about something," Antonin offered, carefully watching to see how his father would react.

The older man looked at Antonin with a somewhat vacant expression.

"No I'm not," he said, helping himself to a second helping of apricot dumplings. But then, as if forcing himself back from his private reverie, he fixed Antonin with an icy gaze.

"I hope you've been keeping your head down in Prague, son. It won't be long now before the final curtain comes down on the Dubcek circus."

Antonin lowered his head.

"You know my views," he said.

His father spat out a stone and then lowered his empty fork menacingly in Antonin's direction.

"I didn't ask for your views, son. I asked if you were keeping your head down. Everyone involved with this whole business is going to be in serious trouble when the Warsaw Pact comes in and restores order. I don't want you getting tangled up with the police, that's all."

Antonin could feel the anger welling up inside himself at the obvious emotional jibe. It was as if his father had written off all chance of his son thinking the right way. Now all he was bothered about was keeping up appearances. Completely forgetting all his carefully constructed plans to break the news to his parents gently, he turned to his father with scarcely concealed contempt.

"But that's the whole point, father. I am tangled up with them. And I'm not just tangled up with them, I'm going to marry one of them. And if you and mother don't like it, that's just too bad."

For a few moments there was a numbed silence. But then Antonin's mother rose to her feet, her face cold and emotionless, and she silently started to gather together the empty dishes lying on the table. Her husband watched her forlornly as she disappeared into the kitchen.

"Sorry," Antonin murmured, suddenly realising what he had done. He had not planned to hurt his parents gratuitously by delivering his difficult news in such an aggressive tone. So now he felt he needed to justify himself.

"Dubcek's only trying to win the free consent of the people for socialism, father," he began. "That's what you want too, isn't it? That's what you've always wanted?"

He had spoken the words without daring to look directly at his father. But as the silence which followed became longer and longer, he could not help but glance furtively towards him. And to his surprise he saw that he had slumped back into the same distant and distracted mood from which he had so recently emerged.

"Father . . ." he began.

His father's eyes rose slowly to meet his. And for a brief instant, no more than a fraction of a second, it was as if he were trying to reach out to his son and tell him what was on his mind.

* * * * * *

"Antonin . . ."

The call seemed far away, floating across a sea of distant memories.

"Antonin, wake up."

The memories began to drift slowly away and Antonin opened his eyes.

"Katrina . . ." he murmured, seeing her face before him.

The girl smiled gently.~

"I'm not Katrina," she said.

At her words all trace of sleep vanished. He shook his head and straightened himself up in the armchair.

"Sorry," he said, "I must have fallen asleep."

The curtains were drawn, but he could see that it was already dark outside.

"What time is it?"

"Midnight. You've been asleep for a long time."

Antonin remembered the papers he had been reading earlier. With a shock, he realised they were nowhere to be seen.

"It's all right," she said. "They're safe. I put them back in the briefcase and took them upstairs."

Antonin studied her for a moment. She was sitting in an armchair opposite him, her feet curled up beneath her, and she seemed to be eyeing him thoughtfully.

"Did you reach any conclusions?" she asked presently.

He thought for a while before replying.

"Yes," he said slowly. "On balance, I think you're right. I think we should destroy them."

She shifted her position slightly and cocked her head to one side.

"Why the change of heart?"

Antonin grunted.

"I think I may have worked out what they'd stumbled across. Not in detail of course, but the broad outline."

She said nothing, waiting for him to continue.

"We already know it was a research institute investigating various ways of using sonic impulses to disorientate and confuse enemy ground troops. As well as military applications such techniques could also have been useful in civilian crowd-control as a more sophisticated alternative to something like tear-gas. But I think it's possible they might have been too successful in their work. They might have discovered some way of using these impulses to actually control what people thought, to induce a state of heightened suggestibility in the human brain. A kind of mass hypnosis, you might say."

Nadja unfolded her legs and leant forward in her chair.

"You think they found a way to control people's minds?"

Antonin slowly nodded his head.

"Perhaps," he muttered. "My father was a sincere communist. A rather stupid and old-fashioned man in many ways. He was not only convinced that communism was the right way forward but also that people would in time come to share his opinions of their own free will. He would have utterly rejected the very notion of such a device being used by the government to brainwash people. He would have done anything to stop that. So it makes his behaviour plausible. And your father might have shared his conviction that whatever technique they had inadvertently stumbled across had to be strangled at birth."

Antonin rose to his feet.

"Where did you say you put the briefcase?" he asked.

She rose to her feet and led him upstairs into one of the two small bedrooms. The briefcase was lying on the old wooden double bed which nearly filled the room. Antonin reached out his hand towards it, meaning to carry it downstairs and burn the papers in the stove, but as he did so Nadja suddenly leant forward and touched his hand.

"And what will you do when you've burnt them, Antonin?" she asked faintly.

He looked up at her.

"I'm sorry," he said uncertainly.

"What will you do?"

Her face looked lonely, as lonely as Katrina's had once looked lonely a long time before. He swallowed hard, unsure precisely how to react.

"She's gone, surely you know that," Nadja murmured.

Antonin dropped his hand limply to his side. Then he sat down wearily on the bed and looked up at her standing before him.

"What do you want me to say to you?" he said.

106

Nadja didn't reply immediately. She walked to the small window overlooking the moonlit clearing beyond and flung it wide open, gazing out at the dark shadows of the Slovakian forest stretching away beyond. Several long minutes elapsed before she finally turned to face him.

"I've never met anyone like you before," she said. "Perhaps I never will again. Now do you understand what I mean."

The chill air coming in through the open window made Antonin shiver. He shifted uncomfortably on the bed.

"It's no good, Nadja," he said miserably. "It's not your fault, but it simply can't be."

"Is it because of her?" she said. "Is it because of the girl I remind you of? Is it because of Katrina?"

"Yes."

"But she's gone. She went a long time ago. Why can't you let her go?"

"I don't know," Antonin said, trying to avoid her gaze, "but I simply can't."

Nadja silently turned and closed the window. Then she turned again to face him.

"But I am the first since her, aren't I?" she murmured.

Antonin could feel his stomach turning inside out. Every glance, every turn of phrase, every mannerism of this young girl reminded him so powerfully of Katrina. On one level it made him angry, angry that she should dare disturb the memory of someone so dear. But on another level it paralysed him with a burning desire to reach out to her and assuage the pain he had carried within himself for so many years.

"You are the first," he replied.

He could see that tears were running down her cheeks. She whispered something he didn't quite catch.

"I'm sorry," he said.

"I said I'm prepared to settle for second best," she muttered. "If you simply burn my father's papers and walk out of my life again I really don't know how I'll cope with it."

Antonin rose to his feet and took a step towards her.

"Are you really so very unhappy?" he asked.

"I didn't think I was," she said, "until you turned up."

"But why me?"

She shrugged, wiping the tears away with her hand.

"It makes some kind of sense, doesn't it? I'm just like the other girl, you've said I am. And I know full well that although you're

107

trying your best to distance yourself from me a part of you is drawn to me just as you were once drawn to her. But don't you see that she was attracted to you too. She loved you once just as you loved her. So perhaps my feelings towards you shouldn't come as such a very great surprise."

Her words stopped Antonin in his tracks. He had been so obsessed with his own reactions towards her that he hadn't really stopped to think about her feelings towards him.

"I suppose you're right," he said slowly.

"So I can't understand why you are resisting me so strongly. Why are you so determined to go on tormenting yourself?"

Without really knowing why, Antonin reached out and took her gently by the hand. The recognition that her feelings towards him were no more than a reciprocal of his own feelings towards her had caused a strange tranquillity to come upon him. It was comforting to know they were in the same boat together, and now he knew that he had to begin to speak the truth.

"Everything you say is true, Nadja," he said. "When I first met you I was shocked by your similarity to Katrina. The way you look, the way you speak, the way you move. It was both uncanny and disorientating for me. It made a part of me cross, as if you were some kind of fraud. But I've slowly come to realise that you're not a fraud. You really are like her, and were I as young now as I was young when I first met Katrina then I really think I might have fallen in love with you just as I once fell in love with her."

He hesitated, uncertain how she would react to what he was about to say. But before he could speak she had interrupted him.

"But surely age doesn't change the important things. Why should the fact that you're older than me affect how we can feel about each other?"

Antonin held her hand more tightly.

"There's something you should know about me, Nadja," he said softly. "It's not something of which I'm proud and it's not something of which I often speak."

He hesitated, and this time it was he who could feel bitter tears running down his cheeks, for the silent grief and suffering of twenty long years seemed as nothing compared to the overpowering sense of worthlessness and self-pity which he could now feel engulfing him.

"Ever since the day Katrina left me," he said simply, "I've not been able to function as a man."

Far away in the darkness of the forest night an owl hooted. There was no curtain across the small bedroom window, and from where he was lying on the bed he could just make out the tops of the forest-covered hills beyond the clearing. For most of the night the sky had been dark, broken only by the stars, but now the bright yellow orb of the full moon was rising above the crest of the hills. He wondered why dawn had not yet come, because he seemed to have been lying awake for so very long, but other than the ghostly rays of moonlight there was as yet no sign of the approaching day.

He turned away from the window and gazed again at Nadja as she lay fast asleep beside him on the bed, her hair strewn haphazardly across the soft pillow. There was a look of quiet contentment on her face, a tranquillity which he dearly wished he could share. But try as he might, he could not find the peace of mind he craved.

It was no more than he would have expected of Katrina, of course. She too would have soothed his troubled brow, told him that a sexual relationship was unimportant to either their present or their future. She too would have persuaded him to lie silently with her on the bed until they drifted off to sleep together.

Antonin smiled wryly as he remembered how careful she had been to conceal her own sexuality from him as they had prepared for bed. Like a thoughtful host offering a reformed alcoholic an orange juice, she had tried to shield him from the horror of his own incapacity. And so now they lay together, both still fully clothed, seeking comfort merely from the fact of each other's presence.

He tried to imagine how she must feel when she thought of his impotence. Did she perhaps suppose that he did not find her sexually arousing, perhaps even that he found her physically repulsive? If she did imagine such a thing she would have been horribly wrong, for in reality his whole body yearned to reach out towards her, to touch and caress her as he had once touched and caressed Katrina, to draw her to him and find release from the concealed frustration of twenty years. Even now, despite her careful attempts to remain hidden beneath her rough walking clothes, he could imagine only too clearly in his mind's eye every curve and crevasse of her young naked body. He turned away and gazed once more through the window. It was no good, a hopeless dream, and it would only be a matter of time before she would come to tire of his piteous state.

Yet the simple question which she had asked him before still remained unanswered. What was he going to do now? As soon as the papers in the briefcase were burnt there would be no further point in his staying in Slovakia. His immediate priority would have to be making arrangements for his grandfather, who was still living illegally in Jiri's Bratislava flat. For a few months or years Antonin would have the solace of the old man's company in his Oxford rooms as a last reminder of his childhood life. But then it would be a straightforward case of the *status quo ante*, life as it had been before, and the strange experiences of his visit to Slovakia and his encounter with Nadja would gradually fade away into his memory. It should not have been a frightening prospect, for an Oxford college was a gentle place in which to live out the closing decades of his life.

Or was it? He turned again and looked thoughtfully at Nadja. She wanted him still, that much was clear. Even knowing everything, which was more than most people did, she undoubtedly still wanted him. And the thought crossed his mind that he could still agree to take her back with him. She was young, in her mid-twenties, nearly two decades younger than he, and it was only reasonable to suppose that in time her feelings for him would gradually fade. But in the meantime he could help her to find a new life in England, discover wider horizons for herself than she would ever be likely to know in the drab and dingy world of a post-revolutionary Slovakian industrial town. And even if he could never be her lover, he could at least aspire to be her mentor, a feeble replacement for the father she had never had.

He rose silently from the bed. He knew that dawn could not now be far off, that soon she would awake. Stealthily, so as not to disturb her, he slipped on his shoes and crept down the stairs to the tiny hallway below. He was just preparing to slip outside into the night, planning to walk and think a while in the crisp night air, when he suddenly remembered the briefcase.

It was still upstairs, still lying where it had been cast aside next to the bed in which Nadja still lay. He had meant to dispose of it the previous evening, as soon as he had taken the fateful decision to destroy whatever evidence it might contain, but then Nadja's words had completely distracted him. And so it was still there, a small piece of important unfinished business. He glanced at the stove in the tiny kitchen and for a moment hesitated, uncertain whether to go up the stairs again and fetch it down so that he could dispose of it straightaway. But with a frown he realised that if he went up again he would most likely wake her and thereby deny himself the chance he needed to reflect quietly on what he was going to say to her in the morning. And so, resolving to burn the documents immediately she awoke, he turned and walked out into the night.

Outside the moonlight was still bright, casting eerie shadows from the nearby trees across the clearing, but far away in the east he thought he could just detect the first faint glimmerings of dawn. He walked slowly towards the narrow stream which ran across the centre of the clearing, hoping that the sound of the water as it rushed and tumbled towards the valley far below would help to clear his thoughts. When he reached the water's edge, he sat down on a rock and began trying to work out whether or not to allow Nadja to return with him to Oxford.

But he didn't have long in which to think. For suddenly, coming along the rough track leading out of the forest towards the house, he became aware of a slowly approaching vehicle. It must have been a four-wheel drive, its frame raised well above the ground, and all its driving lights were extinguished. With an unconscious shudder of fear, Antonin slid off his perch and sank down into the protective cover of the bushes which flanked the stream on either side.

The doors of the jeep swung silently open and six men emerged. Two of them were carrying what appeared to be light machine guns, the others small handguns. They stealthily approached the building and surrounded it. Then one of the men, a tall fellow wearing a long grey raincoat, produced from his pocket a small torch and flashed it twice in Antonin's direction, as if making a prearranged signal to someone on the far side of the clearing. Antonin cowered low in the undergrowth and then, when the light was gone, raised his head and glanced cautiously behind him. There was no returning signal. After a few moments the man by house flashed his torch again. This time, from the direction in which they had come on foot the previous day, there was an answering flash in the dark.

There was no time to think. As soon as the exchange of torchlight messages had been completed there was a loud crash as four of the men smashed through the unlocked door and into the tiny building. Antonin could hear the sound of them rushing from room to room, and then – almost simultaneously – Nadja's startled and terrified scream as she awoke.

Antonin's first instinct was to break cover and run towards the house. But he checked himself, for although the building was not far off, one of the men armed with a machine gun was standing directly between him and the door. In the bright moonlight, there was no possible way he could reach the house undetected.

The commotion in the house seemed to have abated somewhat. Upstairs in the bedroom, he could see that a gas lamp had been turned on. The small window was flung wide open as the man who appeared to be the leader leant out and yelled angrily in Slovak to the guards outside that the man they were looking for was not there.

Then he disappeared inside again, and Antonin could hear him shouting at Nadja to tell him where the briefcase was. He could hear her just beginning to deny any knowledge of it when one of the men must have spotted it on the floor, because the general commotion abated again, leaving an ominous silence in its wake. And then the man's voice again, more controlled now, this time demanding that Nadja tell him what had happened to the Englishman.

Antonin strained his ears. Now that he was speaking more normally, he was sure he had heard the voice before. But try as he might, he could not quite place it.

"Well, Nadja," he demanded, "where have you hidden your fat English boyfriend."

Suddenly Antonin remembered the voice. It was the well-dressed man who had met him at Zilina station and offered him the use of his room, the man who had made a pass at Nadja while she was still at school.

"I don't know, Bohumil."

There was a deep tremor of fear in her voice as she spoke.

"He was here last night. I don't know where he's gone."

"We know he's gone. But where has he gone? He cannot simply have vanished into thin air."

"I don't know."

There was the sound of a sharp slap followed by a cry of pain.

"Enough stalling. Tell me now, or next time I'll really make you hurt."

"I don't know. He must have gone outside during the night. Perhaps he went out for some fresh air."

There was silence for a few moments. Then the man's face appeared at the window and he yelled across the clearing in the general direction of the path down the mountain. Moments later, a young man carrying a torch appeared and headed towards the house, crossing the stream only yards from Antonin's hiding place in the thick undergrowth beside the stream.

112

"Did you see anyone moving outside?" he called to the newcomer.

"No. No one has gone down the path since I arrived."

"Why did you not respond immediately when I signalled you? I had to flash you twice. Are you sure you were attending properly?"

There was a brief silence.

"A call of nature, Bohumil," came the embarrassed reply. "I was only gone for a moment. He could not possibly have vanished in so short a time."

The leader swung back towards Nadja and there was the sound of another slap. But this time there was no accompanying scream.

Her assailant laughed, harshly and coldly.

"You always were a brave girl, Nadja," he sneered. "But we know your friend has not gone down the path, and also he did not go down by the road. And what's more it is also strange that he would leave in the dead of night without taking his precious brief-case. So I do not think he can be very far away."

If Nadja replied, the reply was inaudible. But a few moments later the leader reappeared at the window.

"Antonin Ziegler," he called in a loud voice, as if addressing the whole forest. "Antonin Ziegler, I think you can hear me, so listen carefully to what I have to say."

There was a long pause, his words echoing round the hills, and Antonin strained to make sure he correctly heard the man's words.

"We already have most of what we want. Now it is only you we need. If you give yourself up, I will personally guarantee that no harm will come either to you or to the girl. We wish to talk with you, that is all."

There was a long silence, filled only with the rushing sound of the water in the stream.

"All I want is to talk. Then we will release you both."

Antonin wondered at the man's apparent supposition of his own naivety. But as the silence which followed stretched from seconds into minutes, he could begin to feel a small nagging doubt entering his mind. For cowering in the undergrowth he could achieve pre-cisely nothing. He could neither destroy the briefcase nor help Nadja. Yet if he gave himself up, then despite the overwhelming odds he just might find a way.

"Do you really want this poor girl to suffer needlessly?" the man shouted angrily. "You and I both know she has a sensitive soul. She will feel it all the worse for that."

Antonin could sense that the man's patience was nearly

exhausted. He disappeared from view for a few moments and Antonin could again hear Nadja's voice pleading desperately with him to leave her alone. Moments later the four men appeared at the front door. The first one to emerge was clutching the briefcase under his arm. After him the tall man appeared, pushing Nadja roughly before him. He looked around accusingly at the forest before roughly grabbing her hair and pulling her head upwards.

"You can see she is powerless in our hands," he screamed. "But she is also worthless compared to you. It is you we have orders to take. Come out from whichever tree or rock you are lurking behind and we will release her."

Through the tangled undergrowth, Antonin could just make out Nadja's terrified face. But then she suddenly seemed to draw a deep breath.

"Get away, Antonin!" she yelled at the top of her voice. "If you can, for God's sake get away!"

For a few moments her tormentor froze, as if her sudden intervention had taken him completely by surprise. But then, his face contorting into an expression of uncontrollable anger, he pulled her face roughly round and punched her so violently that she must have lost consciousness, for she slumped down heavily in his grip, her body dangling limply by the hair.

Her assailant looked up accusingly at the forest.

"You really are a stupid man, Ziegler," he roared angrily. Barking an order at the other men to search the house and forest, he began dragging the still unconscious Nadja with him towards the jeep.

Antonin shrank down as low as he could into the undergrowth beside the stream. There was nothing he could do now, nowhere he could run without being spotted.

Minutes passed. At one point he heard the sound of a man quite close by, pushing a stick into the undergrowth as he went, but in the dense mass of foliage beside the stream he missed him. And then, after about half an hour, the jeep's engine sprang into life and it drove off down the rough track.

For a while Antonin remained motionless, straining to hear if any of the men had stayed behind at the cottage. Yet there was no sound of movement, and when eventually he did dare lift his head, he could see to his relief that no one was still standing on guard outside the house. He crouched silently for several minutes longer. And then, numb with silent despair, he began to scramble along on his hands and knees towards the cover of the nearby trees.

There was a faint click as the phone was picked up.

"Jiri?"

"Antonin? Where the hell are you?"

There was an urgent tension in his voice which Antonin hadn't been expecting.

"Jiri. I can't say. Is everything all right?"

"Like hell it is. Your grandfather's gone. Someone must have come and taken him while I was at work. They've left a note addressed to you."

Antonin winced. It meant the noose was closing fast.

"Say something, Antonin. Do you know what's happened to him? What the hell's going on?"

"What does the note say, Jiri?"

"It's written in German. and says that if you want to see your grandfather or somebody by the name of Nadja Markov again you must go at once to Vienna and book into the Hotel Imperial. You will be contacted when you arrive. It also says that no harm will come to you. Does any of this make sense to you?"

Antonin thought fast. They might be bugging Jiri's phone, possibly tracing his call at this very moment.

"I'm in serious trouble, Jiri, but I can't explain anything right now."

There was a short silence.

"What do you want me to do, Antonin?" Jiri replied, his voice more controlled now.

"For the moment, do nothing. Do precisely nothing. As soon as it's safe, I'll contact you again."

He replaced the receiver and stepped out of the callbox into the stillness of the early evening air. Looking briefly at the cluster of tiny houses nestling at the foot of the hills, he examined the bus stop beside the telephone box and saw to his relief that a bus was due in half an hour. Lowering himself wearily down onto a low stone wall, he began to wait.

It had taken all day to reach the hamlet. Not daring to return to the main valley from which they had approached the cottage the previous day, he had climbed up and over the crest of the high wooded mountain range behind the cottage and descended on the far side. It had been a long and wearisome trek, for the blister which had first become apparent the previous day had re-appeared with a vengeance, causing him to wince with every footfall as he had crossed the rough terrain. Fearful of taking any obvious paths, he had struck out cross country, clambering over fallen trees and through low thorny bushes until his clothes were torn and his hands scratched and bleeding. Yet despite the hunger and exhaustion which were now threatening to engulf him, anger and guilt at his own foolishness still remained the dominant emotions.

He pulled out his wallet and checked to see how much cash he was carrying. It was enough to reach a main city, and from there he could probably use his credit card to get him to wherever he wanted to go. But where could he go? For whoever had moved in so effectively on the briefcase and Nadja was clearly trying very hard to find him.

Antonin frowned. The strength of their interest in him personally struck him as odd, for even if they had somehow become aware of the glittering prize the contents of the briefcase might represent, it was hard to see why they should attach any particular importance to him. Yet instead of being pleased at recovering the briefcase intact, the man at the cottage had been consumed with anger, almost as if capturing Antonin had been the central objective of the raid.

The thought faded from his mind, overlaid by other more pressing concerns. Even though he only had the vaguest idea of what the ideas contained in the briefcase might be, he was already beginning to sense the gnawing stench of evil which must have eventually driven his father to mass murder and suicide. For although it was still possible that the briefcase was a red herring, that when subjected to proper scientific analysis the information within it would prove to be irrelevant or incomplete or both, there remained a distinct possibility that it really would unlock the ideas which his father and Nadja's father had tried so desperately to conceal. And if that were true, then the consequences of his failure to destroy the briefcase and its documents just a few hours earlier could have awesome and untold consequences.

He looked up at the road and suddenly realised that he had no idea of the direction from which the bus would be coming. It would simply arrive and he would get on it, irrespective of where it was going. But thereafter he would have to make some more difficult decisions about where he would then go.

His predicament was uncomfortable. He couldn't go back to Jiri's flat in Bratislava, that much was obvious. But for exactly the same reasons he couldn't go back to Oxford either. For he was pretty sure that whoever was pursuing him would be able to pick him up in England as easily as in Czechoslovakia. Provided he remained in the anonymity of the crowd he stood a chance of remaining free, but as soon as he resurfaced again they would have him.

He thought of turning to the authorities, either in Czechoslovakia or more likely in Britain. He could report everything that had happened, tell them of his fears about the briefcase. They would not only be able to offer him personal protection but also be able to use their own formidable resources to try and recover the missing documents. But no sooner had Antonin conceived of the idea of going to the security services than he immediately rejected it again. For even if government agencies did manage to recover the brief-case they would not simply hand it back to him as if it were a lost necklace. They would keep it for themselves. All that would happen is that any secrets contained within it would be transferred from one agency to another. He would have achieved precisely nothing. Somehow or other, he would have to do better than that.

Far away in the distance, out beyond the furthest houses in the village, the bus had swung into view, bumping and swaying through the woods along the small uneven road. Antonin stood up and waited beside the bus stop, fearful that the bus would drive by without stopping. But it slowed and then stopped, and moments later the automatic doors clanked open. He waited patiently while a frail old lady in a black dress alighted from the bus, carrying in her wrinkled hand a heavily laden shopping bag. When she had gone he stepped on board and started to pull out his wallet. But before he had had a chance to pay the driver he swung round sharply and stared after the old lady, who was by now hobbling off slowly towards one of the nearby cottages. And suddenly, with a sense of overwhelming clarity, he knew exactly where he was heading.

* * * * * *

As he stood before the wooden door he realised that he did not even know her name. He raised his hand to knock, but before he could do so the door creaked slowly open.

"I've been expecting you," the old woman said, her small deep-set eyes examining him with probing intensity.

Antonin returned her look.

"I somehow suspected you might be," he mumbled.

Without further words, she stood aside for him to pass. From the tiny sitting room beside the hallway he could see the black cat padding softly towards him, rubbing up sensuously against his legs. He knelt down and started gently stroking the tiny animal's fur.

117

"She told me she liked you last time you came," the woman said. Antonin looked up.

"You can tell her I return the compliment."

His hostess started to hobble slowly towards her kitchen.

"No need," she said without turning round. "She already knows."

Antonin straightened himself up and followed her. He felt comfortable in her presence, reassured by the knowledge that he did not need to explain what was troubling him, confident in the unspoken rapport he had established with this strange old lady on his last visit.

Inside the kitchen her ancient kettle was just coming to the boil on the stove. She lifted it off and poured some water into a teapot.

"I thought you'd like some tea," she said, "and then I will help you mend your clothes."

"Thanks," he replied.

She indicated that he should sit down at a small wooden table near the ancient kitchen range. Then she sat opposite him and eyed him carefully.

"I read a great deal of confusion in you," she said at last. "Confusion, despair, fear, guilt, frustration. These are not good feelings to carry around with you."

Antonin shrugged.

"It's what I feel. I'm pleased you can see it."

"You found the woman you sought and then lost her again. Am I right?"

"Not quite," he said, shaking his head.

For a few moments he hesitated.

"How much can you see?" he asked. "I know you see a lot, but I don't understand your limits. Sometimes you make me think you can see everything."

The old woman cackled silently to herself.

"And that is why you came."

Once more it sounded like a question but it wasn't.

"I came because I sensed you might be able to help me. Perhaps it was a foolish notion, but I couldn't really come up with anything better."

She stood up and collected the teapot and some chipped earthenware mugs, placing them on the table between them.

"The best way to think of my second sight," she said presently, pouring the tea into the mugs, "is to pretend you are walking along in a thick autumnal mist. Sometimes you cannot see two yards ahead, sometimes you can see vague shapes and shrouded patterns looming up before you, while occasionally the banks of mist clear completely and you can see even quite distant objects with extraordinary clarity."

Antonin frowned. He'd been hoping for more.

The old woman's thin lips cracked into a faint smile.

"I do not understand these things you have found any better than you do, if that is what you mean?"

Antonin looked at her sharply.

"What things?"

"The things in the bag, of course. In the black briefcase."

"You can see them?"

"Yes. It is a black briefcase. I see it quite clearly in your mind's eye. It is lying on a bed. And there is someone with you, someone I took to be the woman you were seeking."

Antonin gulped.

"There is a girl. She's reminds me of Katrina. She was with me."

The old woman raised her eyebrows slightly, as if satisfied about something which had previously puzzled her. Then she leant forward slightly in her chair, peering deeply into Antonin's eyes.

"So why have you come?" she asked.

"I thought you'd know."

"I see nothing. I see no clear plans."

Antonin lifted the mug of herbal tea to his lips and sipped the strange brew slowly for a while.

"Do you think it would be possible to tamper with the way people think?" he asked at last.

"You mean by using the things in the briefcase? You think there is a way of controlling people's thoughts?"

He nodded.

"It's a hunch. Nothing more, really."

She inclined her head slightly to one side.

"I have sometimes wondered whether such a thing might be possible – through something such as my own second sight but stronger. When I was a child I even tried to reach out and do so myself." She cackled quietly to herself, as if recalling some distant memories. "All my attempts failed dismally, which was probably no bad thing. Do you not find the idea of such a power frightening?"

"Of course I do. That's why what has happened to me is so dreadful. That's why I came to you."

Without waiting for her to ask, he gave her a full account of exactly what had happened to him since his last visit. She sipped

119

her tea and watched him, making no attempt to interrupt. Only when he had finished did she speak.

"I'm afraid I do not see how I can help," she said flatly.

"So you can't tell me who these people are who came in the night?"

"No. I can see them clearly enough, presumably because they are clear in your mind. But I know no more than that."

Antonin frowned. The old woman was certainly sympathetic to him, reaching out to him and trying to help him, but for all her extraordinary powers of clairvoyance there seemed to be no way in which she could do so. All she could do, it seemed, was read his mind.

And then, quite suddenly, the idea occurred to him. For perhaps the answer to his present dilemma lay precisely there, locked away in his own mind. And if that were indeed true, then the old woman might just possibly be able to provide the vital key he needed to unlock the door.

* * * * * *

He took the ice-cream mechanically from the fresh-faced girl behind the stall and started pacing once more along the broad tree-lined promenade beside the lake. The weather had been gloriously warm since he had begun his vigil early that afternoon, and the high ranges of limestone mountains rising beyond the further shores of the lake were bathed in the soft pink glow of late summer. With a wry smile he mused that at least in his choice of rendezvous he had made a wise decision, for the small town of Gmunden was everybody's dream of a summer holiday centre, a picturesque little resort lying on the fringe of the northern Austrian lake district where the mountain scenery was idyllic, the water sports superlative and the hotels both numerous and of a high standard. It was a perfect place for a late summer break.

He finally reached the end of the promenade and wearily turned back towards the centre of town. There were wooden benches every few yards facing out towards the lake, but despite the fact that he had been pacing up and down for over two hours he still preferred to keep walking. He knew that if he stopped he would become melancholy again, just as he had become melancholy sitting in the railway carriage on the long train journey from Slovakia. If he sat still he would fall back from the manageable world of plans and actions into the dark shadowy world of dreams and nightmares. It was better to keep walking.

He glanced anxiously at his watch, fearful that they would not turn up at all, but then he spotted Vanessa's slightly hunched figure a few hundred yards away, sitting on a bench under the shade of a chestnut tree and gazing out across the lake. And with a sigh of infinite relief, he also saw that she had done what he had asked and somehow persuaded Nathaniel Harrison to accompany her, for he was sitting next to her on the bench, idly throwing the remains of his ice-cream cone towards a small flock of hungry swans which were patrolling the nearer shore of the lake.

They had not seen him yet, but just as he was about to call out he checked himself. He had been so fearful that Nathaniel would refuse to come at all that he had not really rehearsed in his mind how he would begin what was undoubtedly going to be a difficult encounter.

But it was too late now, because Vanessa had looked up and spotted him.

"Antonin!" she called out, rising to her feet and walking briskly in his direction. Nathaniel also rose to his feet, but approached with considerably more hesitation, as if he too did not quite know what to say.

As soon as she reached him she raised her head and pecked him gently on the cheek.

"Are you all right, Antonin?" she whispered. "Ever since you phoned I've been so worried."

He returned her kiss and nodded. Out of one corner of his eye, he could see Nathaniel still hanging back awkwardly, waiting while the two friends greeted one another. Vanessa pulled back from Antonin and glanced cautiously backwards and forwards between the two men.

"Come on, you two sillies," she said with a slightly forced smile. "Come and shake hands nicely now, like grown-ups."

At her words Nathaniel smiled thinly and approached Antonin with an outstretched hand. He was a good-looking man in his late thirties, and although only a few chronological years younger than Antonin he gave the appearance of belonging to a completely different generation, for whereas Antonin willingly projected a stolid image of late middle-aged respectability, Nathaniel had conducted a relentless and generally successful battle against the ravages of the passing years. In his dress and in his manner he looked far more like a postgraduate student than a Senior Fellow.

"Antonin, old chum," he said with the slightly roguish grimace which was so distinctly his own, "it was nice of you to ask me all the way to Austria just to apologise for the huge mess you've landed me in this time."

Antonin winced as he took the outstretched hand.

"Hallo, Nathaniel. Thank you for coming. I wasn't sure you would."

Vanessa glanced at Antonin.

"Nathaniel's only here because I managed to talk the disciplinary committee into deferring its hearing," she announced in a matter of fact tone of voice.

Nathaniel grunted, all trace of humour gone.

"It's all your doing, you know, Antonin. Because you made the complaint official it's beginning to look as if I'm going to have to sacrifice my job on the high altar of self-righteous moral purity."

Again Antonin winced. It had only happened because they'd given him that damned job as Moral Tutor. If they hadn't he'd have minded his own business, however much he'd disapproved of Nathaniel's disgraceful conduct with the college's new female students. But Nathaniel had been causing mayhem in the place, getting the whole academic staff a filthy reputation, making the college the laughing stock of the whole university. He couldn't just carry on looking the other way for ever.

"Is she still going to have the baby?" Antonin enquired at last, uncertain what to say. For Nathaniel had selected for his latest amorous conquest the daughter of a prominent government minister, a buxom eighteen-year-old beauty fresh out from boarding school. But this time he had bitten off more than he could chew, because the girl had not only decided to have his child but had also decided to make an enormous political stew out of it amongst the university's large and vociferous feminist community.

Nathaniel grunted.

"It's every woman's right to have a baby if she wants to. I'm the father and it's not my business to stop her so I certainly don't see why it's any of yours."

Antonin frowned. He hadn't asked Nathaniel all the way to Austria to have a stand-up row with him about the conduct of his intimate relations with the opposite sex.

"Perhaps I made a mistake, Nathaniel," he muttered. "I'm sorry. When I get back I'll do everything I can do to undo the trouble I've caused you."

There was a finality about the apology which stopped Nathaniel dead in his tracks. For the repressed anger in his face swiftly faded, replaced by the alert curiosity of the natural scientist. For Nathaniel

Harrison was no more than an extreme version of most scientists, a confusing mixture between the human being and the logician, the flesh-and-blood participant and the detached observer. And if it was the all-too-human Nathaniel with whom Antonin had so recently locked swords at college, it was now the taut intellect of one of the world's leading experts in neuro-physiology which he needed on his side.

Vanessa sensed the change of mood.

"Shall we walk for a bit, Antonin?" she said. "And then you can tell us exactly why you've asked us half-way across Europe to see you."

It took a long time to tell the story. Mindful of Nathaniel's presence, he was careful to suppress any reference to his somewhat ambiguous feelings towards Nadja, seeing no obvious relevance in it. Vanessa and Nathaniel paced along by his side in silence, and only when he finished did Nathaniel whistle silently to himself.

"Whew," he said non-committally, a look of studied concentration on his face.

Vanessa abruptly stopped walking and sat down on another bench and the two men sat down on either side of her. After a while she looked up at Antonin.

"So how do you think they found you?" she asked.

Antonin shook his head uncertainly.

"I don't know for sure," he muttered. "Somehow or other that man in Zilina must have been put on to me. Then he picked me up at the station with the offer of a room. I imagine he must have bugged me, because they obviously overheard what Nadja told me about the briefcase and then decided to move in." He hesitated for a moment, noticing the sudden anxiety in his companions' faces. "Don't worry," he added, "I've searched through everything I'm wearing and can't find anything suspicious."

"Are you sure?" Nathaniel asked.

Antonin nodded.

"I think it must have been in the suit. Before I went out to see Nadja's mother he offered to press it for me. I suppose he must have planted something then. But the next day, when I went up to the hut with Nadja, I left my suit in the room."

Nathaniel eyed Antonin sharply.

"So how come they let you get there first, knowing full well you might destroy the briefcase as soon as you found it? It seems rather sloppy of them."

Antonin shrugged.

"That thought had occurred to me too. They were nearly too late as it was, because I'd already decided the previous night to destroy everything, and if Nadja hadn't interrupted my thoughts I would most certainly have done so. But I can only suppose they didn't know exactly where the cottage was until we led them to it. And then they probably judged it safer to either ambush us as we carried it back down the hill or move in at night, when they'd catch us by surprise. But their behaviour certainly suggests they were gambling on my curiosity preventing me from destroying it straightaway."

Nathaniel frowned.

"You seem to figure rather centrally in their calculations, don't you, Antonin?"

Antonin nodded slowly.

"I don't have the faintest idea why, I'm afraid. But I suppose I'm going to find out soon enough, aren't I?"

Vanessa looked at him sharply.

"You're not going to Vienna, are you, Antonin?"

Antonin glanced at her horrified expression and laid his hand gently on her arm.

"I don't really think I've got an awful lot of choice, have I? That's why I wanted to see you here first."

Vanessa looked as if she were about to contradict him, but then she fell silent. Eventually it was Nathaniel who spoke.

"And before you go you want me to look at the copy of the documents you pieced together. Am I right?"

From within one of his trouser pockets Antonin silently pulled out the tightly folded sheaf of papers the clairvoyant had helped him to reproduce and handed them over Nathaniel, who looked at them with evident distaste.

"But why me, Antonin?" he asked hesitantly. "You don't even like me."

Antonin smiled.

"Two reasons, Nathaniel. First of all, you might just possibly understand what all that mumbo-jumbo is about. And secondly, I trust you not to misuse the information."

At this, Nathaniel flinched physically.

"But why should you trust me of all people?"

Again Antonin smiled.

"For exactly the same reason you drive me to frustration. I trust you because you value the independence of the individual in all things. And I know you wouldn't want anyone tampering about with your or anybody else's mental processes."

This time it was Nathaniel who smiled.

"You're certainly right about that," he observed wryly, carefully unfolding the papers and removing a pair of reading glasses from his jacket pocket.

"I took the liberty of translating them into English," Antonin added, but Nathaniel was no longer listening. His body was stooped slightly over the papers, his face locked into a fixed expression of intense concentration. Vanessa tugged at Antonin's sleeve and they both rose from the bench and moved away.

"You're really frightened, aren't you, Antonin?" she said when they were out of earshot.

Antonin frowned.

"That's the trouble, isn't it? I don't know whether to be frightened or not. But first of all I find out that my father was driven to mass murder and suicide and then I discover that some quarter of a century later a small army of hired thugs appear to still share his opinion about the importance of whatever it was that they'd stumbled across."

Vanessa nodded slowly.

"But how will simply handing yourself over to them help?" she asked.

Antonin looked at her glumly. After what he had been through in the last few days it was so good to be next to someone who actually cared about him, but it still didn't make him feel any happier about what he was proposing to do.

"I don't know for sure," he replied. "I've recruited you and Nathaniel to my side. Unlike me, you can take any work on this forward without interference. If I don't go to Vienna like they ask, I've got to remain hidden or they'll pick me up anyway. But if I hand myself over voluntarily, I just might be able to find out something significant."

Vanessa frowned.

"For goodness sake, Antonin. What if these people torture you or something? You've no idea what might happen."

Antonin looked miserable. Vanessa knew him well enough to know that he was no hero. And he had more than sufficient powers of imagination to make his own list of all the dreadful things they might do to him without her drawing them to his attention.

"Only once before in my life have I been in a personally dangerous situation, Vanessa," he said slowly. "When I was in Prague in 1968 there was real physical danger all around me. And on that occasion I just ran away and hid while others risked their lives. I've always been ashamed of myself for that. So this time I'm going to do what's right and take my chances."

There was a long silence. Finally it was Vanessa who spoke.

"And what exactly do you want us to do?" she asked.

"I could have gone to the British intelligence community but I didn't. I think you understand why, don't you?"

Vanessa nodded. As a lawyer specialising in international affairs she had on a not insignificant number of occasions tangled with the intelligence community. And Antonin knew that her own opinion of them and all other security services in the world was at least as low as his own.

"I need my own team, Vanessa. People who share my fear of brainwashing in all its forms. People who love the bloody-minded independent streak in human beings that stops us all turning into a bunch of mindless automatons ready to dance to the tune of some power-crazed fanatic. You and I know a fair number of people within the academic community who share our views. And if necessary I want you and Nathaniel to organise them."

Vanessa frowned.

"It sounds like you want us to organise our own secret service," she said.

Antonin's face remained set.

"If you want to call it that. But whatever you do keep it as small as possible and under tight control. And in the meantime, if I can find out anything which might be useful I'll try and find a way of getting it to you."

Vanessa looked out uncertainly across the lake. For a long time she said nothing, but then she once again turned to Antonin.

"I must admit I'm still not sure exactly what we're supposed to be doing," she muttered.

Antonin met her gaze for a few moments.

"Nor am I," he said. "And that is precisely why I wanted you to bring Nathaniel along."

Simultaneously they swung to face him. He was still sitting on the bench, still stooped over the papers. But as Antonin stared at him he could see another emotion lying alongside the intellectual curiosity of the scientist. For this time, unmistakably, Nathanial's face was full of fear.

* * * * * *

The gentle strains of 'The Blue Danube' washed gently across the broad expanse of the hotel lounge from the direction of a small chamber orchestra in the far corner. They had been playing for several hours now, whilst several elderly couples cruised unpretentiously around the small dance-floor in the middle of the lounge, relishing the softly muted opulence of one of Vienna's finest hotels. But Antonin himself was not dancing. He was sitting in one of the richly upholstered armchairs with which the lounge was generously dotted, anxiously examining every new person who entered the room.

He had booked into the Hotel Imperial the previous night, using his own name and half expecting to be given a message to go immediately to some other rendezvous. But the reception staff seemed to have no idea he was expected and had simply shown him to a well-appointed room on the first floor. He had eaten dinner alone that night and then returned early to his room, all the time expecting someone to appear and give him further instructions. But no one had appeared, and Antonin had then spent a fitful night tossing and turning in bed, trying unsuccessfully to sleep.

Immediately after breakfast he had come to the lounge and taken up his vantage point in the armchair. Periodically ordering another coffee to help him stay alert, he had managed to remain vigilant for several hours. But lunch-time had come and gone and now he could sense that the exhaustion resulting from his lack of sleep the previous night was finally beginning to overwhelm him. The combination of the warmth, the soft comfort of the armchair and the soothing music was irresistible. Despite himself, his eyelids slowly closed.

"Dr Ziegler."

He awoke with an abrupt shudder to find one of the elderly couples he had previously seen on the dance-floor standing over him. It was the man who had spoken, a thin bespectacled gentleman trimly dressed in a casual beige suit. His dancing partner, a plump lady with her hair tied up in a bun, stood by his side. The man's smile was disarmingly friendly.

Antonin pulled himself up out of the chair.

"Yes," he said.

The elderly man stepped forward and extended his hand.

"Allow me to introduce myself," he said in German. "My name is Schmidt. Hans Schmidt. And this is my wife Marie."

Antonin stared at the couple in silence for a few moments. He shook the proffered hand, deciding it best to play their game. But the woman made no attempt to shake his hand and on closer examination he noticed that she seemed considerably more nervous than Herr Schmidt, for it was clear that a good part of her attention was directed to the rest of the lounge, as if she were trying to see if anyone was watching.

"May we sit and talk for a while," the man asked politely, indicating the armchairs.

Antonin inclined his head and lowered himself back into the armchair. The elderly couple seated themselves nearby. Within seconds a smartly dressed waiter glided silently towards them.

"Since you have not had any lunch may I invite you to join us in a pastry?" Herr Schmidt enquired. "They really are very good here."

Antonin nodded and the man ordered. When the waiter had disappeared he turned again to Antonin with a friendly smile.

"Thank you for coming," he said in his disconcertingly mild-mannered tone.

Antonin examined him carefully for a few moments.

"I judged it for the best," he replied cautiously. "I am concerned about the welfare of my grandfather and the Slovak girl."

The man frowned.

"I know nothing of these things, I'm afraid," he murmured, suddenly tensing up, and Antonin sensed he was telling the truth.

"What do you want me to do?" he asked.

The man relaxed visibly again.

"You must understand that you have come to Vienna as our guest," he said. "My wife and I are merely messengers, sent to explain the practical arrangements for your visit."

"I don't suppose you might like to indicate who my host might be?" Antonin asked. At this the plump woman flinched slightly and looked anxiously at her husband.

"We can't tell you that," she said rather brusquely, as if she were beginning to tire of the excessively courteous manner which her husband had chosen to adopt.

Again Antonin inclined his head to one side by way of acknowledgement.

"What my wife means to say," the man continued hurriedly, "is that everything will be explained to you later on. You have come to us of your own free will and thereby saved us a great deal of trouble. For that we are naturally grateful. In return we are keen to ensure that you are treated well while you are our guest, subject of course to the necessary security arrangements."

"And what precisely does that mean?" Antonin asked with a frown.

Herr Schmidt leant forward slightly in his chair.

"I must now ask you, Dr Ziegler, whether you have come alone?"

Antonin nodded.

"Completely alone."

"I am pleased. But you for your part will understand that we cannot take any chances in this matter. We will therefore have to ensure that you are – how shall I put it – 'clean' – before we can make arrangements for your onward transfer."

"What do you mean 'clean'? As I say, I didn't bring anyone with me."

The elderly man looked, or pretended to look, slightly embarrassed.

"The point is this. We must make sure that you are not carrying any devices which might make it possible for your movements to be traced."

"And how exactly do you propose to do that?"

"It is a relatively simple matter. After we have eaten our pastries we will all go up to your room. There we will gather up your things and I will give you the money to settle the hotel account. After you have paid the bill we will go outside where a car is waiting. We will drive for a little way and then you will be asked to change into some new clothes which we have brought with us. Soon after that we will leave all your things behind for safe keeping in the first car and transfer to a different car. And then, I am afraid, it will be necessary for you to continue with the little nap which you had just begun when we so rudely interrupted you. When you awake you will be safely at our destination."

Antonin frowned. There was a smooth professionalism about the fellow which he found even more alarming than the violent rage with which Nadja's assailant had behaved at the cottage. Despite his best efforts to the contrary, he could feel a thin ripple of fear running down his spine. For he sensed that once he had passed through the elaborate air-lock which his hosts had evidently prepared for him, the chances of his ever being released again were slim in the extreme.

He rose ponderously to his feet.

"Oh well then," he said slowly, completely forgetting about the pastry, "shall we be off?"

* * * * * *

A small candle flickered on a desk somewhere in the far distance. And working at the desk Antonin could clearly make out the slightly hunched figure of Nathaniel Harrison, his head bent low, peering with a look of dark and intense concentration at the papers laid out before him. The desk appeared to be floating in a sea of darkness, unconnected with any of the usual trappings of home or office, but despite this Nathaniel suddenly seemed to look up and stare directly towards him, as if reaching out across an enormous abyss. His lips parted and he appeared to speak, but although Antonin strained hard he could not make out the words. After several attempts Nathaniel seemed to realise his words could not be heard and once more turned his head back towards the papers before him. And gradually the disembodied desk began to fade away, until finally he could see it no more.

His eyes opened slowly and Antonin gradually became aware of another desk, but this time there was no one sitting at it. And this desk was surrounded by a room, although it was a room he had never seen before. Through a window the sunlight was streaming in, bathing the opposite wall with the soft pale light of evening. He raised his head to get a better look and found to his surprise that he felt quite well.

He cast his eye warily around the room. It was spacious and airy, furnished with heavy oak furniture. Besides the desk and the bed in which he presently lay there were several armchairs, a wardrobe, a chest of drawers and a dressing table. Through an open door near the window, he could see an adjoining en-suite bathroom.

He rose cautiously to his feet, aware for the first time that he was dressed in an unfamiliar pair of pyjamas, and walked uncertainly over to the broad picture window through which the low evening sun was streaming into the room. Leaning cautiously against the window-sill lest he be attacked by some sudden bout of giddiness, he screwed up his eyes against the sun's rays and squinted out. The room was on the first floor, commanding an extensive view of the surrounding countryside. Immediately below the window was a broad gravel path, then a neatly tended flowerbed and a trim wooden fence, and beyond that a flat eternity of vineyards stretching away as far as the eye could see.

Antonin lifted the catch and opened the window, leaning out as far as he could. The building itself was two storeys high and of a rather stark modern design. The whole effect would have been rather harsh had it not been for the window-boxes filled to over-flowing with brightly-coloured cascades of pink geraniums.

He glanced around to see if there were any clues as to the usual purpose of the building, but all he could see was a small security camera perched high up on the wall, a security camera which was at this very moment pointing directly at him.

His thoughts were interrupted by a polite knock on the door and he quickly closed the window.

"Come in!" he called in German, turning to face the door.

The door swung open and the elderly Herr Schmidt entered, his smile as friendly as ever.

"Good evening, Dr Ziegler," he said. "I hope you are fully recovered from your journey."

Antonin nodded but said nothing.

His host walked over to the wardrobe and flung the door wide open.

"In here and in the chest over there you should find all the clothes that you require," he announced. "The bathroom you will also find well-equipped, but should you discover anything lacking or if you feel you would like some refreshment, you can reach room service using the telephone on the desk."

"Room service?" Antonin repeated, raising one eyebrow slightly.

Herr Schmidt took no notice. He was already at the door.

"I will leave you now to get dressed," he said. "When you are ready to see Herr Biedermeyer just pick up the phone and let us know."

"Herr Biedermeyer?"

"Yes," Herr Schmidt replied. "Herr Biedermeyer is the man in charge here. I am sure he will be able to answer all your many questions."

Antonin quietly let the man go. He spent a few moments examining the clothes they had left for him, finally selecting a sober grey suit and tie. And as soon as he was dressed he went straight over to the telephone and lifted the handpiece.

"Yes, Dr Ziegler," came the softly-spoken voice of a young woman. "How may I help you?"

"I'm ready to see Herr Biedermeyer now."

There was a pause for a few moments, as if the woman were seeking confirmation from someone else.

"Certainly, Dr Ziegler. Herr Biedermeyer will be with you right away."

Antonin sat down at the desk and waited. A few moments later there came another knock at the door, but this time it seemed an altogether louder and more decisive knock than the obsequious Herr Schmidt's.

"Come in!" he called again, and this time the door swung open to reveal a tall rather elderly figure with the upright bearing of a military man.

He entered the room and carefully closed the door without speaking. Then he turned to examine Antonin.

"I am Franz Biedermeyer," he said frostily in German, and Antonin immediately recognised the distinctive Prussian lilt of a Berliner. His tone was not rude, but there was a disconcerting coldness about him, a complete lack of emotional contact.

"I understand you're in charge here and that you will be able to answer my questions," Antonin said in as businesslike a tone of voice as he could manage.

Biedermeyer smiled, although there was no humour in his smile.

"Indeed," he said. "And I for my part hope that you will be able to answer some of mine."

The newcomer had made no attempt to sit down and so Antonin now stood up, although he was still several inches below the height of his adversary. Suddenly, for the first time since he had handed himself over to these people, he found himself wishing he had followed Vanessa's advice and stayed in hiding.

"My grandfather and the girl," he said. "Are they both all right?"

Biedermeyer frowned.

"We took the liberty of leading your grandfather to believe you had employed our services to get him away from the jurisdiction of the Czechoslovakian authorities," he explained. "He is presently quite comfortable and expecting you to collect him from us as soon as you have successfully arranged asylum for him in England. The girl is also quite comfortable now, although I regret to say that our contact in Zelina over-reached himself a little when he apprehended her."

Antonin flinched inwardly.

"May I see them?" he asked.

Biedermeyer smiled thinly.

"In due course," he said. "But first I would like to ask you some questions."

Antonin drew a deep breath. This was where he was going to have to start playing a difficult hand with extreme care.

"I'll do my best to answer them," he said.

"You have displayed considerable interest in the activities of the Oblanov Technical Research Institute," Biedermeyer began. "I wonder if you could explain why?"

"I knew my father worked at Oblanov. When I came back to Slovakia to try and trace my parents I found out about the unusual circumstances of their deaths and naturally started asking some questions. That's how I found out about the girl and through her about the briefcase."

"Precisely how much did you know about Oblanov when you were in Czechoslovakia in 1968, Dr Ziegler?"

Antonin breathed an inward sigh of relief. From their behaviour he had guessed they thought he knew more than he was letting on, and Biedermeyer had not wasted any time in getting to the point. It was his only trump in a very weak hand.

"Nothing other than that my father worked there. He was always reticent in talking about his work because it was so highly classified."

"So he told you nothing?"

"Nothing at all."

Antonin watched Biedermeyer's face carefully to see how he reacted. But he didn't flinch.

"Let us turn to the subject of the briefcase then," Biedermeyer continued.

"You probably know more about it than I do. I did cast my eye over the material before your men arrived but I'm afraid I didn't understand a word of it."

"Yet despite our man in Zilina's inexcusable delay you made no attempt to destroy the briefcase and its contents," Biedermeyer observed dryly.

"No."

"Why not?"

Antonin hesitated.

"Why do you suppose I should have wished to destroy them?" he asked. "I was curious to know just what had made my father kill himself and all those other people. The contents of that briefcase were my best chance of finding out."

"So you were intending to show the papers to other people before making any decisions?" Biedermeyer continued relentlessly.

"I wasn't sure. I hadn't made up my mind yet."

Antonin hesitated. Biedermeyer was so poker-faced he gave no indication of whether he was taking the bait. He pulled out a gold cigarette-case from his pocket and offered one to Antonin. When he refused he lit one himself and returned the case to his pocket. It was only after he had drawn a few deep breaths that he again permitted his cold eyes to lock onto Antonin's.

"You will understand, Dr Ziegler, that we have already spoken to the girl. I am afraid her account of what transpired in the cottage that night differs in various significant respects from your own."

Antonin flinched

"In what respects?" he asked.

Biedermeyer smiled.

"Oh come now, Dr Ziegler. Surely the important thing is that she does not corroborate your account."

Antonin said nothing for a few moments. Then he rose and walked over to the window, carefully positioning himself so that the sun's rays were falling full onto Biedermeyer's face, forcing him to squint whenever he looked towards him.

"What exactly do you think they were doing at Oblanov?" Antonin asked.

This time it was Biedermeyer who flinched.

"We believe they had stumbled across a scientific discovery of major importance and then for reasons of their own tried to conceal it," he said.

"And what do you propose to do with the briefcase now you have it?"

"It is now our duty to find out the precise nature of the discovery they had made so that it may be successfully developed in the service of humanity."

"I find 'humanity' such a vague concept, don't you?" Antonin observed dryly.

Biedermeyer fell silent for a while.

"In the circumstances," he said at last, "perhaps it would be wise for me to introduce myself properly. You should understand that I am co-ordinating this investigation under the auspices of the Federal German Government. And I should add that we are working on this matter with the full knowledge and support of both our American and British colleagues."

He delivered the line in such an authoritative tone of voice that Antonin could not help but wince. He had supposed himself to be up against a freelance group, but now Biedermeyer was claiming to represent the intelligence community of a respectable European government. It was a shocking notion which had not previously occurred to him.

"We have recently reopened our file on Oblanov," Biedermeyer continued. "As you know, the East German secret police archives have only just become available to our scrutiny. Back in 1968, the authorities in East Berlin had been greatly puzzled by what had happened at Oblanov, very suspicious of the rather lame explanation offered by the Czechoslovak secret service in which they blamed the deaths on Western Intelligence. Since we of course knew for certain that we were not responsible we decided to follow up the odd circumstances of the case. Our subsequent enquiries led us on much the same trail as you yourself have followed, leading directly to that bartender in Melnik."

Antonin frowned.

"And it was he who told you of my interest?"

Biedermeyer nodded.

"The poor man is trying very hard to rehabilitate himself in the new political environment, I think. He wishes to ingratiate himself with us so that we will provide him with some employment more commensurate with his undoubted technical skills."

"If you're from Western Intelligence," Antonin said, "why this subterfuge? You're supposed to be on my side, aren't you?"

Biedermeyer smiled.

"Exactly, Dr Ziegler. And that is precisely the point of our present conversation. That is why we are now hoping you will grant us your full co-operation. We are clearly both aware that whatever discoveries were made at Oblanov may potentially be of great scientific significance. They may also be dangerous ideas if they fall into the wrong hands. So we can hardly publish this whole matter in the newspapers for all to see."

Antonin squirmed inwardly. If indeed this man did represent a western intelligence agency, and he wasn't yet certain that he did, then it was going to be hard to explain why he didn't regard them as any more trustworthy than the communists who had developed the idea in the first place.

"Just how much do you know about what they were doing?" Antonin asked.

Biedermeyer hesitated for a moment, as if unsure of whether to reply.

"Our technical staff have examined the documents you found carefully," he said eventually. "We now believe that in the course of their work the Oblanov team stumbled across a way of using carefully coded sonic impulses to produce an interference pattern in the electrical impulses which orchestrate the various parts of the brain. Their original objective with this work was merely to confuse and disrupt, but instead they found a way of creating a subconscious state in which the individual would be susceptible to introduced ideas, a kind of long distance hypnosis if you like. It would certainly have been a most powerful tool in the hands of a frightened and insecure communist regime."

"Or indeed anyone," Antonin murmured softly.

Biedermeyer inclined his head as if to acknowledge the validity of his observation.

"I said right at the beginning that we fully accept how dangerous this scientific development might be," he said. "And that is precisely why we had to move so ruthlessly to intercept it once it appeared to be re-emerging. To return to your previous question about our cloak and dagger methods, that is precisely why we acted so quickly to contain both the briefcase and the two people who were aware of its existence."

Antonin could feel Biedermeyer's cold logic slowly beginning to undermine his resolve. He had never stopped to think that others would react in the same way as he had, that by impounding the briefcase and apprehending him and Nadja they too were trying to stop a dangerous idea from spreading rather than themselves spreading it. Wearily, he walked away from the window and sat down in an armchair.

"With you we simply had no choice," Biedermeyer continued, as if reading his mind. "You were a wild card, uncontrolled and therefore dangerous. We had to find you before you went and handed the briefcase and its contents over to some amateur Oxford academic research club."

"So why haven't you destroyed the contents of the briefcase?" Antonin asked weakly. "I nearly did, so why haven't you?"

Biedermeyer came over and sat down beside him. He seemed more relaxed now, as if he felt confident he was making headway against Antonin's resistance.

"The intelligence community is aware of many things which are dangerous. It is our job to control them so that they are not at some future date used against us. But to do so requires knowledge, not ignorance. The important thing is therefore to understand this technique properly and ensure it does not ever fall into the wrong hands."

"It would appear my father didn't share your view," Antonin commented.

"And I for one am very relieved he acted as he did," Biedermeyer continued. "If he had not suppressed the idea the communists may well have successfully developed it. And if that had happened the course of subsequent history might have been very different."

136

"So what exactly are you intending to do?" Antonin asked. "What will you do with this thing when you have explored it?"

Again Biedermeyer hesitated before replying.

"Neither you nor I are scientists, Dr Ziegler," he said at last, "but we are both astute enough to recognise that science is a fickle friend. I think we both understand that it must at least be entertained as a theoretical possibility that this Oblanov technique is as potent a force in its own way as the Atom Bomb. It has awesome dangers associated with it. Your father's solution was to try and bury it, but as our experience with the science of nuclear reactions illustrates his approach overlooked two very important possibilities. For one thing, the scientific development of nuclear technology has brought in its wake many perfectly safe civilian benefits. All these would have been lost if the idea had been suppressed. But even if that were not the case and nuclear technology was destined to unleash nothing but destruction, then it would still have been foolhardy for scientists in the free world to deliberately try and suppress the invention. In the 1930s and 1940s the scientific world was on the brink of inventing the Bomb. If the Americans had not got there first then Hitler or the Japanese or perhaps the Russians would have done so, with potentially unspeakable consequences. You cannot indefinitely push the scientific genie back into the bottle as your father tried to do."

Antonin remembered Nathaniel's astonishment at the mind-blowing mental jumps the researchers had made at Oblanov.

"My father seems to have managed to do just that for nearly a quarter of a century," he muttered.

Biedermeyer smiled.

"A heroic achievement, and as I have already said one for which I am truly grateful. But do you not see that it is that very fact which means we are living on borrowed time. Since 1968 science has made huge leaps forward. We have had the information technology revolution, we have seen genetic engineering emerging as a potent force in human affairs. It seems reasonable to suppose that a revolution in the world of the human mind itself is long overdue. And if this phenomenon exists in nature and had already been discovered as long ago as 1968, then it can only be a matter of time before it is independently discovered again. And when it is, it is vital that we have already learnt to neutralise and control its power. Your father's heroic sacrifice has bought us the time we need, but now it is the job of our generation to try and tame the beast."

Antonin could feel his world beginning to spin. He had come to these people with a clear purpose in mind, meaning to trick them into believing he knew more than he really did in order to persuade them to reveal their hand to him. Yet now he had to admit that everything Biedermeyer had just said made perfect sense. For if his words were to be believed then they were attempting to do no more than he himself had asked Nathaniel to do. They too were trying to take the idea and develop it with the express purpose of neutralising and controlling whatever dangers it might inherently possess. And as he looked at Biedermeyer the thought crossed his mind that it might after all make sense to join forces.

"I must think about what you have said, Herr Biedermeyer," he said. "But first I must satisfy myself that you represent who you say you represent. You will forgive me, but other than your word for it I have no proof."

"What you ask for is perfectly reasonable," Biedermeyer said, his lips parting in a thin smile. "I did not for one minute expect you to believe the word of a complete stranger. But fortunately there is someone in this building right now who might be able to persuade you that we are sincere in our intentions. Someone you will perhaps find yourself able to trust."

Antonin stared at him uncertainly, unsure exactly of whom he might be speaking.

Biedermeyer rose to his feet and moved silently towards the door.

"If you will be so kind as to come with me, I will lead you to my referee."

Without a further word, Biedermeyer led him out of the room and along a deserted corridor. At the end of the corridor some stairs led down to a small hallway adjoining the front door of the building. There were several internal doors leading off the hallway. When he reached the bottom of the stairs Biedermeyer stopped and indicated one of these doors.

"If you wait in there he will come to you," he said quietly, and then he silently turned and climbed the stairs again.

Antonin watched him until he had disappeared from view along the top corridor. The hallway was deserted, no sound at all disturbing the evening peace. He walked uncertainly to the door Biedermeyer had indicated and pushed it gently open.

There was no one in the room. It was a large study, its walls covered from floor to ceiling with bookshelves. To one side of the room was a mahogany desk, somewhat incongruously sporting a sleek white computer terminal, while the other side of the room was filled with several low sofas surrounding an ornate wooden coffee table. Antonin quietly pulled the door closed and glanced quickly along the bookshelves. In the main they seemed to be technical reference books of a broadly scientific nature, bound back issues of academic journals and the like. Some were in German, but he noticed that many were also in English.

He walked quickly over to the desk. Apart from the computer terminal the top of the desk was completely empty, so he sat down and pulled open one of the drawers. Amidst the general clutter of pencils and pens and rulers, there were several sheets of paper. He pulled one of them out and glanced at it. It was written in German, and seemed to be an internal office memorandum relating to the routine expenses involved in the maintenance of the building. He pulled out another sheet: This time it was an invoice submitted by a firm of landscape gardeners for the upkeep of the gardens. The bill was addressed to the Natural Science Study Centre, Pamhagen, Burgenland and came from another address in the same town. Noticing a small atlas of Austria lying in the same drawer, Antonin swiftly pulled it out and began to search through the index. He had already guessed from the view out of his bedroom window that he might be somewhere on the flat plains which lie between Vienna and the Hungarian border, but now he knew the name of the town he would probably be able to pinpoint his exact location.

But he had just found Pamhagen in the index when all thoughts of finding where he was suddenly vanished from his mind. He froze, listening intently to a faint sound which was gradually becoming louder and louder. It was a soft tapping, the sound of a stick falling on the ground at regular intervals. And suddenly, with a strange strangling sense of almost overpowering emotion, he knew exactly who Biedermeyer was sending to meet him.

The tapping of the stick stopped and the door slowly swung open. A tall man in middle age stood silently at the door, the taut handsome lines of his intelligent face strangely enhanced by the slightly hunched posture of the rest of his slender body. Antonin rose incredulously to his feet.

"Stepan!" he mouthed, hardly able to say the word.

His younger brother moved towards him, leaning heavily on his stick as he walked. He had not really changed much in twenty years. The same reserved charm emanated from his whole being, the charm which had so effectively entranced the young women of East Berlin society in days long past, days when they had lived together

in a cramped student hostel in the years prior to Antonin's departure for Prague.

"It's good to see you, Antonin," Stepan said softly.

Antonin walked over to him and they embraced.

For several moments they held each other, but then Stepan
stepped back and smiled.

"How strange that we should meet like this," he said. "I always
imagined that when I was free to find you it would be at your
college in Oxford, stooping over an ancient desk in a book-lined
library. You would have your back to me and you would not notice
I had come. And I would walk up to you and watch you at work
for a while before I would finally tap you on the shoulder and tell
you I was there."

Antonin could feel the tears forming in his eyes. He turned away
and walked over to one of the bookcases, strangely embarrassed
lest his brother notice the strength of his own emotions. Only when
he had regained his self-control did he turn again to Stepan.

"At least there are books in here," he said weakly.

Stepan walked over to one of the sofas beside the coffee table
and eased himself gingerly into it, carefully placing his walking stick
beside him.

"You must excuse me," he said apologetically. "Of late my back
has been troubling me a little, particularly if I stand still for too
long."

"Is it bad then?" Antonin enquired. "You can still walk, I see."

He wasn't sure, but Stepan seemed to flinch at his words, as if he
found all memory of his childhood incapacity painful. Antonin
quickly changed the subject.

"I thought you were with the communists," he said flatly.

Stepan smiled.

"So did they," he said quietly.

Antonin stared at him in utter amazement. For over twenty years
he had supposed he could not contact his brother because he was
an East German apparatchik. Yet now it suddenly seemed there
was a very different explanation.

Stepan rearranged his body carefully on the sofa. Despite sitting
down, it was clear that his back was troubling him more than he
was letting on.

"I started working for the West Germans even before you left
Berlin," he said, as if in answer to Antonin's unspoken question. "I
gave them small pieces of information about the university when
I was there. After that I was instructed to go into what is known as

140

a 'deep sleep'. For nearly twenty years I really was what you supposed me to be. I modelled myself on Dad, the ideal East German official, and gradually ingratiated myself up the hierarchy. When I was finally activated a few years before the Wall came down, I had crawled a pretty long way up. But in the few years I was doing active work for the Federal Republic, I like to think I made some small but valuable contribution to our cause."

Antonin stared at his little brother and gulped. In East Berlin their differing views about communism had always stood as a silent barrier between them, yet now it seemed the barrier had never been real.

Again Stepan read his thoughts.

"I would have told you if I could, Antonin," he said with a sigh. "But what good would that have done? I knew all along we worshipped the same God, but you were destined for a contemplative life while I preferred a life of action. You were never cut out for the dangers of the world of spying so I judged it better you didn't know."

Antonin flinched. Stepan hadn't meant to hurt him, but hurt him he had.

"You could have trusted me, Stepan. Your secret would have been safe with me."

Stepan lowered his head.

"I know that," he murmured. "But I thought you might go crazy in Berlin. I thought the frustration you felt for the system might have overflowed into a futile gesture of contempt. And if that had happened they would have picked you up and dragged it out of you somehow. The Stasi had ways of making even the most loyal of people talk. As it was you nearly wrecked everything by suddenly disappearing to England like that after the Czech uprising."

Antonin shrank down into the chair. Again he felt as he had felt with Jiri when they had met a few weeks before in Bratislava. He felt pathetic, a runaway who had hidden for two decades in the tranquil safety of an Oxford college while others were risking their all in the real world.

For a long while neither of them spoke. But then Stepan looked up at him.

"You must think me an unfeeling bastard, Antonin," he said softly.

Antonin looked at his brother in surprise, and suddenly noticed that beneath the rather suave exterior there lurked a deep sense of emotional vulnerability.

"Why, Stepan? Why do you think that?"

"Because I could perhaps have stopped all this happening. If only I'd been more perceptive, if only I'd realised what Dad was planning, then I could perhaps have helped him find a way out without all that frenzied killing. I had the right contacts, I could have helped him."

Antonin frowned.

"I don't think you should feel guilty about that, Stepan. Frankly, I don't think Dad wanted to be helped by the West Germans any more than he wanted to be helped by the Russians. He didn't want anyone to know about Oblanov."

Stepan met Antonin's gaze. It was if he were unburdening himself of a deep sense of guilt which he had carried with him for a long time.

"I know that. But that's not really the reason why I feel bad. I feel bad because of my feelings at that time. I didn't even try to help him because I was so determined to succeed in my own chosen career as a master spy. After you disappeared I was in a mess. I was questioned for weeks by the East German authorities about my relationship with you. And then just when I thought I'd finally satisfied them that I wasn't tainted by your counter-revolutionary revisionism all these dreadful things started happening in Slovakia. First my parents died under mysterious circumstances, then a few months later my grandfather went mad and started threatening innocent people with an axe. And since there was nothing I could do to stop it I just cut and ran."

Antonin suddenly remembered his grandfather. Stepan had never once contacted him, never even tried to help.

"Have you seen him, Stepan?" he asked. "Have you seen Grandpa since he arrived here?"

Stepan shook his head.

"No," he said. "I thought it would just confuse him to see me after all this time. And anyway, he never really liked me, did he?"

Antonin wondered whether he'd hold his tongue, but then decided he'd better say it now, because otherwise he'd always wonder why.

"You could have helped him, couldn't you, Stepan? For twenty years he was all alone. Twenty wasted years."

Despite his attempt to speak the words without undue censure, Stepan looked away.

"What could I do in the circumstances, Antonin? I knew he was all alone, of course. And I knew you couldn't help him. I could have fetched him to Berlin, I suppose. But he didn't even speak German. He would have hated it and he would have hated me in the role I had chosen to adopt."

"But you could have visited him. You could have told him about me."

Stepan's eyes lifted wearily to meet his brother's.

"I could have done that, I suppose," he said. "But I don't think you really appreciate just how paranoid the upper reaches of East German officialdom could be. Grandpa was a marked and labelled counter-revolutionary and I was a rising star in the Socialist Unity Party who had only just shaken off the stigma of a brother who'd fled to the West. As a loyal Party member I was expected to submit every detail of my personal life to the inspection of the Party. So I followed the stipulated procedure and consulted my superiors about the whole situation."

"And they told you not to see him."

Stepan nodded.

"They told me that for my own good I should leave well alone, so that is what I did. At the time, I justified it to myself by arguing that it's what the old man would really have wanted me to do if only he'd known the truth about what I was doing."

Looking at Stepan's crestfallen expression Antonin could suddenly see the sad and lonely face of the little boy he had for so long wheeled around the ruins of post-war Berlin. He felt consumed by a strange mixture of pity and pride, pity for the years of self-denial that Stepan had inflicted on himself in order to restore freedom to his country mingled with pride in the nobility of his brother's sacrifice. And now, he knew, it was right that his grandfather should be given the opportunity before he died to give Stepan his blessing.

Antonin rose to his feet.

"I think we should go and see him together, Stepan. This very minute. Now at least we can wipe the slate clean."

Stepan looked at him, and Antonin could see the fear in his eyes. For a moment it looked as though he might refuse. But then he picked up his stick and slowly rose to his feet.

"You should know that as a child I was always frightened of Grandpa," he said softly. "But since you think it for the best we will go and see him straightaway."

* * * * * *

Antonin knocked gently on the bedroom door before entering.

There was no answer, so with a reassuring glance at Stepan, who was waiting nervously just down the corridor, he slipped quietly into the room.

His grandfather was sitting up in bed reading a book, a pair of wire-rimmed spectacles perched delicately on the end of his nose, and he did not at first notice that Antonin had entered the room. His ancient but intelligent eyes were studying the book intently, filling his wrinkled face with a look of taut and eager concentration which made him look far younger than his nine decades.

"Is it good?" Antonin asked gently, approaching the bed.

At his words his grandfather looked up and his eyes lit up with obvious relief.

"Ah, my boy, you've arrived at last."

He laid the book down on the covers. Antonin picked it up and examined the title. It was a newly published history of pre-war Czechoslovakia.

The old man watched him examining the book.

"You've no idea how refreshing it is to read an honest account of the times of my youth," he said. "Your friend Jiri gave it to me before I left."

Antonin put the book down and sat on the edge of the bed.

"How are you?" he asked.

"Haven't felt better for years," his grandfather replied, and the alertness of his face confirmed that he spoke the truth. "They're a clever bunch, these friends of yours. They just drove me straight over the border without any fuss or bother."

"Do you know where we are, then?"

His grandfather nodded.

"Of course I do. Pamhagen. It's near the Neusiedler Lake in eastern Austria. I sometimes came to this area on swimming holidays with my parents when I was young. Mind you, it's all changed a bit since those days."

"Pamhagen?" Antonin repeated, remembering again the landscape gardening bill he'd seen in the office.

"It's the last village before the Hungarian frontier," his grandfather continued. "That's probably why these spy friends of yours kept this place. I suppose they used it as a monitoring station or something."

Antonin examined him thoughtfully for a few moments, uncertain exactly how much his captors had told the old man.

"I must say, Antonin, you're remarkably well connected. I really wasn't expecting to be spirited out of Czechoslovakia by West German secret agents."

Antonin looked away. He hated lying to his grandfather, but it really did seem better not to burden him with the truth.

"I know a few of these people. They said they'd help me out."

For a few moments the conversation lapsed.

"There's someone else here you know," Antonin said at last, "someone you haven't seen for a long time. He's waiting outside."

His grandfather looked puzzled.

"Me? Someone who knows me?" he said.

Antonin nodded.

"It's Stepan, Grandpa. He's been working for the Federal Republic's secret service all along. He was active in East Berlin, pretending to be working for the communists, but really he was working for our side. That's why he couldn't come to see you."

As he spoke the prepared words, Antonin looked at the old man's face with growing concern. He had been expecting to see surprise, annoyance perhaps at his other grandson's neglect during the long years of his incarceration in the old people's home. But once he had overcome these initial reactions he had supposed that his grandfather would be relieved to find that his second grandson was not the time-serving communist they had both hitherto supposed him to be. Yet now a dark cloud seemed to pass over his face as he absorbed the news of Stepan's presence, wholly replacing the good humour he had displayed when Antonin had first entered the room.

"Stepan?" he mumbled, his face suddenly confused. "What's Stepan doing here?"

"He just wants to see you, Grandpa. He wants to make amends."

"Why?" the old man growled.

Antonin suddenly wondered if Stepan might not have been right. His grandfather was a very old man and had recently been put through an enormous amount of strain. Perhaps bringing Stepan into the picture as well had been a mistake.

"Stepan just wants to say sorry to you for neglecting you all those years when I was in England. He wants you to understand why he didn't come."

His grandfather shrugged contemptuously.

"I don't wish to see Stepan," he said with an air of gruff finality.

Antonin was shocked by the intensity of his grandfather's feelings. He had always known that there was no love lost between the two, but this suggested a far more deep-seated resentment than he had ever supposed existed.

"But don't you see how much he was risking for the cause we both believed in, Grandpa? He was taking enormous personal risks. Doesn't that put him in a slightly different light?"

For several minutes the old man said nothing. But then he looked up intently at Antonin.

"You never understood your brother," he snorted. "Stepan works for no one but himself. Quite frankly, I've always been ashamed he is of my flesh."

Antonin stood up, examining his grandfather with a slightly annoyed expression. He knew perfectly well that Stepan was waiting just outside the door, that he would be able hear every last word the old man spoke. He glanced hesitantly in the direction of the corridor, uncertain quite what to do. But then, his mind made up, he moved towards the door. Perhaps, if Stepan would only come in and apologise for his lack of care in person, his grandfather would finally agree to make his peace. He pushed his head outside and looked down the corridor towards the place where he had left his brother waiting.

But Stepan was no longer to be seen.

He turned back to face his grandfather again, trying hard to conceal the growing anxiety he now felt.

"I won't be long," he said with as reassuring a smile as he could muster, and then without waiting for an answer he turned and left the room. Moments later he was back down the stairs and once more in the office where he had first met Stepan. His younger brother was sitting at the desk with his head slumped low and a thoroughly miserable expression on his face. He made no attempt to look up when Antonin entered the room.

"Sorry," Antonin murmured apologetically, sitting down heavily in one of the armchairs. "That was my fault. I really didn't think he'd react like that."

Stepan shrugged.

"Don't blame yourself, Antonin. He's very old. He didn't much like me when I was a kid and since then he's had twenty lonely years in which to confirm his poor opinion." He looked up at Antonin and tried to force a smile. "Why don't we just forget it?"

Antonin decided to do just that. His grandfather's mind was obviously set and there was nothing he could do to change it.

"So what's your connection with Biedermeyer?" he asked, changing the subject.

Stepan grunted.

"Biedermeyer's a senior officer in the service. He's got a reputation for getting results, although his methods can be rather unorthodox."

"And what exactly is your role?" Antonin asked.

"I don't know I've got much of a role any more," he muttered, clearly misunderstanding the thrust of Antonin's question. "I was being nurtured all those years for a particular purpose, but now that the East German state has collapsed I'm rather out on a limb. They just give me odd jobs to do."

"And is this just an 'odd job'?"

Stepan shook his head.

"I was questioned about Oblanov long before you became involved, Antonin. I'm as intimately involved as you are, aren't I?"

A small carafe of water and several glasses were standing on the low table in front of Antonin. He picked up the carafe and poured himself a glass of water. Only when he had taken a sip did he turn again to Stepan.

"Why exactly am I here, Stepan? Did they tell you that?"

Stepan didn't say anything for quite a long time. Then he looked wearily at his brother.

"Biedermeyer's convinced you know far more than you're letting on. He thinks you found out something important from Dad before he died and that you came back to Slovakia to pick up the thread."

Antonin stared at him in open astonishment.

"But Dad killed everyone who knew. If he'd told me anything he'd have damned well killed me too, wouldn't he?"

Stepan hesitated. When he spoke it was in a whisper.

"But you weren't there to kill, were you, Antonin? You were in England."

Antonin shivered. There was something that didn't make sense about what Stepan was saying. He understood the words but not the meaning.

"But surely you told him that's rubbish, Stepan. Surely you told Biedermeyer that Dad didn't speak a word to his children about what was on his mind."

He was expecting no more than that Stepan would confirm he had told Biedermeyer exactly that. But instead Stepan picked up his stick and rose silently to his feet. Walking painfully around the desk, he came and sat down again on the sofa beside Antonin.

"You haven't worked out what really happened, have you, Antonin? You really don't know?"

Once again Antonin could feel the ground shifting beneath him. It was always the same. As soon as he thought he had begun to grasp what was going on something would happen which made him start from scratch again.

"Dad told me everything," Stepan murmured.

At first Antonin wasn't sure he'd heard properly. But as he looked into his brother's weary eyes he knew he had.

"About Oblanov?"

Stepan nodded.

"But why?"

"Because he was frightened. Because he didn't know what to do."

Antonin could feel a tightening in his throat. It was just about plausible he would have confided in Stepan. Stepan had always been much closer to his parents than he had been. Yet now the logical implications of his brother's admission were crystal clear.

"Just how much did he tell you?" Antonin asked desperately.

Stepan saw his meaning and nodded.

"Enough, Antonin. He told me enough. He showed me things. One evening he even contrived to take me to the Institute. I think he wanted to prove how serious it all was."

The question lay between them on the sofa, unasked and unanswered.

"And you told your West German control?" Antonin asked.

Again Stepan nodded.

"I thought Dad might have decided he wanted out. When I judged the moment right, I was planning to tell him it was an option I could help him with."

"But before you could persuade him he made up his own mind?"

Stepan nodded. Still the question lay unasked and still it lay unanswered.

"And Biedermeyer knows all this?"

"Of course. As I said, the West Germans knew of the existence of Oblanov a long time ago because I told them about it. Then after Dad went on the rampage the trail went completely cold and the whole thing was put on hold. It was only when the East German state collapsed that Biedermeyer was appointed to go through the files and try to discover what exactly had been going on there. He was told to leave no stone unturned."

"Starting with you?"

Stepan shrugged.

"They knew everything I had to say about Oblanov a long time ago. Dad had showed me a lot of technical stuff but I didn't understand it and I didn't write anything down. My control in Berlin had just equipped me to go in and start taking the photographs they needed when Dad and Markov started killing everyone. So you see I wasn't really much use to Biedermeyer."

"But then I turned up and found the briefcase."

Again Stepan shrugged.

"That was just a lucky break, although from what I gather one that has already yielded useful scientific insights."

In his mind Antonin suddenly remembered the night when they had come to Nadja's dacha in the hills. And he remembered the man's anger because he had found only the briefcase and not him. At the time he had wondered why. Now it all made sense.

"Exactly, Antonin. Now I think you see. Biedermeyer's a thorough man. As soon as he was appointed he decided he wanted to question you about Oblanov and sent a team over to Oxford to talk to you. He reckoned that since Dad confided in me it was quite likely he'd also confided in you. You might even have taken something away with you, an English version of the Slovakian briefcase perhaps. But when Biedermeyer discovered you'd already left Oxford and were poking around in Czechoslovakia asking all sorts of leading questions his original hunch that you might know something gradually grew into a conviction."

Stepan was breathing more easily now. Perhaps he was hoping the unanswered question would quietly go away. Antonin looked at him with a heavy heart and wondered whether to let it go, to bury it firmly in some dark recess of his mind as he had tried to bury so much before in his life. But he knew that if he didn't ask the not knowing would haunt him for evermore. He took a deep breath.

"You killed him, didn't you Stepan? You killed Dad."

There was a long silence which seemed to stretch out towards infinity. Then Stepan slowly nodded his head.

"I'd gone to Slovakia that weekend to persuade him to show me the papers again. I'd brought a special camera with me and was going to photograph them so I could pass them on to the West. I was also planning to try and persuade him to flee, although I never really thought I stood much chance of that."

Antonin could feel a sense of almost infinite pity towards his brother. It was a cruel jest indeed that life had played on him.

"It was about six o'clock on the Sunday morning. I'd arrived from East Berlin late the previous evening and Dad was already out. I was anxious and couldn't sleep. But then I became aware of Mother's footsteps: She was pacing about the house, obviously unable to sleep herself, and so I got up and went to talk to her.

"We went and sat together in the study. If she knew about exactly what was going on at Oblanov she didn't say, but she knew that Dad had become increasingly frightened. She knew he was in some kind of deep trouble, although she didn't know what it was. And now he was still away from home in the early hours of the morning, which was highly uncharacteristic of him. She was beginning to worry that something had happened.

"Soon after we started talking we heard the click of the front door and shortly afterwards Dad entered the study. His face was white with fear and anxiety, and we could immediately see something terrible had happened. He looked shocked to see us talking together.

"When it happened it happened very fast. He asked Mum to fetch him a drink from the wooden cabinet on the far side of the room and as soon as her back was turned he pulled a small revolver out of his pocket and shot her. Then he swung it on me and pulled the trigger again. But the second shot must have misfired, because he angrily hit the gun and aimed again, but before he could pull the trigger I'd grabbed him. There was a brief struggle and the gun fired once more. Then he fell limp in my arms."

Stepan fell silent.

Antonin laid his hand on his brother's shoulder and tried to say something, but no words came out. Eventually it was Stepan who spoke.

"I'm sorry Antonin. I wasn't trying to kill him. I must have forced the gun round in the struggle and then he must have fired it by accident at himself."

Antonin watched his brother's face and it was once again just as it had been when they were children. Once again Antonin could feel an overwhelming desire to hold and comfort his little brother, as he had so often held and comforted him in his wheelchair as a child. And he would have done just that if Stepan had not suddenly reached for his stick and risen to his feet.

Antonin suddenly remembered his grandfather.

"Is that why Grandpa won't speak to you?" he asked.

Stepan had returned to the desk and sat down again. He shrugged uncertainly.

"Maybe he suspects. Dad was expecting me to arrive on Saturday night, which is probably why he decided to close everything down that weekend. He might have told Grandpa I was coming, although I hadn't seen him since arriving late the previous evening. And then when it happened I was very frightened. In my bedroom I had a bag full of sophisticated West German espionage equipment and I knew it wouldn't be many minutes before the militia arrived and sealed off the house. So I hurried back to my room before Grandpa appeared, gathered up my things and left over the back fence. Within the hour I was on a train out."

"So Grandpa might not have known you were there?"

Stepan frowned.

"I don't know, although if I'm perfectly honest it was one of the reasons I never came back to see him. But when I heard him talking about me with such venom just now I wondered if perhaps he'd worked it out."

Antonin suddenly remembered his own situation. Stepan's revelations had changed everything.

"But I didn't know anything about Oblanov when I went to England, Stepan. Dad never told me a damned thing."

For a moment Stepan looked at him suspiciously and Antonin sensed inwardly that his brother didn't believe him. But then he pulled himself together.

"I've always told them you didn't know anything, Antonin. I told them that in 1968 and they swallowed it. That's presumably why they didn't interview you then. But Biedermeyer was suspicious about you from the outset, and then when you started prowling round in Czechoslovakia hunting for information about Oblanov you gave him the proof he needed."

Antonin flinched.

"Proof? What proof?"

Stepan frowned.

"Oh, come on, Antonin. Our people in Zilina botched the pick-up. They left you nearly all night in that cottage with the girl and the briefcase. But you made no attempt to destroy it. It's hardly any wonder that Biedermeyer thinks you were making as purposeful a search as he was for something that would complete a picture, something you could use to develop the idea."

"But Biedermeyer's got the briefcase," Antonin blurted out. "What more does he think I've got?"

Stepan looked at Antonin wearily, as if he were humouring him in his denial of any knowledge.

"He's not certain how much you knew originally about Oblanov, although he suspects you may have some papers hidden away in England relating to it. But since he's got hold of the briefcase he's been absolutely convinced he had to track you down."

Antonin shuddered.

"But why? Why would he want me even more as a result of finding the briefcase?"

Again Stepan sighed.

"Don't you see? He knows you've got the tape, Antonin. He knows you've got the encoded tape which was on the machine when you found it in the briefcase. That tape would quite probably unlock this whole project and Biedermeyer knows you've got it."

Antonin started laughing at the sheer absurdity of the accusation.

"But I haven't got any tape, Stepan. The machine was empty when Nadja found it years ago. What makes him think I've got any damned tape?"

Stepan looked at him anxiously, as if he were trying to protect him from himself.

"Don't mess with Biedermeyer, Antonin. He's a determined man who's used to dealing in a rougher world than you are. He's paid to get results and he knows you took the tape."

"But I didn't take any bloody tape," Antonin said, becoming increasingly exasperated. "I don't understand what makes him think I did."

Stepan was looking at him intently.

"He knows you took it because she told us you did," Stepan said.

"Who?" Antonin asked weakly, scarcely believing his ears.

Stepan sighed heavily.

"Why the girl of course. Markov's daughter. It was she who told us you took the tape."

* * * * * *

It was clear that Biedermeyer's patience was finally beginning to run out. He strode over to the window of Antonin's bedroom, a room which was increasingly beginning to feel like a prison cell, and glowered out at the broad plain beyond. Antonin sat in the armchair on the far side of the room and eyed him cautiously, knowing full well that it was a dangerous ploy on which he had embarked. The chances of success were remote, for Stepan had been right about Biedermeyer being a tough operator. His cold grey eyes gave little away about either his thoughts or his reactions.

Biedermeyer suddenly swung to face him.

"I'm beginning to get rather fed up with you, Dr Ziegler," he said. "To be perfectly frank I'm still not absolutely sure who's side you're on."

Antonin tried to glower back, as if he were confronting a fellow historian in an academic dispute.

"And I'm having exactly the same problem with you, Herr Biedermeyer. I have told you I will collect the tape from where I have hidden it and bring it to you of my own free will in order that you may use it for your scientific research. In exchange I have asked you to release Miss Markov and my grandfather immediately from your custody since neither of them can possibly be of any further use to you. I'm afraid your refusal to do so strikes me as little short of blackmail."

Biedermeyer said nothing. He clearly wanted to threaten Antonin openly, but so far he hadn't done so. Yet the thin veneer of civilised discussion was visibly wearing thin.

"The girl and your grandfather are perfectly comfortable with us. When we have collected the tape we will arrange forthwith for your grandfather's transfer to England and the girl's transfer to anywhere she wishes to go. Since it can only take you a short while to collect the tape I cannot see anything wrong with that arrangement."

Antonin wrinkled up his face contemptuously.

"If you like you may call it a matter of principle, Herr Biedermeyer. The impression created is that they are being held as some kind of hostages to ensure my good behaviour. I point blank refuse to co-operate with you under such circumstances."

Biedermeyer had started pacing up and down the room. That he was finding Antonin's principled ethical stand somewhat difficult to counter was clear, but whether he would agree to his terms was quite another matter.

Antonin suddenly rose to his feet. The present stand-off between them had already continued for quite some time. It occurred to him it might be better to try another tack.

"I would like to discuss the situation with Miss Markov," he announced suddenly. "Then I will review my position."

Biedermeyer suddenly stopped pacing up and down and examined him anxiously for a few moments.

"Why?" he asked.

Antonin puffed himself up as much as he could manage.

"Because I feel personally responsible for involving her in this unseemly business. She was brought here against her wishes. I am naturally concerned for her welfare."

Biedermeyer looked away.

"I'm afraid it is not that straightforward," he muttered under his breath.

"Why not?" Antonin asked.

Biedermeyer shuffled uncomfortably.

"The agent who arranged to have her picked up in Slovakia was not personally known to me, Dr Ziegler. As I explained to you before he overreacted a little when she refused to co-operate with him."

Antonin flinched.

"What do you mean he 'overreacted'?" he asked angrily.

"I understand that there was already some personal animosity between them," Biedermeyer muttered, still looking away.

Antonin remembered the way the man had brutally knocked her unconscious when she had called out. There was no telling what he had subsequently done.

"Are you trying to tell me you've beaten her up?" he shouted angrily at Biedermeyer. "Are you trying to tell me that you've been torturing her?"

Despite the anger welling up within him he could tell that he had succeeded in wrongfooting Biedermeyer.

"You damn well let me see her now or you can forget your wretched tape," Antonin shouted.

Biedermeyer looked at him anxiously. Then he inclined his head.

"Very well," he said. "I will think about it."

He bowed slightly and left the room, pulling the door closed behind him. Antonin went over to the bed and lay down wearily on the bedcovers, trying to decide how long he could hold out against Biedermeyer's determined resistance. He was playing a very weak hand and in the circumstances it was perhaps foolish to raise the stakes so high.

Following his encounter with Stepan, there was now very little doubt in Antonin's mind that his captors did indeed represent who they said they represented. The intelligence services of the Western Powers, having so recently emerged triumphantly from the Cold War, were only doing their job thoroughly by attempting to tie up the loose ends in their old adversary's filing cabinet. And in trying to develop and control the invention Nadja's father and the other scientists had stumbled across at Oblanov all those years before they were only trying to protect society from other less scrupulous groups of people. Indeed, he had to admit that he had found Biedermeyer's argument about the inevitability of the discovery being made by other people at some future date a pretty persuasive one. If indeed he had actually been in possession of any useful information he may even have decided to throw in his lot with them of his own free will.

But the problem he now faced was precisely that he didn't have any useful information to contribute. His father had told him precisely nothing of significance, the contents of the briefcase were already known to his captors and of course he didn't have any tape. So, in short, he could be of no use to them whatsoever.

And that, Antonin knew, lay at the heart of his present dilemma. For Stepan had clearly hinted that the truth was not likely to go down well with the poker-faced Herr Biedermeyer. If he continued to deny possession of the tape Biedermeyer would in all probability not believe him and continue to keep him under lock and key. And even if he could eventually persuade him that he knew nothing, he was pretty sure that his captor would not simply agree to his release, certainly not until he had fully completed his investigation.

The only alternative, the only way of securing his freedom long enough to tell Vanessa and Nathaniel what he had found out, was to confess to Biedermeyer that he did indeed have the tape. Then at least he would have a trump on his side, albeit a fictional trump. And all would be sweetness and light with the fish-eyed Herr Biedermeyer until the moment he realised he'd been double-crossed.

Antonin lay on the bed for a long time, but then his thoughts were interrupted by a sudden commotion from the direction of the corridor outside. The building was normally shrouded in a profound silence which made the sounds of agitated shouts and running feet in the corridor all the more surprising. Biedermeyer's veiled warning about Nadja's condition had already alarmed him, and Antonin now rose anxiously to his feet and for the first time since his arrival tried to open the door. But it was locked.

He pressed his ear to the thick wooden door, trying to make sense of the commotion outside. A woman's voice was calling out in German, yelling at someone to fetch a doctor. Someone ran past his door and down the stairs, and then shortly afterwards he became aware of the sound of a heated conversation between two men taking place some way away down the corridor. But try as he might, he could not make out what was being said.

Suddenly the conversation stopped and there were footsteps in the direction of his room. The footsteps stopped and there was a sound of a key being pushed into the lock. Antonin stepped quickly backwards.

The door swung open and Stepan stood outside, his face ashen. Biedermeyer stood slightly behind him, his expression revealing an uncharacteristically flustered anxiety.

"You'd better come," Stepan said quickly, and then led Antonin down the corridor towards his grandfather's room.

155

Inside were several people – a woman in a white nurse's uniform, several besuited young men who looked like security guards and a doctor who was stooped low over the bed. Just as they entered the doctor straightened up, and something about his manner told Antonin that he had arrived too late.

The doctor saw Antonin's anxious face and sadly shook his head.

"A massive heart attack," he said apologetically, his gaze shifting uneasily between Antonin, Stepan and Biedermeyer. "There was really nothing I could do."

And with that he nodded at the nurse and the security guards and they all filed solemnly out of the door. Biedermeyer hesitated for a few moments and then followed them.

But Antonin took no notice of all this movement. He walked forward and sat down beside the inert figure lying in the bed, and suddenly he felt engulfed by a great emptiness. There was no emotion – no anger, no regret, not even any sadness – just an enormous gap which was no longer filled.

Stepan had silently approached and was now standing beside him. Antonin turned to face him, and gradually he became aware that tears were flowing freely down his younger brother's face.

"This is my doing," Stepan murmured.

Antonin looked at him uncertainly.

Stepan frowned.

"I decided you were right, Antonin. So I came to see him, to tell him the truth about what happened."

Antonin swallowed hard. For Antonin knew that he had encouraged his younger brother to do just that.

"I thought about what you said and decided I owed him an apology for the way I'd behaved towards him after Mum and Dad's death . . ."

His voice trailed away. Antonin took one last look at his grandfather's body and rose to his feet, steering his brother away from the corpse and over to the window.

"You don't have to blame yourself, Stepan," he said. "You weren't to know this would happen."

Stepan laughed bitterly.

"Well if I didn't know I should have known. He was so old. I should never have allowed myself to come."

His brother pulled out a large white handkerchief from his pocket and wiped his eyes. Then he turned again to stare miserably at his grandfather's body.

"I came to see him because Biedermeyer's agreed to your terms," he said abruptly. "I knew if I didn't say something soon he would have left and the chance would be gone."

Antonin looked up at him sharply.

"He agreed?"

Stepan nodded.

"Biedermeyer and you don't operate on the same wavelength," he explained. "He was suspicious that you were trying to pull some kind of stunt. I told him you were straight."

Antonin could feel a sense of almost infinite relief seeping through him as Stepan spoke. For the inner emptiness he had felt was gradually being replaced by a sense of almost unbearable claustrophobia. He badly wanted to break free of Biedermeyer and Oblanov and all the sordid paraphernalia of this closed world of intrigue, manipulation and death. After all, if anyone was going to have the damned invention it might as well be the government of a responsible democratic state. He would take Nadja and hide somewhere until the whole thing had died down, and then re-emerge and resume his contemplative life as an Oxford academic. He for one had had his fill of his brother's sordid world.

"Can I see her now?" he asked.

"She was never here," Stepan replied. "Since you said you'd left the tape in England she'll be taken straight to your college. Biedermeyer and a few of our men will accompany you so that you can hand the tape to them on your arrival. And then our business with you will be complete."

Antonin frowned.

"Why don't you come, Stepan? I'd rather you came instead of him?"

Stepan shrugged.

"I'm afraid I'm just the office boy. This is so important that Biedermeyer wants to supervise the handover personally. And I have other duties in Berlin to return to."

Antonin looked sadly at his brother. It sounded like goodbye.

"Can we at least visit each other now, Stepan? Can we at least have that?"

Stepan hesitated.

"It's not easy," he muttered unhappily. "Until the situation in East Berlin is fully stabilised I'm still involved in a fairly complex double game. It might be better to wait a few more months."

Antonin nodded silently. Then suddenly he leant forward and embraced his brother.

"You must know I'll be always be there when you need me, Stepan," he whispered.

And as he spoke the words he was sure he could feel his brother's thin frame shudder beneath his touch.

* * * * * *

"Dr Ziegler, what a pleasure! We were expecting you back."

Antonin cast a wary eye in the direction of the portly chief steward who had come out from his cubby-hole beside the college entrance to greet him.

"Oh yes, Scudder. And how is that?"

Scudder glanced at the three odd-looking gentlemen accompanying his favourite member of the academic staff and leant conspiratorially in Antonin's direction.

"Well, it was the girl who told me," he whispered discreetly. "She said she had met you whilst you were overseas and that she had arranged to meet you here. I put her up in Room 73, one of the postgraduate rooms down in the lower quad."

Antonin nodded, glancing apprehensively round at Biedermeyer and his two heavies. But they were standing some way off and appeared not to have heard.

"Quite so, Scudder, but a little discretion if you please," he whispered softly, winking at the by now somewhat confused chief steward.

"And you say you've had fine weather these last few days," he said in a louder voice.

Scudder, who was not a stupid man, seemed to have recovered from the shock of the college's amiable but rather prudish Moral Tutor returning from his continental holiday with a petite young girlfriend in tow.

"Very good weather, sir. A little on the warm side perhaps, but we really haven't been able to complain."

Antonin suddenly turned to Biedermeyer and beckoned him over.

"Mr Biedermeyer," he said in English. "Allow me to introduce Mr Scudder, our chief steward. Mr Scudder will arrange for you to find a good hotel in town. I will phone you as soon as I have some news."

Biedermeyer stepped forward anxiously.

"Dr Ziegler," he said quietly but forcefully, "this is not what we agreed. We agreed that we would accompany you immediately to collect the tape."

Antonin scowled at him.

"We agreed I would first speak with Miss Markov," he said. "Only then did I say I would collect the item you are looking for."

"But the girl's already here," Biedermeyer exclaimed. "I was assured by our people that she was dropped off two days ago with instructions to wait for you here."

Antonin turned to Scudder.

"You don't know anything about a girl asking after me, do you Scudder?" he asked.

Scudder shook his head with great solemnity.

"A girl, Dr Ziegler? No. As far as I am aware no one has enquired after you recently. But I will certainly ask the other staff."

Antonin turned to Biedermeyer with a scornful expression.

"Sorry, but it looks a bit like this might be another botch-up, doesn't it? However, I'm sure she'll turn up soon enough, and as soon as she does you may be sure I'll get in touch."

And with that he picked up his bags and strode off in the direction of his rooms without glancing back.

He arrived at his flat unmolested, quickly unlocked the door and stepped inside. His captors, for that is how he thought of them, had thoughtfully retrieved his things from Slovakia, and he now threw them down in the corner of his small hallway and headed gratefully for his compact little kitchen. Putting on the kettle, he bustled around preparing to make himself a cup of tea.

Antonin had felt much more in control of events since he had left the rather up-market prison he had briefly occupied in eastern Austria. And now he smiled to himself smugly at the rather neat way in which he had wrong-footed Biedermeyer and his chums by the college entrance. Unable to restrain his curiosity until the kettle had boiled, he strode across his living room and peered cautiously out into the street. Sure enough, one of Biedermeyer's two 'colleagues' was waiting on the corner in the sweltering summer heat, rather awkwardly clutching a copy of 'The Times' and looking as if he was settling in for a long wait. If Antonin's guess was right, Biedermeyer and the other fellow would have declined Scudder's hotel-finding service and would by now be pacing anxiously around the perimeter of the college trying to cover all the other possible entrances. Within a few hours they would no doubt have summoned up reinforcements, either from German Intelligence or indeed from their British counterparts.

The kettle started to whistle and Antonin returned to the kitchen and poured the water into the teapot. Then he went back to his living room and picked up the phone. As he had hoped, it was Scudder who answered. He was on the point of asking him to bring the girl up to his room when it suddenly occurred to him that the line might not be secure. It was a rather sobering thought, for he realised with a shock that if the Germans were really working with the co-operation of British Intelligence then they might possibly have the whole college staked out already, both inside and out.

He felt hungry after his long journey. Pulling a small tin of chocolate biscuits out from a cupboard, he started to munch his way through them while he sat down by his little kitchen table and started to think through exactly how he was going to proceed.

But he didn't think for long. Not even waiting for his tea, he slipped into the bedroom and changed his clothes, pushing some more clothes into a small travelling bag. Then, after confirming once more that the minder outside had not moved from his position on the street corner, he walked out of his flat, down the stairs and off across the quadrangle to the room where Scudder had said Nadja would be waiting.

The postgraduate flats were in a relatively new block at the back end of the college and were slightly more spacious than the rather pokey undergraduate quarters. Antonin climbed the stairs to the first floor and knocked politely.

"Who?" Nadja called in English with an accent so heavy it was scarcely comprehensible.

"Scudder, miss," Antonin replied in Scudder's broad West Country accent.

The lock clicked and the door swung open. Nadja was standing there, her drawn expression showing all to visibly the mistreatment she had received at the hands of her captors. For although there was no obvious external sign of injury, her previously alert and slightly playful eyes looked frightened and drawn.

Antonin stepped briskly into the room and raised his finger to his lips. Silently putting the bag down on the bed, he pulled out some casual clothes, indicating to her with his hands that she should take everything off and put them on instead.

She looked at him uncertainly and then started to undress. Uneasily, Antonin turned to face the wall.

A few moments later she lightly touched his shoulder and he turned to face her again. She looked absurd in Antonin's oversized clothes, but neither of them felt in the mood to laugh.

Antonin poked his head out of the door to check there was no one there. But since it was the middle of the summer holidays most of the students were away and the block was largely deserted. He beckoned her to follow and led the way down the corridor until he found an empty room. Only when they were both safely inside and he had shut the door did he turn to her with an apologetic expression.

"I'm sorry," he said in Slovak, "but I thought they may have wired you up."

She didn't reply. Instead she flung her arms around him and clung on tightly, her body racked by silent sobs.

He held her close to him until the deluge had passed. Only then did he move his head away so that he could look into her face.

"You're all right now, Nadja," he said, wishing to a confidence he certainly did not possess. "I'll make sure you'll be all right now."

His words had started her crying all over again, and as he held her he sensed that whatever they had done to her would leave some permanent scars behind. When she had once again stopped crying he stepped back and looked at her sadly.

"What happened?" he asked.

She said nothing.

"Did he rape you?"

She said nothing but nodded.

Suddenly Antonin remembered Biedermeyer's eyes as he had tried to apologise for his man's 'overreaction'. At the time he had guessed what he had meant and now she had done no more than confirm his suspicions.

"Was it just him? Just the man who came to the dacha?" he asked.

She nodded again.

"We haven't got much time, Nadja. I know it's not easy for you, but you've got to tell me what happened since then."

She sat down miserably on the unmade bed in the corner of the room and looked at him with bloodshot eyes.

"I always knew he was a snake," she said. "He did no more than confirm it."

Antonin sat down beside her and gently held her hand.

"What happened?" he asked.

"He'd tried molesting me before, when I was at school and he was a youth leader. But that time I managed to avoid him."

Antonin frowned. He was puzzled that her captor had raped her. It seemed like oddly uncontrolled behaviour for a man who had presumably been employed by the West German intelligence services as some kind of double-agent under the communist regime.

161

"So what exactly happened?" Antonin asked again.

Nadja stood up and walked over to the wash-basin, turning on the cold tap and throwing some cold water over her face. She looked around for a towel but there were none, so Antonin handed her his handkerchief.

"He knew you'd been up at the dacha with me, Antonin. He thought you were hiding and that I knew where you were. So he hit me about a bit when I refused to tell him. But later that night he came back drunk to the room where I was being held. That was the first time."

Antonin winced.

" 'First'?" he repeated.

She nodded.

"It happened several times. First that night and then several times over the next few days. Only later did he stop, after a German called Biedermeyer turned up and spoke to me.

"Biedermeyer?"

"Yes. A tall man. I don't speak much German so Bohumil had to act as interpreter. But I think Biedermeyer must have told him to lay off, because after that he became much more cautious in his behaviour towards me."

"And all this happened in Zilina?" Antonin asked.

Nadja shook her head.

"Oh no, not in Zilina. They moved me out of there straightaway. I was blindfolded but I think they took me to Vienna."

Antonin looked at her sharply.

"Why do you think it was Vienna?" he asked.

"I'm not sure. It was some kind of tenement building. I was in a room quite high up but I couldn't see anything out of the window except a scruffy courtyard with a lot of bins in it. But my room led off another bigger room and if I pressed my ear up against the door I could hear when people were talking. Once I heard Bohumil say to one of the Slovakian guards who'd come with us that he was meeting someone in a cafe near the Praterstern. That's the name of the big open-air fairground in Vienna, isn't it?"

Antonin nodded.

"So Bohumil came with you to Vienna?"

She nodded.

"Bohumil and several of the other Slovaks stayed with me throughout, but I was interviewed several times by Biedermeyer and once by another man."

Antonin looked at her.

"Who?"

"I don't know. He was middle-aged. He carried a stick and walked with a limp."

Antonin couldn't help but flinch.

"The man with the stick? Did he say anything?"

Nadja flashed an intelligent glance at Antonin, and as she did so her expression once again reminded him powerfully of Katrina.

"You know him?" she asked.

Antonin looked away, trying to summon up the strength to lie to her. But Nadja was not going to have it.

"Come on, Antonin. I've been through living hell. If you know what's going on then I've every right to know."

Antonin sighed.

"He's my brother," he said at last.

She looked at him with a nonplussed expression.

"What? The man with the stick? Your brother?"

Antonin bowed his head.

"Yes. My younger brother. I haven't met him for years, not since 1968. I always thought he was an East German official. Now it turns out he's been working for West German Intelligence all this time."

Antonin began to tell her everything that had happened since they had parted. She listened silently, making no move to interrupt, and only when he had finished his account did she speak.

"And you believed what your brother said about who these people were?"

The words came as a shock. He looked at her as she stood before him by the sink, and as she spoke he suddenly realised that she had only said what any right thinking person would have said in the circumstances.

"I . . .er . . .yes," he mumbled.

Nadja looked at him uncertainly.

"Your brother mixes with some pretty unpleasant people," she commented dryly.

Antonin looked at her.

"Did my brother say anything to you?"

She shook her head.

"Not much. Biedermeyer did most the talking. I just told him what I thought he seemed to want to hear. I was terrified that if I didn't he'd let that filthy animal loose on me again."

Antonin frowned.

"So is that why you told them I had the tape?"

She nodded.

"How was I to know you'd gone and handed yourself over to them, Antonin? I thought you'd have more bloody sense."

Antonin stood up and started nervously pacing up and down the room. Nadja hadn't really told him anything surprising, nothing that would make him change his plans.

"Nadja," he said. "We've got to disappear for a bit. Do you understand?"

She forced a smile and looked down at the oversized men's clothes Antonin had told her to put on.

"If you're saying you want me to keep a low profile," she said, "then I think you'll have to come up with something better for me to wear."

Antonin peered out of the window at the deserted quad below.

"That's the least of our problems," he said. "First of all we've got to work out how we're going to get ourselves out of here."

And then, just as he was trying to come up with a realistic plan, a slim figure in a jogging outfit swung into view through an archway on the far side of the quad. It was Danny, his Glaswegian history student. Antonin had always liked and trusted Danny, and now he suddenly realised that the time had come to put the trust to the test. As Danny jogged round the quad towards him, Antonin opened the window and leant out.

"Danny!" he called out as softly as he thought he could get away with.

Danny stopped jogging and looked up, surprised to see his history tutor's head protruding from one of the postgraduate rooms.

"Dr Ziegler!" he replied with a smile. "I didn't know you were back."

"Could you come up for a few moments, please, Danny?"

Danny disappeared beneath him and a few moments later reappeared outside the room. He looked more than a little surprised to find Antonin holed up in an unoccupied bedroom with a young girl dressed in oversized men's clothes.

"Come in, Danny," Antonin said. "I want you to meet Nadja, a friend of mine from Czechoslovakia. I'm afraid she doesn't speak much English."

Danny extended his hand.

"A pleasure to meet you," he remarked in passably good Czech.

Antonin stared at him in amazement as Nadja returned the greeting.

"I didn't know you spoke Czech, Danny."

Danny blushed.

"Didn't you?" he replied in English. "Picked it up during my gap year after visiting Prague – I suppose you might say learning languages is a hobby of mine. But I'm afraid I don't speak it very well."

Danny's manners were always immaculate, and now he stood politely before them, waiting for Antonin to explain why he had been summoned.

"Why aren't you off for the vac, Danny?" Antonin enquired, still uncertain quite what to say.

"I wanted to spend some extra time in the library, catching up on a few things I didn't get time for last term," he replied, although Antonin could tell that wasn't the whole story.

The awkward silence descended again.

Danny looked at Nadja, who was still standing there looking ridiculous in Antonin's clothes.

"I'm in a little spot of trouble, Danny. Well, quite serious trouble really. And if I may I'd like to ask you for your help."

Danny quietly pushed the door closed behind him.

"What kind of trouble?" he asked.

Antonin shuffled uncomfortably. He knew he was asking Danny to become involved in something dangerous, potentially something very dangerous. But he didn't really feel he had any choice.

"I don't really want to explain all the ins and outs to you, but something cropped up while I was in Czechoslovakia. Nadja and I have washed up here but the outside of the college is being watched by some rather unpleasant people who don't want us to leave without them. Now we need some help to get out and disappear for a bit."

Danny glanced backwards and forwards between them for a few moments, his intelligent young brain silently assessing the situation on the basis of the hopelessly inadequate information with which it had been provided.

"Exciting," he commented.

Antonin shook his head.

"Not exciting, Danny. Dangerous. I'm very much afraid I've got myself involved in something that's far too big for me and now I'm completely out of my depth. What I'm asking you to do may not be entirely safe."

Danny smiled, and Antonin recognised immediately the impetuous smile of youth. It was precisely the same smile that his fellow students in Prague had so often smiled during that heady long summer of freedom in 1968.

"Oh well," Danny said, "I guess it'll make a change from the Risorgimento. Are they watching all the gates, do you suppose?"

Antonin nodded.

"They sound like spies," Danny said with a faint grin, until the sight of Antonin's stony expression made him check himself.

"Oh dear," he said, correcting himself, "they are spies, aren't they, Dr Ziegler?"

"Yes, Danny, they are. And they're probably very good at their job. But if you don't mind I really don't want to go into the full circumstances just now."

Danny frowned.

"If you get out, where are you going to go?" he asked.

Antonin shrugged.

"I don't know. A hotel, I suppose, or perhaps a rented house somewhere."

Danny thought for a bit.

"Annie's parents' weekend cottage in the Cotswolds is free all summer while they're in the States. She has the key. If you don't mind me telling her then perhaps you could both stay there."

"Is Annie your girlfriend?"

"Yes. She lives in Oxford."

Antonin frowned. This business of telling more and more people was dangerous. It would only take one inadvertent remark by one person in the chain to give the whole game away.

"Do you trust her?"

Danny smiled wryly.

"I'm going to marry her next summer, so I suppose I must do," he said.

Antonin turned to Nadja and quickly explained to her in Slovak what was going on. She nodded her assent and he turned back to Danny.

"OK, you can tell her. And you can also tell her we'd very much like to stay in the cottage for while."

Danny nodded slowly and then walked over to the window overlooking the quad.

"And if you give me a few minutes," he said thoughtfully, "then I think I may just have thought of a way of getting you both out of this place."

* * * * * *

The grandmother clock in his living room struck the half hour and Antonin glanced anxiously at his watch. He had already been sorting out his things for too long, trying to remember everything he would need for what might be a fairly long absence from college. In ten minutes time they were all supposed to be meeting up at Annie's room to begin executing Danny's extraordinary escape plan. And if all went well, all four of them would be safely tucked up at the cottage in the Cotswolds before nightfall. And then, for the first time in quite a long while, he would perhaps be able to take stock of the situation and devise some sensible way to proceed.

He finished gathering up his papers and went casually over to the window, fully expecting to see Biedermeyer's hatchet man still standing on the corner clutching his unread copy of 'The Times'. But he was no longer there. He peered up and down the street, trying to work out if he had simply moved to a better vantage point, but there was still no sign of him. Then, with a vaguely uneasy feeling in the pit of his stomach, he returned to his desk and started to sort out his papers.

But he had not sat there long when there was a brief ring at the front door. He stood up and walked out into his small hallway.

"Who is it?" he called out anxiously.

"Scudder," came the reply, and with relief Antonin started to pull back the safety chain.

But no sooner than he had started to open the door than it was pushed violently open and he found himself staring straight into the barrel of a revolver. The man he had previously seen on the street corner was holding it, pushing Antonin back against the wall of the tiny hallway as he shoved his way into the flat. Close on his heels was Biedermeyer, pushing Scudder roughly in front of him with the barrel of another revolver.

"I'm sorry Dr Zie . . ." Scudder began.

"Shut up and go in the other room!" Biedermeyer snapped, closing the door behind him and herding everyone through into Antonin's living room.

Antonin watched Biedermeyer in silent terror. Already in Austria he had sensed he was a brutal man, but then he had been trying hard to control his instincts in order to secure Antonin's co-oper-ation. Now it was abundantly clear that the kid gloves were off.

Biedermeyer turned to Scudder.

"Face the wall!" he barked.

Scudder obeyed. Biedermeyer immediately swung his gun on Antonin and flicked a glance towards his accomplice. An almost imperceptible grin seemed to pass over his face as he walked over to the college steward, and then he raised his gun and brought it down hard on the back of his head. Scudder sank unconscious to the floor.

Biedermeyer looked at Antonin's horrified face with quiet self-satisfaction.

"The poor man is an innocent party to all this, Dr Ziegler. It wasn't very kind of you to involve him in such unpleasantness."

Antonin said nothing. He felt like a trapped animal, unable to speak because he could think of nothing useful to say.

"I treat you with respect and you repay me by treating me like an idiot," Biedermeyer snarled, angrily pushing Antonin back towards the desk with the gun.

"What do you mean?" Antonin began, knowing he just had to say something.

Biedermeyer pushed Antonin's large body roughly back over the desk so that his feet were lifted off the ground. Then he lent down over him and peered into his face.

"Enough of your clever little tricks, Dr Ziegler. We already have the girl."

Antonin stared up at his assailant. Something inside him told him he wasn't bluffing.

"Now you will give me the tape without further delay," Biedermeyer continued.

Antonin gulped.

"I don't have it," he said breathlessly, for Biedermeyer was holding him in such a way that he was finding it pretty hard to breathe.

Biedermeyer laughed a sour hard laugh.

"That's sad," he said. "Sad for you, Dr Ziegler, but sadder still for the girl."

Antonin stared at his frenzied face and for the first time it crossed his mind that Biedermeyer might possibly be mad. There was something wild and deeply disturbing about his eyes. But it wasn't a thought that comforted him greatly.

"It's the truth," he said. "There wasn't ever any tape. She only told you that because she was frightened. If you don't believe me ask her."

Biedermeyer lowered his face until it was only inches away from Antonin's.

"Like I said, if that's true it really is a pity for you both."

Antonin was struggling to think straight. Spy or no spy, surely Biedermeyer wasn't authorised to act in this outrageous fashion.

"If you're from German Intelligence you can't behave like this," Antonin managed to say.

Biedermeyer laughed dryly.

"Can't I?" he sneered. "They employ me for results, Dr Ziegler, not for the niceness of my manners." He turned to his colleague, who was still standing nearby.

"Turn the place over," he barked. "It's just possible he's foolish enough to have hidden it in here somewhere."

The man disappeared into the bedroom and silently started work, pulling out drawers and emptying cupboards.

Biedermeyer turned back to Antonin.

"I won't ask you nicely again, Dr Ziegler. Tell me what you've done with that tape."

Antonin could feel his warm breath on his face. And he could feel the man's anger almost as powerfully. He hesitated for a moment, wondering what to say. As Stepan had already warned him, Biedermeyer was thoroughly convinced he had the tape. Denying it again would almost certainly elicit a violent response.

"It's not here," he muttered.

Biedermeyer seemed to breathe an inward sigh of relief. The pressure on Antonin's chest loosened a little.

"That's better," he said softly. "So where precisely is it then?"

"At the bank," Antonin lied, noticing on the grandmother clock that it was already a quarter to six and that the bank would therefore be closed until the following morning.

Biedermeyer must have followed his eyes.

"The bank," he repeated suspiciously, making no move to call off the search of Antonin's room. "Which bank?"

"National Westminster Bank in the High Street," Antonin mumbled, hoping that Biedermeyer wouldn't ring up some chum in British Intelligence and get the place opened up immediately.

Biedermeyer eyed him cautiously for a long time.

"You'd better not be lying to me again, Dr Ziegler," he said, finally pulling away and allowing Antonin's feet to return to the floor.

"Fritz!" he called, and the other man returned from the bedroom.

"It's at the bank," he said. "We'll have to get him out of here and wait until tomorrow morning. Go and tell the others to get a car ready outside. Then come back."

Fritz jerked his head towards Scudder, still lying inert where he had dropped.

"What about him?" he asked.

Biedermeyer flicked a hesitant glance at Scudder's inert body. Then his eyes veered round to Antonin and a thin smile spread over his face.

"Kill him," he ordered softly, not taking his eyes off Antonin for a second.

Antonin stared at Biedermeyer in horror.

"No," he cried, trying to force himself to think. "You can't kill him. If you do I certainly won't co-operate."

Biedermeyer cold eyes were still fixed on Antonin. And now a sneer spread across his face.

"Kill him!" he repeated.

Fritz was already fixing a silencer to his gun as Biedermeyer pushed his own hard into Antonin's stomach.

"More ethical acrobatics, Dr Ziegler? But this time it won't work, I'm afraid. This time we play the game by my rules. You can think of it as an object lesson in what happens to people who lie to me if you like."

Fritz walked over to Scudder and knelt down beside his head. There was a muffled shot and it was over, leaving nothing but a cold silence in its wake.

Antonin tried to control the feeling of nausea welling up inside him. But he didn't want Biedermeyer to see how frightened he was. At least he wanted to deny him the satisfaction of that.

It was at that moment that he became aware of a faint sound of someone moving in the hallway outside. He glanced at his two assailants, but in the drama of Scudder's execution neither of them appeared to have heard anything. Fritz had already gone over to the window and was peering outside while Biedermeyer was still training the gun on Antonin with one hand and leafing through the papers on the desk which Antonin had been preparing to take with him with the other. So neither of them was looking towards the door as Danny's face appeared briefly around the doorframe.

Antonin tried to forget Scudder and think fast. There was no cover in the hallway, nowhere that Danny could hide if the man called Fritz left to organise the car. But Danny was already one step ahead of him. He raised his finger to his lips and silently pulling off his shoes crept stealthily across to the bedroom while Biedermeyer and Fritz were looking the other way.

Fritz suddenly turned.

"They're already waiting outside," he said.

Biedermeyer nodded. He jerked his head in the direction of Scudder's body.

"Put it in the bedroom," he ordered, speaking as usual in German.

"Why do you want to hide the body in my bedroom?" Antonin repeated loudly in English, fearful that Danny's linguistic skills might not extend to deciphering Biedermeyer's heavy Berlin accent.

Biedermeyer looked at him with a slightly puzzled expression but didn't reply. Fritz was already dragging the body across the room.

Antonin tensed. He was pretty sure Danny would try and jump him. So the tricky thing would be Biedermeyer. His gun was still trained on Antonin, but Biedermeyer did not appear to be expecting anything to happen. Half his mind was still on the papers he was rustling through on the desk.

"I'll need my identification at the bank," Antonin muttered darkly.

Biedermeyer scowled.

"What identification?"

Fritz was getting close to the bedroom door.

"You always need identification at English banks," Antonin mumbled. "Mine's down in the bottom drawer."

His heart was pounding. Fritz had disappeared from view into the bedroom. Biedermeyer reached down to the bottom drawer, trying to keep the gun trained on Antonin at the same time. It had to be now.

Bracing himself as firmly as he could against the desk, Antonin kicked Biedermeyer as hard as he could in the face. The force of the blow knocked him backwards onto the floor, but the gun was still firmly in his hand. So Antonin stamped down hard with the heel of his shoe onto the wrist clutching the gun and Biedermeyer roared out with pain. But to Antonin's horror the pain of the second blow seemed to help him recover from the shock of the first. And before Antonin could do anything he had pulled away fast, backing off in the direction of the hallway door, the gun still trained on Antonin.

If Danny had done anything Antonin had not heard it. But the silence from the bedroom spoke for itself. Biedermeyer flicked an anxious glance towards the open bedroom door.

"Fritz!" he called, now fully recovered, his eyes flicking backwards and forwards between Antonin and the bedroom door. Antonin held his breath. It seemed as if Danny had managed to immobilise Fritz and now was trying to entice Biedermeyer into the same trap.

Biedermeyer hesitated, still standing in the hallway door.

He made no move towards the bedroom door. Instead, he indicated with a jerk of his pistol that Antonin should approach him.

Reluctantly, Antonin moved forward as Biedermeyer's eyes continued to flick backwards and forwards. Only when he had nearly reached Biedermeyer did he himself back out into the little hallway. When Antonin too had left the room he stopped.

"Close the door behind you," he ordered.

Antonin did so. Biedermeyer continued to back up towards the external door of the flat.

Antonin followed because he had no choice but to follow. He was pretty sure that Biedermeyer would have taken great pleasure in killing him there and then if he hadn't thought he needed him to recover the tape. Therein lay the only reason he was still alive. Now he was planning to get Antonin away to the waiting car.

But then, just when Antonin had given up all hope of escaping, he suddenly saw a long dark shape appear high above the doorframe of the open external door of his flat. Biedermeyer must have seen it, because he started to turn, but before he could do anything the shape descended, cracking down hard onto his head. He slumped unconscious onto the floor.

A young girl appeared at the door, clutching a wooden lacrosse stick in her hand. She looked at her victim carefully to make sure he wouldn't get up. Then she glanced anxiously at Antonin.

"Where's Danny?" she asked, her voice full of fear, but no sooner had she said the words than Danny appeared from the living room, clutching in his hand Fritz's revolver.

"Holy shit!" Danny muttered under his breath, coming up and examining Biedermeyer. Then, without a further word, he dragged him back to the bedroom and deposited him on top of Fritz's limp body beside the bed.

Annie was staring in horror at Scudder.

"He's dead," Antonin said, pulling her away. "There's nothing you can do."

Annie was shaking, and Danny drew her silently towards him.

"They have Nadja," he said. "We only left her for a few moments to get some of Annie's clothes. When we came back we saw them marching her across the quad. They must have forced Scudder to tell them where she was."

Antonin nodded, nervously examining the various bodies littering the floor of his bedroom. Danny must have seen what he was thinking.

"You've really got only two choices now, Dr Ziegler," he said, sensing Antonin's confusion. "Either we call the police and explain everything to them or we take you out alone just like we arranged."

Antonin's mind was racing. He was so weary of all this horror and violence. It seemed so appealing to just phone the police and let somebody else sort it all out. But somewhere deep within him, a small voice prevailed.

"Let's go," he said. "I can't stay here."

* * * * * *

If it had been winter a log fire would have been crackling in the ancient fireplace. But it was high summer and the evening sun was only just setting over the rose bushes at the end of the cottage's tiny garden, casting a pale glow through the lace curtains onto a large vase of pastel-coloured dried flowers nestling in the grate. The quaint rural surroundings, the knowledge that for the moment at least he was beyond Biedermeyer's reach, the soft warmth of the evening sunlight, all these things were comforting and strangely soothing, and despite the recent traumas Antonin could feel the unremitting tension of many days beginning to abate. And soon, he knew, he would at least be able to find some sleep.

Annie appeared from the tiny kitchen adjoining the living room bearing a tray laden with three mugs of hot chocolate. She handed one to Antonin before settling down on a small sofa beside Danny. Ever since they had arrived at the cottage just over an hour earlier a strange silence had descended upon them, and now they continued to sit without speaking, each sipping their hot chocolate and watching the shadows of the window-frame move slowly but inexorably across the fireplace.

After a while Annie looked up at Antonin with a concerned expression.

"Are you feeling any better yet?" she asked.

He put down his mug and stretched out his still aching limbs.

"A little," he replied.

He glanced distastefully at the large trunk still sitting in the corner of the room, the trunk in which his friends had carried him from the college to Annie's waiting car, right under the noses of Biedermeyer's waiting men. Squeezing Antonin's rather corpulent figure into the trunk had been a painful and far from straightforward task which he sincerely hoped he would never have to repeat.

He looked gratefully at his hosts and realised that he still hadn't thanked them properly for what they had done.

"I just want to say . . ." he began rather solemnly.

"Please don't thank us, Dr Ziegler," Danny interjected, his young eyes rising to meet Antonin's own. In the high drama of the afternoon Danny seemed to have aged several years, as if he had somehow completed the process of turning from a boy into a man. "A difficult situation arose and we reacted. That's all."

Antonin fell silent. He knew what Danny wanted from him. It wasn't thanks, but rather an honest explanation. Danny was dying to know the truth but was far too polite to ask.

"If I tell you what's going on you'll be in even more danger," Antonin muttered uncomfortably.

Danny frowned.

"More than Scudder?" he observed dryly.

Annie looked at him sharply.

"Sorry," Danny corrected himself. "I didn't mean that."

Antonin rose to his feet. He really had no choice but to trust them, if that was what they wanted. He stood by the fireplace and looked down at them sitting together on the little sofa. They were just a couple of young students, from the perspective of a man in his forties little more than kids. But in the circumstances they still had every right to know.

"Do you really want me to tell you?"

Danny was about to speak but Annie interrupted him.

"Not if you don't want to tell us," she said firmly. "You don't have to tell us just because we helped you. But if you do tell us I suppose it's just possible we may be able to continue helping you. And frankly, Dr Ziegler, right now you look as if you could use a little help."

Antonin smiled.

"You're right about that," he murmured, and without further ado began to outline his extraordinary experiences since returning to Slovakia.

By the time he had finished it was already dark and a bright half moon had replaced the sun outside the cottage window. Annie got up and quietly closed the curtains before switching on the light. Then she turned to Danny.

"What do you make of it?" she asked.

Danny scowled.

"I agree with your Slovakian girl," he said. "In the light of what's happened there's no way those people can have anything to do with a reputable intelligence agency. I frankly don't believe it."

All the time he had been telling the story Antonin had been standing up. Now he sat down again. Danny first reactions were the same as Nadja's. And what's more he understood perfectly well why they both thought what they did.

"You think I've been duped by my brother, don't you?" Antonin said.

Again Danny frowned.

"It's possible. Or maybe he's been duped, too. You said he told you he'd never actually met Biedermeyer before. It's possible, isn't it?"

Antonin picked up the unfinished hot chocolate from the little table where he had put it. It was stone cold now, but still he took a sip.

"Stepan wouldn't lie to me. I'm sure he wouldn't lie."

Danny shuffled uncomfortably.

"But he did before, Dr Ziegler," he said softly. "You told us he admitted lying to you when you shared a room in East Berlin as students."

Antonin could feel his world spinning. Stepan had only lied then to protect them both, to make sure that if he fell into the hands of the Stasi they wouldn't be able to make him talk. Was it perhaps possible he was lying again for the same sort of reason?

"If Biedermeyer isn't from German Intelligence, then where is he from?" Antonin asked, not wishing to pursue his faith in his brother to the point where he started to look stupid.

Danny shrugged.

"It's difficult to know for sure, Dr Ziegler? Lots of people would like to have something which could control the way people think. But from what you've said I'd say everything points to a group with heavy connections with the communist intelligence organisations, not the West Germans."

Antonin looked at him sharply.

"Think about it," Danny continued. "Your brother's East German connections, that Czech agent in Melnik who you spoke to about Oblanov, the man who arrested Nadja in Slovakia. What do they all have in common?"

Antonin shrugged. Looked at from that point of view it seemed pretty plausible.

Annie had been sitting quietly all this time. But now she looked at Antonin intently.

"Remember the group who remained loyal to Hitler in the closing months of the last war," she said quietly. "Things weren't going their way, but instead of giving up they pinned all their hopes on a new wonder weapon, a kind of magic wand which could make all their problems go away."

Antonin nodded.

"Well," she continued, "the communists are in a similar mess at the moment, aren't they? I'd say they need a lucky break. Maybe they think they've found one. It looks as if the Oblanov research your father was involved in might have thrown up some sort of technique for long distance brainwashing. Perhaps some of the communist old guard have decided to attempt to develop the technique."

Antonin shifted uncomfortably in his seat. If what they said was true, then it seemed to imply that Stepan was either a fool or in it up to his ears, and that he simply refused to believe.

He rose to his feet.

"I'm tired," he muttered, looking down at his two new friends. "You may be right about what's going on. The only problem is, I'm not sure how it helps."

* * * * * *

The Prague spring had long since turned into high summer. At the far end of the platform, Antonin could see a thin figure struggling to step down from the train.

"Come on," he said nervously, glancing sideways at Katrina, "that's him."

Katrina had been uncharacteristically quiet ever since they had got up that morning and he could sense how nervous she was about meeting her future brother-in-law.

Antonin reached out and put his arm reassuringly around her slender body.

"Please don't be frightened," he said, giving her a squeeze.

He glanced at her and she forced a smile. But although he could see it was a false smile the time for reflection had long since passed, for they were now only yards away from him. Stepan had finally managed to clamber down from the train and had just spotted Antonin approaching with his wife-to-be.

Antonin embraced Stepan warmly. Then he stood back and formally introduced Katrina.

Stepan stepped backwards slightly and gazed into her eyes intently for a few moments before speaking. It was Stepan's way, and he had used the same technique with great effect on many occasions during the times they had shared in their student lodgings in East Berlin. For Stepan understood that to speak to a person too quickly was a mark of profound disrespect, a mark of a relationship that was doomed for ever to the superficial, the kind of relationship one might have with a shopkeeper or a bus conductor. To look at a person square in the eyes was a way of showing them that they were important.

"Katrina," he said at last. "I have heard a great deal about you. You have managed to quite melt my big brother's heart."

He leant forward on his stick and kissed her gently on the cheek.

Antonin glanced anxiously at Katrina. Yet despite her best efforts, he could see that none of her earlier ill-ease had vanished.

"Antonin's spoken a lot about you too, Stepan. It's nice to meet you at last."

Stepan smiled.

"You look a little frightened of me, Katrina," he said lightly. "I hope Antonin has not been telling you untrue stories about his poor little invalid brother."

Antonin laughed and embraced Stepan again.

"What nonsense you talk, Stepan!"

Stepan laughed too.

"You should know that Antonin thinks I'm not serious enough about life. And he worries about my politics as much as I worry about his. But despite it he must have told you that we are really very close and have been since our earliest childhood. So if Antonin says you're the one for him, then that's good enough for me."

He paused for a moment, once again fixing Katrina with an intent look. But then he bent down to pick up his case.

"But enough of this," he said. "Now why don't you show me a bit of your beloved Prague like you promised."

It had been the start of a long and tiring day, a day which had lived for a long time in Antonin's memory. Under the blazing sun the three of them had tramped the narrow lanes and broad thoroughfares of Prague. They had walked for many miles, occasionally stopping in a coffee-house when their feet became weary before moving on. They had visited museums, ambled round parks, sometimes taken a ride on a tram. And all that time Antonin had watched a kind of silent inner struggle developing between Katrina and his little brother. And gradually he had come to see that however hard they both tried, they would never really come to accept each other's place in his affections.

It had been a painful sight, for the greater part of Antonin had so much wanted them to get on. Apart from his old Slovakian grandfather, they were the only people alive who he loved. For if

Katrina was his future, Stepan was his past, the salvation of his childhood just as much as he knew Katrina would be the salvation of his adult years.

Yet despite it all a small part of him rejoiced that try though they might Katrina and Stepan could not seem to develop a bond with each other. For he knew deep down that a part of him was frightened of Stepan, that one of the reasons he had left East Berlin was to escape his brother's growing success in every aspect of his life. And if he was totally honest with himself he had to admit that a tiny part of him was actually frightened that Katrina might prefer Stepan to him.

The slow burning tension had finally come to a head late that night. They had all been drinking rather too much beer, attempting perhaps to force a sense of jollity where none in fact existed. But the alcohol had been a bad mistake, for Katrina had finally allowed her guard to fall. She fixed Stepan with an icy glare.

"Antonin says that if the chips are down you would fight against us," she murmured.

Antonin swallowed down his beer and stared at her in astonishment. But Stepan did no more than raise his left eyebrow.

"Why should I fight you?" he asked non-committally.

"When Brezhnev comes. Everybody knows Brezhnev will come soon."

Stepan frowned.

"And will Antonin fight?"

The remark was not addressed to him but to her, and try though he might he felt he had no choice but to let her answer.

Katrina turned and smiled savagely at Stepan.

"He does not think so. But when he sees a Warsaw Pact tank smashing its way through the streets of this beautiful city then I believe he will fight. I merely asked whether you will be driving the tank?"

Antonin looked backwards and forwards between them with growing despair. He had known full well the risks of them meeting face to face. They were both such powerful people, and their politics were hardly compatible. But despite it all he had hoped that they would have had the sense not to let it come to this.

He tried to force a laugh.

"Stepan can't join the army. He's got bad legs," he offered desperately, yet neither his brother nor his girlfriend seemed to take any notice of him. Instead they continued to stare aggressively at each other.

"Antonin knows he is a thinker. Antonin knows he should keep out of politics," Stepan murmured. "If you truly love him you would not try to stir him into this dangerous pot of intrigue that is developing in Prague."

Katrina was about to speak but then she suddenly checked herself. It was as if the effects of the alcohol had temporarily abated, allowing her to see how foolish her earlier remark had been. She sank back into her chair and looked at her feet.

Antonin looked at Stepan, and as he did so he suddenly felt a slight shiver of fear running down his spine. For his younger brother was still looking at Katrina intently, and he could see that Stepan's eyes were examining her with an intensity which was more than merely curious. And with a sudden shock Antonin realised that Stepan too had been infected by her power.

* * * * * *

The sound of Annie's car arriving roused Antonin from his sleep. He rose quickly and pulled aside the curtain to see if they had come, but the car had already pulled round to the far side of the cottage and was out of sight. Too impatient to get dressed, he fumbled around in the room's only wardrobe and found an extravagant silk-embroidered dressing gown which must have belonged to Annie's father. Pulling it quickly round his shoulders, he walked to the bedroom door and down the stairs.

He arrived in the living room just as Annie was coming through the front door, and with a look of tremendous relief he could see that she was closely followed by Vanessa. But of Nathaniel Harrison there was no sign.

Vanessa hurried over and hugged him. It was not a display of affection in which she normally indulged.

"Poor Antonin," she said, as if she were addressing a little child who had been through a difficult time.

Antonin gratefully accepted the hug and then pulled away, gazing uncertainly into her face.

"It's all right, my dear," she said, "Annie explained everything to me. It's all quite dreadful, quite horribly dreadful."

It was Annie who filled the momentary silence which descended.

"The college is crawling with police," she said. "Scudder must have told the cleaner you were back in college. She found his body this morning when she went in to make the bed."

Antonin looked at her with consternation.

"Oh my God," he said. "You didn't talk to the police, did you?"

179

Vanessa shook her head.

"Goodness me no", she said. "Annie didn't, but I did. Everybody at college knows I'm a personal friend of yours. So when Annie told me what happened I thought I'd better go round and be my usual nosey self. I found the inspector most charming, if a bit perplexed."

Antonin looked at her numbly.

"You gave the police a statement!" he exclaimed.

Vanessa nodded.

"But of course. It would have looked a bit odd if I hadn't, wouldn't it? Naturally I denied all knowledge of what's happened to you since you left England.

During the exchange Danny had silently appeared in his pyjamas at the bottom of the stairs.

"Did they find the others?" he asked.

"No," Vanessa replied. "Some of his accomplices must have come and extricated them before Scudder's body was discovered. But from our point of view that's probably just as well."

Antonin nodded in silent agreement. Scudder's death would completely baffle the British police. And every force in the land would be looking for him.

Again they all fell silent. Then Annie quietly pulled Danny away by his sleeve in the direction of the kitchen. As soon as they were alone, Vanessa sank down gratefully onto the sofa. As Antonin joined her he suddenly became aware of how weary she looked.

"Where's Nathaniel," he asked.

Vanessa grunted.

"In hiding."

"In hiding? But why?"

Vanessa looked at him anxiously.

"You probably know there are only about a dozen top scientists in Nathaniel's field. Naturally he's on first name terms with all of them. He told me he thought it for the best to approach Professor Langbury at Cambridge with your Slovakian paper. He's known him for many years and trusts him completely. Since Professor Langbury had been dabbling in a similar kind of research for a number of years without success he thought it might make sense for them to join forces. Anyway, he asked me whether he could speak to him and I agreed. But when Nathaniel telephoned him at his home a few days ago to arrange a meeting Langbury's wife told him that he'd completely disappeared together with their ten-year-old daughter. No letter, no phonecall, nothing. So then he started ringing round to see who else he could contact, only to discover that three other scientists have disappeared during the past week, all of them specialists in exactly the same field. All of them had been taken with hostages."

She fell silent.

"So Nathaniel pre-empted them by disappearing."

"Yes. As far as I'm aware I'm the only person who knows where he is. But I did speak to him yesterday."

"And what did he say?"

"He admitted he's making some limited progress. The papers you brought with you from Slovakia do indeed suggest a premature scientific breakthrough. He explained that in the 1950s and early 1960s a great deal of work was being undertaken in the United States and Western Europe to influence the behaviour of the human brain through the use of directly applied electrical stimuli. The idea behind the research was that the human brain was akin to a sophisticated computer system. It was therefore believed that a way might be discovered to use electrical impulses to adjust the programming of the brain, resulting in emotional and behavioural modifications. Nathaniel told me that although much of the research was done in civilian institutions a great deal of the funding came through what can only be termed military sources, since there was at that time a belief in some government circles that such techniques could have applications in the defence and espionage fields. But although a few useful ideas emerged from the research, especially in psychiatry, the steam began to go out of it all with the development of artificial intelligence in the late 1960s."

Antonin looked at her uncertainly.

"And Oblanov?" he asked.

Vanessa frowned.

"Essentially an accident. They weren't using electrical impulses, but rather sonic impulses. But somehow they managed to produce a much more effective response in the human brain than they'd reckoned on. And an added bonus was that because of the delivery system the implanted instructions could be delivered easily over long distances to large population groups."

Antonin drew a deep breath.

"So they were right," he murmured, more to himself than to her, for Nathaniel's description of the invention was broadly the same as Biedermeyer's had been.

She nodded glumly.

"All you would need to control an entire society would be a radio transmitter," she muttered. "Frightening prospect, isn't it?"

Antonin looked at her numbly, trying not to dwell too long on his own personal responsibility for rediscovering the contents of the briefcase.

"So who do you think Biedermeyer is involved with?" he asked presently.

She shook her head.

"Your guess is as good as mine," she said. "This thing's not a crude weapon like a nuclear bomb. It doesn't destroy anything other than human mental freedom. Big companies, religious fanatics, governments frightened about re-election, opposition groups trying to win support for their own ideologies. I think they'd all welcome such a technique. And those of us who fear for our mental freedom enough to oppose its use would make up a very feeble army by comparison."

Again Antonin could feel his spirits sagging.

"So what do we do now?" he asked. "Did Nathaniel have anything positive to suggest?"

"Fortunately he did," she replied. "He offered the tentative view that we should abandon your father's approach to all this. In other words, in the long run we should stop trying to repress the method. Instead we should concentrate on developing some way of rendering it ineffective, rather in the way that sufficiently careful programming can prevent a computer virus from attacking vital software."

Antonin frowned.

"And did Nathaniel think he was capable of doing such a thing?" he asked, hoping the scepticism he felt would prove ill-founded.

But Vanessa shook her head.

"No," she replied. "Frankly he doesn't, certainly while he's holed up on his own without a laboratory or even a decent library to work in. He would certainly need a lot more information than the papers you gave him."

Antonin rose ponderously to his feet. For several minutes he walked backwards and forwards in the tiny living room. Then he stopped and turned to face his friend.

"So where does my brother fit in to all this?" he asked point blank.

Vanessa pursed her lips and thought for a while before replying.

"I guessed that was bugging you, Antonin. So why don't you tell me what you think? You always seemed to have a high opinion of him. In fact I don't think I've ever heard you say a word against him."

Antonin shrugged.

"Because of his terrible injuries we were very close as children. We've always trusted each other."

She looked at him sharply.

"You trust him to take your side?"

He nodded. It was a simple fact that however odd the circumstances of his reunion with his brother had been, he still did trust him. But he knew that Vanessa's words were hinting at something which had already occurred to him, a way forward which might yet produce results. And the more he thought about it, the more he knew she was right.

*   *   *   *   *   *

It had been far simpler than he had supposed. As soon as he had arrived at the airport in East Berlin he had walked into a phone booth and found Stepan's number in the telephone directory. He lived in a modern block of ten or so storeys in what was by East German standards a smart residential district. The car park outside the building was singularly lacking in the usual shabby assortment of clapped-out Trabants and Ladas, sporting instead a more than respectable collection of Western models.

Antonin dismissed the taxi which had brought him from the airport and glanced round apprehensively to confirm that no one was following him. But the few people he could see were taking no notice of his movements and he felt sure that thus far at least he had remained undetected.

He straightened his suit and pushed through the glass doors of the building's rather imposing main entrance. Behind a desk, a uniformed doorman was slouched in his seat reading a magazine. When Antonin entered he looked up.

"Can I help you?" he asked with a bored expression.

Antonin walked over to him.

"I'm looking for Stepan Ziegler," he said purposefully.

The man shook his head.

"Herr Ziegler?" he said. "He has a flat here, but he hasn't been around for ages."

Antonin frowned.

"Oh," he said. "Do you have a forwarding address?"

Again the man shook his head.

"I'm afraid not."

"When did he move out?"

"Last time I saw him was last winter, about ten days after the Wall collapsed. I think he left in a bit of a hurry."

"Why?"

"Herr Ziegler worked for the Stasi. Quite a high-up gent, I think. Many of his type seem to have decided to lay low until the flak dies down."

Antonin examined the man carefully for a few moments. Stepan had explained that he worked in the East German administration and somehow or other he had not got around to asking which branch. Yet the chances were that the doorman himself had been Stasi, probably charged with keeping track of the movements into and out of the building. He probably knew what he was talking about.

"What exactly did Herr Ziegler do in the Stasi?" Antonin asked.

The man looked at him suspiciously.

"Who are you?" he said. "Are you trying to arrest him or something?"

Antonin forced a smile, trying to copy the confident manner he had seen Andreas display towards the barman in Melnik.

"I'm investigating Herr Ziegler's activities under the old regime. In your own interests I would strongly advise you to give me your full co-operation in my enquiries."

It worked perfectly. The man's rather offhand manner disappeared. He bent down and fumbled around nervously in a drawer for a few moments, finally pulling out a key.

"Look," he said. "I'm just the doorman. I didn't know much about the people who lived here, but if you want to go and look through his flat, be my guest. I told you Herr Ziegler left in a hurry. He just took the things he could fit into the back of his car. Ever since then the rent's been paid regularly every month, so technically speaking the flat's still his. Why don't you go up and see for yourself? It's Number 17, on the fifth floor."

Antonin thanked the man and took the key, heading quickly for the lift before the doorman overcame his anxiety and thought to ask him for proper identification. A few minutes later he found himself outside Stepan's flat.

He pushed the key into the lock and turned it gently. The door swung silently open, and Antonin entered an imposing hallway with several opulently carved oak doors leading from it. He pushed open the one immediately in front of him, revealing a spacious living room filled with modern white furnishings of the highest quality.

The room was immaculately tidy, if a little dusty, but other than that gave little away about the personality of the occupant. In fact it looked more like the kind of flat loaned to business executives on short stays in foreign cities than an ordinary home.

Antonin walked over to the desk and pulled open the drawers, but besides a few pens and pencils there was nothing to be seen. When he left Stepan had clearly been careful to take with him any papers which he had kept there.

Antonin walked back into the hallway and pushed open each of the other doors. Besides the bathroom and toilet, there was a large double bedroom and a smaller guest bedroom with a single bed. All were as smartly furnished and immaculate as the living room had been.

He cautiously entered the double bedroom. The beds had been left made up when Stepan had gone, two duvets neatly puffed up as if they were waiting for someone to return home. Or rather, as if they were waiting for two people to return home.

In itself the double bed should not have been puzzling. Perhaps because he himself was a single man he had assumed that Stepan was too. And Stepan himself had not mentioned anything about a wife or family. But even if he was not married, there was absolutely no reason why his younger brother should not have had a girlfriend.

Antonin pulled open the wardrobes and examined the clothes. Some of them were men's things but there were also women's clothes, the clothes of a smartly dressed lady of substance at that. It looked as if the girlfriend, if that is what she had been, was a fairly permanent fixture in the flat. It was odd that Stepan had not mentioned the fact.

Anxious lest the doorman come to his senses and stop him, he left the master bedroom without further ado and went into the smaller single bedroom next door. Here the bed was stripped back, but there was a large cupboard to one side which Antonin now pulled open.

But as he did so his mouth fell open in astonishment, for the cupboard was filled to overflowing with children's toys. Antonin knelt down and started pulling them slowly out, numbly fingering the Lego, the train sets, the toy soldiers and other assorted clutter which he had found. There was a blank cardboard box at the back of the cupboard and he heaved it out. It had been carefully sealed up with sticky tape, as if it had been put away for posterity. Antonin pulled it off and opened the box, which was filled with school exercise books. He pulled one of them out. It was an ordinary junior level maths book containing simple arithmetic exercises in childish handwriting. But on the cover was some writing in the same hand: 'Ernst Ziegler, Class 5, September 1977.'

Antonin lifted the box up and put it down on the bed, sitting down beside it. He flicked through some of the other school books. They all seemed to belong to the same boy, this Ernst Ziegler. So Stepan did have a family, after all. He appeared to have at least one child who bore his name, which suggested that the woman whose clothes he had found in the other room was perhaps his wife, the mother of the child. It was strange indeed that Stepan had mentioned neither wife nor son when they had been reunited after so many years apart.

Antonin picked up the maths schoolbook again. Class 5 in 1977. A quick mental calculation suggested that the child had been born around 1969, not that long after Antonin himself had left Czechoslovakia. The wife, if that indeed was who she was, would have been pregnant in 1968, yet as far as Antonin was aware Stepan had not even had a steady girlfriend at that time.

"Excuse me, sir."

Antonin looked up to see the doorman standing behind him.

"Yes."

"Excuse me, but it occurred to me I ought to have seen your identification before letting you in."

Antonin flinched, but only for a moment.

"You should know where I'm from," he said.

"I'm sorry, sir, but I don't even know your name. Are you from the police?"

Antonin stood up, realising that the fellow had decided to insist this time. He handed back the key and returned the box of exercise books to the cupboard.

"I've just about finished anyway," he said.

With relief the man took the key and followed him to the door, carefully locking it as they left.

Only when the door was safely closed and they were waiting for the lift did Antonin turn to the man.

"Did Herr Ziegler leave with his wife and child?" he asked.

The doorman shook his head.

"No. Just his wife. Their child left home ages ago."

"Ernst?"

The man grunted.

"Not before time, either. He was a right pain when he was young, the bane of my life."

186

Suddenly the doorman's face grew serious again.

"About the identification," he said. "I really do think I should take down some details . . ."

His voice trailed away slowly as Antonin pulled out his wallet. But instead of the identification the man was expecting Antonin started pulling out a high denomination West German banknote.

"Just a few more questions?" Antonin asked.

The man was silent, staring anxiously at the banknote.

"Tell me about Herr Ziegler and his family?" Antonin continued.

The lift arrived. But neither of them got into it. Instead, the man opened the door of Stepan's flat again and gently edged Antonin back inside.

"What exactly would you like to know?" he asked.

"Tell me about his wife and child, for example? He had a wife and one child, didn't he?"

"Yes. That's right. They moved here when the boy was about eight, I suppose."

"A tearaway, you say?"

The man shook his head.

"Not so much a tearaway. More a bit strange. He always seemed to be staring at me. I used to find it uncomfortable and chased him away. And even when he got older, he never seemed to have any friends. He'd just sit around by the door doodling on a pad of paper. Frankly I was pleased when he left."

"Where did he go?"

The man shrugged.

"How should I know? He left several years ago, when he was around eighteen."

"And did he come back to visit his parents?"

"No. Not that I saw."

"So then it was just Herr Ziegler and his wife?"

"Yes."

"Tell me about her."

"Tall. Fair-haired. A good-looking woman."

"What was her name?"

The man shrugged.

"Look," he said, "I'm just the doorman. To me she was Frau Ziegler."

"Tell me what sort of person she was? I don't mean her looks, I mean her personality."

"She was quiet, I suppose you could say, especially when she was together with her husband. Always polite, mind you, but quiet. She didn't really have much of a personality, if you want my honest opinion."

Antonin pulled out several West German banknotes and handed them to the man, being careful to reveal how many more were still in his wallet.

"Can you think of anything else about the Zieglers which might be of interest to me?" he asked.

The man thought for a moment.

"Are you trying to trace him?" he asked.

Antonin nodded.

"You could try Vienna," he said.

"Why Vienna?"

"It might be nothing, but when they left I helped carry their things out to their car. I happened to notice a street map of Vienna on the front passenger seat. It's a place I'd always wanted to visit and I knew that with the Wall coming down I might finally get my chance. So I asked Herr Ziegler in passing whether that was where they were going. But he just snapped my head off and told me to mind my own business. And later, when I brought the next load down, I noticed the map wasn't there any more."

Antonin frowned. He was sure he recalled Stepan saying he was still living in Berlin. He'd certainly implied that he'd only been called to Austria at Biedermeyer's request shortly before his reunion with Antonin.

Antonin handed him another banknote.

"Anything else?"

The man shrugged.

"It's difficult to know what you want. Herr Ziegler was generally courteous towards me, but he didn't exactly chat. He struck me as a solid and purposeful man, I suppose. He appeared to have a doting wife and a son who he didn't get on too well with, but other than that we didn't have much to do with each other."

Antonin nodded silently. He had already reached the conclusion that a direct search for Stepan was unlikely to succeed. As a spy he would have been far too experienced to leave a trail behind him. But Stepan appeared to have left behind a wild card, and now Antonin decided he would try and play that card.

"I need to look in the small bedroom again?" he said.

The man stood aside to let him pass and within minutes he was back with what he wanted carefully tucked into his suit pocket.

"Thank you," he said, handing over yet another banknote.

"You've been most helpful, but I don't think you should mention my visit here if Herr Ziegler should by chance return."

The man smiled wryly.

"Don't worry," he said, "I won't."

* * * * * *

It seemed a strangely foolish notion. As Antonin walked across the playground into the district school which Stepan's son had once attended he was not absolutely sure what he could hope to achieve by it. But the boy had apparently seen eye-to-eye with neither his father nor his mother. If the doorman had been right, and he was certainly in a position to have noticed, young Ernst Ziegler had not even visited them after he had left home. If Antonin could find out where he was, there was just a chance he would talk to an uncle he had never met.

Lessons were still taking place and the playground was quiet. Antonin entered the main building and headed straight for the reception.

There was a slight elderly woman in the office, typing on an even more elderly typewriter. She looked up as Antonin entered.

"Hallo," she said politely. "Can I help?"

Antonin nodded.

"Perhaps," he said. "I'm trying to trace a former student of yours, a young man by the name of Ernst Ziegler. I'm his uncle."

The woman thought for a few moments.

"Ernst Ziegler. Yes, I remember him. But he left quite a few years ago."

"Do you know where he went?"

The woman shook her head.

"Not a clue, although I think he left under something of a cloud. He was a rather quiet fellow. One of life's loners."

"Is there anyone here who might be able to help me trace him? Anyone who might know what became of him?"

Again she thought.

"Frau Riemer might. She taught him German."

The woman briefly consulted a miniature timetable on her desk.

"She's not teaching now. Would you like to speak to her?"

Antonin nodded and woman picked up the phone and spoke briefly. After a few minutes a thin, rather prim looking woman in her fifties appeared in the office. She inclined her head cautiously in Antonin's direction by way of greeting.

Antonin introduced himself, but the look of caution on Frau

189

Riemer's face did not disappear. Instead, she led him out of the office and along the corridor to a small tutorial room. Only when she had closed the door did she turn to meet his gaze.

"You say you are Ernst's uncle?" she said non-committally.

"Yes."

"I didn't know he had an uncle. He once told me both his parents were only children."

"Perhaps his parents didn't tell him about me. I left for the West before he was born."

Her face seemed to relax a little, as if she found the explanation satisfactory.

"You're trying to trace him?"

"Yes."

"Presumably you've asked his parents where he is?"

Antonin shook his head.

"No. I can't find them. They moved away from Berlin about six months ago without leaving a forwarding address. It was the doorman at their old flat who referred me here."

The woman's face seemed to relax still further.

"And why do you want to find Ernst?"

"He's my nephew. I just want to find him."

He said the words bluntly, and as he did so he suddenly realised they were true. Having no children himself, the idea of the Ziegler blood flowing in the next generation did fill him with a certain sense of excitement.

"I'll be perfectly frank with you," Frau Riemer said. "Ernst was always a disappointment to his parents. His father was high up in the administration, but Ernst was a bit of a rebel at school. It didn't make for a happy mix."

Antonin nodded.

"He probably took after me. I went to school here too and I never fitted in very well. Was Ernst disobedient, then?"

Frau Riemer smiled.

"Disobedient? No, he wasn't exactly disobedient. But he allowed people to see he didn't approve of things. He had strange eyes, and he'd strip people apart who tried lying to him. It was as if he were trying to prize the truth out of them. As you can imagine, many of the teachers didn't much like that."

"But you didn't mind?"

Again Frau Riemer smiled.

"I liked your nephew," she said, "and I think he liked me."

Antonin returned the smile.

"He didn't stare at you, then?"

"He did stare. The difference was I didn't mind."

For a few minutes they said nothing. Yet Frau Riemer didn't take her eyes off him for a moment, as if she were silently assessing him. And Antonin was careful not to look away.

Finally she spoke.

"Ernst told me before he left school that he didn't want to see his parents again," she said bluntly.

Antonin looked at her sharply.

"As bad as that?" he asked.

"I'm afraid so. And as far as I'm aware it's pretty mutual, certainly as far as his father is concerned."

"And his mother?"

Frau Riemer pulled a grimace.

"His mother was a total wash-out. A kind of non-person. Whenever I saw her she would sit silently and let her husband do all the talking. And she would invariably take her husband's side against Ernst."

Antonin hesitated for a few moments before he spoke again.

"You seem to have known him pretty well?" he observed.

She smiled.

"It's like that when you're a schoolteacher," she said. "Most of the time the kids you see just roll past you. You do your job and that's that. But sometimes a child makes more of an impact. Something in the chemistry of the relationship, I suppose. It was always like that with me and Ernst."

Antonin nodded.

"Do you know what happened to him when he left here?" he asked.

"Ernst was actually a rather clever boy," she said. "But he left here without many qualifications, and because he wasn't very popular with the staff he didn't have much of a reference either. So they gave him a manual job in a local factory. Six months later he was gone."

Antonin looked at her sharply.

"Gone?"

"Yes. He vanished."

"But this was East Germany. You didn't just vanish."

Frau Riemer smiled.

"But I know where he is?" she said proudly. "You see, about six months ago, after the Wall had gone, he sent me a letter. I've been corresponding ever since."

Antonin didn't ask. He knew she would tell him only if she wanted to.

"Is he all right?"

"He went to the West."

"What? Three years ago? How did he manage that?"

"I don't know. He didn't say and I didn't ask. But if you want my opinion his father might have had something to do with it. He was Stasi, I think. Perhaps he fixed it for Ernst. Or maybe he just found a way by himself."

Again the silence descended. And this time it lasted a long time. But finally Frau Riemer spoke.

"You want me to give you his address, don't you?"

Antonin nodded.

For a while her face remained stern, but then it suddenly broke into a gentle smile.

"He told me quite explicitly not to tell his parents," she said, "but he didn't say anything about uncles."

She reached into her handbag and pulled out a small address book and a piece of paper. She leafed through the book and scribbled something down. Then she folded the piece of paper together and handed it to Antonin. Only then did she look at him again, the rather fierce look of a kindly schoolmistress who cared.

"Be kind to Ernst," she said. "He always struck me as a boy who could do with a kindly uncle."

Antonin looked at the folded piece of paper in his hand and then gingerly unfolded it. And as he did so a thin shiver of fear ran down his spine.

For once again the same place was cropping up. At every turn of the drama it kept cropping up.

For his nephew Ernst had gone to live in Vienna.

* * * * * *

The tall tenements still carried with them the faded grandeur of the dying days of the Austrian Empire. The elaborate stonework of the window-sills, the ornate iron balustrades surrounding the first floor balconies, the fin-de-siècle craftsmanship of the high tiled roofs, all indicated that these had once been the homes of the wealthy Viennese patrician class. But those days were long since past. The stonework was crumbling, the iron balustrades were rusting and the tiled roofs were urgently in need of repair. And the bourgeois families who had once inhabited these homes had long since been replaced by a motley collection of Turks, Slavs, Hungarians and those poorer Austrians who had failed to keep up with the rapid pace of post-war economic growth in their homeland.

As Antonin walked along the litter-strewn pavement, the sounds of a large group of children playing an impromptu game of football in the street mingled with the dull rhythmic chant of a Turkish melody which was wafting down from one of the open windows. With a gentle thud the football hit Antonin's chest and landed by his feet. Bending down, he threw it back in the general direction of the children before brushing down his suit with his hand and pulling out from his pocket the little piece of paper Frau Riemer had handed him in Berlin. Carefully checking to see if he had found the correct address, he pushed open the door of the building beside him and started to climb the stairs.

Four storeys up he arrived at the front door of Ernst's flat. Stuck to the outside of it with sticky tape was a large poster advertising a forthcoming jazz concert on the outskirts of Vienna, and written in felt pen across the front of the poster – in a scrawny handwriting – was an invitation to apply within for tickets.

Antonin knocked gingerly on the door. He felt a little nervous, uncertain quite how to introduce himself, unsure whether his nephew would welcome a family intrusion into his new life.

He waited. But there was no reply. He knocked again, this time more loudly than before.

"The door's open. Come in."

The voice was subdued and seemed somehow frail. He opened the door and stepped inside, peering cautiously around the primitive little kitchen in which he found himself. The old white sink was cracked and dirty, filled to overflowing with an accumulated debris of grubby pots and dishes. And the whole dreadful mess was accompanied by an almost overpowering stench, a ghastly mixture of blocked drains, decaying food and old grease.

Trying not to breathe too deeply for fear he would be sick, Antonin walked through the deserted kitchen to a door at the far end. Pushing it gently open, he entered what served as a living room, and as he did so he could not help but be struck by the sharp contrast between the room in which he now found himself and the antiseptic apartment in East Berlin in which this young man had grown up.

For despite the absolute untidiness of the room, despite the filth on the floor, despite the dirty clothes lying draped over the scruffy furniture, despite the general grime of the place, Antonin had to admit that the room possessed a certain sort of charm. For just as the kitchen had been filled with dirty dishes, so this room was filled with a huge assortment of musical instruments. There were saxophones, trumpets, a set of drums, a violin, a double bass and, in the far corner of the room beneath an open window, a large if very dirty grand piano. But the strangest thing of all was that under the grand piano was a mattress, and lying on the mattress, dressed only in a stripy blue and red pair of old pyjamas, was a young man.

"Hallo," said the young man in a voice which despite its frailty was remarkably open and friendly. "Have you come for some tickets?"

Antonin looked at him uncertainly for a few moments. His face was lean and angular, the face of a young man who didn't eat too well, yet despite a certain bleariness which suggested fever, his eyes were filled with an unmistakable clarity.

"No," Antonin replied.

"Oh yes, of course," said the young man, as if he had just remembered something.

He seemed to slump back onto his mattress. Antonin took another step into the room.

"Are you all right?" he asked.

The young man tried to smile.

"No," he replied. "I feel lousy. You wouldn't mind getting me a glass of water, would you?"

Antonin nodded and went silently to the kitchen. Rummaging around in the dirty sink, he found a large wine glass, washed it out and filled it with water. Then he returned and crossed the room to the grand piano. Bending down, he handed the glass of water to the young man.

"Thanks," he said weakly, sitting up and sipping the water gratefully. After a few sips he put the glass down and lay back on his impromptu bed, momentarily closing his eyes.

Antonin watched him in amazement. Having discovered he didn't want any tickets he had made no move to ask him who he was and yet seemed entirely relaxed in his presence, grateful to have a visitor to fetch him a glass of water. He seemed so overwhelmingly trusting that Antonin didn't really want to disturb the tranquillity.

"May I sit down?" he asked.

The young man looked at him and nodded.

"Of course, just push the stuff on the floor."

Antonin selected a scruffy armchair nearby and lifted the clothes gingerly onto the floor before lowering himself into the seat.

"Are you Ernst?" he asked.

The young fellow nodded.

"Yup," he said. "I expect you've come to see Helmut, haven't you?"

Antonin looked at him uncertainly.

"Helmut?"

Ernst propped himself up on his elbow.

"Oh, sorry, when you said you didn't want tickets I thought you must have been coming to see my flatmate Helmut. He mentioned he was expecting a tenor saxophonist to drop by this afternoon for an audition."

Antonin smiled.

"Sorry," he said. "Saxophones were never my strong point."

Ernst eyes narrowed, as if he had suddenly focused on Antonin.

"Have you come to see me then?" he asked.

Antonin nodded.

"Yes. I've just flown in from Berlin. Frau Riemer at your old school gave me your address here."

Ernst looked at him suspiciously.

"Do I know you?" he asked warily.

Antonin shook his head.

"Don't worry, I didn't tell your parents anything."

He could not help but notice that Ernst relaxed a little. But he said nothing.

"Did you know your father had an elder brother?" Antonin continued.

"No. He always told me he was a single child."

"Well, he wasn't and I am. That's to say I'm your uncle, your father's elder brother."

Ernst looked at him long and hard. Then, despite the fever, his face broke into a wry smile.

"Holy smoke!" he muttered.

Antonin smiled. Ernst's face was now completely relaxed again, the acceptance of the fact absolute and unquestioning.

"You really don't look very well," Antonin said.

Ernst lay back on the mattress.

"It's flu," he said. "And we've only got eight days left to the big day."

"The one on the door."

"Yup. I've gone and got flu and our tenor saxophonist has run off with his girlfriend to Tibet. It's all rather bad timing, don't you agree?"

Antonin looked round the room.

"Do you play all these?" he asked, indicating the array of musical instruments.

"With varying degrees of competence," his nephew replied. "Why, do you play?"

Antonin smiled. There was no interrogation, no quizzing on Antonin's background or circumstances. Just an open-minded friendly acceptance of an uncle he had never known.

"No," he laughed. "I'm afraid I can't play a thing."

There was a brief silence.

"Frau Riemer sends her regards," Antonin said at last.

Ernst smiled.

"How is she?" he asked.

"She's well. She hoped you wouldn't be cross with her for giving me your address."

Ernst shook his head.

"Look," he said, "I know Dad's a pro. If he wanted to find me here so bad he would. I'm not stupid."

You had to be perceptive to spot it, but there was a tension in Ernst's voice when he mentioned his father which contrasted oddly with the young man's otherwise relaxed manner.

"So you think he's not trying?"

Ernst frowned.

"Frankly, I think Dad was as pleased to see the back of me as I was to see the back of him."

As Ernst spoke the words Antonin suddenly remembered his own childhood. In a flash it all passed before his mind. The coldness, the mutual embarrassment, the total lack of anything which could remotely be called love. And suddenly, with a deep and profound shock, he realised that Ernst had been through exactly the same himself.

After a while he stood up and walked towards the closed window near the piano. For despite his best efforts to ignore it, the smell wafting through from the neighbouring kitchen was becoming over-powering.

"Do you mind if I open it?" he asked.

Ernst slumped back on the pillow and closed his eyes again.

"Be my guest. It pongs a bit in here, I'm afraid. Since I got ill I haven't been able to clean up. And you'd have to wait a very long time before Helmut would do it."

After opening the window Antonin absent-mindedly started picking up the clothes off the floor and gathering them together into piles.

"You can't shock me," he said. "I'm used to students."

Ernst opened his eyes again. After tracking Antonin around the room for a few moments he wedged himself up on his elbow.

"How come Dad never mentioned you?" he asked.

"Perhaps because I was the black sheep of the family. Like you are, maybe."

Ernst grunted.

"Did you go to the West then?"

Antonin nodded.

"An embarrassment for Dad, I suppose."

Again Antonin nodded.

"Now I'm an academic at Oxford University in England. But I was a student in Prague when the Soviets invaded. That's when I left. So I imagine your father just decided it would be best to forget about me."

Ernst slumped back on the mattress again.

"So have you seen him since?" he asked.

"I didn't see him for a long time."

Despite the fever Ernst's eyes narrowed.

"And you met up again recently?"

"Yes. We kind of bumped into each other, you might say."

"And he told you about me?"

Antonin shook his head.

"No. He didn't even mention he had a family. Then when I went to see him in East Berlin I found he'd moved out six months ago. It was while I was there that I found out about you."

Ernst was now making a serious although not entirely successful attempt to fight the fever and concentrate.

"You couldn't find Dad so you went to my old school and spoke to Frau Riemer. And now you've come all the way to Vienna to see me."

All this time Antonin had been standing. Yet now he sat down again uncertainly. Throughout the flight to Vienna he'd been wondering quite what to say once he'd found him.

"I urgently need to speak to your Dad, Ernst. Do you know where he is?"

Ernst's face fell, as if he had somehow been hoping that Antonin had genuinely been seeking him for himself.

"I'm afraid I don't know where Dad is," he said. "If you say he's left the flat without leaving a forwarding address then I'd say he was on the run."

"On the run? Because he was Stasi?"

"Yes. Dad was pretty high up in internal security. He and his friends must have made a lot of enemies over the years. Some of them might want to settle old scores."

Antonin frowned. None of what Ernst was saying, in fact nothing he had discovered recently, established that Stepan had been lying to him about his West German connections. The things that didn't add up about Stepan were personal, not political. That was where the story didn't match up.

"When I saw him your father told me he was working for the West all along," Antonin said softly, carefully studying Ernst's face to see how he reacted. But he just lay back and grunted.

"Was he really?" he mumbled.

"You believe him?"

"That Dad was a double agent? He might have been, I suppose. He wouldn't have told me, would he?" He hesitated, and then a thought seemed to cross his mind. "But if he was, why's he run away now?"

"He told me he had some unfinished business to conduct."

Ernst suddenly seemed to lose all interest in the conversation.

"Oh well, what the hell. What difference does it make anyway?" His body slumped back heavily onto the mattress and he closed his eyes. "I'm sorry I can't help you find him."

Antonin looked sadly at his nephew. He looked so forlorn lying there under the grand piano, so deeply and profoundly unloved. Antonin stood up and took a deep breath by the window before walking purposefully into the kitchen. Silently turning on the tap, he started mechanically doing the washing up.

For three hours he worked solidly, scrubbing and cleaning Ernst's disgusting crockery, wiping surfaces and organising cupboards. From the other room came not a sound, for clearly Ernst had fallen into a fevered sleep. Eventually, after finally finding the strength to clean out the filthy toilet adjoining the kitchen, he put on the kettle and started to make himself a cup of the rather odd-coloured herbal tea he had discovered in the further reaches of one of the cupboards.

The kettle had just come to the boil when his nephew appeared at the door leading from the living room.

"Holy smoke!" he said. "You've been busy."

Antonin felt genuinely tired from the physical work. But nevertheless he got up and pulled out another mug.

"Do you want one too?" he asked, holding up the packet to show his nephew the tea.

Ernst came into the kitchen and sat down at the table.

"Please," he said, looking round admiringly at the clean kitchen. "And thank you for all this."

"Are you feeling better now?"

"Yes. I think I must have needed the sleep."

Antonin smiled, allowing his eyes to meet Ernst's.

"I'm sorry I gave you the impression I just wanted to find your Dad," he murmured. "That was a bit crass of me."

Ernst nodded but said nothing. Although the fever had passed, the sadness was still there.

"Don't you even want to see your mother any more?" Antonin asked gently.

Ernst grunted uncertainly.

"Do you know her?" he asked.

"No. Stepan must have got married shortly after I left for the West."

"She's a strange woman," Ernst muttered. "I could never make her out."

"Didn't she love you?"

Ernst frowned.

"When I was a child I used to like to fool myself she did. I suppose you have to. But eventually I decided she couldn't."

Antonin looked at him askance.

"Couldn't?"

"That's right. She only really loved Dad. I don't think she could love anyone else. She'd sometimes try, I think, but when the chips were down she'd always choose him. At the end of the day I decided she was useless."

Antonin winced. He could so well remember his own feelings of childhood rejection. Now it seemed the next generation had been destined to suffer the same fate. So now he told him a little about his own childhood experiences.

When he finished speaking there was a long silence. Antonin was expecting a question about what had become of his own parents, Ernst's grandparents, a question to which he had almost decided to give a truthful answer, but no such question came.

"Do you have a family in England?" Ernst asked instead.

"No. I never married."

"Oh. That's sad."

Antonin tried to smile.

"I manage. Do you plan to marry then? Or have your parents put you off?"

Ernst's face hardened.

"If I marry," he said, "I won't marry someone like Mum."

The resentment was deep and hard, if anything deeper and harder against his mother than against his father.

Antonin glanced at his watch. Evening was approaching and he couldn't stay all night. And pleasant though it was to have discovered a nephew he hadn't known he had, it didn't seem as if there was any way Ernst could help him track down Stepan.

"Ernst," he began cautiously, not wishing to return to the subject.

His nephew looked up at him.

"Yes."

"I don't want to explain exactly why, but it really is very important that I find your Dad. Are you sure you can't think where he might be?"

"I told you I don't know."

"The doorman at your old home in Berlin thought he might have come to Vienna."

Ernst looked faintly alarmed.

"Why did he think that?" he asked.

Antonin told him and he shrugged.

"I suppose it 's possible," he said.

"Why do you think so?"

"Because my Dad knew Vienna. He used to come here quite often with his work."

"I thought you said he was internal security."

Ernst nodded.

"He was. But maybe there were dissident groups operating out of Vienna who the Stasi had infiltrated. Anyway, I know he came here because he used to bring Mum and I presents."

Antonin nodded, deciding to try another tack.

"Did he by any chance know a man called Biedermeyer?"

Ernst shook his head.

"It's not a name I know. But he didn't bring a lot of people home with him."

As his nephew spoke he could feel an oppressive sense of powerlessness beginning to overwhelm him. He knew he shouldn't have expected to find anything useful, nothing which would help him find Stepan. He had taken a great liking to Ernst, but Ernst knew no more than he, less perhaps. Back in East Berlin, Stepan had obviously kept his private and public lives well separated. He had confided no more in his son than Antonin's own father had confided in him.

But then perhaps it made no difference. Perhaps Stepan would not help him even if he did find him. His role in the whole operation was so mysterious, his moves so totally unfathomable. And Antonin had no guarantee that he would agree to help a brother with whom he had had no contact since the distant days of his childhood.

Ernst interrupted his thoughts.

"I don't know your name," he said.

Antonin forced his sombre reverie to a close.

"Antonin."

"Antonin. How odd!"

"Why?"

"When I was little I had a pet dog called Antonin. A chubby little fox terrier."

"How come you called him Antonin?"

"Ernst shrugged."

"How should I know? Really it was my parents' pet. I suppose they must have chosen the name."

Antonin looked at him with curiosity. It was odd that Stepan had chosen to name his pet dog after his vanished elder brother. Or maybe, perhaps, it wasn't odd at all.

"I hope it was a nice dog," he muttered.

"Oh yes, a real sweety," Ernst said with a smile. "Just like you really."

The remark was batted off casually, without any advance planning. Yet somehow it suddenly made Antonin want to cry. Ernst must have seen him flinch.

"You're not at all like Dad?" he said wistfully.

Antonin thought for a moment.

"No," he said presently. "No, I don't think I am. Even during all those years he spent in a wheelchair he was always more worldly than me. More capable, I suppose you'd say."

Ernst looked at him sharply.

"A wheelchair?" he said. "Dad was in a wheelchair?"

This time it was Antonin who was shocked.

"Yes. For about ten years during his childhood and adolescence. Surely you knew that?"

Ernst shook his head.

"That's odd. Neither of them ever mentioned it."

Antonin looked at Ernst in amazement. It was an obvious enough fact. Nothing to be ashamed about. Stepan had always been such a brave little fighter.

"Look, Ernst," Antonin said after a while. "Your father didn't

201

mention me, he didn't mention his childhood disability. It sounds like he didn't talk about anything much."

Ernst nodded.

"That just about sums it up."

"Didn't he have old photograph albums, that sort of thing?"

"If he did I never saw them."

"Did he tell you about his parents?"

"No."

"And you didn't ask?"

"I did. He said they were dead." He hesitated for a moment. "They are, aren't they?"

Antonin nodded.

"Yes. Around the time you were born, shortly after I left for the West."

A temporary silence descended.

"Did you know you're only three-quarters German?" Antonin observed, suspecting that Stepan might not have revealed to his son the Czechoslovakian side of the family.

Ernst looked at him with a puzzled expression.

"Three quarters?" he queried.

"Yes. Your Dad's mother was a Slovak. We grew up in Berlin, which is why we speak German, but at home my parents always spoke Slovak with each other." A thought crossed his mind. "I'll bet you didn't even know your Dad spoke Slovak."

As he was speaking he noticed an amused smile cross his nephew's face. He rose slowly to his feet, picked up the two mugs and started busying himself with his back to Antonin preparing some more herbal tea. And then, quietly, he did something quite unexpected.

"I take it you'd like another cup, uncle," he said, and this time, instead of speaking in German, he was speaking in pure accent-free Czech.

Before Antonin could react he turned and smiled.

"Surprised?" he said, continuing in Czech.

Antonin continued to look at him, still utterly speechless, for this was no school-learned language. This was flawless, accentless. The language of a mother's lap.

Ernst smiled.

"Why did you assume my mother was German?" he asked.

Antonin lips tried to move but nothing came out.

"But . . ." he said at last, but the word gradually trailed away.

"She's a pure blooded Czech," Ernst continued. "When my father

202

was there we always spoke German, but with me she always spoke Czech. So as you see, I'm completely bilingual."

But Antonin wasn't listening any more. His mind was over twenty years away, in a student hostel room in Prague.

"Your mother's first name," he asked, his voice scarcely more than a whisper. "What was your mother's first name?"

Ernst had suddenly become aware of the fear which had spread over his uncle's face.

"Are you all right?" he asked anxiously. "You look as if you've come over ill."

Antonin stared helplessly at Ernst.

"Just tell me her name," he repeated. "For Christ's sake tell me your mother's first name."

Ernst looked at him uncertainly for a moment, but when he spoke the word it was open and clear, leaving no room for uncertainty. And as he did so, Antonin could feel his whole life collapsing beneath him. And the dull numbing ache which had filled his soul for so many years was suddenly transformed into the sharp stabbing pain which it had been so long before.

"My mother's first name," Ernst said softly, "is Katrina."

* * * * * *

Antonin paced up and down the tiny room he shared with her in the student digs and looked impatiently at his watch. It was already nearly eleven in the evening and she still hadn't returned from the university. He threw himself down on the bed and absent-mindedly picked up a textbook lying on the bedside table, meaning to read for a while to pass the time until she returned. But soon he realised that it was a pointless exercise, that although his eye would pass obediently along the words no meaning would enter his brain. For in truth there was only one subject about which he could think nowadays, and that was Katrina herself.

As he lay on the bed and waited Antonin was not angry with her for being late but rather impatient. Since they had fallen in love they had both been consumed by a passion so all-consuming that everything else seemed to have faded from their lives. His academic work, her political efforts on behalf of the Dubcek reform movement, all seemed like a distant memory of an earlier life. For in love they had found something far more important than either of these things, a force which seemed to give a higher meaning to their lives.

Soon, he knew, she would be beside him on the bed, their bodies and minds melted once again into a single whole. And even when all physical passion was spent they would simply lie in the intimacy of the night and whisper sweet secrets to each other, anecdotes of their previous lives apart, plans for their future lives together. And he knew it would be long after dawn when they would finally fall asleep.

There was a faint click from the hall outside. Antonin could feel his heart fill with joy and anticipation at her return. He reached over and quickly switched out the light on the bedside table, meaning to trick her into believing that he had fallen asleep whilst waiting for her. Then he lay back on the bed and closed his eyes.

In the blackness he could hear the door to their bedroom opening but there was no other sound. He waited for several moments, expecting to hear the sound of her voice, but there was no sound to be heard. He wondered if she too were playing a trick on him, waiting to see whose nerve would break first. He lay completely still, determined to wait until she came.

But as the seconds stretched out there was still no sound, still no indication that she was present. And finally, deciding that if indeed she was playing a game she had won, he opened his eyes and looked towards the door.

He immediately saw that she was there, her slim figure silhouetted in the doorway against the light shining in the hallway. She was perfectly motionless.

"Katrina!" he whispered anxiously, for something about her made him fearful that something was wrong.

But still she said nothing. Still she remained standing where he had first seen her, a rigid statue framed in the lighted doorway.

Suddenly frightened that she had been attacked, he sat up and leant across to switch on the bedside lamp.

As soon as the light flooded her face the feeling that something had gone horribly wrong was transformed into a certainly, for still she didn't seem to react to him. Her face was completely numb, as if she had seen some terrible horror.

"Katrina!" he said anxiously, swiftly rising from the bed and approaching her. "Katrina what's wrong?"

He was still assuming that the cause was external, that she had been frightened by something or someone. But as he touched her a new fear gripped his heart, for she stepped backwards slightly, as if he were a complete stranger.

In his shock at her physical rejection of him he himself stepped backwards.

"Katrina!" he repeated uncertainly.

She seemed to draw a deep breath.

"I've come to say . . ." she began, her voice strained and oddly subdued, but then her words petered out.

Again Antonin reached out towards her, but this time she pulled back more sharply.

"Don't touch me!" she ordered.

By now the fear Antonin could feel inside was growing so powerful that he found himself scarcely able to draw breath.

But Katrina suddenly seemed calmer.

"I've come to tell you it's over," she said in a voice completely devoid of all emotion.

Antonin stared at her in utter confusion.

"Over?" he whispered. "What do you mean it's over?"

Katrina stared directly at him, her eyes cold and oddly inhuman.

"I mean," she said, "that I will not see you again. I have come to collect my things and leave."

The shock of her words was so complete that Antonin did nothing but stand motionless and stare at her with blank non-comprehension. And before he could think of anything to say she had walked past him to the small wardrobe and started gathering together her clothes, pushing them into a small suitcase she had pulled out from under the bed.

But the paralysis gradually passed. He stepped forward and grabbed her forcibly from behind, pulling her round so that she was facing him.

"Why?" he demanded, but his voice revealed no anger, only total confusion.

This time she made no attempt to pull away but instead remained limp in his grip.

"It was a mistake," she said passively, allowing her eyes once again to meet his. "You were a mistake. And now I must leave."

It was not her words but the look in her eyes which finally made Antonin release her. She turned away and rammed down the lid of the suitcase. And then, without so much as a glance in his direction, she picked up the case and walked swiftly out of the room.

* * * * * *

He only gradually became aware of Ernst's presence again. The young man was sitting opposite him at the small kitchen table, watching his uncle's reactions in silent confusion.

"Katrina!" Antonin repeated slowly. And then, without another

205

word, he reached into his wallet and pulled out a small faded photograph which he had carried with him for over twenty years. It was a photograph he had not shown to any other person since the day he had left Czechoslovakia. Silently, he handed it to Ernst.

He examined it for a moment.

"It's definitely my mother," he said presently, laying the photograph back down on the table.

Antonin picked it up and stared at it for a long time. He could remember every second of their brief life together, every superficially trivial moment which at the time and ever since had assumed for him such profound importance.

Eventually he laid the photograph down and looked at Ernst. For something had suddenly occurred to him.

"When is your birthday?" he asked.

Ernst's look of bewilderment magnified several times.

"My birthday?"

Antonin nodded.

"April 10th"

"Yes, but in which year?"

"1969."

Antonin stared at him in amazement. For the calculation was not a hard one to make.

Ernst picked up the photograph again with redoubled interest.

"You knew my mother?" he asked cautiously.

Antonin looked at him.

"When I was young she was my fiancée. We lived together for a while. Suddenly one day – only a short while before the Warsaw Pact tanks invaded Czechoslovakia in August 1968 – she left me."

Ernst looked at him in astonishment.

"What? With your brother?"

Antonin looked at him sadly.

"So it would seem," he murmured.

Ernst was counting something out on his fingers. When he had finished his eyes looked up and met Antonin's.

"Is it possible . . ." he began, but the words just petered out.

Antonin nodded slowly.

"I always thought," he said, "that the legacy of Katrina in my life was entirely negative. But now I see that maybe it was not."

And as he said the words he could suddenly feel an overwhelming happiness spreading through his mind. It was a joy so complete that he dared not believe it would last, for it was sweeping away a great emptiness which had been there for many years. For the young man before him was almost certainly his son.

Ernst was clearly struggling to control the enormity of the revelations Antonin was throwing at him.

"But what on earth did you see in my mother?" he asked abruptly, the words those of a young man who was still finding it difficult to come to terms with a loveless childhood.

His question forced Antonin's mind back to Katrina. For she was no longer history, she was real again, quite possibly walking around somewhere in the very city in which he now found himself.

He looked at Ernst.

"She was so vivacious, so independent of spirit, and yet so warm. It's hard to describe." He spoke of her as he chose to remember her during all except his darkest nightmares.

Again Ernst frowned, and when he eventually spoke there was no trace of sentimentality in his voice.

"No she wasn't!" he announced with a sharp finality that permitted of no contradiction. "She wasn't like that at all."

* * * * * *

Ernst stood by the window and watched the street below with scarcely concealed impatience. He looked older than when Antonin had first arrived, the fresh and rather carefree manner he had displayed on their first encounter replaced by strained and cautious anxiety. Antonin watched him silently from the door of the kitchen and then stepped quietly into the living room, laying down the tray of sandwiches he had prepared on top of the French horn case which doubled as the room's coffee table. Only then did he subside into the nearby armchair.

After a while Ernst turned away from the window and came to join him, sitting cross-legged on the floor. He picked up a tuna fish sandwich and started mechanically munching through it, his mind far away. Then he looked up.

"Even if she hears I still don't think she'll come," he muttered.

Antonin frowned, for he was none too sure himself.

"Any better ideas?" he asked softly.

Ernst picked up another sandwich but said nothing. Three days earlier a brief message had gone out over the Austrian national radio networks, a message that a young man called Ernst Ziegler was unwell and trying to get in contact with his estranged mother, one Katrina Ziegler, last known to be living in the Vienna area. At around the same time Ernst had contacted all the people he knew in Berlin who had been acquainted with his parents, asking them to make contact with her if they possibly could.

"Stepan's got very long ears," Antonin muttered, taking a large bite out of his sandwich. "I think he'll get to hear about it one way or another."

Ernst looked glum.

"What if he comes instead?"

Antonin shook his head.

"You told me Stepan never bothered with you. But you also said Katrina did care for you after a fashion, provided that Stepan's interests weren't affected. So as long as Stepan doesn't suspect my involvement, and there's no reason to believe that he'll have worked that out, then I think there's a good chance he'll either let her come, or perhaps find a way to let you go to see her. Either way we're ready."

Ernst put down his half finished sandwich and walked over to the window again to examine the morning bustle in the street outside.

"But it's already been three days since the broadcast."

Antonin remained seated, for they had already agreed he would not approach the window lest he be seen from outside.

"We'll just have to hope," he said quietly, remembering how his previous plan had come to nought. Ernst must have read his mind.

"Are you thinking about your trip to Pamhagen?" he said, turning round.

Antonin nodded silently, because he was indeed thinking of the professionalism with which the so-called Natural Science Research Centre in which he had been detained with his grandfather had been quietly closed down, leaving no clue as to where its occupants might have gone. For although it seemed likely that the centre had been intended to be the place where the research into the Oblanov technique could be undertaken, the group with whom Stepan was involved had clearly decided that Antonin's escape required the complete relocation of their operations to a new and secure premises.

But all thoughts of the empty building in Pamhagen were abruptly cut short when he noticed Ernst's body suddenly tensing. Moments later he pulled back from the window and flicked an anxious glance towards Antonin.

"A Mercedes has just pulled up outside," he said apprehensively.

"Katrina?" Antonin asked, rising to his feet.

"No. An elderly man, not Stepan. It might be nothing."

Ernst was trying hard to conceal the rising tension in his voice. Antonin edged over to the empty wardrobe standing in one corner of the room which was his prearranged hiding place.

Moments later, their was a sharp knock on the front door and Antonin stepped inside, pulling the wardrobe door firmly shut behind him.

A few moments later he could hear the click as Ernst opened the front door of the flat.

"Ernst Ziegler?" came a voice which Antonin instantly recognised as that of Herr Schmidt, the polite little man who had escorted him to Pamhagen on his previous visit to Vienna.

"Yes," came Ernst's voice.

"I've been sent by your mother. She heard you were unwell and were trying to contact her."

There was a pause.

"Where is she?" Ernst asked.

"She's here in Vienna, staying with your father, but she couldn't come herself. She asked me to pick you up."

There was a short silence.

"Why couldn't she come herself?" Ernst asked, his voice slightly slurred as if he were ill.

"She's not very well herself, I'm afraid," Herr Schmidt replied. "That's why she asked me to come."

"What's the matter with her?"

"Nothing serious, just an attack of flu. I expect she'll be over it in a few days."

There was a long silence. Then Ernst's voice again.

"Where exactly is she?"

This time the silence was brief.

"I'm afraid I can't tell you that," came Herr Schmidt's softly spoken reply.

"Why not?"

"It's a little difficult, to do with your father's situation. You know it's been a difficult time for him."

He could hear Ernst grunt.

"You mean Dad's gone into hiding, is that what you're saying? Is that why nobody knows where he is in Berlin?"

"Shall we say he's just waiting to see how events develop."

"But I'm his son," Ernst replied angrily. "I might not always see eye to eye with him but I'm not going to turn him in, if that's what you mean."

"Your Dad thought it best if you didn't know," Herr Schmidt said apologetically. "I'm not authorised to say where he is."

"But if I come with you I'll know where they are anyway," Ernst retorted.

There was a long silence, and Antonin suddenly realised that Ernst was being invited along the very same road he had once travelled with Herr Schmidt, a one-way road down which there would be no immediate return.

Then he could hear Ernst's voice again.

"Since mother's so keen to keep her whereabouts a secret from me you'd better give her this," he said rather crossly. "When she feels able to, she should come and see me here herself."

Antonin listened anxiously, his ear pressed against the wardrobe door. For he knew there was an outside chance that the older man would have instructions to take him along by force.

"Very well then," Herr Schmidt replied, if anything faintly relieved, "I'll give her the note. Is there anything else I can do for you before I leave? I have money if you need some."

"No. I'll be all right. Just tell her to come when she can. Tell her I want to see her again."

There was the sound of the door closing. Moments later, the wardrobe door flew open.

"Come on," Ernst called, already running to the front door, "we've got to go."

* * * * * *

Fortunately the Mercedes was not travelling too fast. Seeing it slow down as it approached a set of traffic lights some way ahead, Ernst gently applied the brakes.

"Where do you think he's heading," Antonin asked.

"He's indicating left – that might mean he's going out of town. If he is, then he's probably heading west."

They drew to a halt some eight or nine cars behind Herr Schmidt. Ernst's face was drawn and tense.

"If he's good at his job then he'll spot us," he muttered.

Antonin smiled grimly. Of late he had been becoming increasingly used to this kind of activity. Perhaps, after all, a little of Stepan's taste for the cloak and dagger had rubbed off on his older brother.

"I don't think they've connected you with me yet," he observed dryly. "That probably means Schmidt won't be concentrating too hard."

The traffic lights started to change and Ernst eased his car into gear. Moments later they were speeding down towards the next junction.

Now the Mercedes indicated right.

"That's it," Ernst declared. "Now we know. He's heading for the motorway to Salzburg."

Antonin tried to relax in his seat as Ernst followed their quarry onto the broad dual carriageway leading out of town towards the motorway. For they were both hoping that the messenger would lead them straight back to the source of the message.

Suddenly Ernst tensed.

"Why's he slowing down again?" he asked anxiously.

The Mercedes was indeed slowing down for no apparent reason. Ernst braked gently.

"Damn," Antonin said. "He must have been doing this kind of thing for so long that he checks for tails instinctively."

The Mercedes had slowed down to about thirty kilometres an hour, far too slow for the broad dual carriageway along which they were travelling. Ernst had already taken the decision to overtake him along with the other traffic, for any other course of action would undoubtedly have drawn attention to their presence.

They approached the Mercedes and overtook it. And as they did so it was Antonin who tensed. For Herr Schmidt was quietly examining the occupants of each and every car which drove past.

"Damn!" he exclaimed. "I think he might have seen us."

He could sense the shiver of fear running through Ernst beside him.

"He's probably phoning through right now," Antonin muttered.

But already the Mercedes was moving again, this time behind them. Ernst started to accelerate, but as he did so the Mercedes also began to speed up.

And with a dreadful sinking feeling, Antonin realised that suddenly the tables had been completely turned, that now it was Herr Schmidt who was following them.

Ernst's eyes were constantly flicking backwards and forwards between the road in front and the rear view mirror.

"Holy smoke," he muttered. "Now what do I do?"

Antonin glanced back again.

"Turn off when we get to the next junction and head back towards town. It'll be easier to give him the slip where it's crowded."

The Mercedes was rapidly gaining ground on them.

A slip road loomed up ahead. Ernst pulled out into the fast lane, as if he meant to go straight on. But then, right at the last minute, he forced the wheel round and pulled the car violently across into the slip road.

"Damn," he exclaimed, as the Mercedes succeeded in swerving after them.

In front another set of traffic lights loomed. They were at red, with waiting cars completely blocking the road ahead.

Ernst had no choice but to slow down and stop. As he did so the Mercedes drew up beside them in the neighbouring lane. Inside Herr Schmidt was looking at them and smiling, the small revolver in his hand aimed directly at Ernst's head.

The lights were still red. Ignoring the terrified look on the faces of the nearby motorists, he climbed quietly out of the Mercedes and pulled open the rear door of Ernst's car, his gun not wavering for a moment.

"Look," he observed with a smug smile as he settled into the back seat, "the lights have changed."

Ernst drove on, following Herr Schmidt's softly spoken instructions to rejoin the main road towards the west.

Antonin glanced round, hoping that a police car alerted by one of the startled motorists would intercept them.

"In my experience the police usually take a little time to get themselves organised," Herr Schmidt observed, as if reading his mind. "And by the time they do we'll have left this car far behind."

He pulled a small mobile phone out of his pocket and exchanged a few words.

"Pull off at the next junction," he ordered, indicating a large out-of-town shopping centre several hundred yards ahead.

Ernst did as he was told, bringing the car to a halt as instructed in the car park.

"Now get out," Herr Schmidt continued. "And remember, I will use this weapon if I need to."

Antonin and Ernst stepped reluctantly out of the car. Moments later a large Range Rover drew up beside them.

Herr Schmidt opened the rear door.

"After you," he said, waiting for them to enter before doing so himself. And then the car moved quietly off and rejoined the main road.

For a long time nobody said anything. Then Antonin, who was sitting in the middle of the rear seat, turned towards Herr Schmidt.

"Where are we going?" he asked.

Herr Schmidt turned and smiled the same courteous smile which never seemed to leave his face.

"I think, Dr Ziegler, that you know that as well as I."

They travelled on in silence for many miles along the motorway, climbing high through the wooded hills which lay to the west of Vienna. The weather was dreary and overcast, making the densely packed fir trees appear dark and sombre, like some evil forest from a medieval fairy tale. They reminded Antonin of that other forest, far away in Slovakia, where he had first encountered the sinister group of people with whom his brother had chosen to make common cause. He remembered the gratuitous brutality with which their Slovakian agent had attacked Nadja, the cold calculating rage with which Biedermeyer had ordered Scudder's execution back in his Oxford rooms. And now, most recently, he thought of the way in which Stepan had stolen Katrina from him following that fleeting visit to Prague all those years before.

Antonin flinched at the thought of seeing Katrina again, for he was sure that that was what would soon be in store for him, perhaps even this very day. It should have been a happy thought, for often enough over the long years they had been apart he had wished for another glimpse of her, but he knew that the quiet fancies of his waking hours were but an illusion, that the reality of their reunion when it came would be a far from happy one. For Katrina would no longer be the vivacious young student he had known and loved, she would instead be the dull and passive woman he had seen on the day she had told him she was leaving, the woman whom Ernst had known as a mother, the woman Stepan had turned her into.

He looked sideways towards Ernst sitting beside him. He was a handsome young man in many ways, rather like Stepan had been as a young man, his aquiline features enhanced by an alertness which did much to improve his looks. In the few days Antonin had spent with him in Vienna they had already grown close, both happy to fill the vacancy in the father-son relationship which fate had thrust upon them. And now Antonin hoped that his son would not live to regret the day his natural father had chanced upon his life.

The motorway swept gracefully round the brow of a high hill, and as it did so a new vista of high forested hills opened up before them. Far away to their left, nestling in a small wooded valley, Antonin could just make out a small chateau, its steeply sloped roof projecting high above the tree tops.

"Our destination," Herr Schmidt announced softly.

Antonin eyed the building unhappily.

"And is my brother there?" he asked.

Herr Schmidt smiled his enigmatic smile.

"Be patient, Dr Ziegler," he said, "and soon you will see for yourself."

* * * * * *

He had been separated from Ernst as soon as they had arrived, and now Antonin was alone. The room in which he found himself was small yet comfortably appointed, overlooking the central courtyard of what must once have been the hunting lodge of a member of the Viennese aristocracy. The building was on two storeys, with an arcaded balcony running around the first floor of the central courtyard. The somewhat plain effect of the whitewashed walls was softened and enriched by a well-tended garden filled with bright red geraniums, whilst at the centre of the garden a gently tinkling water fountain provided a focus for the wandering eye.

The actual room in which he was being held prisoner was decorated in the richly decorated Gothic style so popular with the Austrian aristocracy at the turn of the century, its dark sombre furniture overlooked by austere staring eyes protruding from the stuffed heads of hunting trophies hanging from the walls. For several hours now he had paced up and down in this room, locked in a private world of doubt and insecurity. Outside in the courtyard there had been no movement since their arrival, and the whole place seemed to exude a forlorn atmosphere which matched exactly his own mood.

Suddenly there was a click and the heavy wooden door swung open. And there, before him, he could see his younger brother once more, leaning on his stick, his eyes fixing Antonin with a strangely enigmatic look.

Without a word Stepan entered the room and closed the door behind him. He seemed both tired and exalted, as if he were keeping himself going on caffeine, laced perhaps with other less natural drugs.

This time Antonin made no move to embrace him as he had done the previous time they had met. Instead he stood silently before his brother and captor, reluctant to speak the first word.

Stepan inclined his head by way of greeting.

"Are you comfortable?" he enquired.

Antonin nodded but said nothing. Oddly enough, despite the circumstances of their encounter, he was sure he could detect a slight tremor of fear in Stepan's voice, an uncertainty as to quite how to deal with his older brother.

Stepan shifted uneasily on his cane. He seemed to want to sit, yet Antonin remained standing.

"So you know," he said at last, and again there was the slight tremor of fear in his voice.

Antonin frowned.

"I know about Katrina, if that is what you mean," he said. "What I don't know is why."

The pain in Stepan's leg was clearly troubling him despite whatever drugs he was taking. Giving up the attempt to remain standing, he hobbled over to a chair and eased himself into it. Then he looked up at Antonin with weary eyes.

"Haven't you worked it out yet?" he asked. "When I realised you'd discovered Ernst I really thought you might have seen through the whole thing."

Suddenly the latent anger within Antonin flared.

"Maybe I have worked it out, Stepan," he snarled, "but even if I have I still want to hear it from your own mouth."

Stepan looked at him with a strained face.

"It was really nothing more than a kind of joke," he muttered.

Antonin wasn't sure he'd heard right.

"A joke?"

"Maybe not a joke. More an experiment, I suppose you'd say."

This time Antonin's speechlessness was not feigned.

Stepan shifted uncomfortably in his seat.

"I wasn't planning to keep her," he said glumly. "I was just testing it out to see whether it really worked."

Antonin stared at him.

" 'Whether it worked'? Whether what worked?"

Stepan frowned.

"I thought you knew. That little trick they'd stumbled across at Oblanov, the device which could manipulate people's thoughts."

Antonin nodded, for Stepan's words only confirmed a theory he had begun to formulate in Vienna several days before.

"So you had it in your possession? Back in 1968, you had it?"

Stepan smiled grimly.

"Had it, then lost it," he muttered.

He paused for a moment, as if trying to decide whether to continue.

"There's really no reason you shouldn't know everything now, Antonin," he muttered at last with a finality which made Antonin shiver, "so I might as well tell you the whole story."

He paused again, this time removing a small pill from a tin in his pocket and popping it into his mouth. Only when it was gone did he continue.

"It was near the end, shortly before Dad's death, but at the time he was still uncertain what to do. He wasn't a strong man, and as I told you before I think he wanted to share the secret with someone. So one day he told me exactly what they'd discovered at Oblanov. He wanted to convince me he was telling me the truth, so late one evening he connived to take me to the institute with him."

Stepan stood up painfully and hobbled over to the window. He gazed out at the courtyard for a few moments before turning back to face Antonin.

"While I was there, at the institute, I managed to steal one of the prototypes."

"You just picked it up and took it?" Antonin asked. "Just like that?"

Stepan looked at him with a wry smile.

"It wasn't very big, just like the one you found in the briefcase, except my one came complete with the tape. While Dad's back was turned I just pushed it into my bag and took it along. It was really as easy as that."

Antonin looked at his brother numbly. For what had happened next was really transparently clear.

"And then you tested it on Katrina?"

Stepan nodded.

"I wanted to try it out, see if it worked. And when you introduced me to her she seemed like the perfect challenge."

Antonin remembered his previous words.

"A joke, perhaps?"

Stepan looked away.

"Perhaps, Antonin, perhaps."

Despite all his efforts, Antonin now found himself beyond rage. He stared blankly at Stepan, unable to comprehend how such an idea could possibly have come into his head. For it seemed a very strange way to reward the loyalty he had always shown to his little brother when he had been a defenceless disabled child.

"I didn't mean to keep her from you," Stepan continued, as if by way of excusing himself. "Believe me that was never my original intention. All I wanted was to see if I could persuade her to leave you, because that was something I was sure she would never have done of her own free will. So after I saw you that last time in Prague I returned and asked her to visit me at the hotel where I was staying. She came up to my room and I told her I wanted to play her a tape recording I thought she might find interesting. I sort of intimated it might have had a political content."

Stepan's face darkened.

"When we were alone in the room I turned the thing on just as Dad had told me to do. The room was filled with a high-pitched stream of white noise. While it was playing I instructed her to love and obey me. Then I turned it off. It was as simple as that, but I could immediately see in her face that Dad hadn't been joking about the power they'd discovered. Before she had been wary of me, only there at all because of her loyalty to you, yet now she was looking at me with slavish devotion. And even before I spoke again I knew she would do whatever I asked. But just to be certain I told her to go to your room and tell you that she was leaving you for good. I said she should pack her things and return to my hotel."

Antonin looked at him numbly, for it seemed to him incredulous that for so many long years he had been the victim of nothing more than a cruel practical joke.

Stepan must have read his thoughts.

"I swear I was planning to reverse it, Antonin. I didn't really intend to take her away from you for good. When she got back to the hotel I was going to reprogramme her, wipe her memory free of her encounter with me and simply send her back to you again to say that it was all a little joke. But when I turned the machine back on again nothing came out. It was a complete blank. As some kind of security precaution the tape had been constructed so that it automatically wiped clean once it had been played."

Antonin looked at his brother thoughtfully, for suddenly Stepan's subsequent behaviour towards her was beginning to make sense.

"So Katrina was your only chance to use this power?" he said.

Stepan nodded, a grim smile slowly spreading across his face.

"Yes, Antonin. Until now she was my only chance."

For a while they both remained silent, but then Antonin looked at his brother glumly.

"That story about working for Western Intelligence was rubbish, wasn't it Stepan?" he said.

Stepan nodded.

"I'm afraid that was Biedermeyer's idea. He thought you might agree to co-operate if we could only persuade you we were working for your side."

"Biedermeyer?" Antonin asked, not relishing another encounter with the man. "Is Biedermeyer here too?"

"No, Antonin," Stepan replied, and as he spoke the words

Antonin was sure he could detect a faint triumph in his voice. "Biedermeyer's dead, but he was useful while he lasted."

Antonin decided to ignore the implications of his last remark.

"Biedermeyer was East German intelligence, wasn't he, Stepan? A Stasi man on the run. Just like all the others involved in this little club of yours."

Stepan nodded.

"They're not just East Germans. Some are from Czechoslovakia. There are a lot of frightened people running around in Eastern Europe at the moment. It was Biedermeyer's idea to set up the group and it was under his own command. But now he's dead it's effectively mine."

"So is that why you want the Oblanov technique?" Antonin asked uncertainly. "Do you have some plan to use it to help restore communism?"

Stepan smiled enigmatically.

"That's why Biedermeyer wanted it. He was a man of the old school, a backward-looking man. A device to control the fickle political mood of the masses would have been very useful to him and his fellow communists."

Antonin frowned.

"You sound as if you have a different agenda," he observed.

Stepan smiled again.

"But you forget I was Stasi too, Antonin. If I'd wanted to hand Katrina to the communist political establishment I'd have done so many years ago. But I always knew they would just have taken her from me and cut me out."

"So you bided your time," Antonin murmured.

"I'm not quite sure yet what I'll do," Stepan continued, as if he hadn't heard Antonin speak. "But what I do know for sure is that I want it."

Antonin shook his head sadly.

"Why?" he said. "Is it really that you want more Katrinas? Was your conquest of her so very satisfying?"

Stepan suddenly looked away, clearly hurt by Antonin's remark.

"You always were so insufferably pure," he retorted, the anger in his voice sharp and clear.

The sheer force of his words caught Antonin by surprise.

"And what do you mean by that?"

"Nobody else but you would question why someone would want to possess power. Everybody wants power. Every businessman trying to carve a market, every politician trying to win an election, every priest and every mullah trying to hoodwink the masses into believing their version of reality, every man trying to win the affections of a woman. History is nothing more nor less than the story of people using all their wit and guile to win control over other people's minds and actions. It's fundamental human nature. I am at least no different to all the others of my species. It is only you who thinks you can stand above the rest of us in your moral purity and lecture us about the fragile sanctity of the human mind. You really are insufferable."

Antonin stared at his little brother in utter amazement, for the hatred was clear to behold. It ran deep and hard, the resentment of a lifetime bursting forth. And suddenly it made Antonin want to cry.

"What have I ever done to you to deserve all this?" he said. "You stole my wife and my dignity. You even stole my son. And now you stand there and lecture me about moral purity. Is this really what I deserved for all those years I pushed you around in that wheelchair?"

At this Stepan suddenly turned to face him, his face now white with anger.

"Oh yes," he said, almost spitting out the words. "You loved that little wheelchair of mine, didn't you? You could push me around and feel the righteous glow of your own insufferable goodness. You could bask in the pale reflected light of my own misery, relishing your glorious generosity while I remained trapped."

He stopped for a while, as if wondering whether or not to continue.

"I've sometimes even wondered," he said, "whether you actually pushed me into that pit."

The deluge suddenly stopped, Stepan's anger subsiding into a kind of passive vacuum. Antonin stared at him in total horror, remembering the long years of Stepan's childhood as if they were only yesterday. He had always been so kind, nothing but kind. And yet all that simple kindness had been twisted and distorted in Stepan's mind into a deep and burning resentment, as if his own childhood powerlessness had all been his older brother's fault.

For a long time neither of them spoke. Stepan remained by the window, staring out into the courtyard. Antonin remained standing on the far side of the room, watching Stepan with silent despair. For it was not in Antonin's character to fight back against his younger brother's accusations. Instead he searched his own conscience to find a way in which he himself could take the blame for everything that had since happened. For in a sense Stepan had been right, there had been a psychological pay-off for him in their childhood relationship, the moral glow that came from always being the giver and never the receiver. And if it had really caused such deep pain, then surely it had been at least partly his fault.

"Is Katrina here?" he asked softly.

Stepan didn't turn. He remained motionless, staring numbly out through the window.

"Yes," he said presently.

"Can I see her?"

"You can see her if you want to. I've finished with her now."

His words brought Antonin up with a jolt.

" 'Finished with her'?" he repeated uncertainly.

Still Stepan didn't turn to face him.

"Surely you worked out there were scientists here," he murmured. "Katrina had been subjected to the original Oblanov technique. Her brain was the vital clue in the research."

Antonin stared at him numbly.

"What have you done to her, Stepan?" he said, the fear in his voice scarcely concealed.

Now Stepan turned to face him, and as he did he could see immediately in his eyes how utterly unimportant Katrina had been to him as an individual. She was, probably always had been, nothing more than a vital tool to help him rediscover the technique she carried locked within her mind. And he had lived with her as man and wife for over twenty years merely to prevent a valuable asset from being mislaid."

"Don't worry, Antonin," he said, "they didn't hurt or damage her in any way. But it was her brain as much as the briefcase you helped us find which enabled us to unlock so quickly the secret which Dad tried to bury."

The past tense was unmistakable, the implication clear.

"And have you now succeeded in recreating the device?" Antonin asked.

Stepan's thin smile returned.

"Oh yes, Antonin, my efforts have not been in vain."

Antonin eyed him unhappily, for he remained utterly uncertain what Stepan proposed to do with the awesome power he now possessed.

"So are you saying you have a device here, Stepan? Do you now have the power to indoctrinate others as you once indoctrinated Katrina?"

Stepan nodded.

"And what will you do? Sell it?"

Stepan smiled.

"You're certainly right there'd be a market. But I don't intend to sell my research. At least not immediately. For the moment I thought it might be more interesting to simply hang on to it, see where it takes me. You see, for the time being I'm proposing to be the only person around who possesses this thing. I alone shall decide when and on whom it is to be used."

Antonin turned away. That Stepan was in one sense mad there was little doubt. A megalomania born of childhood incapacity perhaps. But if it was indeed true that he had recreated the power which had wrested Katrina away from him so many years before, then there was equally little doubt that he would have the intelligence and cunning to use his new toy with discretion. And in one sense, of course, his plan made every sense. With such a device there could be no business partner because the machine could so easily be turned on its creator. Stepan knew full well he was dealing in a world without patents.

"Stepan," he said. "Now you have the power you wanted, what exactly do you propose to do with me and all the other people you've incarcerated?"

Stepan remained silent for a few moments.

"It is not what I will do, it is what I already have done. Do you not notice how quiet it is here?"

"Have you killed them?" Antonin asked softly.

Stepan shook his head.

"No, no, Antonin. Why on earth should I have done such a thing? The technique itself renders such a crude course of action completely unnecessary."

"So you have used the technique to wipe the slate clean. It is I imagine a straightforward enough matter to induce people to forget."

Stepan inclined his head sideways by way of acknowledgement.

"Indeed, Antonin," he said quietly.

There was a long pause during which neither spoke.

"And despite my earlier remarks, Antonin, it is not my desire to heap further personal misery on top of that which I have already caused you."

Antonin looked at him for a moment, unsure if he had correctly understood the implications of his words.

"Are you saying you will release Katrina?" he murmured.

Stepan nodded.

"You may have her if you wish, Antonin. And as a gift, I will programme her to total loyalty if that is your desire." As he spoke he must have seen Antonin flinch, for an impish smile suddenly flashed across his face. "I'm sorry, Antonin, but I forgot your predilections. So if you prefer I will simply restore her to what she was before. I will do now what I had intended to do all those years ago and release her from her somewhat blind loyalty towards me. And then her future will simply be up to her."

Antonin stared at his brother in astonishment. Was this the true extent of the power play in which he was now engaged, the first tentative pulling of the strings? For he could see in Stepan's eyes how much he enjoyed manipulating the feelings and desires of others as if they were nothing but childish toys. Yet he was careful to say nothing which might offend Stepan.

"Thank you," he said instead. "I would very much like to see Katrina again."

Stepan hesitated for a moment, glancing quickly at his watch.

"All right, Antonin," he murmured. "I suppose you've waited long enough. I'll go and see if I can organise something right away."

He moved slowly and painfully towards the door and was just about to leave when he hesitated, turning back to face Antonin.

"There's just one thing I'd like you to know about Katrina," he murmured.

Antonin looked at him uncertainly.

"During all the years of our marriage," Stepan muttered, "I never touched her once."

* * * * * *

The hours passed. Day turned into night. Antonin waited forlornly in his ornate yet sombre prison cell, wondering if Stepan would keep his promise. For the thought of seeing Katrina again after all these years was almost more than he could bear. The void she had filled in his younger days had been so vast, the desolation he had subsequently experienced after her abrupt departure from his life so utterly devastating, that he wondered how he would react when she finally returned to him.

And there was no doubt in his mind that if Stepan freed her she would return. The whole emptiness of his being for the two long decades of their separation had arisen precisely because she had betrayed such a total trust, a trust so deep and enduring that even now he knew that she would be true to him. Yet despite that confidence he was still afraid, still afraid that somewhere deep down their love would be blunted and hardened by the long years of separation. For it was not just their physical looks which would have changed, they had also been separated by twenty years of totally different experiences of life, she the neglected wife of an East German apparatchik, he the life of a lonely bachelor academic. Neither of them were the idealistic young students they had been in Prague in 1968. She would probably have been as sorely wounded by the fate life had inflicted upon her as he had been by his own silent misery, and it was the effects of those wounds on their future relationship together which Antonin now dreaded.

He looked through the window at the empty courtyard outside. It was eerily silent, the moonlight reflecting on the whitewashed walls creating a ghostlike feel to the place. High above a sonorous clock began to strike. There were eleven deep chimes. And then the silence returned.

Suddenly Antonin tensed. For a door was slowly opening on the arcaded balcony running around the first floor of the courtyard. Then, slightly unsteadily, a woman appeared in the moonlight and Antonin knew that it was her. She was older than she had been before, the slim vibrancy of her youth turned into the more reserved poise of middle age. But Antonin's heart nevertheless thrilled at the sight of her, for he had feared that she would somehow have become unrecognisable to him, that the passing of the years would have prevented him from even recognising her if he had chanced upon her in the street.

And then, behind her, Stepan too appeared. He stepped in front of her and led her slowly around the balcony towards the steps leading down to the small garden in the centre of the courtyard. Yet as they approached Antonin could feel a shudder of fear ripple through his body, for as he saw her face more clearly in the moonlight he could clearly make out the same expressionless stare which he had seen the last time he had been with her, and he knew with sickening certainty that Stepan had not yet fulfilled his promise.

Moments later they re-entered the building and were gone.

For ten minutes he waited but nothing happened. But then the door swung slowly open and Stepan was there again. Of Katrina there was no sign.

Stepan stepped into the room, leaning heavily on his cane.

"Where is she?" Antonin asked, for despite himself he was unable to contain his impatience.

Stepan eyed him carefully.

"I thought you might like to see," he muttered.

Antonin stared at him.

"See what?"

"I thought you might like to see just how simple it is to use this device you have helped me recreate."

"Katrina!" he called softly, his voice nothing more nor less than a gentle command.

Moments later she appeared, carrying in her hand a small briefcase. Unlike the last time they had met she looked at him quite calmly, as if she had been thoroughly prepared for the encounter. And yet the very calmness of her manner made Antonin wince.

"Hello Antonin," she said. "It's been a long time."

The courtesy was not forced, the quiet repression in her voice gentle and restrained. And Antonin could see that for her at least the prison cell in which she had been incarcerated had not been overly harsh. It was almost as if she were on a heavy dose of tranquillisers, calming and soothing her every thought.

Antonin threw a desperate glance towards Stepan, but his younger brother only smiled.

"Don't you even want to say hello to her?" he asked.

Antonin shook his head, for it was clear that Stepan had only brought her down in this pathetic state so that he could gloat. He wanted his older brother to know the full extent to which he was now in control. And he also wanted him to know that what he gave he could also take away.

"Why should I say hello?" Antonin asked. He jerked his head towards Katrina.

"She's not Katrina. She never was."

Stepan smiled dryly.

"No," he said. "I don't suppose she is."

Antonin stared at him helplessly. For here he was, utterly dependent on Stepan's will. And there was nothing at all he could do about it.

He could see that Stepan was enjoying his discomfort. He held his hand out to Katrina and she quietly handed him the briefcase. Laying it down on a small carved table, he opened the lid and lifted out what looked like a portable CD player. He picked it up and smiled with scarcely restrained triumph.

"It's so small, isn't it?" he murmured, fingering the machine in his hand. "An appropriate invention for our times."

Antonin stared at the device miserably. For he had no doubt in his mind that Stepan was telling the truth, that the tiny object in his hand possessed in its own way as much power as a nuclear bomb. More perhaps, since unlike the nuclear bomb there was no real reason why the possessor should exercise restraint.

"And is that it?" he asked, although he already knew the answer. Stepan smiled.

"Yes," he said. "Essentially its the same as the one they developed at Oblanov, although now the technology permits a smaller carrying case. You see, it is nothing more nor less than a way of transmitting the correct sonic code to the chosen subject. While the code is being emitted the human mind becomes susceptible to suggestion. There is really no more to it than that."

"So anyone could use it?"

Stepan smiled, his once handsome face distorted by the faint sneer which spread across it.

"Oh yes, anyone at all. Even you could use such a device if you were minded to do so. That is precisely why I have been so careful to ensure that there is only one functional copy. And it is also why I have been careful to ensure that only I know how to activate it. It is not the sort of thing one would wish to leave lying around. It is to be treasured, held in reserve for occasional and very special use."

Antonin stared helplessly at Katrina. His hope that Stepan was simply going to release her was fading fast, overlaid by a dawning realisation that he too was about to be programmed.

"And now you're going to use it on us?" he asked in a voice so faint it was scarcely audible, for a sudden fear had filled his whole being, rather like the fear of death. It was the fear that his mind itself was going to be ripped away from him, as Katrina's had been ripped away from her so many years before, torn out by its roots by way of punishment for the perceived wrongs he had inflicted on Stepan in his childhood.

Stepan smiled, as if enjoying his final revenge. He seemed almost reluctant to turn on the machine and finish the job. It was as if he wanted to relish Antonin's growing fear.

"Yes," he said. "I'm afraid you must both forget all this."

"Everything?" Antonin asked.

Stepan shook his head.

"No, not everything. For you the last six months should suffice, although for Katrina it must necessarily be a little longer. A simple memory block should be sufficient. But there will also have to be a few additional instructions. Before you are released you will naturally have to give me a full account of your movements over the last few months, but also I will try to programme you in such a way that neither of you suffers unduly as a result of your dramatic memory loss. It would seem a pity to release you into each other's arms only to be tormented by the stress of unexplained amnesia. You will perhaps be a little puzzled when you reappear into your new lives, but other than that I would predict no serious side-effects."

Antonin swallowed. He felt like a man condemned to be hanged. And at this very moment the executioner was beginning to fasten the rope around his neck.

For a fraction of a second Antonin wondered whether he could lunge at his brother and somehow overpower him. He was standing some way away on the far side of the room, near the door, with Katrina close beside him. Stepan was not a fit man, he would be easy to bring down. Gingerly he took a step forward.

Stepan suddenly tensed, and immediately Antonin knew that he had seen what was in his mind.

"Katrina," he whispered softly, and she quietly withdrew a small revolver from a pocket in her jacket and aimed it straight at him. All the time her face remained quite expressionless.

"Oh Antonin," Stepan murmured. "You surely wouldn't want to attack me, would you?"

Antonin stepped back again. Strangely enough, the sight of Katrina pointing a gun at him did not distress him any more than he had already been distressed. For she was only the outward form of the Katrina he had loved. The woman who stood before him was a stranger.

"I would if I could, Stepan," he murmured.

Stepan had visibly relaxed, and Antonin could tell that despite the hatred, despite the desire to see Antonin squirm before him, Stepan did not actually wish to see him dead. Somewhere, far beneath the hatred, it suggested the presence of other more complex emotions.

He eyed the small CD player in Stepan's hand warily.

Stepan smiled, and again it seemed to Antonin that he was reluctant to begin the process.

"I used it first on Biedermeyer," he said, his face cold and emotionless.

"Biedermeyer?" Antonin asked. "You said Biedermeyer was dead."

Stepan smiled faintly.

"Yes. An unfortunate accident. Would you believe it but the

strain of our joint enterprise was so great that he climbed out onto the roof of this very building one night and jumped off."

Antonin grunted, for although he felt no love for Biedermeyer the manner of his demise still made him wince.

"Oh yes, I think you'll agree it was a pretty conclusive test," Stepan continued. "You see there are two kinds of command. I call them primary commands and secondary commands. For a primary command the machine itself must be used. So with Biedermeyer I used the simple primary command of obedience, just as with Katrina I once used the twin commands of love and obedience. Thereafter, provided that a primary command of obedience has been applied, secondary commands no longer require the machine itself. The obedience is sufficient. So one day when I was ready I simply instructed Biedermeyer to take his own life."

He paused, eyeing Antonin suspiciously for a few moments.

"Does my action seem callous?" he asked. "Biedermeyer wasn't a very nice man. Had he been allowed to live he was planning to transmit the necessary sonic codes over the airwaves. It would have been crude indoctrination on a mass scale."

Antonin eyed his little brother angrily as he spoke, unable for a fraction of a second to control his feelings.

"Unlike the great and glorious Stepan Ziegler, I suppose?" he observed. "How grateful we all should be."

He regretted the words as soon as he had uttered them. For it was the angry rebuke of the older brother, the very older brother against whom Stepan was so insanely jealous.

Stepan's face clouded, his earlier bragging expression replaced by cold anger.

"I tire of your tedious pomposity," he said. Then, without so much as a glance in her direction, he spoke to Katrina.

"Take out some tape," he commanded.

Katrina turned to the briefcase and took out a large roll of black masking tape.

"For obvious reasons it is necessary that you cannot speak while the machine is switched on," he observed.

Katrina handed the revolver to Stepan and began to approach Antonin. He stepped involuntarily backwards and she paused, sensing he might resist.

"Would you really rather I shot you, Antonin?" Stepan asked coldly. "You know I cannot simply let you go."

Antonin stared at him helplessly, for in truth he knew that Stepan had no choice. He stepped forward passively and allowed Katrina to bind his hands and mouth. The act seemed to amuse Stepan.

"Silenced at last, eh," he muttered.

Again the fear, this time even stronger than before.

"Right," Stepan said, "now, Katrina, bring the tape here."

She did as he said and he bound her too. And as Antonin watched him do so he tried to fill his mind with the thought of her, for like the condemned man who turns to God in his final moments she was his final solace. For if Stepan was as good as his word, then soon at least they would be together again.

He finished his work and sent Katrina back to stand beside Antonin, while he himself began fiddling with the controls on the device, apparently typing in some kind of personal code.

He looked up.

There was not even a glance at Katrina. His eyes were locked on Antonin's, as if he were still relishing every moment of his quiet revenge. And silently, without really knowing why and despite the fact that his hands were bound, Antonin gently edged round so that he could take Katrina's hand in his own.

Stepan glanced quickly down at the machine again.

"Goodbye, Antonin," he murmured, his finger hovering over a small button on the machine. "I don't think we'll be meeting again."

And then with a slight movement of his finger he silently pressed the button.

* * * * * *

Antonin awoke slowly but didn't open his eyes, relishing the comfort of the bed, resisting as he often did the moment when full consciousness would return. He felt warm, his body wrapped snugly in a clean white duvet, and he was dreaming as he often dreamt of Katrina. In his dream they were lying in a large double bed. She was fast asleep beside him, the regular sound of her breathing gentle and reassuring. Her close presence made him want to cling onto sleep a little longer, listening quietly to the regular pattern of her breath. He didn't dare open his eyes, for if he did a part of him sensed that she would vanish, that she would leave him alone once more, leave him as she had left him so many times before.

The breathing beside him became less regular, as if she were waking up herself. It somehow annoyed him, because although he understood that sooner or later he would have to awake fully and leave behind the twilight zone he now inhabited, he regarded it as his prerogative to determine the precise moment at which he would do so. It was after all his dream.

"Antonin?" came an uncertain whisper beside him, and it was indisputably Katrina's voice. The voice was so close that he could feel the warmth of her breath on his face. It frightened him in a strange sort of way, because he could not remember a time when Katrina had spoken gently to him in his dreams.

It was the apprehension which caused him to open his eyes. He didn't want her to speak, because the only time she ever spoke to him it was in the cold emotionless voice with which she had told him she was leaving. As he opened his eyes he was fully expecting her to disappear, to find himself alone in his Oxford rooms, engulfed once more by that suffocating sensation of loneliness which was always the daytime legacy of his dreams of Katrina.

But she was still there. Her face was only inches away from his. It was an older face than the one he remembered, but it was still the same face. It was still Katrina.

"Antonin, is that you?" she asked uncertainly, and this time he could hear a distinct shiver of anxiety in her voice.

Her anxiety caused all vestiges of sleep to leave him. He suddenly became aware of the fact that not only was Katrina really beside him but also that he was in an unfamiliar bedroom, smartly appointed but slightly impersonal, rather like a hotel room. Even the pyjamas he was wearing were not his own.

Katrina was looking at him with uncertainty and confusion in her face.

"What's happened?" she asked. "You look so . . .so different, so old. What's happened to you?"

Antonin wondered if it really were a dream after all. Why was Katrina with him now? How had he found her? But try as he might he simply couldn't remember a thing.

"It is you, isn't it, Katrina?" he asked, although he was sure that it was.

She nodded, but as she did so a thought seemed to occur to her. Wearing only her night-dress, she rose from the bed and walked to the nearby dressing table. As she looked at herself in the mirror he could hear her draw breath sharply. She turned to him with fear in her face.

"I . . .I must have lost my memory. I . . . I can only remember being young."

Antonin stepped over to her. Unlike her, the anxiety in his mind at his own loss of memory was mixed with an almost uncontrollable joy. For she was with him, and nothing else seemed to matter.

"What year do you suppose it is?" he asked hesitantly.

She looked again at the mirror, then turned to him anxiously.

"I remember it as being 1968, but it isn't, is it?"

For a while he said nothing. For his part he thought it was December 1989, but outside the sun which was streaming though the curtains was not a dull wintry sun, it was the bright strong sun of summer. He walked over to the window and pulled open the curtains. The room they were in was fairly high up, on the fifth or sixth floor perhaps, and outside was a busy city street full of shops. There were trams on the street and the signs on the shops were all in German.

"I'm not sure, Katrina," he said, reluctant to compound her own alarm by his own obvious loss of memory.

There was a television in the corner of room and he quietly switched it on. There was an advertisement for some kind of catfood, the price displayed in Austrian schillings. He flicked over to teletext to see the date.

"It's September 1990," he murmured uncertainly, "and the most recent thing I can remember is December last year."

He was straining hard at his memory. But it was definitely December 1989. He was in Oxford and it was the end of the autumn term. He remembered he was thinking of going to Slovakia the following summer. Had he gone and somehow found her there? Was that why they were together again?

Katrina stared at him.

"1990," she murmured, her eye falling back incredulously onto the image of her own face in the mirror.

"But I can't remember a thing, Antonin," she said. "If it's really 1990 then the last twenty-two years of our marriage has simply been wiped out from my mind."

Her words were uttered with such innocence. Even in her present state of total confusion it was something she clearly took for granted. They had been engaged in 1968, he was with her now, it was pretty obvious that they had been married all those years.

"But do we have any children?" she asked uncertainly.

"No," he said quietly, unsure how to tell her what he knew. "No we haven't."

She looked at him sadly, as if the news came as a disappointment. And Antonin suddenly realised he had to tell her what he knew.

It was several hours before he finished speaking. He told her of the way she had left him, of his departure for England and his rise to a position of respectability in the English academic establishment. He told her of his loneliness over the years, and of how he had always dreamt of her returning to him. And finally he told her of his theory that he had somehow been successful in his quest.

"And that," he concluded, "is everything I know. Of what happened to you in the intervening period I have no idea."

"And you don't know why I suddenly left you?" she asked.

Antonin shook his head.

"I don't know. I simply don't know. I think that was why I could never really build a new life."

She glanced at him unhappily.

"Perhaps," she said in a quiet voice. "Perhaps that is why I have forgotten. Perhaps that is my punishment for being so unspeakably cruel."

Antonin looked at her and nodded. It was as good a theory as any. And perhaps after all she was lucky to have forgotten the twenty-two missing years of their separation, years which he himself had found so very hard to endure.

"Why don't we simply forget the past, Katrina?" he continued. "The whole of my adult life I've been locked up in the past. Now all I want is to live for the present and the future."

She thought for a while and then rose up from the chair beside the dressing table. She stood silently before him. It was almost as if she too had made an inward decision not to probe the missing years of her past life too deeply.

"I look so old," she said uncertainly. "Do you still find me attractive?"

Antonin could feel tears of joy running down his cheeks. He reached out to her and drew her gently towards him, lowering her onto the bed. And as his hands began to caress her, he knew with inner certainty that the silent nightmare of impotence which had haunted his adult years was very soon about to end.

* * * * * *

Katrina lay on the bed and stared morosely at the ceiling of their hotel bedroom. She seemed distant, as if she were engaged in an intense internal struggle. Once or twice Antonin had tried to speak to her, but she had brushed his remarks aside before returning to her own private world. So now he had given up trying to talk to her and was standing by the open window, lost in silent thought.

For some reason he didn't quite understand, certain things

seemed perfectly self-evident. They needed time together, time when they could be alone and rebuild their relationship. So he would not take her back to Oxford yet. They were now in Vienna. So perhaps they should go south, to Italy, rent a small villa somewhere in the depths of the countryside.

He glanced round at her lovingly, intending to ask her what she thought.

"Katrina," he began, but no sooner had he opened his mouth than she suddenly rose to her feet and went into the adjoining bathroom. For a while he could hear the sound of her splashing cold water over her face. Soon however she returned, and again, just as before, she seemed to be conducting some kind of internal struggle.

"Antonin," she murmured, "I'm not sure, but something strange is happening. I keep seeing shadows I don't understand."

Antonin looked at her with a faintly annoyed expression, for he didn't really understand why she didn't seem to be sharing in his overwhelming sense of happiness.

"What kind of shadows?" he asked, giving up the attempt to tell her about his honeymoon plans.

Her face was strained.

"They're like faint images. There are rooms. The rooms are very modern and clean. And I can see a child in my mind, a little boy."

She suddenly sat bolt upright, rigid and alert.

"Ernst!" she said. "That's his name! It's Ernst!"

Antonin looked at her blankly, for none of what she said made any sense at all to him. If he felt anything at all, it was that he was a complete idiot.

Again she went to the bathroom, splashing yet more cold water onto her face. It was as if she were struggling to clear her brain.

She returned and pushed her head through the open window, drawing the fresh air deeply into her lungs. Then she turned once again to face him. She looked at him anxiously.

"Who is Ernst?" she asked uncertainly.

Antonin shook his head. He didn't want to hurt her feelings, but he certainly wished she'd just relax a bit and enjoy his company. After twenty-two years of separation he wasn't really interested in talking about anyone called Ernst. He'd rather she was talking about him.

"You don't know a boy called Ernst?" she persisted.

Again he shook his head.

"No, Katrina, I don't. Perhaps it's a faint memory coming back."

Katrina was staring at him hard, as if he were the only fixed reference point in a blurred and confusing world. For unlike him, she didn't seem at peace with herself at all.

"I remember him so clearly," she said. "I remember a baby, and a little boy, and then a teenager. Perhaps he was my son."

Antonin frowned. If she had a son she had a husband. And if that was the case it would make everything so much more complicated. He thought wistfully of the little Italian villa, of sitting on the terrace with Katrina and watching the evening sun setting over the warm Mediterranean landscape. He really didn't want all this pointless probing into the past.

"Does it really matter, Katrina?" he said tentatively. "We're together, that's what matters. Why can't we just enjoy it?"

But Katrina didn't seem to be listening. Instead she seemed to shudder inwardly, as if a great wave of returning memory had suddenly washed over her.

"Oh my God!" she exclaimed, staring at Antonin with a horrified expression.

He took a sudden step towards her, worried that she might faint.

"Now I remember," she mouthed.

She looked at Antonin in consternation.

"It was Stepan," she announced.

Antonin met her gaze with blank non-comprehension.

"Stepan? Stepan who?"

"Your brother Stepan. All this is his doing."

He looked at her and swallowed, having no idea whatsoever what she was talking about.

"My brother Stepan," he murmured. "But I haven't seen Stepan for decades."

Katrina's face was changing. The perplexed confusion was gradually clearing, gradually being replaced by a look of hard cold anger.

She looked up at Antonin.

"Now I can remember everything," she announced quietly.

He stared at her blankly. Intellectually it struck him as odd, but he didn't want her memory to return. He knew it was only polite to ask her what she could remember, but still he didn't want to.

But now, somewhat to his surprise, he saw that she was looking at him with a face full of pity.

"You don't want to think about the past, do you Antonin?" she said softly.

He shook his head. In the face of Katrina's new-found vitality he

233

felt like a little child beside her. He really didn't know what to do or say.

"Not really," he mumbled.

"Poor Antonin," she said softly.

He flinched at her words. He didn't feel like poor Antonin. He felt happy, happy beyond measure. After all, he had her back.

"Me," he said. "I'm all right, Katrina. I'm so pleased we're ..."

His words trailed away, for again he could see the pity in her eyes.

"I suppose it's as if you've been drugged, isn't it, Antonin?" she said.

This time Antonin really couldn't help but be surprised.

"What do you mean I've been drugged?" he asked faintly.

Katrina approached him and steered him towards the bed.

"Sit down," Antonin," she said gently, "and I'll do my best to explain."

* * * * * *

Katrina sat quietly by the window in the small coffee house, maintaining a watchful eye on the apartment block on the other side of the street. The coffee cup in front of her was long since empty.

"Do you want another one?" Antonin asked, eyeing the empty cup absent-mindedly, "or perhaps something to eat?"

She glanced at him quickly and tried to smile a reassuring smile, rather as a frightened mother might throw a reassuring smile at a small child.

"No, Antonin," she said, "but you go ahead and have something if you want."

Antonin summoned the waiter and ordered a small beer. Then he slouched back morosely into his chair and watched Katrina as she maintained her silent vigil.

Her attempt at explaining everything had left him feeling quite numb. She had started saying such extraordinary things to him. What she had said should have been interesting, of course. But somehow it wasn't interesting, somehow he just didn't want to know. Eventually he had told her so.

So Katrina had suddenly stopped telling him, given up he supposed. Instead she had just asked him to trust her and do exactly what she said. That was easier. He had agreed. So now he found himself sitting in this rather quaint coffee house in a smart district of Vienna while Katrina watched the block of flats opposite.

Suddenly she tensed.

"There he is," she murmured, more to herself than to him.

Antonin looked out of the window. And there, just entering the building, was a middle-aged man walking with the help of a stick.

Antonin stared after him uncertainly.

"Stepan?" he asked.

Katrina nodded but said nothing, knowing it was utterly pointless talking to Antonin in his present state.

"Good," she muttered, "he's alone. That means I'll have a chance."

She looked at Antonin.

"Do you remember what to do?" she asked.

He nodded.

"Stay put until you return," he said.

Katrina stood up and came round the table, kissing him gently on the cheek.

"Remember that whatever happens I'll always love you, Antonin," she said.

Antonin looked up into her face like a frightened child. Things were happening to him, things he didn't understand. But he knew that Katrina he could trust.

"I love you too," he said, but she had already turned and left.

As he watched her cross the road and disappear into the apartment block after Stepan, Antonin tried to work out why he didn't really seem to care about anything that was happening around him. Katrina had said nothing to him about the purpose of her visit, or indeed about anything else. And he for his part had not asked her what she was proposing to do. She had asked for his trust and he had given it freely, and that was quite enough for him.

Half an hour elapsed before she returned. She came swiftly back out of the door through which she had entered and came over to the join Antonin, a kind of triumphant savage smile on her face.

"Come on Antonin," she said, pushing some money rapidly into the hand of a passing waiter, "he's waiting for you."

Antonin rose to his feet and followed her quite passively into the apartment block. There was a lift inside and they went up to the second floor before walking down a short corridor to a door. Then, pulling out a set of keys from the pocket of her jacket, she swiftly opened the door and stepped inside.

Antonin followed her and then stopped dead in his tracks. For there, lying on the floor with his hands and feet tightly bound and with a large piece of brown parcel tape across his mouth lay his brother Stepan.

He was about to open his mouth and say something when Katrina put her finger to her lips and he relapsed into silence. She swiftly closed the door to the flat and approached Stepan's prostrate body. Antonin watched her blankly as she did so, for he could see that she was filled with an anger more extreme than any he had ever seen in her before. Even in his present state it frightened him.

She stood beside Stepan and jerked her head towards Antonin.

"Is this what I was like all those years?" she asked, although with his mouth so tightly bound it was impossible for him to answer.

Stepan lay completely still, staring up at her with frightened eyes.

"You were so confident I wouldn't return you even forgot to take my key away," she growled scathingly.

Stepan was staring at Antonin with pleading eyes, as if trying to tell him something. Katrina must have noticed.

"Oh yes, Stepan. That's what you'd like to do, isn't it? You'd really like to tell Antonin to come over and pull me away. For all I know you'd tell him to kill me."

Katrina suddenly knelt down beside Stepan.

"Is he what I was like all those years, Stepan?" she repeated. "I can remember everything, you know. Our flat in Berlin, the things we did together, my son Ernst. But I can't remember any feelings from those years other than a blind slavish loyalty towards you."

The fear in Stepan's eyes was growing with every passing second.

Katrina stood up and walked over to a small table which Antonin had not noticed before. Lying on the table was what looked like a small portable CD player.

"This is it, isn't it, you arrogant bastard?" she said, holding it before him. "This is your little toy."

Stepan hesitated for a few moments and then nodded.

"There's a code, isn't there?"

Again he nodded.

"And probably if I get it wrong the whole tape will erase."

This time Stepan lay still.

Katrina backed away from him, still holding the CD player in her hand. From the pocket of her jacket she removed a small kitchen knife.

"Let me make myself perfectly clear, Stepan," she said. "I would very much like to kill you for what you have done to Antonin and I."

She paused, holding the knife over him. And only when he had finally stopped squirming and was lying quite still did she continue.

"In a few moments I am going to unbind your hands and give

236

you a piece of paper. Then you will have just one chance to instruct me exactly how to free Antonin's mind from whatever mental strait-jacket you have locked him into. If you make a mistake and give me the wrong instructions, whether by accident or design, I will slowly and methodically skin you alive. But if you do what I have said and I can successfully release Antonin then I will give you the opportunity to bargain for your life. Do you understand me?"

Stepan lay still for a few moments and then nodded.

Katrina cautiously cut the binding away from his hands. Stepping quickly back, she dropped a piece of paper and a pen by his hands.

"Remember, Stepan, I want clear instructions."

He picked it up and scribbled for a while before looking up and holding the paper out to her.

"Throw it to me," she ordered.

He did so. She read the instructions carefully and then picked up the CD player.

For a few moments she cautiously fiddled with the controls, care-fully cross-checking every step with the instructions Stepan had given her. There was a faint murmur, and then a strange kind of white noise filled the room.

Antonin looked at Katrina blankly, but then she started to speak.

"Antonin," she said calmly and clearly, "henceforth you will com-pletely disregard all instructions that have been given to you by your brother Stepan while this machine was running."

Outwardly nothing changed. Antonin still stood opposite her, apparently listening to the strange sound that filled the room. But inside his mind it was as if a great torrent were washing across him, a torrent of memory and emotion. He could remember his former placidity but no longer experience it. Katrina was no longer the calming mother-figure she had been before, she was suddenly the victim of an enormous outrage. An outrage caused by the man lying bound on the floor before him.

And now it was as if he were back in the chateau again, moments before Stepan had activated the machine. For everything since that moment was fast fading into a dream. And now, suddenly, he remembered the fear of death he had felt as Stepan's finger had hovered over the button.

"Antonin," Katrina asked uncertainly.

He looked at her and smiled. But this time it was not a docile drugged smile, but instead a savage smile of triumph.

Katrina kissed him gently on the lips, for she could tell from his face that it had worked.

But the initial euphoria was fading fast. There were other memories as well, memories of having told Stepan everything before their release. Everything about Nathaniel and Vanessa, about Danny and Annie, about all his experiences during the last six months.

Antonin stepped away from Katrina and stared down at Stepan.

"Can I let him speak now?" he asked.

She nodded.

He bent over and pulled the tape roughly away from Stepan's mouth.

"Where are they?" he demanded.

"Who?" Stepan asked sullenly.

"You know damn well who?"

Stepan scowled.

"Everyone who was at the chateau is free. I had no wish to see any of them harmed."

As he spoke Antonin knew it was no more than the truth.

Stepan looked at Katrina.

"So it didn't work on you a second time?" he observed dryly, and there was even a touch of genuine curiosity in his voice.

She scowled.

"At first it worked. But then it faded rapidly. Perhaps after all these years I have developed a certain immunity."

He frowned.

"Do you know," he observed. "Because you had been under my spell for so long I never really considered the possibility that the effect might only be temporary."

Katrina looked down at him lying helpless before her.

"This device," she said roughly. "Can we use it to free the others too?"

Stepan smiled a faint sarcastic smile.

"If you wish," he said. "For the moment it would seem you have possession."

As his younger brother spoke Antonin could not help but feel a certain wry admiration towards him. For even in defeat he retained his boyish charm. And suddenly, despite everything, he could feel once again a faint echo of the unbounded love he had once felt towards him.

"Oh Stepan," he murmured. "Why did you do all this? You were always so talented, so able to win people's hearts without all this? Why?"

Stepan looked up at Antonin, his face suddenly crestfallen.

"Was I?" he said softly.

Antonin gazed back at him sadly. For all his many talents it was clear that Stepan had never seen them. He had only ever seen in himself the crippled twisted failure of his childhood years. And that lay at the very heart of his tragedy.

"So what do we do with him now?" Katrina muttered anxiously, glancing at her watch.

Antonin looked at Stepan uncertainly, but before he could say anything Stepan himself spoke.

"You must kill me, I suppose," he said.

Antonin stared at him in horror.

"Kill you? Why would we kill you?"

"It is the only way you would really be safe. Even if you use the device to wipe my own mind clear there would no guarantee my memory will not return. Katrina has proved that. And if it did I would pursue you to the ends of the earth to recover my prize."

Antonin glanced at Katrina standing beside him. Something about her manner told him that she agreed with Stepan's analysis. But as yet she said nothing.

It was classic Stepan. Sooner or later they would have to decide what to do with him, sooner or later they would consider the possibility of killing him. So he had taken the offensive, forced them to consider the possibility sooner rather than later. Yet inwardly of course he was gambling on Antonin not having the nerve.

Although his hands and mouth were now free his legs were still tightly bound with tape, making it impossible for him to stand. And now he looked up at Antonin with plaintive eyes.

"I'm in some considerable pain, Antonin," he said. "While you decide my fate please could you allow me to sit in a chair."

Antonin was about to step forward and help him up onto a nearby chair when Katrina suddenly caught his arm.

"No," she said firmly. "Let him stay on the floor. He's dangerous." She picked up the roll of tape she had used on him before and approached him cautiously, meaning to tie his hands once more behind his back.

She bent over him. But then, suddenly, he grabbed her roughly and pulled her over onto the floor beside him.

Antonin leapt forward to snatch her free, but Stepan had already managed to pull the little knife with which she had earlier threatened him out of her jacket pocket.

"Don't!" he warned, holding the knife across her throat.

Antonin froze.

The limp pitiful expression on Stepan's face was now replaced by the taut alertness of a cornered animal. Still gripping Katrina firmly with one hand and holding the knife to her throat with the other, he lay on the floor and challenged Antonin with cold expressionless eyes.

"And now," he said, "we play again by my rules."

Stepan flicked a glance down at his bound feet. He could have cut himself free with the knife, but only by removing it from Katrina's throat.

So instead he looked towards Antonin.

"Undo my feet," he ordered slowly and calmly, and there was a strange confidence in his voice, a smug certainty that Antonin would do exactly what he was told. He didn't even bother to tell him that he would kill Katrina if he tried anything.

Antonin stepped slowly forward and knelt down by Stepan's outstretched legs. His hands reached out as if to remove the tape. But then, with one almighty heave, he pulled Stepan's feet sharply towards him. There was only a moment, but in the fraction of a second during which Stepan was disorientated he lunged upwards towards the knife just as Stepan began tensing his hand to plunge it into Katrina's neck.

And as he did so Antonin experienced something which he had never experienced before. As he saw Stepan's muscles tense to once again rip Katrina away from him he felt consumed by an uncontrollable wave of raw undiluted anger. There was no time for the intellectual reflection which normally governed his every action, only Stepan, his hand tensed to tear the life out of the woman he loved.

He grabbed the knife and twisted it angrily round, plunging it deep into Stepan's heart.

* * * * * *

It was a dark overcast day in November when the gathering began. In a small and rather scruffy flat in one of the poorer districts of Vienna the guests had started arriving early. But only when they had all assembled in Ernst Ziegler's Viennese home did his father Antonin rise to address them.

"Welcome to our annual meeting," he said in the rather ponderous tone into which he invariably lapsed when addressing a group of people.

The room fell silent. Some of the visitors were sitting on dirty armchairs, others were cross-legged on the floor, but all looked up attentively as Antonin began to speak.

"It is now several years since we held our first meeting," he began, "and I think we are entitled to feel a certain modest pride in our achievements. The secret which we share in our group has remained just that – a secret – and although there are twelve of us here who could win fame and fortune beyond our wildest dreams by compromising that secret not a single one of us has done so."

He hesitated, casting his eye around the room. Most of the people present were scientists, men and women like Nathaniel Harrison who knew and understood the secret of Oblanov. They were amongst the leading practitioners in their fields, and Antonin was well aware that some of them had been deliberately feeding disinformation into scientific journals for many months in order to deflect other scientists from probing too deeply.

"I think those amongst us who are scientists have proved that as a profession they need not be as socially irresponsible as they are sometimes portrayed to be. Just as we do not expect musicians to play music that will offend the ears we do not expect scientists to devise things which will damage the world. We must understand that there are many different projects on which scientists can choose to work, some good and some bad. Science is not and never can be just a random search for knowledge which can be thrown thoughtlessly at the rest of society without even a health warning attached. Like all other fields of human endeavour it must be based on certain decent moral precepts."

He glanced at Nadja, who was sitting cross-legged beside Ernst not far from where he was standing.

"My father and Nadja's father believed that scientists could not be trusted to keep their mouths shut. They did not even trust themselves to keep quiet. They sensed that once the Oblanov technique was released into the wider world the temptation to use it would be too great to resist. They also understood that by the nature of the discovery there could be no public debate on the matter. So they concluded that everyone involved including themselves had to die.

"Standing here today with our own experience of how it is perfectly possible to keep a secret, I wonder what would have happened if instead of killing the other scientists they had simply confronted them with the wider social consequences of their actions and asked them to desist from all further development of the idea. Would they have agreed? More importantly perhaps, would they all have agreed? For it would only have taken one of them to reveal the secret and it would have been out, then just as much as today."

He looked around and smiled.

"But I think all present will agree," he continued, "that from a strictly personal point of view our own less dramatic approach is infinitely preferable to my father's."

There was a faint ripple of amusement around the room. Only when it had died down did he continue.

"And now," he said, "I would like to hand you over to Nathaniel, who will begin our review of the technical developments which have taken place during the past year."

Nathaniel rose to his feet and came to the front of the room. Over the months he had become an unofficial second-in-command to Antonin, taking responsibility for all matters of a strictly scientific nature, matters which were by their nature beyond Antonin's grasp. For the work of their little group was not strictly passive. They were also committed to monitoring and where possible manipulating the course of future scientific research to try and ensure that the ideas inherent in Oblanov did not independently resurface elsewhere. Some of the scientists present were also engaged in a secret programme of research to try and develop effective counter-strategies should their attempts at repression ultimately fail.

The technical exchanges lasted late into the evening. But eventually the discussion drew to a close and the delegates once again began to disperse.

Vanessa was one of the last to leave. But before she went she drew Antonin aside.

"Well, Antonin, how are you enjoying your new post?" she asked, for he had recently left Oxford to become Professor of Modern History at Charles University in Prague.

He smiled at her fondly, for she knew that he had been initially very uncertain about leaving Oxford. Oxford had always been for him a gentle sanctuary, and he had left it with considerable sadness. But Katrina had not been happy in Oxford as Antonin's appendage. She had wanted to be herself again, to achieve in the second half of her life a little of the work that Stepan had prevented her from achieving in the first. And so he had agreed to return to the city of their youth when the chance arose. But although he had gone for Katrina's sake he had to admit that he had been surprised by the extent to which he had been pleased to be back. In a way, no less than Katrina, he too felt that he had returned home from an exile which had lasted too long.

"There are only two things I really miss about Oxford," he said. "One is the food and the other is your helpful little hints for getting through the day ahead."

Her lip puckered into a smile.

"And does Katrina look after you properly, or is she a modern woman?"

Antonin smiled.

"Thoroughly modern, I'm afraid. But that's the way I like her."

Vanessa's face suddenly became serious again, for as always she could tell when something was preying on his mind.

"Are you still thinking about your brother?" she asked.

He nodded.

"He haunts me still, I'm afraid. In the moment I acted I wanted him dead. I suppose it was mainly fear, fear that he would somehow succeed in killing Katrina, but there was also a feeling of violent revenge mixed in with it. A part of me feels terrible remorse because of that."

She looked at him sadly.

"He deserved your revenge," she said softly.

He looked at her kindly face and a part of him knew that she was right. But there was another part, deep down inside, which didn't accept that obvious version of the truth.

"I sometimes wonder," he said, speaking words which he never dared speak to Katrina because he knew they would only make her angry, "I sometimes wonder if Stepan was right to blame me, if I really did have something to do with him turning out the way he did."

Vanessa put her arms round his still generous form and hugged him affectionately.

"You really are too gentle for this world," she whispered softly, and then she kissed him tenderly on the cheek and turned away to bid the others farewell.

It was only when Vanessa had gone that Katrina took Antonin's hand in her own.

"You miss her, don't you?" she said.

Antonin looked at her fondly.

"Vanessa was always kind to me, but now I've found you again I think it's better she's not there. Somehow she reminds me of a past I'd rather forget, when I really want to be looking to the future."

Katrina smiled but said nothing, for nothing needed to be said. Their relationship was now again as it had been before, and words were frequently unnecessary. They had rebuilt their shattered lives with the confidence and determination of those who have stared disaster in the face and successfully overcome it. And it could be said that they were truly happy.

Katrina turned and looked at Nadja, who was tidying away the wine glasses in the living room.

"Looking back, it's strange that you were drawn to her too, isn't it?" she said, careful to keep her voice down so that she could not be overheard.

Antonin inclined his head to one side.

"Don't you think she's like you," he said. "I found it so uncanny when I met her. But I suppose that explains why Ernst liked her too."

Katrina smiled. For as a married couple Ernst and Nadja were as close in their own way as Antonin and Katrina had ever been.

But Ernst had spotted them talking. He called them through to living room. Everyone else had left, and now Ernst took Nadja's hands in his. He looked uncharacteristically formal.

"What's up, Ernst?" Antonin asked.

Ernst pulled Nadja closer towards him.

"We," he announced smugly, "are going to have a baby."

Antonin and Katrina both looked at the young couple and smiled with unrestrained pleasure. For in their son and daughter-in-law they could see themselves as young people, living a stage in their lives which they themselves had been denied.

Antonin leant forward and kissed Nadja gently on the cheek. And as he did so he could feel some small tears forming in his eyes, tears which he felt were not entirely appropriate to the occasion.

He pulled himself together and shook Ernst warmly by the hand.

"By way of celebration," he said, "I propose we put on some music and dance."

Ernst had seen the tears in Antonin's eyes but said nothing, for he had inherited in full measure his father's quiet sensitivity. So now he walked over silently to his extensive collection of CDs and started looking through them.

"I think," he said, carefully selecting one and turning to face his family, "that it would be appropriate to dance a Viennese Waltz."